Praise for **BREATH AND MERCY**

"In *Breath and Mercy*, we watch the emergence of the HIV epidemic and witness a health care system buckle under the destructive power of a hurricane. Powers skillfully portrays the role of religious framings on medical decision making, the intensity of medical training and practice, and the fatigue and strain it engenders. Compelling from start to finish, *Breath and Mercy* quickly draws the reader into a richly layered series of action-packed medical adventures."

— Kim Talikoff, MD, Pediatrician, Educator, and Documentarian

"Through the character of Dr. Phineas Mann, Dr. Powers explores the complex responsibilities of the medical profession — to speak the truth, to improve health, and to relieve suffering, even in the face of extreme hardship and imminent death. The story is riveting and kept me guessing until the last page."

— John A. Bartlett, MD, Professor of Medicine and Global Health, Duke University, and Co-Director, The Center for AIDS Research

"Dr. Powers sets the fictional Dr. Phineas Mann in a cauldron of ethical dilemmas brewed in a raging New Orleans hurricane. Mark Powers writes as one familiar with facing the challenges of life and death issues. As a former co-chair of a hospital ethics committee, I recognize a similar compassion in Phineas for patients and families as the author has. I already want Phineas in a third novel."

— The Rev. Dr. Ralph Bright, Retired Director of Chaplaincy, Durham Regional Hospital

"Dr. Mann's role as a physician in a New Orleans community hospital during a Category 5 hurricane is a harrowing account of doctors and nurses and other hospital personnel trying to provide humane care under inhumane circumstances. Readers interested in the humanity of health care, health education, and the human condition will find this novel interesting and compelling."

— Nancy ⬚⬚⬚⬚⬚⬚, MD, Professor of ⬚⬚⬚ternal and
Fe⬚ ⬚⬚⬚⬚⬚⬚⬚ Carolina

D0911969

"For readers who have not read *A Swarm in May*, I suggest that they read *Breath and Mercy* first, as it will add to its suspense and set the stage for Phineas' subsequent adventures and exploits. Dr. Powers had a long and successful career as an outstanding and widely respected physician. He is now well into a second career as a skilled and successful novelist."

— Daniel J. Sexton, MD, Professor Emeritus of Medicine,
Division of Infectious Diseases, Duke University

"Mark Powers' new book *Breath and Mercy* left me breathless while reading the hospital scenes during the storm. He captured the emotion and exhaustion that I would feel in such a desperate situation. I applaud his courage in addressing a quandary well-known to health care providers who must navigate the intersection between religious faith, hope, and medical futility with each patient and family."

— Carol Dukes Hamilton, MD, Professor Emeritus of Medicine,
Division of Infectious Diseases, Duke University

"Wow, you will not want to put this one down! I felt like I was making evening rounds with Dr. Mann during his early career and experiences grappling with the fragility of human life and then again, when he is tested under the most extreme circumstances, to be true to himself and uphold his commitment to his patients and the woman he loves."

— Celeste Mayer, RN, PhD, Patient Safety Officer, Retired,
University of North Carolina Hospitals

"Powers' fast-paced novel begins with a medical journey through the early days of the HIV epidemic. Powers beautifully captures the uncertainties and challenges of doctoring in that difficult time by weaving together carefully crafted vignettes of individual patients living with HIV. Powers' protagonist, Phineas Mann, is skillfully imbued with great passion for service and humanistic care, still core qualities in health care during our current challenging times."

— Peter Kussin, MD, Professor of Medicine, Division of Pulmonary,
Allergy, and Critical Care Medicine, Duke University School of Medicine

BREATH
AND
MERCY

BREATH
AND
MERCY

A NOVEL

MARK ANTHONY POWERS

HAWKSBILL PRESS

HAWKSBILL PRESS

www.hawksbillpress.com

Edited by Dawn Reno Langley, President of Rewired Creatives, Inc.
Book design by Christy Day, Constellation Book Services
Author photo by Amy Stern Photography, www.amystern.com
Cover image by istockphoto.com

ISBN (paperback): 978-1-7370329-2-2
ISBN (ebook): 978-1-7370329-3-9

Printed in the United States of America

To all healthcare workers:
Thank you for all your sacrifices during the pandemic.

PART ONE

BOSTON

And divided tongues as of fire appeared on each of them.
And they were all filled with the Holy Spirit and began to
speak in tongues as the Spirit gave them utterance.

ACTS 2:3

The woman threatened passersby with her cigarette. She was wretched,
even for Boston's Combat Zone on a Saturday in 1976. Engulfed against
the frigid January predawn by layers of grimy coats and a knit hat under
a black shawl, she watched the medical center's morning shift personnel
trudge by and lingered on the edge of the sidewalk against a shopping
cart stuffed with plastic bags. Phineas Mann saw her take the cigarette
into a toothless mouth and create a long, glowing ash. She raised it in her
clenched fist, an orange flame against a gray sky, and thrust it toward the
forehead of a young woman trying to hurry past.

Phineas swung his backpack to deflect the glowing cigarette ash. It
sizzled in the snow at the attacker's feet. She glared at him while she
traced a cross with her fist from her forehead to her waist then shoulder
to shoulder as she latched onto her cart and was swallowed by the crowd.

Phineas pursued the young woman. "Holy Smokes..." he couldn't stop himself from exclaiming. "Are you OK?"

"Too early in the morning for drama...or puns." She turned to face him while adjusting a Tiffany patterned scarf over her long auburn hair. "I'm fine. She missed. She's been there about every day recently. Usually stares and points her cigarette at me. First time she's attacked me." Her words were from the South, probably the Deep South, warm pralines, nothing like the staccato of Boston. "Oh—and thank you."

She stared into Phineas' eyes, level with hers. Her two-inch scuffed boot heels lifted her to his five-foot ten. Her irises were the blue of sunlight illuminating a National Geographic glacial crevasse.

I must look a fright. His breath always condensed in the freezing temperature and salted his thick coal-black beard with glistening specks of ice. He lowered his down-filled hood, uncovering his nearly shoulder-length hair and tried to appear less intimidating.

The young woman abruptly pivoted and called back over her shoulder, "Well, work awaits. Thanks again and have a nice day." She hurried along the sidewalk.

He followed a few paces behind her toward the Tufts New England Medical Center, watched her enter, remove her scarf, and shake out her long hair, now gleaming under the lobby's brilliant overhead lights. She pulled open the stairway door.

He rode the elevator to the seventh floor. For reasons unknown to him, architects had placed the block of Intensive Care Units near the top floors, causing personnel to always arrive breathless when a Code Blue was called after hours.

The Coronary Care Unit team members were hanging coats and stowing backpacks in cubbyholes. Phineas had barely enough time to review the medical student admission note he'd written last night, and to memorize his patient's labs and nursing notes. He'd admitted ninety-year-old Mr. Goodman for recurrent ventricular tachycardia. After Phineas had finished his workup, they chatted about the Red Sox.

Hank Norton gathered the team at Mr. Goodman's door. Hank was the resident and led today's team of two interns and two medical students. Under their short white coats, the interns wore pale green scrubs, and the students, ties and button-downs.

"Mann, give us a *concise* presentation on your patient." Hank sounded tired. "You can do the long version at attending rounds."

Hank was a no-nonsense bestower of wisdom, empathy, and Xeroxed articles and a master of the "What am I thinking?" learning method. One could always tell how long Hank had been in the hospital, because he shaved every other morning before his night on call, and by the second day, he sported the beginnings of a thick black beard. Hank had proudly graduated from Harvard Medical School but missed the Residency Match for Harvard's Beth Israel, known as 'The House of God', the Massachusetts General Hospital, and The Brigham. He'd ended up at his fourth choice, Tufts. When Phineas checked out last night, Hank told him that he hoped to get back to Harvard for a nephrology fellowship. Boston was the epicenter of medicine for him.

Phineas pulled himself to attention. "Mr. Goodman is a 90-year-old admitted yesterday for recurrent ventricular tachycardia. He had myocardial infarctions at ages 80 and 87 and has had congestive heart failure since the second one. His cardiologist saw runs of ventricular tachycardia on Mr. Goodman's Holter monitor after he complained of palpitations and feeling lightheaded. His exam revealed an enlarged heart with a mitral regurgitation murmur, as well as rales and edema. Last night, we started him on intravenous Pronestyl for his VTach, and potassium supplements and diuretic for his heart failure."

"So, what happened during the night?" asked Hank. *Again the "What am I thinking?" approach.* Hank had been there.

"From the notes, it looks like he had longer runs of VTach."

Hank shook his head. "I thumped him twice and, incredibly, he converted to normal sinus rhythm each time. Never worked for me before last night." The precordial thump, performed with a fist or open palm on the lower breastbone sometimes delivered a modest shock to the heart that might convert a rapid arrhythmia to a normal rhythm. "Let's go see your patient."

Phineas led the team to Mr. Goodman's bedside. "Good morning, Mr. Goodman. I understand Dr. Norton had to intervene for your rhythm last night. How are you this morning?"

"Other than a very sore chest, not so bad. That liquid potassium you gave me—could anything taste worse? And the laxative hasn't worked yet. Maybe after breakfast. And when does that get here?" He sat propped up in the hospital bed, looking every bit his 90 years, completely bald with bruised, paper-thin skin on his hands. "When does my cardiologist come see me? Can I get a newspaper? I prefer *The Globe*."

His bedside monitor alarmed as a wide complex tachycardia appeared on the screen like coarse teeth on a brush saw. He stared at Hank with his pale grey eyes wide open.

"Don't hit me..." He wailed and collapsed back, eyes closing.

Hank's fist pounded Mr. Goodman's chest. The old man grimaced before he lost consciousness. Hank thumped him again. He felt Mr. Goodman's neck for a pulse. "No pulse. Get the defibrillator!" Hank, his brow deeply furrowed, hit him again, looking frustrated. "Call a code. Get anesthesia here so we can intubate him!" He whirled on Kirk Mills, the intern on Mr. Goodman's case. "Mills, check his airway and start mouth-to-mouth respirations. Someone find an Ambu bag and mask!" Mills fished out Goodman's upper and lower dentures.

"ABC. Airway. Breathe. Circulation!" Hank pointed at Mr. Goodman's nurse. "Give him 100 milligrams of lidocaine IV STAT!" He pulled the code blue board from the foot of the bed and shoved it under Mr. Goodman. "Mann, the med student does the compressions. Make sure you push hard."

Phineas placed his right palm on the back of his left hand and compressed Mr. Goodman's breastbone. The first compression produced a sequence of cracking sounds as at least half a dozen ribs fractured. Phineas cringed and hesitated. He'd never broken anyone's bones before. The sensation gave him the creeps.

"You should be able to do better compressions now. Keep going," Hank instructed. Phineas pushed on Mr. Goodman's broken chest.

Hank led the code blue protocol through the standard drugs: epinephrine, lidocaine, and finally bretyllium. He shocked Mr. Goodman after each dose of drug, his frail body convulsing each time. The anesthesiologist inserted an endotracheal tube to ventilate him. Hank interrupted Phineas' compressions to insert a central IV catheter under Mr. Goodman's collarbone, and again when he inserted a six-inch cardiac needle directly into the heart to instill more epinephrine. The rhythm steadily deteriorated from the ventricular tachycardia to ventricular fibrillation to flat-line asystole as Mr. Goodman's spirit took wing from its splintered cage.

A gurgle followed a rumble, then a pungent stench filled the room as Mr. Goodman's bowels emptied, more with each chest compression. Phineas gagged. It took little force to compress the chest, yet Phineas' brow dripped sweat.

Hank checked for a pulse in Mr. Goodman's groin. "I feel good pulses with your compressions. Hold for a minute and let's check his rhythm. Make sure all his leads are attached." The monitor displayed a straight line.

"Call it. We've done enough," Hank announced. "We did the best we could for Mr. Goodman. The next time we code someone, we may save a life. I'll page his attending."

The intern, Kirk, a shy and thoughtful UMass medical school grad, glided to the sink and spit. He asked the nurse for mouthwash in a whisper. He spit some more.

Phineas stared at Mr. Goodman then at his own hands. A tingling began behind his nasal passage and spread upward behind his eyes, like a carbonated drink that had gone the wrong way. His eyes moistened. Emptiness filled his chest. These were sensations he hadn't experienced in years.

Hank put down the phone. "First one you've lost?"

Phineas blinked back tears. "I liked him. We talked for a while after I finished my work-up. Made me think about my grandfather." He pulled tissues from a box next to the sink then pressed them into his eyes.

"It's OK to feel bad about it. Shows you're still human."

✤ ✤ ✤

Mr. Goodman was the first person Phineas watched die. He'd seen corpses in anatomy class and funerals but had never observed life leaving someone. He'd seen animals die. As a child, he'd watched trout that he and his father caught flop in the creel until they suffocated. When he indicated concern for their suffering, his father showed him how to break their necks, after which the gasping ceased. As a medical student, he was troubled to realize the fish had still been conscious, but unable to breathe.

Phineas learned at age seven to shoot on a .22 rifle. At YMCA summer day camp, he fired their .22 rifle well enough to earn a Marksman badge. When he was fourteen, he unwrapped a deer rifle on Christmas morning, a coming-of-age gift in rural Vermont. The next fall, he and his father hunted without having an acceptable shot, until the last day of the season, the only day taking a doe was legal.

As dusk approached, his father walked one side of a ridge and Phineas the other when Phineas spotted a large doe loping fifty yards away at the edge of a clearing. He placed the cross hairs on the doe's chest and squeezed the trigger. The doe collapsed but struggled mightily. Phineas jogged closer and realized the doe was dragging her paralyzed hind legs. His shot had severed her spinal cord. He shot again, striking her in the chest. She lifted her head, bleating. He raised his rifle again and, despite his wobbly legs, silenced her with a final shot. Her head exploded behind her terrified doe eyes.

Phineas' chest pounded then felt empty. His nasal passage tingled before his throat tightened and his eyes moistened. He knelt at the dead doe's side to recover. *Why didn't he feel triumphant?* It was such a messy kill. She'd suffered, and he'd inflicted that on her. If only his first shot had missed.

His father arrived moments later, puffing. "It sounds like you had a war going on over here." His eyes opened wide when he saw the mangled doe. "Let's tag her and get her registered. We'll butcher her tomorrow."

After that day, deer season was an excuse for a solitary hike. During his first year of medical school, Phineas convinced his father that he needed the money from the sale of his rifle to purchase the expensive required textbooks.

Work rounds with his resident seemed interminable after Mr. Goodman died. Then rounds with the supervising cardiologist were longer. Phineas had to present Mr. Goodman's case again, this time in excruciating detail. The cardiologist reviewed the diagnosis and treatment of ventricular arrhythmias, and the team went through the code step by painful step. Hunger finally, mercifully, intervened and they recessed.

Phineas descended the stairs to the cafeteria, carrying his lunch in a recycled bread bag. He bought a tall coffee and searched for a seat. The young woman he'd encountered earlier on the Combat Zone sidewalk sat by the window and spoke with an older woman. The winter sun lit up the young woman's face, and those brilliant ice blue eyes framed a slender nose. Her skin maintained a healthier color than the pallor most wore during a Boston winter.

Phineas approached and asked hopefully, "Do you mind if I sit here?" She couldn't turn away from him this time.

The young woman looked up, "Of course not. This isn't private. Do *I* know you?" That accent again.

"We met briefly early this morning. The bag lady with the cigarette."

"I was just telling Mary about that pitiful woman."

The older woman smiled. "Sir Galahad, I presume?"

"More likely Don Quixote. Pleased to meet you, Mary. I'm Phineas."

"Phineas, this is Iris."

He shook both their hands, lingering a second longer with Iris and savoring the warmth that came through her silky palm.

Mary stood and brushed wrinkles from her bulky gray sweater and black skirt. "Iris, I need to go back and review the forms you filled out earlier. Take your time."

"Mary's helping me learn to write up FL-2 nursing home referral forms for the doctors to sign. Tedious necessities," Iris explained.

He held up the bread bag. "Brought my lunch. Nothing fancy, but happy to share."

"I noticed. You go ahead. I'll watch you eat." An empty brown paper bag was neatly folded in front of Iris. She sipped coffee between full, unadorned lips and glanced at his student nametag.

"My friends call me Fin or Finman." *Those eyes. Without direct sun rays striking them, they shifted toward a deep-water ocean blue.* He could not look away.

"Iris Babineaux." The first hint of a mischievous smile. "*My* friends call me Iris."

Phineas rallied for another try.

"I'm in med school here at Tufts. Just started on the Coronary Care Unit. So, you work here too?"

"I have a part time job here Saturdays, sort of a paid internship. I'm in grad school at BU in medical social work."

"How long does your internship last?" With luck, as long as his medical school.

"It's temporary, to help out while a woman is on maternity leave. Hope she decides to stay home with her little angel. I like the job and need the money—but I don't care for that walk through the Combat Zone." She sipped more coffee. "So, Phineas, how was your morning after our encounter with the weaponized cigarette?"

"Not good after I left you." His voiced softened. "I lost my first patient." His shoulders slumped forward, and he told her about how he admitted Mr. Goodman last evening and then about the code. He stared at the olive Formica tabletop, and his speech evened out as he started to go through the CPR protocol.

Iris raised her hand. "Stop. Right. There. I may be working in a medical center, but I am *not* by nature a medical person. I get queasy easily. I don't think you want me to get all swimmy-headed—or to hurl. That would *not* be lady-like."

Phineas suppressed a smile, grateful for re-entry. He inhaled steam from the coffee, tasted a sip, and then bit into Swiss cheese on pumpernickel. Spicy mustard ignited his palate.

"It seems to me the important question is why y'all would do all that to try to bring a ninety-year-old back from a painless, sudden death." Iris pressed on. "If you'd somehow managed to start his heart up again, Mr. Goodman would still be ninety—with his bad heart." She folded her hands and looked straight into Phineas eyes. "Tell me, Phineas, what sort of shape would Mr. Goodman be in, if he made it through the code, and by some miracle, made it to discharge? Do you think he could go home? I'd guess at best he would require skilled care nursing care for the rest of his life." She set her coffee cup on the table and folded her hands together. "So, Phineas, when do *you* consider a life fully lived?"

That question would require more reflection, more time. For now, he'd pivot back to Mr. Goodman. "He'd had a good life. More than most. But maybe he'd still get to watch his Red Sox on TV with his family."

"That might have been enough for him—if his brain recovered. What qualifies as a good quality of life is a moving target." She drained her coffee and set the cup on the table. "By the way, how's your quality of life, Phineas?"

Phineas wished he'd packed more for lunch. He wanted to listen to her voice and look at her face as long as he could. He swallowed a bite of his oatmeal cookie and summoned his courage.

"I'm hoping you might help me improve it. Iris, do you know where the Exeter Theatre is?"

"On Exeter."

"Right." *Got me again.* "I saw a poster at the trolley stop. They're replaying Orson Welles' 1938 radio broadcast of the *War of the Worlds*

Friday evening. I've always wanted to hear it." His pulse pounded in his ears. "Would you like to go with me? My treat."

Her eyebrows lifted for a few of his heartbeats. "You must really want to hear it. I know the Exeter. Good place if you have a tight budget. I live a few blocks from there."

She must know that tickets are only a dollar. He was surprised that a grad student could afford an apartment in Back Bay. "When Orson Welles first read it over the radio, it caused a nationwide panic. Listeners were convinced Martians had invaded." Had he sold her on it or convinced her his tastes were too weird?

"And then there was public outrage."

"You know the story?"

"It *is* famous. I suppose it is my duty to experience it at some point."

"So, you'll go?" Did he hear right?

"It just so *happens* I'm free Friday evening. I'll meet you there."

Phineas' day had turned around.

❦ ❦ ❦

On Monday, images of Mr. Goodman's death still hovered in Phineas' thoughts and pulled him to the med student dorm for a talk with Dr. MacSweeney. Ian MacSweeney MD was a staff psychiatrist on the medical school faculty and wore a trimmed salt and pepper beard and Irish wool cardigans "for credibility". After a medical student committed suicide several years earlier, the school arranged for Dr. MacSweeney to camp out in the dorm lounge one afternoon a week. Students were free to drop by and informally chat. Medical records were not created. The primary goal was to identify a possible crisis before it became one. The common outcome was that many of the students learned to release pent up stresses in a secure setting. Dr. MacSweeney's affable personality and relaxed schedule led to loose friendships, and a few students even considered the field of psychiatry.

While listening, MacSweeney sometimes held an unloaded meerschaum pipe that was formed into a Wampanoag Indian Chief's head. He might take the mouthpiece, or bit as he called it, between his teeth while he listened. He told Phineas he had succeeded in kicking the nicotine addiction but enjoyed the memory.

The first time Phineas found his way to a Dr. MacSweeney's lounge session was after a second-year Psychiatry class. Phineas was studying the obsessive-compulsive personality disorder and sought reassurance he was not barreling along that highway. Dr. MacSweeney advised, "Conscientious is not OCD. Your behaviors are not pathological, only adaptive. They'll be good for your patients...So, Phineas, how's life outside of medicine?"

"It could use some work," Phineas had responded.

Dr. MacSweeney had then returned his pipe to his sweater pocket. "Don't think of it as work, and don't let me keep you from it. Go forth and have some fun."

During today's second visit to Dr. MacSweeney, Phineas sat forward, elbows on knees and head in hands, staring at the floor, as he recounted Mr. Goodman's death. When he concluded, he looked up to meet Dr. MacSweeney's gaze.

"Phineas, it's okay to feel. It's great that you do. I'm glad you're talking about it. Always do that when you feel this way. There's no getting around that this is your job. Death will happen. It sounds like you did everything correctly. You may not have saved Mr. Goodman, but you were someone to talk to during his last night. That made a difference." He handed Phineas a tissue from a box on his end table. "And it's okay to let the tears out."

The Exeter Theatre was once a classic beauty but now was reduced to recycling older movies for a dollar admission fee, making it popular with cash-challenged students. On his way there, Phineas' confidence ebbed. Some choice for a first date with Iris. *I should have done better.*

As he stood on the top step of the theatre entrance, he exhaled steam in the cold night then spotted Iris crossing the street, wrapped in a puffy royal blue parka. He descended the steps to greet her. "I'm glad you came. I was worried you might think I was some kind of a nut, asking you to this."

"I'll defer my judgment on *that* question for now, but I have to say this certainly *is* the most unusual first date I've ever had."

⚜ ⚜ ⚜

They sat in the dark theatre minutes past Orson Welles' last lines, "Isn't there anyone on the air? Isn't there...anyone?" until the final scene when all the Martians succumbed to Earth germs, and the human survivors of the attack were left to rebuild the planet.

The lights came on and revealed bordello style wallpaper as Phineas and Iris rose from the balding burgundy velvet seats. "It's astounding people could believe all that happened in sixty minutes." Phineas offered his enthusiasm for the drama. Did she feel it too?

"The awesome power of the media. People tuned in part way through and freaked out during the attack." Her voice was at least a little bit animated. She seemed intrigued.

"It was clever for H. G. Wells to use Earth germs to defeat the aliens, since their systems had no immunity. All Earth's weapons didn't defeat them, but a brand-new infectious agent did." Even to his own ears, he was beginning to sound like a science nerd.

"Like our government did to the American Indians when they gave them blankets covered with smallpox?"

Wow! She doesn't hold back. "We learned about that in Microbiology class. Not a history to be proud of."

She slipped her parka on and began sidestepping toward the aisle. A coin-sized patch of silver duct tape sealed the elbow of her coat. "There *has* to be something better we can talk about."

"May I treat you to ice cream?"

"Proper use of 'may I' instead of 'can I'. Yes, you may. It's *way* too cold for a Southern girl to eat ice cream though. I'll accept a decaf."

✧ ✧ ✧

They found a ground level snack shop on Newbury Street, where Phineas ordered the decaf and a scoop of pistachio. Iris peeled off her parka and emerged, as if from a cocoon, in a light blue sweater over faded jeans. Phineas had to force himself to look only at her eyes as he set the coffee before her and asked, "So, how did you find your way to Boston?"

"I went to LSU to be a marine biologist. I eliminated the *marine* part when I discovered terrible seasickness at the end of a scuba certification course. They had an open water dive in the Gulf for the final, and conditions were choppy." She chuckled, a low rolling sound. "I *barely* got the regulator out of my mouth before I hurled."

Phineas winced at the image.

She continued, "I still loved studying biology though. I took most of the 'ologies. I met another problem as I was finishing my junior year and exploring career options."

"What was that?"

"The only jobs advertised for someone with a B.S. in biology were as lab techs. So, I went on a summer job interview. I was told my first duties would be to dissect freshly 'sacrificed' rats and *grind their brains* for analysis. On the tour of the lab, I had to excuse myself to keep from throwing up." She pushed her fist against her lips, as if to suppress a gag.

"So, you switched to social work."

"I took some sociology courses and decided to give it a try. Maybe I can make a difference—or at least a living."

"And BU has a good program?"

"I wanted to get out of Louisiana and see somewhere else. Boston looked interesting, and BU had the best program. They gave me a partial scholarship, and I have a student loan. It's still *way* too expensive here though." She sighed and crumpled her napkin.

Phineas answered, "Tufts helped me find a good loan package, and my folks help with rent and some with tuition."

"Lucky you. Even with my paid internship, my finances run on *empty* most months." She stared into her coffee.

"No help from Mom and Dad?"

"My father told me he sent me to college to get my 'MRS' degree." She added air quotes. "Having failed that, I should come live at *home* and look for a job. With my younger brother coming along, Dad said he was finished paying for my education."

"Seems pretty harsh."

"My father is a high school teacher, and my mother *was* a teacher, but became a stay-at-home mom." Iris chuckled again. "She taught home economics, but *none* of it rubbed off on me. Dinner was always ready when I got home. *I* can't cook a lick."

"Hard to imagine going home after college."

"I'd rather be cold and hungry in Boston than live at home." Iris set her empty coffee cup on the table and focused on Phineas' eyes. "I stopped here once after I first came to Boston. The cookies looked so good, and I was *sooo* hungry, I just *had* to have one." She looked down at her hands. "I counted my money. Seventy-eight cents. It wasn't enough." She was almost whispering. "The clerk scraped a pile of crumbs together and gave them to me. Crumbs. That was a low point."

He'd never been that broke. *Hungry and broke. Ouch.* "Sorry, you had to experience that."

He wanted to keep Iris talking, but the shop workers conspicuously began sweeping the floor.

She rose to her feet. "I declare, it's getting late, and *this* girl needs sleep."

Phineas helped with her coat and followed her out the door. They had walked two blocks when she announced, "This is it."

"Nice neighborhood." They were on the edge of the upscale part of Back Bay.

"It's nothing fancy. In fact, it's the opposite. I live on the top floor in a cramped apartment that's seen better days, and I have two roommates." She climbed a step and turned. "I had a nice night, Phineas. Thank you."

Phineas murmured, "May I kiss you good night?"

"Yes, you may."

He hugged her gently and lightly kissed her silky lips. He tasted coffee and inhaled lavender perfume. When he began letting go, her eyes caught him in a whirlpool, and he mumbled, "I hope you'll go out with me again."

"I'd be pleased if you'd ask."

❧ ❧ ❧

During one of a handful of dates, Phineas extracted the news that Iris had a birthday soon. He convinced her that such an event warranted a splurge, and she agreed to let him take her to No Name Seafood, where whatever came off the boats that day made it onto the menu boards.

He could barely contain his excitement on the way there. "I've only been there once, and the seafood was cooked perfectly. I think you'll like it. The décor is basic. Picnic tables covered with brown paper. You order at the counter, and they bring it to you. It's 'bring your own wine or beer'." He held up a bottle of Blue Nun he'd wrapped in a brown bag. He'd also picked up a bouquet of daisies from a sidewalk booth on the way to Newbury Street. She shook her head but looked pleased when he handed them to her.

They took their place in line while Iris studied the menu on the chalkboard. When it was their turn, she asked, "*What* in heaven's name is scrod?"

The woman at the counter answered, "Today it's cod. Sometimes it's haddock. How'd you like it cooked? I'd recommend broiled."

Phineas requested the deep-fried platter of shrimp and clams with a side of onion rings. Iris grimaced. "Good thing you don't eat like that every day."

"I think they use peanut oil. It's crisp on the outside and moist on the inside, so they must deep-fry it at 400 degrees or higher. I want to own a deep fryer someday."

"Might be your undoing."

They found a remote corner table in the bustling restaurant to wait for their meals. Phineas placed the daisies in a glass of water and poured wine. He then excused himself under pretense of using the restroom to arrange Iris' birthday dessert.

They savored the seafood and sipped the wine as long as they felt they could take up space in the busy restaurant. Iris stood as plates were removed, but before she could don her parka, a cluster of employees marched out of the kitchen singing 'Happy Birthday Iris'. The lead person held a tray aloft with a 6-inch cake covered with dark chocolate, a single candle in its center.

"It's Boston Cream Pie. I hope you like it," Phineas watched her for a sign of approval. Had he embarrassed her?

She mouthed "Thank you" to each of the servers then appeared to admire their offering from different angles. "The chocolate icing is a good start. My philosophy has always been that if it's not chocolate, it's not dessert."

At least Phineas got that part right. He cut the cake in half. "There's cream filling in the yellow butter cake. It's a Boston tradition."

"What a wonderful tradition! This is *so sweet* of you. Thank you." She squeezed his hand.

"Dig in." He held a forkful to her mouth with his other hand.

"Mmmm." She swallowed. "That's really good, but I can hardly eat another bite. I already ate *way more* tonight than usual."

"We'll get a box for the leftovers. A treat for tomorrow."

Phineas rose to pay the bill, while Iris located the restrooms. He draped her coat over his arm and stood in the line for the cashier. A bright yellow t-shirt was for sale behind the glass cabinet. A smiling cartoon fish winked and proclaimed, "I got scrod last night at No Name Seafood!"

"How much for the t-shirt?" he asked.

Before the cashier could answer, Phineas felt Iris lift her jacket from his arm. She shook her head and exclaimed, "I declare, who would buy *that* shirt?"

The cashier shot a glance at Phineas. "You'd be surprised."

❀ ❀ ❀

On the way back to her apartment, Iris explained, "Jean works in a small restaurant. She sometimes brings back leftovers. She has to go in at 4 AM."

"We should go there sometime," Phineas replied.

"Elizabeth works in a lab at Boston Children's Hospital varying days of the week on the 3 to 11 shift."

"Sounds like you three are on different schedules."

"Sometimes we go days without seeing each other. Would you like to come in?" She caught him off guard.

"You bet, of course." *Too enthusiastic. Sounds like a puppy dog drooling and wagging its tail. Stay cool. Don't blow it.*

He followed Iris up three narrow and dimly lit flights. At the top, she unlocked an ancient wooden door carved with names and the initials MM+JD in a heart. She led him to a windowless kitchen where she placed the daisies in a plastic cup with water. The kitchen appeared to be the only common room. Its small table was covered with red plastic and surrounded by three rickety chairs. The appliances looked ancient. The range lacked two knobs. Iris put the cream pie in the mostly empty refrigerator.

The quiet suggested her roommates were either asleep or out.

"We drew straws and I had first choice of bedrooms. We figured my room used to be the living room." She opened the door to a room on the street side of the apartment. The moonlight shone through a row of windows overlooking Newbury Street. "I heard a woman screaming down there one night. When I peeked out, I saw police trying to get her and another woman into a paddy wagon. She was *handcuffed*. Then I understood why I see so many dressed-up women near here, and why cars sometimes slow down next to me as I walk home."

She turned on a floor lamp. Phineas noticed a painted nail protruding from the windowsill. On closer inspection, he found it penetrated the biggest cockroach he had seen outside of a biology lab. There were at least two coats of paint over it.

Iris laughed. "I'm guessing the prior occupant considered that one a trophy. It seemed too much trouble to dig it out of the paint. This *isn't* a place I'm proud to show off. It may be the least elegant apartment in Back Bay."

A 'desk' was constructed of a beat-up door perched on cinder blocks. A folding metal chair, tucked against it, faced the windows. A few textbooks and paperbacks with 'used book' stickers surrounded a mechanical type-writer. The radiator banged out a series of notes, not exactly the beginning of the Anvil Chorus.

Phineas sat in a massive, overstuffed chair with worn arms. He imagined Iris cuddled in it, reading for hours at a time, but at that moment she perched on the end of her narrow bed like in a goddess on a pedestal, beyond his reach. They talked until he thanked her for a wonderful evening, kissed her goodnight, and left.

⚜ ⚜ ⚜

Iris watched Phineas descend the first flight of stairs then closed her apartment door. *Well, that was surprising!* She had expected him to at least make a pass at her in her bedroom. She might have even allowed it. *Not even a grope.* All he'd done was talk. She had felt warm and affectionate with good food and Blue Nun in her belly. *And the dessert!* She wasn't one for desserts generally, but the way it was served and all. And it was delicious, especially the creamy filling.

He finally kissed her and held her for the first time without her bulky parka. She pressed into him, and his hand began to slide down her lower back. But he retrieved it before it reached her bottom. *Could it be he had taken some sort of vow of celibacy until marriage?*

She'd learned to be on guard in college. Alcohol, pot, frats, and the 70's had given her dates expectations. They were usually trying to get her out of her clothes on first dates. Those became last dates. She didn't want those kinds of complications. Not after that date with Purple Jesus.

At the beginning of her sophomore year, she'd moved into Tri-Delt sorority, pledging along with a few of her close freshman friends. She liked that it was near the gym where she could swim laps after classes.

After about a month of steady visits, she began to recognize a few other regular swimmers.

Todd often waited for her to finish a lap to start a conversation, then one day, he asked her out. He was blond, athletic, and a strong swimmer. They had a few pleasant dates until he asked her to his fraternity formal at Sigma Chi. Formal meant he wore a tie and jacket, and she, her one long dress, a leftover from her high school prom. There was a band and dancing. Then there was Purple Jesus in large punch bowls. It was so smooth going down, that she hadn't thought to ask what was in it. When she finally asked the recipe, she was told grape juice, ginger ale, and Everclear.

She later learned Everclear was 95% pure alcohol.

She woke up late the next morning in bed at tri-Delt in her long dress. Her head felt woozy, and she was nauseated. Her sorority sisters joked about how drunk she'd been when Todd brought her back. She could barely stand, they said, and he'd recounted how she kept falling asleep, how her low alcohol tolerance had surprised him.

When she finally dragged herself out of bed to pee, she was horrified to discover her panties had been pulled down to the top of her thighs. Had she failed to pull them all the way up last night during a drunken trip to the bathroom, or had she been groped and ogled?

That was her last frat party. She decided she'd had a wakeup call and was at college for better reasons. She wanted to avoid drama or complications. She stopped swimming, took up running, and became the 'serious sister' at Tri-Delt before moving into an off-campus apartment at the end of the year. She found comfort in her studies, good books, and a few close friends.

Todd had never called after that date. She'd spotted him a few times from a distance, but if he'd ever noticed her, he didn't let her know.

Grad school hadn't exactly lined up desirable suitors. Almost all her classmates were women. She had no problem seeing herself single and working, and husbands and kids could complicate her life. She wanted everything simple. Perhaps Phineas was just going to be a good friend. *No way.* He really seemed to enjoy kissing her. Slow and shy weren't bad, only different. It seemed he wanted her to direct. She could play that part. She could bring this along, as she liked. He might even be decent looking under all that facial hair, and untapped warmth resided in those brown eyes.

Before Phineas, Boston had become a cold and lonely place. Well, the amount of time she had for him was about right. She still had much to accomplish.

⚜ ⚜ ⚜

"I ga-ron-tee!" Justin Wilson, a Cajun chef from Southern Louisiana, had just dumped oysters into a jambalaya. Phineas had discovered Wilson's Saturday afternoon cooking show on public television soon after he met Iris. PBS was one of three channels the rabbit ear antennae on his ten-inch black and white TV captured from the airwaves. Phineas timed study breaks to the show's beginning. Wilson's dishes and humor sent Phineas to used bookstores more than once to find a Cajun cookbook to add to his embryonic culinary library.

The last time, Phineas purchased a used hardcover copy of *The New Orleans Cookbook* by Rima and Richard Collins for two dollars. In it was another recipe for jambalaya, using chicken, ham, and sausages. He wrote down the essential ingredients and planned to improvise with whatever he could find at Haymarket. He'd invited Iris for a shopping expedition there today, after which he would cook for her for the first time.

While he listened to Justin Wilson, Phineas had the Collins' cookbook open to the jambalaya page. He precisely measured out the herbs and spices and arranged them and utensils on the tiny counter, like soldiers lined up at attention.

He chuckled at Justin Wilson's closing words. "You can tell I ain't poisoning anybody. I eat what I cook." Wilson then took a big forkful, chewed, and smiled.

※ ※ ※

Phineas gave Iris the two-minute tour of his apartment in Beacon Hill. It was officially a one bedroom, but included a separate tiny room, *his* bedroom.

"And *this* is my humble bedroom." He nodded his chin toward the room that featured an armoire instead of a closet. The red plaid bedspread was stretched wrinkle-free over his full-sized bed. A twelve-inch window offered a view of a nearby brick wall.

Iris peered in from the doorway. "Cozy. Do you ever stub your toes?"

He explained that his apartment mate was a senior medical student who had the real bedroom, the one behind the other door. "It will be mine after Tim graduates." The apartment had been handed down through medical students for years. It was traditional for the more senior student to advance to the larger room.

※ ※ ※

When they arrived at Haymarket, Phineas had to raise his voice to be heard over the hubbub. "Hope you're ready to shop!" Rows and rows of stalls displayed colorful fruits and vegetables. Vendors hawked wares, often in Italian accents, as Phineas and Iris meandered along the rows. Breezes brought hints of onion, garlic, and fresh fish through the frigid air. Iris' head swiveled from side to side as they walked. She proclaimed that she hadn't yet discovered the expansive outdoor food market.

"Hey! You two looka like you need to take home some of my home-made sausage, the best in Boston!" A middle-aged man with a pencil mustache.

Phineas eyed the sausages. "I'm looking for Andouille sausages."

"I gotcha your mild Italian, your spicy Italian, and these Polish Kielbasa. You look Italian with your Roman nose. How about Italian sausage? I didn't make the Kielbasa."

"The Kielbasa will have to do for what I'm cooking. It's smoked, right?"

"Of course, my friend."

Phineas next gathered onions, a green pepper, a bunch of scallions, a head of garlic, and fresh parsley as they walked. He debated between chicken and shrimp.

"Here, young man. Inspect this beauty." The seafood salesman handed him a crustacean on a sheet of newspaper. It shimmered and smelled light and salty. No ammonia.

"I'll take one pound."

The sun began a rapid descent from its apex during Phineas' finicky shopping. He considered himself lucky to find a decent baguette late in the afternoon. A second was half off, so he took two.

While he was thinking of a sweet pastry for dessert, Iris chatted with a wiry sixteen-year-old boy at a nearly empty fruit stand. The boy blew into his hands and stamped his feet. His black hair was slicked back, and he wore a lined denim jacket and tight jeans.

"Sir, you've got to taste these grapes to believe them!"

Iris turned to Phineas. "He said he'll sell us five pounds of grapes for a dollar. Our appetizer and dessert?"

The young vendor shrugged. "I have a date tonight. I'm done here when I sell out."

Phineas tasted a firm and juicy green grape before handing him a dollar. "Where can we get a good price on cheese?"

⚜ ⚜ ⚜

Back at his apartment, he took Iris' coat and poured her a glass of Chenin Blanc. He washed the grapes and placed them in front of her on a plate with a knife and the block of gouda cheese. He hovered for a moment, hoping she was pleased.

She plucked a grape from the stem and inspected it. "Phineas, I can help, but I'm happy to watch and learn. I'm not up to your cooking standards."

"There's only room for one in this miniscule kitchen, so relax and enjoy."

The ingredients formed a grid on the counter, with the foods, herbs, and spices taking the place of numbers in a matrix, each to be added at just the right time.

"Wow! I've never seen anyone so organized while cooking."

"The French have a term for it."

"What?"

"I forget. Saw it on a cooking show. All the ingredients measured and in order, so I don't screw this up."

He chopped vegetables and sautéed them in olive oil. Next came the sausage, a handful of chopped parsley, then the rest of the herbs and spices, carefully mixed in. He named each one for Iris. She nodded and acted interested. The bouquet of onions, garlic, sausage, and spices filled the apartment and lifted his spirits. It had to lift her impression of him.

Iris offered him a wedge of cheese. "You mind if I hold my head over the pot and sniff for a while?"

She approves!

He added four cups of water and two cups of long grain white rice then brought it all to a boil before he covered it to simmer. He then washed, peeled, and deveined the shrimp, taking care that each precious one was perfect.

"We'll add these after the rice is done and the heat turned off. The hot jambalaya will cook them just right."

He felt triumphant after he washed his hands and plopped a grape in his mouth.

While the rice cooked, he explained to Iris how at his small-town high school, sports made you popular. He played baseball. Studying made you a geek.

"I was able to get good grades without working at it. College was a total shock. Everyone was smart *and* studied."

"Imagine that."

"My first mid-term grades were way below what I was used to in high school. I began to regret going to an Ivy League school. One guy on my hall, Mike, transferred to an easier school. Another, Peter, dropped out. Jeff, a sophomore I knew from my high school left on academic probation. I was terrified I'd have to go back to Vermont with my tail between my legs."

"Wait. You have a tail?"

"Surgically removed." He winked. "Let me pour you another glass of wine."

"Oh my. Go on. How did you resurrect yourself?"

"I became a grind." *Not the best impression to give her.*

"We should work on that." The 60-watt overhead kitchen light produced shadows that accentuated the elegance of her face.

"No playing except Friday and Saturday nights. The library was my home the rest of the time. I became conscientious, boringly conscientious. I learned how to learn."

"Glad it extends to your cooking. I'm getting hungry."

A good sign. "Do you mind if I put garlic butter on the baguette?" Phineas began slicing half of the loaf at precise angles.

"Fine with me. Whatever you like. I'm usually not a bread person. I can't afford a new wardrobe."

A ravenous Phineas plated the jambalaya and lit a candle between them on the small kitchen table. He turned off the overhead light and sat. Before he could take a bite, the apartment door burst open, and a booming voice followed. "Finman, what masterpiece have you concocted this time? Smells heavenly!"

Phineas gestured at the intruder. "Iris, this savage and unkempt human being is my apartment mate, Tim. Hard to believe he is *almost* a doctor. Tim, this is Iris."

Tim bowed deeply, which wasn't far since he stood at most five foot four. He had shaggy blond hair and would have benefited from a shave of his wispy attempt at a beard. Behind him was a thin woman with unnaturally blond hair almost to her waist. At first glance, she appeared the epitome of Tim's personal philosophy of life. "Life," he once told Phineas, "is made up of two parts. Sex is one part. All the rest is foreplay."

"And I'd like to introduce my date, Hanna. Finman, you'll work with her when you do OB. She's a nurse in Labor and Delivery."

Iris rose and shook their hands. "Pleased to meet you. Will you join us in this feast?"

Tim grabbed two plates from the cupboard before he inquired, "You sure you have enough? Mann, I'll miss your cooking when I'm at Dartmouth next year." He handed the dishes to Hanna and found two forks, glasses, and napkins. She scooped servings of jambalaya. Tim peered at one plate. "A little more for me, please."

Iris pushed bread toward Hanna. "Have you been dating long?"

Hanna's forkful of jambalaya paused in front of her scarlet lips. "A few weeks. This looks wonderful. Thank you for sharing."

Iris turned to Tim. "How did you and Phineas wind up as roommates?"

Tim swallowed and reached for the bottle of wine. "Yeah, thanks. Phineas was one of the second years who answered my ad. He said he mostly just studied and cooked, so I took a chance on him." He grinned. "Haven't been sorry. He'll soon have to find my replacement."

"So, he's been easy to live with?" Iris tilted her head toward Phineas.

Tim pointed the half loaf of bread at Phineas then tore off a generous piece. "He's no party animal. Studies a lot and keeps things neat. And I haven't had to deal with him having women staying over all the time like my last roommate."

Phineas felt flushed and on display. "How do you like the jambalaya, Iris?"

"Delicious." She had just managed to swallow her first forkful. "Tim, you're confirming my impression of Phineas. And it's nice that he has your senior guidance."

"Haven't talked him into radiology yet."

Phineas laughed. "Not sure I want to stare at x-rays in a dark room all day. And you don't get to know patients."

"The lifestyle is better. You work shifts, and most are days. Most nights you don't take call. And there's the pay..."

Iris glanced at Phineas and said, "Hard to argue with that." She smiled at Hanna. "Hanna, how'd you end up in obstetrics?"

Hanna sat tall and pushed her silky hair behind surprisingly prominent ears. "It was my favorite rotation in nursing school. So many happy parents and cute babies. But my nursing school hospital didn't do high risk OB like they do at Tufts."

"How's it different?"

"At the medical center we see the tough cases referred from smaller hospitals. Often there's no prenatal care. More social problems. More complications. More damaged babies. I'm not sure how long I'll stay there." Hanna glanced expectantly at Tim.

He broke off another piece of baguette and shifted the subject. "I heard you two met when Phineas kept a bag lady from attacking you with a cigarette."

Phineas gestured with his fork. "I used my backpack."

Iris reached for his other hand. "He was truly gallant."

Tim guffawed then grabbed his napkin to dab at the wine that leaked out of his nose.

⚜ ⚜ ⚜

Tim and Hanna fled into the night after they'd eaten their fill and profusely thanked Phineas and Iris. Phineas sighed. "Well, I thought I had cooked enough for leftovers."

He gratefully accepted Iris' offer to help tidy up. He began washing. She dried. "You're a man of many surprises. A talent for cooking, and you prepared my native comfort food. What led to your culinary interest?"

"Started in college." He handed her a plate. "My apartment mates and I took turns cooking dinner. I began thinking about it like a meal was a mix of an organic chemistry synthesis and artwork. It got competitive after a while. We each gained about fifteen pounds during our senior year."

"So, you're self-taught?"

"My mom too. She's Italian, so it's in the blood. When I was home from school, I hung around and watched her chop, sauté, and even make pasta from a volcano of flour with egg lava. I asked her to teach me. She said, 'you can read, can't you? Well then, you can cook.' Hah! That's Mom." He held out both wet hands, palms up.

"My mother would have loved to teach me. I wasn't interested."

"Mom must have been amused at my interest though because she began measuring her handfuls, pinches and dashes. She then wrote them down in letters, which contained recipes of my favorite dishes."

"What I just ate wasn't Italian." She dried the last glass and handed him the dish towel.

"I found this Cajun chef on PBS and have been watching him since I met you. He pronounces onion with long o's and says 'ga-ron-tee'." He draped the towel over a bar next to the sink. "I remembered the phrase I was searching for earlier. Mise en place. Everything in its place. Works for cooking—and medicine."

Iris moved closer to Phineas, silently meeting his gaze. He placed his hands on her hips and kissed her. She pulled him closer and kissed him back. He pressed the tip of his tongue against her lips and was pleased as she relaxed them enough to let him caress her tongue. He eased his right hand under her sweater. *How smooth her skin is!* He found the clasp of her bra, struggled to unfasten it, and failed miserably. Iris grasped his arm and gently pushed it down.

"Iris, I'm...I'm sorry."

She peeled off her sweater, unhooked her bra and slipped it off. When she whispered, "It's cold in here. We should get under the covers," he forced his spellbound gaze from her ample breasts back to her captivating eyes.

One by one, she turned off the lights and led him to his room. The night sky outside his window offered just enough light to outline her profile while she stripped off her jeans and panties and slipped between the sheets.

"Your bed is freezing!" Get under here! I need you to warm me up."

He had to remind himself to breathe.

❀ ❀ ❀

Phineas awakened at first light and lay as still as he could. Iris' toasty skin was pressed against his back. He lingered divine minutes before he slipped out from under the covers, emptied his bladder, brushed his teeth, and started the coffee percolator. Then he crept back into the now chilly sheets and pressed his chest into her warmth.

She stirred. "Umm. I smell coffee."

Phineas kissed her cheek, her lips, her neck. A hint of garlic remained. He lifted the sheet and admired her body and her long, athletic legs in the daylight. She was the most beautiful being he'd ever seen. She pressed her index finger on his lips and whispered, "I need to pee first."

❀ ❀ ❀

Over coffee and toasted leftover baguette smeared with his grand-mother's wild blueberry jam, Phineas began, "You know, Tim will be moving out in June. I'm expected to advertise my room at school and move into Tim's room." He paused to steady his nerves. "Iris...we've been dating for almost three months, and I think we're great together...I...I wish you'd move in instead of another medical student." He put down his toast. "If you want to."

Iris hesitated. "I've never lived with a man."

"I've never lived with a woman."

"It might put a lot of stress on us. I've gotten used to alone time. What happens if it doesn't work out? Where do I live then?" Her words came out in a rush.

"I'll give you as much space as you want. You can have the smaller room as a study." Phineas swirled his coffee cup. "You know, I'll be in the hospital a lot with rotations, at least until next winter and spring when electives start. And you'd have the apartment to yourself for the weeks while I am away on out-of-town rotations. And I have to travel to interview for internships in the fall. You should have plenty of alone time."

"I hope you wouldn't expect sex every moment you're in the mood."

"Now and then would be nice. I hope you enjoyed it." His first-time clumsiness and overexcitement flashed back to him. His cheeks felt hot. He hoped she didn't notice.

"It did get better the second and third times." She smiled warmly.

Wow! He wanted to kiss and hug her right then.

Iris sipped coffee and swallowed. "When would I have to decide? I don't know what my roommates' plans are."

"I probably don't have to announce the room for a month or two. Whatever you decide, I want to see as much of you as our schedules will allow." He hoped she would feel the same.

When the roux attained the color of peanut butter Phineas added chopped onions, green peppers, shallots, and garlic. The garlic and onions' essence filled the apartment as he hummed and assembled gumbo. Today, Saturday, was a red-letter day, despite the background of a grey week on psychiatry.

Though Phineas neared the end of that rotation, he'd realized quickly it wasn't going to be his career path. Morning inpatient rounds featured tragic young people, suddenly psychotic with new onset schizophrenia or manic-depressive disorder. Phineas saw little progress day to day. Medications failed to return them to their healthy and happy younger selves. The older folks on the wards were so depressed, that Phineas' duty was to assist with their electroconvulsive therapy.

He spent some afternoons in clinic with therapists, seeing people with everything from neuroses and depression to 'assisting' with marriage counseling.

When he'd explained his duties to Iris, she'd commented. "Imagine *you* doing marriage counseling,"

"One afternoon, I started to fall asleep during a session. The psychologist I was paired with, Dr. Nakayama, brought me back into the conversation, so I think she noticed. Not sure about the couple...I don't do well listening to others go on and on."

Phineas reread about the obsessive-compulsive disorder. He quoted a descriptive passage in his text to Iris.

"... a preoccupation with orderliness, perfectionism and control..."

Iris nodded. "Jury's out. Do go on."

"... at the expense of flexibility, openness and efficiency."

"Not guilty, yet."

"I've become more compulsive since I began college,"

She'd leaned over and tickled his ribs. "Just don't drift into obsessive. *That* could be a slippery slope."

Her warning from that day came back to him as he surveyed the perfect grid of gumbo ingredients on the counter. Food was too precious to chance mistakes. *Mise en place.*

Today's red-letter day launched after Phineas acquired tickets in the bleachers for the Red Sox game that afternoon. It was Iris' first Major League Baseball game and her first spring in Boston; a city she thought might never warm up again. The Red Sox demolished the White Sox 9-1 and Fenway rocked. Twenty-ounce draft beers were fuel. A home run landed two rows in front of them. The entire section stood and screamed.

Iris apparently saw that as the right time to say, "I'd like to take you up on your offer to move into your apartment."

"That's fantastic!" He hugged her. Could his life get any better?

"I have some more news I think you'll like."

Really? "More?"

She whispered in his ear. "I went to the BU infirmary and started birth control pills."

The crowd noise drowned her words. Phineas shook his head. "What did you say?"

She yelled into his ear. "I started birth control pills."

Phineas' mouth fell open.

The older couple in the seats in front turned and surveyed Iris and Phineas. They both had round faces and ruddy cheeks. The woman said, "Good idea" and returned to shelling peanuts.

On a Saturday afternoon in late May, Phineas settled into his bunk in the windowless basement call room in the Concord Hospital in Concord, New Hampshire. He had one more week of his Obstetrics-Gynecology rotation there.

He'd started the Ob-Gyn rotation as an observer on the high-risk pregnancy service in Tufts New England Medical Center. The second half was an hour up Interstate 93 on the front lines as one of the students on first call in the Concord Hospital, where there were no interns or residents. He reported to and assisted the staff Ob-Gyn MDs directly. Seven MDs practiced in two private groups. He and two other students worked all day weekdays and shared call nights and weekends. The students delivered the uncomplicated babies as the MDs and Labor and Delivery nurses coached. Phineas even helped with a breech and a twin delivery. On two other occasions, he delivered babies before the MD could get there. Students were allowed to first assist on the infrequent Caesarian sections. Constantly immersed in the work, they slept when they could. They felt useful. Healthy babies meant happy parents. One of the other students, seduced by the upbeat atmosphere, had declared she wanted to go into Ob-Gyn.

The MDs put in lengthy days and nights. Some labors progressed slowly. The nurses and students tried not to call them until the moment was near. Weekdays, the MDs put in full days in clinic, sometimes after sleepless nights.

Phineas had been up most of last night with Dr. Senior for a firstborn. Labor had taken sixteen hours, a Pitocin drip to strengthen contractions, and a forceps delivery. They then made work rounds on the inpatients, after which Dr. Senior had gone home to try to steal recovery sleep.

Phineas retreated to his assigned bedroom in the hospital basement. It had been three weeks since he'd seen Iris. He was too tired to write another letter. One more week in Concord.

An hour later Phineas was jolted awake by the shriek of his pager. The only light oozed under the bottom of the door. He turned on the lamp and dialed Labor and Delivery.

"This is Phineas Mann."

"Phineas, this is Janie in L&D. Dr. Senior wants you to give him a call." She relayed a phone number. Phineas sat up on the edge of his narrow bed and dialed.

A gravelly voice answered, "Phineas? Dr. Senior. Just got off the phone with the ED and Janie Roberts. Clara O'Hara is being admitted after a second trimester miscarriage. I need you to see her." Phineas could hear Dr. Senior yawn. "Just started a nap. I'm running on fumes. Too tired to drive, so I'll have to get my wife to bring me back. Shouldn't be too long."

"Is the patient okay? And what about her baby?"

"She's physically okay; emotionally upset, as you'd expect. The baby can't survive at 22 weeks. Even if we transported it to a neonatal unit, it wouldn't make it."

"What would you like me to do?" *What can I possibly do?*

"Janie can guide you. Check on Mrs. O'Hara. You can make sure she's physically stable. Answer questions and sit with them."

"What should I tell them?"

"I'll explain to her what happened when I'm back there. Probably has an incompetent cervix. We should be able to take care of that with her next pregnancy."

"What about the fetus?"

"Janie will walk you through it. We'll need to record the time of death."

"Anything else?"

"Appreciate you doing this for me."

"I'll head right up." *Thank God Janie's there.* She'd guided Phineas through other first-time crises.

"I'll be in before too long. Should be within an hour."

Phineas paused only to splash cold water in his eyes before he jogged up the stairs. His mouth was sticky from sleep, though he was now fully awake. Janie Roberts, RN waited for him at the L&D door in an immaculate white dress and cap. "Carol O'Hara is 24 and was 22 weeks pregnant; her first. Her husband is with her."

"Is she OK? Any bleeding? Is the placenta out? Where's the fetus?"

"Everything is out. No extra bleeding. The fetus is in a bassinet in a private room. He was out as they arrived. She was too upset to keep him with her. Didn't want to watch him die." Janie had done this before. Her competence helped slow Phineas' rapid heartbeats.

"What'd Dr. Senior tell you?"

"Sounded like he was asleep. Mentioned incompetent cervix probably. Said he would see her as soon as he got back to the hospital. Nothing he could do now. Said the fetus isn't viable at 22 weeks."

"Which room?"

"Patient or fetus?"

He swallowed. "I should talk to her right away, but I'll check the fetus first."

"230, then she and her husband are in 212."

"Have you called the chaplain?"

"Her husband left a message for their priest at the sacristy."

Phineas slipped through the door of 230. The room was undisturbed except for the transparent bassinet next to the window. A miniature head was framed by a light blue baby blanket. Flecks of dried blood dotted the surrounding fabric. The eyes were sealed closed. The head slowly, rhythmically, almost imperceptibly rocked backward.

Phineas lifted the blanket. Skin between ribs retracted in time with the head. The cord was clamped close to the flimsy abdomen. Male genitalia were displayed between splayed legs. Petite, perfect fingers and toes were dusky grey. Phineas could have held him in one cupped hand. He covered him to his chin and smoothed the wrinkles.

As he approached 212, Janie Roberts whispered, "Such a shame—a beautiful boy."

Phineas' heart pounded in his ears as he entered the room. He wiped his sweaty palms on his scrub pants.

"Mr. and Mrs. O'Hara, I'm Phineas Mann, the medical student. I am so sorry for your loss. Dr. Senior is on his way. Is there anything I can do for you?"

Carol O'Hara gazed at him between puffy, red eyelids. What Phineas could see of her eyes was vacant. Her words were ragged. "I...I can't think of anything." He wished he could.

Her husband sank into the chair on the far side of the bed, his forehead lined. He was a large man who looked beaten. "Can you tell us what happened?"

"Dr. Senior will give you a full explanation after he examines you. From what I understand, what probably happened may be prevented in future pregnancies with a simple procedure, allowing the pregnancy to proceed to term. But he should be the one to explain it to you."

Mr. O'Hara looked over at his wife. "That I'll want to hear."

Phineas pulled a chair to the bedside and sat. "Are you having any pain?"

"Just cramps."

"Mind if I check your heart, lungs and tummy?"

"Go ahead." Her head settled into her pillow.

Phineas found only clear lungs, a healthy sounding heart between swollen breasts, and her deflated abdomen. "Cramps are to be expected and should subside. We'll check your bleeding the next time your nurse changes the pad."

The near silence that followed was painful, punctuated only by her erratic sobs and sighs. Her husband kept his eyes trained on her, his lips pressed in a tight line. Phineas could think of nothing helpful to say. He finally stood. "I'll be right outside. Please let us know if you want anything." He touched her forearm. "Would you like to see your son?"

"I said goodbye in the emergency room. I'm praying for him." She folded her hands and bowed her head.

"Call us right away if you change your mind."

Mr. O'Hara leaned forward and covered both of his wife's hands with one of his. "We already saw him."

Phineas returned to room 230 and slid a chair next to the bassinet. He raised his watch. 3:24 PM. He counted eight seconds between head and chest movements. The familiar sensation began in his nasal passage. He blinked back tears. Janie Roberts' head appeared in the doorway.

"What's happening, Phineas?"

"I didn't think he should be alone."

"Let me know when it's over. I'll make footprints on the certificate, and a plaster impression of his feet, in case they want it. And I'll ask her again if she wants to see him." She closed the door.

Phineas sank onto the seat. *Was this a life, if it was never viable?*

This was not his question to answer.

His time as an altar boy suggested one final task. Phineas hurried to the sink and drew a teaspoon of cool water into his palm. He cradled it back to the bassinet and let a few drops dribble onto the tiny forehead. "I baptize you in the name of the Father, Son, and Holy Ghost."

He settled himself at his post and counted ten seconds. Twelve seconds. He rubbed his eyes. Sixteen seconds. Twenty. The delicate lips, now grey, sipped hospital air. Then the softest escape. Phineas opened the window. The smell of lilacs and fresh cut grass entered. Another sip. A gentle shudder. Stillness. Phineas listened for a heartbeat. Nothing. 3:42.

⚜ ⚜ ⚜

"My God, Phineas. It's hard to imagine you had to go through that alone." Dr. MacSweeney extracted his empty pipe from his sweater pocket and sucked on the bit.

"Janie, the nurse, was there, and Dr. Senior came within the hour. He was exhausted." Phineas sat back and sank into the spongy sofa. "They taught me so much there. I'm not upset that I was alone that day. I did what thought was right when I baptized him before the end…Probably accomplished nothing though. Maybe it was more for me than him."

"Are you familiar with Pascal's wager?"

Phineas shrugged. "Heard his name in math classes."

"He decided it made no sense to bet against the existence of God. One might be wrong." Dr. MacSweeney pocketed his pipe and sat back.

Something for Phineas to ponder later. "So, when will the dreams stop?"

"Tell me about your dreams."

Phineas pressed his fists into his eyes. "I dream I'm the husband, and it's Iris who miscarries. I'm alone with her. No nurses or doctors. And together we watch our baby die slowly…in the palm of my hand."

Dr. MacSweeney waited for more before responding. "Preoccupation after an event like this is common. You're so busy with work during your days, that it surfaces when you sleep."

"How long will it continue?"

"Hard to say. We talk to *parents* who lose babies about relinquishing, readjusting, and reinvesting. You might want to contemplate these three R's and tuck them away for the future." He wrote the words on a scrap of paper. "Tell me about your Iris."

Phineas shoved the paper in his shirt pocket. He sat up on the front edge of the seat cushion. "Doc, where do I begin?"

❖ ❖ ❖

The early July morning hadn't yet heated up during his walk to the emergency room at Boston Children's Hospital. There was already someone in every bay and a line outside triage. Families stood in hallways where they had to listen to crying, screaming, and puking.

Phineas reported to Claudia, the resident on his pediatric rotation, to discuss Roberto, a ten-year-old suspected of having a ruptured spleen. Roberto had fallen from a jungle gym while trying to imitate Olympians competing on the high bar. Claudia had called the surgical consultant who requested they place a nasogastric tube to suction. The surgeon would be there before long.

"Have you placed an NG before?" Claudia asked, all efficiency and focus. She wore a short lab coat, close-cropped brown hair, and wire-rimmed glasses.

"On surgery, in adults. Where they understood what I was doing."

"Roberto seems pretty together for a ten-year-old. I'll bet he'll let you do it, once you explain it'll help his pain."

While he gathered gloves, K-Y jelly and the nasogastric tube, Phineas ran through the procedure in his mind. He steadied himself before he prepared Roberto and his parents.

Roberto put on a brave face while his hands trembled. "You're going to do what with what?"

"The tube will enter your nose and advance to your stomach where it will decompress your distended gut."

"My what?"

"Your intestines are over-distended from irritation, making it like a stretched balloon. Reducing the stretch with suction through the tube should help with your pain."

Roberto scrunched his face. "Up *your* nose with a rubber hose!" He studied Phineas face for a response before he added, "That's from a TV show."

"Which one?"

"It ain't *Good Times*!"

Phineas tried not to grin as he introduced the tube into Roberto's nostril.

⚜ ⚜ ⚜

Claudia and Phineas worked through case after case of respiratory infections and viral gastroenteritis trying not to miss a serious bacterial infection that demanded aggressive intervention. The next chart indicated that, hidden under the sheets in the next bay, Leigh was a 14-year-old girl with abdominal pain and fever. The nurse's notes indicated that the patient had also reported a vaginal discharge and admitted to being sexually active. The nurse had collected items for a pelvic exam. Family had vanished.

Claudia and Phineas peeled back the top sheet and found a sweaty and disheveled adolescent with bleached blond hair leading to dark roots. The curved outlines of the gown suggested she was physically mature.

"How many days have you had fevers?" Phineas asked.

"Two."

"And the pain?"

"Three, mebbe four."

"We need to examine you to find out what's wrong, OK?" He watched her face for a sign that she understood what he meant.

"OK." No sign, only a passive tone.

"Do you know where your parents are?"

"Probably home or on their way there."

"I'll call them, OK?" Claudia offered.

Leigh seemed to be studying the ceiling. "Phone's disconnected."

Despite his gentlest touch, Phineas found her lower abdomen rigid, and she winced when he removed his hand.

"Leigh, we need to examine you internally." He showed her the metal speculum.

"Internally where? How?" Her wide eyes suggested she'd never seen one.

"I'll insert this small tube in your vagina to get samples." Phineas answered. "Then I'll take it out and use two fingers to check your ovaries and tubes inside. I'll wear gloves. Okay?"

She sighed and closed her eyes. "If you have to."

Claudia touched Leigh's arm. "Leigh, have you ever had a PAP smear?"

Leigh shook her head. She was biting her lower lip.

"We'll be as gentle as possible."

The nurse helped Leigh put her feet in the stirrups and Phineas, grateful for his recent gynecology training, did his best to be gentle as he inserted the lubricated speculum in her vagina. This produced a whimper then a scream. "Ow! Ow! Please stop!"

The stench of anaerobic decay, like a two-day old roadkill deer on a summer day, assaulted Phineas. He pulled his head back and battled his gag reflex.

Claudia placed her hand on Leigh's arm and spoke firmly, "Try to hold on. This will only take a minute. It's very important." Claudia aimed the bright goose-neck lamp over Phineas shoulder and into the speculum.

Blisters and shallow ulcers coated Leigh's vaginal lining. Pus pooled below her cervix. Phineas swabbed her cervix and the pus and stuck the culture swab into a tube of holding medium then removed the speculum.

"Leigh, I'm sorry that was uncomfortable. I need to check your tubes and ovaries for swelling or masses next. I'm going to use two fingers. Let me know if anything hurts. This won't take long."

Claudia hovered while he inserted lubricated, gloved fingers. "There's a soft three-inch fullness to the left of her uterus."

The instant his fingertips moved her cervix, Leigh shrieked and scooted off his hand and almost over the head of the examination table. After calming and repositioning Leigh, Claudia reluctantly confirmed Phineas' findings.

They again inquired about ways to reach Leigh's parents to no avail. Claudia told her they needed to admit her for antibiotics and close observation before she and Phineas took Leigh's chart to the workroom to write orders.

"Herpes?" Phineas asked.

"Herpes, gonorrhea, tubo-ovarian abscesses, and who knows what else. Maybe syphilis. You witnessed what is irreverently referred to as the 'chandelier sign', when the patient leaps off your fingers and grabs the chandelier." Phineas had not seen Claudia angry before. Her voice quivered with rage.

"It's hard to imagine she got all that from someone her age. We clearly need to report this to the Health Department. It would be great if they could pursue contacts and find the bastard or bastards who gave it to her. It's almost certainly statutory rape. She'll be afraid to tell on anyone. That's what usually happens."

She took a deep breath. "So, Phineas, how do you like Pediatrics so far?"

❦ ❦ ❦

Phineas trudged up the steps to the apartment. Iris sat at the kitchen table, typing, as he opened the door. She put her hands in her lap and smiled. "You look wiped out. Hard day?"

"After today in the ER, I decided I'm not going to be a pediatrician. Looks like it's internal medicine for me."

"You sure? Something happen?"

"Just a terrified kid with multiple venereal diseases protecting rapists." He wrinkled his nose at the memory and shook his head in disgust.

A crease formed between her eyebrows and suggested sympathy. "An opportunity for social work to help?"

"How do you find someone before it happens?"

"We don't usually, not the way things work."

"Seems like kids either have grown-up problems, or we have to restrain them in a board with straps, called a papoose, to stick needles in them. Then they think I'm a monster. They don't understand why we're hurting them."

"And helping them."

"I can't stay awake during psychotherapy, so psychiatry is out. It's also so vague and disorganized." Phineas held up his index finger. "I'm not giving up my best years to train as a surgeon. Those guys never sleep or go home." He held up a second finger. "I liked delivering babies, but I'm not sure I can see myself waiting for labor to progress day and night when I'm in my fifties or doing pelvic exam after pelvic exam all day." Three fingers. "And I cringe when I have to do painful things to kids who can't understand I'm trying to help them." Four. "I don't want to stare at x-rays or into a microscope all day. That rules out radiology and pathology." His thumb and his other index finger. "That pretty much leaves internal medicine."

"But do you *like* medicine?"

"Yes. I believe I do."

Iris rose from the table and opened the refrigerator. She removed a cupcake with a candle and placed it on the table. "Happy birthday! *Now* you get to make a wish." She struck a wooden kitchen match and lit the candle.

He closed his eyes. When he reopened them, he blew out the flame.

"So, what was your wish?"

"You know I'm not supposed to tell if I want it to come true." He'd tell her one day—when the time was right.

By November, Iris' mother had somehow determined Iris was living with a man. In a call out of nowhere, Mom expressed great shame and heartbreak before she declared she'd disowned her daughter. The words, "What if the other women of my church were to find out?" still echoed in Iris' thoughts.

Her father called soon after, sadness in his voice, and said, "You know how stubborn your mother is. I don't think I can change her at this point." Before this call, he had been sending short, caring letters sometimes wrapped around ten or twenty-dollar bills. Iris feared his letters, her only contact with him, might stop.

They called while Phineas was away for residency interviews. Iris' tears smeared a freshly typed report. The phone rang a third time. She picked up after the eighth ring. "Hello?"

"Hi Iris. I'm in New Orleans," Phineas was yelling over raucous background noise. "I'm in the French Quarter on a pay phone."

Iris sighed. "Glad *you're* having fun."

"You okay?"

"Just got off the phone with Mom." A pause and another sigh. "She disowned me."

"What?"

"Living in sin with a man, she said."

Phineas was silent for several seconds. "I don't know what to say. I wish I was there for you."

"And you're partying in New Orleans."

"I won't be coming here for residency. Didn't like the program." A pause. "I fly home tomorrow. Can't wait to see you."

The telephone receiver demanded, "Please deposit two dollars for three more minutes."

Iris murmured, "I'd better let you go."

"I miss you. See you tomorrow night."

"Me too."

Iris wiped her cheek on her sleeve before she began retyping the smeared page.

⚜ ⚜ ⚜

Phineas pored over notes from his recent interviews for internal medicine residencies. He had to submit his rankings of the programs to 'The Match' in December. Residents Match Day was in March. Before that day, a computer would match his rankings with the programs that wanted him and tell him where he would train for the next three years.

He had done well enough at Tufts for his advisor to suggest he apply for at least one of the Harvard hospitals. He'd interviewed at Harvard's Beth Israel Hospital and Peter Bent Brigham, both no brainers with great programs. He would rank them first and second, knowing he had only the slimmest chance of the computer going far enough down those hosptals' lists, past the superstars who'd already published in journals, to match him, an unpublished, bookish grind.

"Why didn't you apply to Mass General?" Iris had asked.

"You mean Massive Genitals? Those guys never go home. They live in the hospital. No thanks, and I wouldn't get in anyway."

The happiest visit Phineas had was in Chapel Hill at the University of North Carolina. The residents who showed him around and the faculty who interviewed were friendly, and the training seemed top-notch. He could see himself happy in Chapel Hill, so UNC would be third on his list.

When he'd told Iris about UNC, she raised an eyebrow and said, "Small town North Carolina? You do know Jesse Helms is from North Carolina?"

"I like small towns. I'm from one. And Chapel Hill is a college town. Everyone I met there was nice...By the way, who is Jesse Helms?"

"A scary senator. And you'll be working all the time, so small town won't matter much to you."

He also liked the program at The University of Virginia. The hitch was that its residents were painfully preppy. All the men had been clean-shaven and wore button-down shirts with ties, khaki pants, and Top-Siders. UVA would be his fourth choice.

He'd looked at Charity Hospital in New Orleans, mostly as an excuse to see where Iris came from. He loved exploring the French Quarter, but not his tour of Charity Hospital. It was standard practice for residents to draw all the labs, start all the IVs, and do their own EKGs. He heard interns usually had to take their own patients for x-rays. When he finalized his list, Charity wouldn't be on it. There'd be little time to learn.

Dartmouth and Tufts rounded out his list, but he hoped the Match computer would send him to one of his first three.

While he traveled for interviews, Phineas had admitted to himself that he was in love with Iris. He'd reasoned that if he told her he loved her, and she didn't respond that she loved him, he might sabotage what they had. How uncomfortable would *that* conversation be? And neither knew what would come after their graduations. For now, he had to be resigned to wait for her cues. It did feel like she'd missed him while he traveled though. Maybe she wasn't as solitary a person as she liked to think.

On New Year's Eve, it was biting cold on the streets of Boston after the Greyhound bus ride from Vermont. Iris' new parka and gloves, Christmas presents from Phineas' parents, Norris and Maria, had kept her comfortable in Vermont, the farthest north she'd ever been. Phineas' family had warmly taken her in for their Thanksgiving feast and then again for Christmas, like she'd been orphaned.

The mailbox contained a letter and a Christmas card, both addressed to her. The card was from her father. Two twenties fell out. He wished her blessed holidays and expressed sorrow she didn't share it with them. There was no mention of her mother, confirming Iris' ongoing maternal disinheritance.

The letter was the second she'd received from her sixteen-year-old brother, Matthew. She answered his first letter immediately after it arrived two months earlier. His printing was again neat and precise.

> *Dear Iris,*
>
> *We will miss you at Christmas. I can't remember you not being here for the holidays.*
> *It's still pretty crazy here. Mom never says your name. It's like she's pretending you never existed. And she slams the doors A LOT!*
> *Dad and I talk about you when she's not here, but as you know, she's always here. Dad is holding out hope that Mom will come around, or maybe your 'situation' will change.*
> *Anyway, there is some relief you are not the perfect daughter she always said you were (after you left for college). This should make things easier for me. Ha! Ha! So thank you at least for that.*
> *I wish I could visit you and hang out with you and Phineas in Boston, but that's not going to happen any time soon.*
> *So Merry Christmas and Happy New Year.*
> *Write to me.*
>
> *Matthew*

Iris dabbed at the corner of her eye.

⚜ ⚜ ⚜

Phineas' March visit to the Giant Ocean Tank at the New England Aquarium was one of a handful for him. It was his favorite exhibit. With 200,000 gallons, it was the one of the largest in the world and contained awe-inspiring sharks, eels, and barracuda. The sea turtles were surprisingly nimble in the water despite their blocky forms.

Iris agreed to meet him there after her Saturday shift at Tufts. Immersed in trying to secure employment after her upcoming May graduation and without a single positive response to numerous inquiries, she'd left a message for her supervisor at Tufts, asking whether they could hire her full time in May.

She recently told Phineas how she endured a long unpaid internship at Boston University's hospital in Roxbury as part of her Masters program. The walk from her trolley stop to the hospital was worse than the Combat Zone. She hurried past shabby clusters of men who hooted and whistled. She had also been warned that her supervisor there, Dr. MacDonald PhD, was a creep. The word was that if he circled behind you as he talked, he was trying to look down your blouse. She'd worn turtlenecks since the beginning of her rotation there.

Phineas watched Iris' approach down the giant tank's entrance ramp. Her shoulders slouched forward, and she kept gazing at the floor. Phineas guessed her part-time job at Tufts wasn't going to mushroom into a full-time position. He was afraid to ask. She stared into the tank, her attention on a hammerhead shark circling close. "The director told me everyone liked my work, but they won't have an opening then. She also commented that Boston has so many graduate students, the only way to stand out is to get experience somewhere else, then come back. It's not the first time I've heard that."

"I didn't think you were that crazy about Boston."

"I wasn't at first, but I'm used to it now."

"You know I learn the results of The Match next week."

"And you like Beth Israel and the Brigham here in Boston."

"The odds are against me matching at either."

They stood in the empty observation area without speaking. Phineas shifted his weight from one foot to the other twice before he decided it was time to summon enough courage to face her and say what he'd been holding back.

"Iris, I love you. Will you marry me?"

Iris looked bewildered. "Phineas, would you repeat that please?"

Phineas took a knee. "I love you. I want you to marry me. I don't know where I'm going in June, but I want you with me."

The courage he had summoned began to dissipate as Iris studied his face. If she said, "No," he wasn't sure he'd have the courage to ask again. Had he ruined their happy arrangement? His pulse pounded in his temples.

Iris closed her eyes for a moment before staring into his. "Phineas, I can't imagine marrying anyone else. Yes, I'll marry you." She cradled his face in her hands.

He stood and kissed her. When she rested her head on his shoulder, a wave of warmth washed over him. "I wish I had money for a diamond. As soon as I can, I'll get you one. A wedding ring will have to come first."

"I don't need a diamond. Can't imagine such an extravagance.'

※ ※ ※

That night, after making love, he told her for the third time he loved her. This time she responded, "I love you too."

※ ※ ※

Phineas steadied his hand as he handed the torn envelope to Iris. His sweaty palms had dampened the paper.

She tilted her head forward and creased her brow. "So, what do we have here? Good news? You look like the cat that ate the canary."

"You tell me."

"Harvard?" She opened it. "Phineas, this says you, I guess I should say we, are going to North Carolina."

She said, "we"!

"You will love it there, I'm sure."

"It appears we'll both need to *like* it there. I hope you're right. You spent, what, a day and a half there? I hadn't been thinking much about going south."

"You're from the South."

"That's why I wasn't thinking about going there."

"Will you...Will you still marry me?"

Iris studied the paper, then Phineas' face. "Yes, I'll still marry you—and I'll come to North Carolina."

He wrapped his arms around her. "Iris, there's so much to figure out. We'll need a car. Maybe I can get one soon and drive there to rent an apartment."

"What are you going to use to pay for a car?"

"I'm going to be a doctor. Banks will lend to me."

"If you get a car, I'm going with you to Chapel Hill to pick out the place. I'll be the one who will be there the most."

⚜ ⚜ ⚜

Iris sat at their table as Phineas mix spices in a bowl. It was a Friday in Lent, and he planned to blacken a piece of salmon he'd purchased on his way back to the apartment. He'd promised glazed fresh turnips for the side dish.

The phone rang for the first time in a week. Iris guessed, "Wrong number?" She pressed the receiver to her ear. "Hello?"

"Iris, we are just so excited! Have you and Phineas picked a date? Have you picked out a church?" A woman's voice, laced with a drawl, carried across the kitchen.

He knew Iris had dropped a note to her father Monday to let him know of Phineas' proposal and her acceptance. It clearly reached its destination.

"Well, hello, Mom. So nice to hear from you."

"Tell me about your fiancé. Your father says he's almost a doctor. We have so much to catch up on." Phineas could hear every word.

"Mom, we haven't figured any of it out yet. The only thing we know is that we plan to live in Chapel Hill, North Carolina for the next three years. I only learned this a few minutes ago."

"North Carolina. Oh my! I do hope you want to have the wedding here in New Orleans."

"Mom, we haven't figured anything out yet. Why don't you call me next week after Phineas and I have talked more about everything? And give my love to Dad." Iris hung up. She sighed. "Oh my, indeed."

Phineas watched her expression shift from surprised to anger to tears. He couldn't understand why he felt responsible.

⚜ ⚜ ⚜

Phineas listened to Iris tell how much her mother was pushing for the wedding to take place in New Orleans in the Catholic church where Iris received her first communion and her confirmation. Her mother kept effusing about how all the family friends would want to attend. Not aware of this opening gambit, Phineas' mother offered to arrange the service in Vermont at the church where Phineas had been an altar boy, and Iris and he had attended midnight mass on Christmas Eve. To top it all off, Iris mentioned going to Boston's City Hall for a civil ceremony, a quick fix to the predicament.

Amid the swirling chaos, Phineas sought a solution satisfactory to all parties.

He decided to make his first confession in years at Saint Stephen's Catholic Church in Boston's North End. He and Iris had once admired the building when they had detoured to the Harbor before shopping at Haymarket. At the end of his confession, he asked Father Kelly if he could meet with him. Phineas then knelt in a pew, struggling to remember the words for his lengthy assignment of prayers of penance. The priest seemed to feel that Phineas needed to atone for his many Sunday absences from mass and for premarital sex.

The Catholic Church had once been a cornerstone in Phineas' life. When he was ten, the priest had visited the parents of the ten-year-old Catholic boys in his small town and convinced them their sons should be altar boys. Phineas had found his three years on the altar peaceful. He'd learned the Latin responses his first year before the Church had shifted to English. He memorized the ritual chants and contemplated the scripture readings, the only sounds echoing in the otherwise silent, cavernous building. Phineas even considered the priesthood before hormones had filled his dreams and directed his eyes to the changes girls his age underwent on what seemed like a daily basis.

After his prayers of penance in St. Stephen's, he found himself thanking God he hadn't become a priest, and that Iris had come into his life and consented to be his wife.

"How can I help you, son?" Father Kelly inquired in a soft baritone voice. He was stout under his cassock and crowned with curly gray hair. Phineas explained the situation with the two mothers. Father Kelly suggested a hoped-for solution.

"You should marry in *my* church."

Perfect!

"Thank you, Father." Phineas suspected it wasn't going to be that simple.

"Of course, you and Iris will need to attend weekly Pre-Cana sessions first."

Phineas would have to convince Iris. "We can do that, Father." He hoped.

"I'll find out the dates for you." Father Kelly offered a church bulletin and a pen. "Write down your phone number."

Phineas managed to convince Iris they should walk to the Harbor Sunday after they read the Globe. He steered her by the front of Saint Stephen's and suggested they peer inside. Iris watched Phineas dip his index finger in the holy water and make the sign of the cross, as he had done so many times as an altar boy.

"Are you becoming religious again?" Iris asked.

"How would you like to have our wedding here?" He looked into her face to gauge her reaction.

"It's nice. Probably not available."

"I met with the priest this week. We can have it here."

"Really? You're full of surprises." She cocked her head. "Is there a catch?"

"We'll need to attend Pre-Cana marriage preparation classes."

"We could just go to City Hall."

"Classes are free and only one evening a week for four weeks—and you've always liked learning stuff."

Iris was silent.

Phineas continued, "I think both sets of parents would be happy with it. We could say this is our church."

"At least we wouldn't have to travel."

"So that's a 'Yes'?"

Iris nodded as she took in the simple elegance of St. Stephen's interior.

⚜ ⚜ ⚜

June traffic around Logan Airport was a moving parking lot, except that every other car honked, not just a few wake up beeps, but laying on its horn. Phineas and Iris approached the Arrivals area in their new silver Toyota Corona, secured through the loan officer in Phineas' father's bank in Vermont, and Iris began scanning the crowd for her family. They were coming to Boston for the first time, for the wedding tomorrow.

"There they are." She pointed toward the exit doors.

Phineas pulled to the curb and parked. He soon spotted a cloud of smoke lugging two suitcases. Jerome Babineaux sported a cigarette between his lips and a grey crew cut. Classroom chalk dusted the lapels and around the buttons of his tweed jacket. Behind him was a tall, gangly teenager. Matthew's hair was the same brown as Iris' with an obvious fresh trim.

Iris hugged her father. "You know Daddy, you can't smoke in our new car." She let go and looked over her shoulder. "This is Phineas." The males all shook hands and exchanged hellos. Iris had warned Phineas about her father's smoking. She tried for years to convince him to break his nicotine addiction. He preferred Camels unfiltered. His right index and middle fingers were stained amber.

Matthew exclaimed, "I finally get to see Boston!"

Before Phineas could respond, Iris blurted, "Hi Mom" and began moving toward a woman walking slowly with a garment bag folded over her arm. Sarah Jane Babineaux's platinum hair, her crowning glory, was swirled, stacked, and sprayed into a structure that added at least four inches to her height. She wore a beige satin jacket over white linen pants. Gold shoes glided over the grimy sidewalk. She appeared impossibly thin. Phineas wondered how her abdomen could hold all her organs. *How can she fit a liver in there?* When she hugged Iris and turned sideways, she almost disappeared, like she was in two dimensions.

"Mom, this is Phineas."

"Pleased to meet you, Mrs. Babineaux."

She surveyed Phineas' face with the withering intensity of a health inspector. "You need to call me Sarah Jane, and we in the South hug our family members when we greet them." She held up her arms. Phineas hugged her gently, afraid of cracking ribs. He felt a rattle in her chest when she coughed. He had to resist the instinct to percuss her chest.

She reached up and stroked his thick beard. "My, you're a furry one."

"Mom, I doubt I'd know him if he shaved." Iris rescued him.

Sarah Jane's face lit up. "Let's get out of this old airport and go get you two married!"

PART TWO

CHAPEL HILL

"Throughout the day the doctor was conscious that the slightly dazed feeling that came over him whenever he thought about the plague was growing more pronounced. Finally he realized that he was afraid!"

from *The Plague* by Albert Camus

After the wedding and their graduations, Iris and Phineas packed what they could into the Corona and headed south. On the way to Chapel Hill, they paused for a three-day honeymoon on the Outer Banks' Ocracoke Island where they stayed in the Blackbeard Inn, a fleabag motel with flea market furnishings. When the 'no see ums' weren't biting, they sunbathed on the beaches. When the invisible pests bit, Iris and Phineas dove into the surf. More than once Iris noticed Phineas lost in thought and staring at the waves with a look that made her think of a prisoner inspecting his last meal. He explained to her that his thoughts were about what life would be like as an intern.

❦ ❦ ❦

The heady fragrance of freshly baked bread filled the apartment. Iris resolved to bake bread for Phineas' bag lunches for now. Money was tight. She poked the soft loaf and observed with satisfaction that the crust sprang back. Her earlier attempt was a dense lump that she would chew her way through in private.

Iris had begun job searching the first of July. Since Phineas could walk to the hospital from their Laurel Ridge apartment, she used their brand-new car. So far, she left applications at Duke, UNC, and Durham County General hospitals.

When she wasn't looking for a job, she enjoyed the apartment complex's pool with two other interns' wives, Judy and Ellen. They'd taught elementary school while their husbands were in medical school and both landed Chapel Hill teaching jobs that would commence in August.

⚜ ⚜ ⚜

Iris heard the mail being delivered. When she opened the door, Judy was also standing at her mailbox. Judy called over, "Hey Iris, Ellen and I are going to the pool. Come join us."

"Sounds great. See you in a few."

Iris gathered up the mail and the library novel she was reading, *Oliver's Story* by Eric Segal. By the time she settled onto a chaise lounge at the pool, Judy and Ellen were close behind.

"So, Iris, how's Phineas' internship going for you?" Ellen asked. "I'm not liking Frank being gone so much. And he's so tired when he's home. He's not a lot of fun."

"Feels like I'm easing into marriage. I only get to see Phineas awake every third night." Maybe being a newlywed had one advantage. "On the night after he's been on call, he eats then falls asleep in the recliner with his *Harrison's Textbook of Medicine* on his chest. I thought he'd face plant into his mashed potatoes one night." Iris wondered when she'd next see her husband awake. "This Sunday is his first full day off, the precious one every three weeks. He'll probably sleep most of it."

She sifted the items in the mail. Most of it was junk, but there was one business envelope. The return address read Durham County General Hospital. She carefully removed the letter inside and read it twice. She pivoted to a sitting position. Her bare feet gripped the baking concrete.

"Anything good?" Judy asked.

"They have a position at Durham County General. They want me to call for an interview. The rest is directions."

Ellen lowered her *Glamour* magazine. "Better not do too well, or we won't be able to all hang out at the pool,"

"We need the money. Phineas' $10,000 a year salary barely covers expenses, and payments on our student loans start soon."

Phineas innocently went from an unknown newbie intern to the subject of the residents' amused banter after the second week of his internship. He and Iris had planned their expenses to the last dollar. When it was announced that state employees have their first paycheck withheld, he'd asked his team's resident, Curt Quincy, to cover for him for an hour while he ran an urgent errand.

He hurried on foot to Central Carolina Bank in the July heat and asked for the loan officer. Phineas' sweat-soaked shirt was stuck to his chest when the officer greeted him in a well-pressed poplin suit that matched the gray hair at his temples. They exchanged names and shook hands as the banker asked, "What can I do for you, Son?"

"I'm an intern at UNC Hospital. And I need a loan...they withheld our first paycheck."

"Well, how much do you need?"

"We should be able to get by with fifty dollars. My wife and I need to buy groceries. I can pay you back as soon as I get my next paycheck."

The loan officer pulled out his wallet and extracted fifty dollars in cash and handed it to Phineas. "Pay me back as soon as you can, Phineas."

This would so never happen in Boston.

Curt asked him where he'd been to get so sweaty. When Phineas told him about the generous loan officer, Curt thought it was such a good story he should share it.

The next day, Phineas was paged to the Chairman of the Department of Medicine's office. The Chairman stood up from his desk and welcomed Phineas. His long white coat hung on a stand behind him.

"Phineas, I heard you went to the bank yesterday."

Phineas flinched. "Yes, sir. We needed a few dollars to tide us over until my next paycheck. We didn't know the first one was going to be withheld."

"I'm embarrassed you didn't feel you could come here for help."

"The bank seemed the right place to go."

"So this doesn't happen again, we're establishing a fund for this kind of situation, so none of our residents have to go through what you did. I am sorry you had to."

"That's nice of you, sir. Thank you."

Phineas couldn't imagine asking his chairman, or his parents for that matter, for money. He'd go to the bank again, like a grown person should, under the same circumstances.

The TV ads sang, "I like calling North Carolina home." He hoped this would be true.

❧ ❧ ❧

It was time for early morning work rounds to begin for Phineas' team. They had all gathered except for fellow intern Roger, who'd been up all night with a renal patient admitted in heart failure. The woman needed peritoneal dialysis catheter inserted under her navel to dialyze her and remove her extra fluid. Their team's resident, Curt, scanned the workroom and the ward outside the door. "Let's start with Roger's new patient. He's probably there."

Curt led the all-male team of the two other interns, three medical students, and the clinical pharmacist down the hall to the dialysis ward. The charge nurse, in her brilliant white starched uniform and cap, greeted them at the door. The corners of her mouth were turned up. "Never seen such a thing before."

The patient, a broad-shouldered African American woman, was propped up on three pillows. Wisps of white hair escaped beneath a shiny black wig. A plastic bag of clear dialysis solution was suspended from a hook over her. Her belly made a dome of the sheet. Another bag on the floor collected pale yellow fluid from her abdomen. Roger's head rested on her enormous right breast. His stethoscope stretched from his ears into his right hand draped over her left breast. He snored softly.

The patient beamed at the team, her hand resting on Roger's shoulder. She patted it gently. "He was listening to my heart. He looked *sooo tired...* must have low blood."

Curt grinned. "When your doctor wakes up, tell him to join us on rounds, please Ma'am."

Curt led the team back into the hallway. "Looks like Roger has been studying the Emerson Biggans Syndrome."

Puzzled looks all around.

"'Em are some big uns." He chuckled. "Medicine doesn't always have to be completely serious. Here's another name you may someday hear in jest. Anyone ever hear of Throckmorton's sign?"

Blank faces.

"On x-ray, the penis points to the side of the lesion 50% of the time."

At the next patient's closed door, Fredrick, a medical student from New York cautiously inquired, "Low blood?"

"Anemia." Curt responded. "This would be a good time for you to learn some useful North Carolina patients' medical expressions that they may tell you. How about high blood?"

"Hypertension." Fredrick again.

"Correct. Too easy. Thin blood?"

Another student, Dale, from High Point. "Clotting disorder."

"Right again. You'll hear that one on the Coagulation Service. We are the referral center for the hemophiliacs and other clotting disorders in the region. Let's make this more challenging." Curt's mischievous expression suggested he expected to stump his audience. "How about bad blood?"

Silence.

"Syphilis. Hope you don't hear that one. Gone to Korea?"

Silence again. The interns and students looked at each other and shrugged.

"Gonorrhea. Ticks on my wig?" Curt paused. "Probably too hard. Means a case of crabs." He seemed to be enjoying himself. "How about fireballs of the Eucharist?"

No answers.

"Fibroids of the uterus. Final one." Curt pointed his index finger at the ceiling and gave it a shake. "The smilin' mighty Jesus?"

"Sounds bad," Phineas offered. "Someone on the way out?"

"Maybe. Spinal meningitis."

⚜ ⚜ ⚜

Iris answered the phone on the third ring. She had just arrived home after a long day of work at Durham County General Hospital. "Hi Iris. A bunch of us are celebrating Friday at He's Not Here." Phineas sounded giddy. He had been on call the night before. "Come join us...If you don't want to, I can walk home." He went on to explain how to find the hole in the wall bar.

Before he left yesterday morning, he'd announced to her that this, his third month, was the best month of his internship. Even though he was on hematology and caring for tragically sick leukemics, all the pieces of a great team fell into place. The attending was smart, a great teacher, and supportive. And Phineas found another intern who was the smartest intern or resident he'd run into in his short medical career. Phineas told Iris that he expected miraculous achievements from Franklin, perhaps even a Nobel. And Franklin was going to research human genetics after residency, not one of the usual specialties.

"If Franklin's going to study it, it'll probably turn out to be a groundbreaking area." Phineas told Iris.

Iris figured she'd better step up and rescue Phineas. "Okay, Phineas, I'll head over. Will the rest of your team be there? I'd like to meet them."

"Some of us. Franklin's at the hospital, on call."

Evening temperatures were beginning to be less oppressive in September. There hadn't been an evening shower in a week. The thought that it would be a perfect evening to explore a new part of downtown Chapel Hill provided Iris with a needed energy boost. She parked next to the Central Carolina Bank then walked across the street to locate the grubby bar down an alleyway behind a gas station.

Phineas bounced to his feet, grinning broadly at her arrival. He poured her a plastic cup of beer and introduced her to Ron Bullock, the other hematology intern, and to Holcombe, the resident. Despite his drooping eyelids, Phineas chatted away, riding the crest of beer on an adrenaline rush after being up all night on call.

"Iris, Ron and I have developed a new physiologic fluid balance concept that should make us famous."

"It hasn't already been published?"

"Nope. We'll call it the Mann-Bullock Beer Balance."

Ron, tall, athletic, and looking better rested, cleared his throat. "Bullock-Mann Beer Balance."

"When we got here, we were in negative Beer Balance." Phineas' slurring was just noticeable. "After almost three glasses—that's about a liter—I am now into positive balance." He took another generous swallow.

Ron hoisted his cup. "Whoever writes the paper gets his name first."

Iris laughed at her husband and his new friend. "I won't hold my breath."

After the beer, Iris drove home, and Phineas was asleep before the first red light. In the apartment parking lot, she shook him in a futile effort to awaken him then gave up. She rolled the windows part way up and checked on her husband twice over the next hour before she could finally rouse him and direct him to bed. She fell asleep listening to him snore.

❖ ❖ ❖

Every three weeks interns had a morning when they could sleep in. No pagers. No alarm clocks. Tomorrow, Sunday, was that day. Tonight, Bubba and Martha Sue invited Iris and Phineas to their place for a potluck dinner.

Bubba was one of the most entertaining of the interns. At check-out rounds, he routinely invoked Johnny Carson. Wrapping his head in a towel and holding his patients' index cards to his head, he gave his reports, complete with future predictions. The rest of the interns missed him when he was forced to take two weeks off with hepatitis B from a needle stick. His scrawny jaundiced face scared the young doctors, but after a month, he seemed back to his old self.

Phineas planned to bring red beans and rice tonight. He savored its preparation, even chopping the onions. He laid out the other ingredients in neat piles and enjoyed one of his few chances to cook in months.

Iris laughed when she saw his typical organized countertop. "Are you doing a chemistry experiment?"

"*Mise en place*. Everything in its place." He held up a chopping knife. "Let me show you my new way of chopping onions. I saw it on a cooking show before my nap."

She covered a yawn. "Why do I need to learn it? I have you."

"This is my old way. First you cut off the root end and stem end. Then you cut it in half through the stem." He peeled off the outside layer before he sliced every quarter inch parallel to the stem. Then he squeezed it together with one hand and made cross slices with the other.

"Are you operating on the onion, or chopping it for dinner?"

"And this is my new way." He left the stem end intact on the half onion and peeled the outside layer. He again made slices parallel to the stem but stopped just short of it. The stem held the onion together as he made the perpendicular cuts.

"This way I don't need to pinch the onion together. It's faster *and* with my fingers out of the way, there's a lot less chance of a knife injury."

"If it saves me from carrying you to the emergency room, I'm all for it." Iris crossed her arms and tucked her fingers under opposite elbows as she watched. "You know if you were bleeding, I'd probably throw up and pass out anyway."

Phineas had learned to do his best to shield Iris from all things she might find 'icky', especially those he faced on the job.

Red beans and rice were his favorite covered dish on their tight budget. The most precious part was the sausage. For tonight, he'd even added a half pound of smoked ham. Perfect with the cold six-pack of Dixie beer he'd splurged on.

And there would be no pagers tonight.

Bubba greeted them at the door with a striped necktie for a headband. "Only one more still coming. Chips and dips are on the table. Grab yourselves something to drink."

Dishes of fruit salad, green salad, and banana pudding covered a side table. A cooler next to it was full of ice, beer, and a gallon jug of white wine. Phineas retrieved a beer and poured Iris a paper cup of white wine. They took seats at the table across from Ron Bullock, and the interns and their dates announced their names.

A bakery smell rose from the golden loaves of bread Martha Sue carried on a baking sheet. Long blond hair cascaded over the top of her embroidered dress and framed her flushed cheeks. A macramé belt cinched her narrow waist. She wrapped the bread in a towel lining a wicker basket next to the salads.

Rick, a rotund and garrulous junior resident, pushed through the front door. He sported a dark lumberjack beard and brown pants and matching brown shirt. His clothes looked pressed and new. He offered tubs of Allen and Sons' take out pork barbecue and slaw.

Martha Sue put her hands on his shoulders. "Why Rick, I swear if someone stuck some corn on you, you'd look just like a giant turd!"

Rick looked wounded. "If anyone but you said that, Martha Sue, I'd be turning around and leaving. I'd take this dope home by myself to console my hurt feelings." He extracted three joints from his shirt pocket. "Bubba, you get your own, and one for each side of the table." He filled a plate and settled into his seat. "I'm starving!"

All the interns erupted in raucous laughter. "We know that ain't so," Bubba yelled.

Martha Sue arched her eyebrows. "Am I missing something?"

Bubba explained to Martha Sue how Rick had been busted by one of the well-seasoned waitresses at Ye Olde Waffle Shoppe one Sunday morning after rounds. Other residents witnessed his epic put-down and circulated the story. Rick had asked her for another biscuit, claiming he was starving. The waitress looked him up and down, paused and breathed, "Honey, I've seen starving. You *ain't* starving."

All eyes turned to Bubba when he stood. "You won't believe what happened my first week back. I was lucky to escape without injury. They don't teach you about some things in medical school." He adopted a more somber tone as he began presenting.

"I admitted this twenty-three-year-old woman for uncontrolled seizures. The poor lady was severely retarded and nonverbal, so her mother spoke for her. When—"

Iris sat up straight, like she'd been poked. "Bubba?"

"Iris?"

"'Retarded' is a term that many in my profession frown on. Better to say, 'intellectually handicapped'."

"Sorry. Like she said...So...when I did my review, I asked about Pap smears. Turned out she'd never had a GYN exam. Her mother asked me to do it, 'as long as she's in the hospital'. The nurse got all the stuff and put her up in the stirrups."

He pointed two fingers on his right hand. "When I began the bimanual pelvic exam, her eyes rolled back, and she seized. Next thing I knew, her legs clamped around my hand, and she shook me like a rag doll."

His head bobbed, and all of him followed. "Well, I was in a real fix. Thank God, I'd been smart enough to start an IV when she arrived. I said to the nurse, *p-p-p-push V-V-V-Valium S-S-S-STAT!*"

Iris looked concerned. "How long did it take for her to stop?"

"Seemed like forever. A couple minutes." He stared at his two fingers and sat down. "They're still a little sore."

Rick wiped cole slaw dressing from his mustache. "Hey Finman, that was a nasty code you had yesterday. I heard you had to start mouth to mouth on a cirrhotic alcoholic."

Iris stared at Phineas. Her forehead creased and she raised her hand to her mouth. Her neck muscles tightened. *Is she trying to hold back a gag?*

"You know how it is, Rick," Phineas responded, "ABC. Airway and breathe first, then circulation. Respiratory therapy might not be on the floor, and it takes forever for anesthesia to get there with their damned airway kit during the day when they have OR cases." He looked down at his plate. "There'd be *Hell* to pay if someone died and I refused to give them the Breath of Life. Might as well pack up and leave."

Rick tapped his glass with his spoon. "Kiss of Life."

"What did I say?"

"You said Breath of Life, like in Genesis when God gave the breath of life into the first man."

"The altar boy is slipping through," Iris murmured.

"Some slip, Finman." Rick again. "If you were God, it would always work."

"Meant to say Kiss of Life. Although seems like the Kiss of Death most of the time. Wish they'd study it, to see if mouth to mouth actually helps. They drum it into us. Start it right away. Do it first. It's essential. They should have masks and bags available everywhere instead of only with Respiratory and Anesthesia."

Rick, the only resident among interns at the table, put down his spoon. "Medicine loves miracles. The public sees breathing life back into the dead as a miracle. That's why CPR has been so enthusiastically embraced." He pounded the table with his fist. "One of these days someone will figure out what parts of a code actually help, and which patients can be saved. For now, we're stuck doing everything on just about everybody who codes, even when the chances of success are slim."

Bubba crumpled his napkin. "We can't ask the medical student to do it, 'cause they pay tuition, and the medical school doesn't want them to be exposed to bad shit, or they'd all go into radiology or dermatology. Junior and senior residents have put in their time. Doubt anyone has ever seen a professor work a code. Process of elimination. Interns are what's left, so it's our year to suck it up…so to speak."

"Rank has its privileges," observed Ron. "The foot soldiers lead the way into battle while the officers follow."

"Anyone heard of the Bikini Atoll?" Rick seemed intent on teaching.

"Bikini what?" He had the males' attention.

"United States tested nuclear weapons in the Pacific on Bikini Atoll. Then they sent in enlisted men to clean up while the officers stayed safe on ships miles away."

The military reference shifted the conversation to Vietnam. None of the men in the room had served there. They compared draft lottery numbers. Theirs had all been high enough to be safe.

Bubba declared internship a year to get through. Everything would be better after, besides anything was better than a foxhole in Vietnam.

⚜ ⚜ ⚜

From the moment Rick leaked Phineas' performance of mouth-to-mouth resuscitation, Iris hardly said a word, and she remained silent when she settled into the Corona's driver's seat for the trip home. Was a new marital stress piled on top of Phineas' chronic sleep deprivation? He fought the urge to doze off while she turned the ignition, but he was jolted full awake when she backed into a roadside mailbox post.

"I think I hit something."

They inspected the damage together. The dent in the bumper was minor and cosmetic, a crease. The post had a scratch. Phineas mumbled, "No harm done". During the ride home, she met each of his attempts at conversation with terse one-word responses.

As they lay next to each other in bed, Phineas tried to kiss her. Iris turned her head to the side and whispered, "Not yet."

"How long until I can kiss you again?"

"I'll let you know." She covered her mouth again.

A wave of sadness engulfed him. Duty had ambushed his love life.

⚜ ⚜ ⚜

Phineas heard the mail truck rumble to a stop outside their apartment. He waved at the departing mailman and retrieved an envelope and grocery coupons from their box.

A job that allows one to drive, walk and chat. I'm jealous. He noticed the envelope's return address was Tufts Medical School. He tore it open.

Dear Phineas,

It brightened my day to receive your letter. Feel free to write when you think I might be able to help.

I wish I could help you help Iris get over her squeamishness. That's a tough one. Medical personnel can desensitize themselves to these reactions, but I doubt Iris would go for repeated exposures to gore as a strategy. She may not see it as something she feels the need to overcome. She sees it as the way she is.

So, I'd recommend accepting her the way she is, and don't push her to change. When you can, protect her from repulsive stuff. Don't talk about medical nastiness with her. She has enough on her plate to get you through your internship.

Cheers!
Ian MacSweeney

⚜ ⚜ ⚜

Days after sleepless on-call nights were all caffeine and adrenaline. During emergencies, time seemed to slow. Thought processes and procedures seemed to gain efficiency. Phineas slipped in IV or abdominal dialysis catheters in less time than usual. Once, called away during check-out rounds, he helped resuscitate a gout patient who was bleeding out from a gastric ulcer caused by the new 'miracle' arthritis drug, ibuprofen. Three interns quickly placed three large bore intravenous lines in three different extremities for fluid resuscitation while the resident called the operating room. The four then all ran the patient down the hall in his bed to the elevator and to the operating room. The patient survived after an emergency resection of his ulcerated stomach.

The one thing worse than working all night was being unable to keep up, not getting to the next crisis fast enough. That was when an intern had to ask for help. It was okay to acknowledge fatigue after a superhuman run of work, but not to bitch and moan about it. Interns and residents were in it together. They had each other's back. Training was a temporary state, which would get better each year and had an end in sight.

⚜ ⚜ ⚜

When the redbud trees bloomed in spring, Iris decided they should have a dog. She'd broached the subject with Phineas one evening before he sank into sleep, and he hadn't objected. He did admit he enjoyed dogs. Their apartment neighbor, Judy, had a lovable golden retriever named Cinnamon, her constant companion after she finished her workday at school. Iris knew Phineas liked Cinnamon.

Friends Judy and Ellen had begun discussing when they should have children, which Iris too quickly realized she was a long way away from wanting, if she ever would. Phineas hadn't brought up the subject yet. Iris' gynecologist had recently said it would be best if Iris took a break from birth control pills and fit her for a diaphragm, which meant she'd need to be more careful to avoid a pregnancy. And having a dog might keep the notion of having children out of Phineas' head for a while. She would visit the animal shelter to take a look. Her ex-Navy father would have called it reconnaissance.

The first Saturday in April was sunny and warm. Phineas was on rounds, as usual, and would be on call that night. After morning coffee and perusing the *News and Observer*, Iris found the shelter. The attendant, a young woman in jeans and tee-shirt, directed Iris to a long, bright room with rows of cages on three sides. As Iris entered, the pungent stench of dog shit assaulted her nose. A few of the dogs, barking nonstop, were now hoarse. Several others slinked to the backs of their cages as she approached. She eliminated the dogs that displayed panicky behaviors from consideration, and she eliminated the tiny fru fru dogs. Phineas was polite about them in public, but she knew they irritated him. She also eliminated the huge dogs because they'd need too much space. Their first-floor apartment had a porch with a five-foot high wall, where she planned for their dog to stay while they were at work. By the time she approached cages at the far end, Iris considered abandoning her dog search, but sitting at attention next to the final cage's door was a medium sized black dog whose head and torso favored the looks of a Labrador retriever.

She cooed, "And what's your name and story?"

The dog tilted its head and locked big, brown eyes on hers, as the attendant leaned on her shovel and responded, "That's Amos. He just came in yesterday. His family had to move to New York City and couldn't take him. He's well behaved and should find a home. He has the best chance of any of our dogs. He's two years old and has had all his shots and been neutered. Wanna take him for a walk?"

On the way home from the shelter, Iris and Amos stopped to buy dog food, dog dishes, a pillow, and a real leash to replace the temporary rope from the shelter. She took him for a walk around the apartment complex and knocked on Judy's door. When it cracked open, Iris asked, "Can you and Cinnamon come out and play?"

Cinnamon's golden snout sniffed the gap.

"My what a handsome boy! I bet Phineas is excited," Judy exclaimed.

"Doesn't know yet."

⚜ ⚜ ⚜

Iris would bring Phineas supper that night. They sometimes met on nice days at the picnic area between the hospital and the pathology building. She paged him to find out what time to arrive before packing a basket with salad, leftover Dijon chicken with pasta, and brownies.

When Phineas approached, Iris arranged herself at one of the tables with Amos lying under it. As Phineas leaned over to kiss her, Amos sat up and bumped his head, whining pitifully.

"Whose pooch?"

"Ours."

"'Scuse me?"

"He needed a home, and I *know* you like dogs, and I need some company at night when you're gone. He can stay on the porch when we're at work." She offered her husband her best pleading look. "I'll be doing most of his care. You can just enjoy him!"

Phineas held out his hand for Amos to sniff, while Iris held her breath. Phineas patted Amos' head. Amos stood and wagged his entire back end.

Phineas smiled. "Seems like a good dog. And so enthusiastic...Guess if we are going to have our first dog, might as well be Amos."

"Just don't expect me to wag my backside like that when you come home."

"That I'd like to see."

"Don't hold your breath."

⚜ ⚜ ⚜

Iris quickly learned that having a dog led to more changes than expected. As she arrived home after work one day, she heard Amos barking on their walled porch. From the sound of his hoarse bark, he'd been at it a while. He cowered in the back corner of the porch. Pebbles and a few larger stones, some the size of golf balls, surrounded him. Iris had a notion which of the children in the complex had committed the heinous act and likely escaped when he heard her arrive.

That night, she and Phineas decided Amos would have to be crated in the apartment when they were out, and they, meaning Iris, would immediately begin searching for a rental with a yard.

⚜ ⚜ ⚜

After a week of scouring the *Village Advocate*, Iris found an ad for a small house in the country north of Chapel Hill on Mount Sinai Road with two small bedrooms, one bathroom, but no air conditioning. What caught her eye was the claim of a fenced in area next to the house and a garden area. She met the landlord there after work the next evening while Phineas was in the hospital on call.

Jackson Lee was trim and sprightly in his early eighties and had to look up at Iris' face when they exchanged greetings and shook hands. He made sure to mention that he still kept his real estate license.

"Hard to place your accent, Iris. Where y'all from?"

"New Orleans by way of Boston."

"That 'splains it." He gestured toward the west. "Well, you'll want to take a drive down 86 toward Hillsborough. Lots of history in the county seat. There's the Occoneechee tribal area and the Burwell School for young ladies—goes back to before the war between the states—just for example."

She listened politely as he tossed out additional historical tidbits like they were chicken feed. When he finally took a breath, she asked, "Have you lived your whole life around here?"

"Not yet." He chuckled at his joke. "Guess you'll be wanting to see the house."

"That's what I'm here for."

"Got to apologize for the shape it's in. Previous tenant just left—and in a hurry." He held open a storm door with a torn screen.

The solid wood door creaked when Iris pushed it into what she guessed was the living room. A musky odor accompanied a clutter of trash and random salvaged furniture, including a legless sofa that rested on the floor.

Jackson Lee found a reason to study his feet. "Fellow was a drummer in a band that broke up. You might find a drumstick or two."

She hoped he meant the wooden kind and not poultry bones. "Do you plan on having it cleaned?"

"Yessum. I'll have my nephews haul away this mess tomorrow." He tilted his head toward her and raised an eyebrow. "Give you a rent you'll like too."

She brought Phineas and Amos by the next night. Phineas held Amos' leash close when he saw the scattered bits of mess left by the landlord's nephews. "It's not the brand-new apartment we moved into."

"You saw my Boston apartment."

He poked his head into each room. "Might be an old sharecropper's house, insulated and sheet rocked later on."

His expression and tone improved when they strolled in the yard, with its garden space and generous dog pen. "Are you *sure* you're okay with being way out here by yourself when I'm on call?"

"I have Amos."

"If that's a 'yes', this place is okay with me."

※ ※ ※

Phineas and Iris moved into the house the next Saturday. Phineas was bent on removing all leftover trash, then thoroughly sweeping and mopping before they brought the first of two loads from the U-Haul truck. There were lots more boxes left to unpack by the time they gave up and collapsed in bed.

A curious noise stirred Phineas from deep sleep. Quiet had returned when he finally pried open his eyes. The dawn light peaked through ragged blinds and illuminated tiny dust particles floating near the window.

"Errt-uh-err-uh-errrrrrr!"

Phineas smiled at the familiar sound from his childhood.

Iris rolled over and rubbed her eyes.

Amos rose from his pillow at the foot of the bed and stretched.

"Errt-uh-err-uh-errrrrrrrrrr!"

Iris' eyes were now wide open. "What on earth was *that*?"

"Now I know I married a city girl. Have you never heard a rooster crow?"

"Never in New Orleans, Baton Rouge, or Boston. Is that going to happen every morning?" She yawned and stretched her arms over her head. "And why do they call it crowing?"

As he came to bed the next night, Phineas noticed Iris opening a small case.

"What have you got there?"

"Ear plugs. Since you're in my bed, you can be my ears, my country husband. I'll sleep through the rooster, and you can make the coffee."

With 1979's spring in sight, the medical house staff's spirits warmed. As ward teams anticipated the therapeutic benefits of the precious sunshine they'd missed over the winter months, work rounds at the hospital were completed more crisply on the weekends. Sign-outs to the on-call doctors covering Junior Resident Phineas' service were accomplished before noon. He'd been eager for this Saturday ever since Iris told him what she had arranged for the weekend in their second spring in Chapel Hill.

Jackson Lee now treated Iris like a favorite adopted grandchild. He and Amos had become immediate buddies, inseparable when Mr. Lee stopped by. They would perch on the front steps while he scratched behind Amos' ears and recited soothing verse.

The rental house squatted at the end of two open acres. Scrub pines lined the street on the other end and concealed garden spaces and blueberry bushes behind them. Mr. Lee planned to have the gardens tilled for planting this Saturday before the first day of spring, as was his ritual. He had also arranged for a load of mulch to be delivered for Iris. She'd offered to mulch the azalea bushes and flowerbeds surrounding the front of the house. A tray of pansies waited to be installed.

Phineas had mentioned to Ron Bullock, fellow resident and good buddy, about these planned activities. Ron, another carpetbagger from the North, had departed medical school in New York City for residency in Chapel Hill and fully embraced its more relaxed pace and open air. He wanted in on the gardening, his first experience in agriculture. Phineas had grown up with gardens. His parents' gardens had evolved through Great Depression gardens to Victory Gardens in WWII, to gardens to help feed their young family before their business began to be dependably profitable. In recent years his parents had a small, lush patch for cultivating tomatoes with flavor.

Ron and Phineas arrived to see Iris in jeans and t-shirt wielding a pitchfork in the front yard. She waved before plunging the tines into the waist high mulch pile. A battered horse trailer attached to a light blue pickup truck rested next to the road. Amos greeted Phineas with enthusiastic tail wagging then shuttled the hundred feet between Iris and the garden area. Phineas hurried after him.

Mr. Lee had arranged a lawn chair beside the garden. Next to his chair sat beekeeping equipment: a veil, a smoker, and his hive tool—a handheld flat metal bar used for prying and scraping hive frames. He planned to work the two hives he'd installed behind the garden. He'd explained that not only was honey a golden treasure, but the worker bees pollinated his blueberries, squash, melons, and cucumbers, improving quality and yield. Amos had painfully learned early on to steer clear of the hives. Mr. Lee speculated that Amos reminded the bees of a bear.

Mr. Lee now smiled at the spectacle in front of him while patting Amos and holding his collar. Amos' attention was focused on the action in the garden.

A mule pulled a plow under the direction of a lean white-haired African American man in overalls. The mule driver steered with commands of

"Gee" and "Haw" and the mule kept a steady pace, not slowing even while depositing a pile of turds in its wake. When the plow team made the turn and faced their spectators, Mr. Lee introduced Moses James who responded, "How y'all doing?"

Phineas and Ron went to the house to change into jeans and old t-shirts before they returned to rake the loose soil into rows. Then they started to hoe the straight furrows into uniform mounds for lettuce, peas, carrots, radishes, turnips, scallions, and potatoes.

A piercing scream interrupted their rhythm and raised the hairs on Phineas' neck. He raced, hoe in hand, to the remnant of the mulch pile where Iris stood and shrieked. She'd hoisted the pitchfork high in the air, as high as she could above a leaping Amos. A copper-colored snake, more than four feet long, was impaled on the tongs and writhed with open mouth and visible fangs. Phineas grabbed Amos' collar and handed him off to Ron.

"I stuck the pitchfork into the mulch—and this came out! Do something!" she yelled at Phineas.

Phineas sidestepped around the pile to face her. "Looks like you already have. Pin it to the ground as far from you as you can." As soon as Iris brought the snake down, Phineas swung the hoe hard and decapitated it. The tail continued to writhe and twitch.

Iris dropped the pitchfork. "Ewww! Gross!"

Jackson Lee sauntered over from the apiary. He raised his veil and set the smoker at his feet. It billowed pine straw incense as he knelt. He began handling the snake's parts with care and reverence.

"That's a copperhead, yessir, and a big one at that. 'Twas warming up in the composting mulch." Mr. Lee pointed at the triangular head. "See these pits between the nostrils and eyes? That's why he's called a pit viper. And look at the pupils. They're vertical." He used the beveled end of his hive tool to express venom from the snake's fangs. His finger traced along the decapitated body. "The skin has an hourglass pattern. Beautiful!"

Ron edged in for a closer look. "We should take it in to the Chairman's morning report on Monday. The other residents should see it."

"Might get pretty ripe by Monday." Mr. Lee continued. "Why don't you put the head in a jar and refrigerate it till then? And mind the fangs. They still have some venom. Moses, you got any use for the rest of it?"

Moses James had wrapped the plow reins around a nearby sapling to secure his mule in a patch of grass and followed Mr. Lee to the ruckus. "I believe I know someone who might make a belt and a meal from it. It's big enough. Mind putting it on some ice in a plastic bag till I finish?"

Ron ran his fingers along the scales of the tail end. "If someone makes a belt out of it, I'd like to buy it."

Later in the evening, after grilled burgers, cold beer and cribbage, Ron thanked Phineas and Iris and rose to depart. "Wasn't this an incredible day?" He held up the snakehead in a jar. "Maybe this place can stay Eden, now that Phineas has slain the serpent."

Phineas answered, "The TV ads do say we're in the southern part of Heaven."

⚜ ⚜ ⚜

Phineas awakened to find he'd kicked his side of the sheets to the end of the bed. Iris clutched her side under her chin. "Bad dream again?" She asked.

"A snake. This time it was in our bedroom."

She switched on the lamp. "See? All clear. Now you can go back to sleep." She pulled the sheets over him and kissed his cheek. Amos lifted his head and yawned from the floor next to Iris.

⚜ ⚜ ⚜

Iris placed a plate of sesame chicken with broccoli and rice in front of Phineas. He slouched, head in his hands, after almost 36 hours without sleep following a brutal on-call night. She placed an envelope next to his plate. The return address read Tufts Medical School.

He sliced the edge with his knife and extracted a folded sheet of paper.

Dear Phineas,

> *So good to hear from you again.*
> *There's been much written about snake dreams, and you can pick whichever interpretation you want. These might range from personal energy to corruption and contamination, to healing and resolving a difficult situation.*
> *Jung might suggest a spiritual association, a connection to Christ. Freud theorized repressed sexual desire.*
> *I have to thank you for giving me the chance to say something once in my career that I would never have had the opportunity to say in Boston. My answer to your recent question is: sometimes a snake is only a snake. You beheaded one. That's the connection. Now sleep well, Amigo.*

Cheers,
Ian MacSweeney

Phineas sat up and laughed out loud.

Iris tilted her head and furrowed her brow. "What from Tufts could be so funny?"

He handed her the letter. She studied it before pocketing the envelope. "Now maybe you can stop dreaming about snakes?"

⚜ ⚜ ⚜

Iris parked the Corona and heard Amos pacing behind the side door. He emitted a low growl.

"It's me, Amos."

He whined and wagged his tail as she entered. The roar of a crowd came from the living room. Then, "Fifteen two." Phineas and Ron sat across the coffee table that held a cribbage board, cards, and two cans of beer. The screen of their portable TV revealed that Monday night baseball this July night featured Ron's Yankees and Phineas' beloved Red Sox.

"Looks like you two have been furthering your medical educations."

Phineas smiled. "Look what Ron bought us at a flea market sale." He held up a wooden sign with the letters E D E N carved into it. "How was pottery?"

Iris held out two mugs, a bowl, and a goblet.

"They opened the kiln. My first creations. And thank you, Ron. It's really nice."

Phineas inspected the dishes. "These are great! If you need a break from social work, maybe you have another career option." He turned the goblet over in his hands. "So why did you make a chalice?"

"It's a goblet, for when I have a glass of wine."

"So, it's a goblet if the wine is unconsecrated?"

She shook her head. "Can't take the altar out of the boy."

Iris left them and switched on their only room air conditioning unit, secured in a window in the bedroom. She had learned to like cool sheets in Boston. Phineas must have vacuumed since the vacuum cleaner was in the middle of the tiny mudroom. This meant two things. First, he had arrived home well before Ron came over. And second, he had rare leftover energy and would soon end the cribbage contest; yawning and claiming to Ron he needed sleep. With Ron gone, Phineas would begin pursuing her.

This was a behavior she'd reinforced. On an occasion early in his residency, he vacuumed the house in a desperate effort to stay awake while he waited for her to come home. She told him how much she appreciated this and then took him to bed. Phineas had begun referring to his vacuuming as foreplay, and Iris wasn't going to discourage it. Definitely a win-win.

Her job at Durham County General had worked out, and life was good in Chapel Hill. Even that miserable Jesse Helms hadn't spoiled it, including when he opposed building the North Carolina Zoo, arguing they should build a fence around Chapel Hill instead. Iris would vote for the fence if it would keep that toxic man out.

❦ ❦ ❦

As Phineas approached his Senior Resident year, it was time to decide on a specialty. He liked working with his hands and his head, so he wanted a specialty that had procedures and diagnostic mysteries. Pulmonologists got to perform bronchoscopies, and they placed Swan-Ganz pulmonary artery catheters in the ICU. And many of the cases they saw were diagnostic dilemmas, puzzled out by the astute clinicians. Pursuit of clinical mysteries lit up Phineas' brain. This would be the path he'd pursue.

The residents voted on residents' awards at the end of the year. These were handed out in a light-hearted ceremony. The Senior Resident who received the 'Calm in the Face of Disaster' award had signed on to be a pulmonary fellow. The 'Disaster in the Face of Calm' award went to a resident who was moving on to a dermatology residency.

✤ ✤ ✤

When July and the first month of Phineas' senior resident year arrived, he arranged a meeting with the Chief of Pulmonary, Dr. Kornberg, to discuss fellowship programs. Dr. Kornberg was known as a brilliant man whose administrative assistant, Ruby, kept him organized. Since he didn't wear a watch, she paged him whenever it was time for him to attend a meeting. He called back if he needed directions.

Dr. Kornberg played violin in a chamber music quartet every Sunday afternoon at 2 P.M. When he covered an inpatient service on a Sunday, he frequently ran his thumb across calluses on the tips of the fingers of his left hand and asked the time. His chamber music sessions were his touchstone. Rumor had it that he attended music camps during his vacations.

They sat across his desk after they shook hands and exchanged pleasantries. Dr. Kornberg wore his usual tweed jacket, white button-down shirt, and solid black tie. His shiny forehead extended all the way back and was surrounded by thin gray hair. Frameless glasses rested halfway down the bridge of his long, narrow nose. "Ruby said you wanted to talk about pulmonary programs. We know your work. I talked with others in the division who've worked with you." His words surprised Phineas. "I'd like to offer you a fellowship with us." He stood and again extended his hand.

Phineas was caught off guard, having expected an information gathering session, but thrilled at the unexpected praise. And he liked and admired the UNC pulmonary faculty. He could be happy staying. He stood and shook Dr. Kornberg's hand.

"I'll let my wife know today. I believe she'll be happy to stay in Chapel Hill."

She was.

✠ ✠ ✠

On a sunny December morning in 1981, pulmonary fellow Phineas Mann's pager blared with the usual static and "Dr. Mann, 6337. Call 6337." He and the resident assigned to the pulmonary consult service, Faith Oxendine, were sitting across the table from each other in the tiny conference room reading pulmonary function studies. Faith was a Lumbee Indian from Robeson County, the first in her family to go to college, much less medical school. She wore her shiny, black hair in a single braid tucked under her white coat. Thick lenses in wire-rimmed frames magnified her rich brown eyes.

Phineas dialed the extension at the 6West nursing station. "Dr. Mann here."

"This is Isaac Lerner. I'm the medical student for a patient admitted yesterday, and we need a pulmonary consult for bronchoscopy. Are you the fellow?" Excitement filled his voice.

"I am. Can you tell me more about your patient? I may need to grab a place on the schedule before I see them."

"D'you see the article in the *New England Journal* this week about homosexual men in San Francisco having pneumocystis? Our patient has hung out at the bathhouses there on vacations—and has the same signs and symptoms."

"I saw the article." Phineas hadn't actually *read* that issue of the journal yet. "What's his chest x-ray look like?"

"The radiologist read it as 'within normal limits', but we don't buy it. And a lung scan showed no blood clots. He gets short of breath just walking."

"Name and room please. We'll see him next."

"Daniels. Levi Daniels. Room 6313."

"Thanks. We're on it. Don't feed him in case I can get him on the schedule for later today."

Phineas hung the phone on the wall receiver and turned to Faith. "Let's see this one together, since it's urgent. And we need to find a copy of this week's *New England Journal*. Could be a very interesting case."

Faith opened her backpack and extracted a journal still in its brown wrapper. "I haven't read this one yet...obviously."

Phineas smiled. "Ah! The famous *Brown Journal of Medicine*. Having this issue on hand may help you get an outstanding evaluation for the rotation. Where's the article about the homosexual men with pneumocystis?"

The paper was listed first in the Original Articles section. They read it together and learned that a series of homosexual men had presented with pneumocystis pneumonia, an infection rarely seen, and then only previously in patients with severely compromised immune systems. Most of the men in the series also had oral thrush and had frequented bathhouses in San Francisco, meeting places for sex with multiple partners. The paper raised the possibility that an unidentified agent transmitted by sexual contact damaged their immune systems.

Phineas had heard the emotion in Isaac Lerner's voice. A new and bizarre disease happened to show up on their doorstep. "Let's grab the oximeter and head to 6313 now. Then we'll get his chest x-ray and page Dr. Burney."

Dr. Burney was the attending supervising the pulmonary consult service this month. His responsibility was to review every case and observe every bronchoscopy. He had begun his career as a tuberculosis specialist, as many of the pulmonologists in his generation had. During his long career, he had seen about everything. Phineas felt privileged to have Dr. Burney for an attending.

The oximeter, a massive metal box weighing over fifty pounds, rested on a wheeled cart. Beth, the respiratory therapist who ran the lab, was calibrating equipment there. Beth reminded Phineas of his paternal grandmother with her wire-rimmed glasses, short, silver permed hair. She bordered on being stout, 'big-boned' in North Carolina parlance.

"Beth, I need to schedule a bronchoscopy."

"Whoa, now! Where's the fire?" She cranked a tank valve closed before locating the scheduling notebook. "We can do it at 2 PM today or tomorrow at 9 AM."

"The 2 PM slot. Daniels in 6313. Much obliged."

Faith and Phineas found Levi Daniels propped up in bed watching the news. He had a full head of short blond hair carefully parted on the side. His face was flushed, his cheeks sunken. Rather than a hospital gown, he wore black satin pajamas, soaked with sweat and stuck to his spindly chest.

After introductions, Phineas asked him, "What did you notice first?"

"Short of breath." Levi Daniels' neck muscles tightened with the effort of each breath.

"For how long?"

"A few weeks." His breathing became rapid, and he paused before he could answer, "At first...only hills and stairs." More recovery time. "Now just going from...one room to the next." A dry cough.

Faith asked, "Temperature?"

"102 the last few days...less before." He took several deep breaths. "Then I sweat, really sweat...I'm dripping."

Faith again. "And your weight?"

"Dropping...25 pounds in a couple of months...Clothes just hang off me." He displayed a safety pin that cinched the waist of his pajamas. "Bottoms would fall off me without this...Went right past svelte." He appeared to force a half smile.

"The medical team started you on the antibiotic, cefazolin, yesterday." Phineas asked, "Feel any better today?"

"I wish."

"Coughed anything up?"

"The other doctor said...it was just spit."

Faith and Phineas reviewed the remainder of Levi Daniel's history with him until Phineas asked, "Okay if we examine you now?"

He held up his arms, palms out. "Help yourself."

They counted an elevated respiratory rate at 26 and heart rate at 112 per minute. His forehead felt warm. A shaggy yellow material coated his palate. The stethoscope examination revealed soft scattered crackles, like cellophane. Phineas attached the oximeter probe to Levi's ear. The probe was the size of Levi's hand and had to be secured with a thick headband. While he breathed oxygen from a nasal cannula, its display read 94%. Phineas pushed the oximeter cart and followed Levi while he walked. His oxygen reading fell to 78% after a few steps.

Phineas directed him back to bed and explained. "Mr. Daniels, we need to review your x-rays and bring our boss, Dr. Burney, by to examine you. You haven't eaten yet today, have you?"

"Haven't seen anything yet to tempt me."

"Good. Don't eat or drink anything. We might recommend that we perform a bronchoscopy this afternoon."

Phineas reviewed the bronchoscopy procedure, step by step, including the infrequent chance of complications including bleeding, pneumonia and collapsed lung, before asserting, "We need to establish a firm diagnosis in order to start the correct treatment." He added, "Our therapist, Beth, will have a consent form for you to sign, saying we have reviewed the risks."

Levi nodded and covered his mouth as he coughed. "No problem. Sign my life away...Hope you got good drugs for this."

Phineas offered a smile. "Should be. We'll try to keep you comfortable with Demerol."

"Was hoping you'd keep me high."

Phineas and Faith exited 6313 to retrieve x-rays and meet Dr. Burney. On the way, Faith rehearsed her presentation of Levi Daniel's case with Phineas. As he reached for the doorknob of the lab workroom, he said, "Perfect. Dr. Burney will be impressed."

Dr. Burney sat at the table reviewing and signing pulmonary function studies. He looked up. "Greetings, team. What fascinating cases do you have for us today?"

His white coat was crisp and starched. His left hand rested on his lap. Its deformity was evidence of a childhood farming accident. He usually wore a smile and loafers. Phineas had been impressed when he witnessed Dr. Burney tying his knit tie with his good right hand one Saturday before rounds. Rumor was that Dr. Burney could also tie shoes with one hand if he had to.

Phineas took a seat. "We may have something very unusual. Faith?"

Faith reported Daniel's history and examination then extracted his x-rays from their thin folder and hung them on the light boxes. "Radiology read these as within normal limits."

Dr. Burney studied the front and side views. He pulled the films down and walked to the window, holding each up to the low winter sun. "Faith, look at them again in this brighter backlight, and tell me what *you* think."

Faith studied the films before pointing at the lung peripheries and the usual clear space behind the sternum. "I think there's more here than is normal."

"Well done, Faith. I'd describe these findings as soft nodular densities. They probably reflect an alveolar process. Now tell me your differential, please."

Faith pulled the *New England Journal of Medicine* from her backpack. "We think he fits with this series." She put her index finger on the title. "We suspect pneumocystis."

Dr. Burney glanced at the journal and chuckled. "Ah, the Aunt Minnie approach to differential diagnosis!"

Her expression shifted from excited to puzzled. "Aunt Minnie?"

"It looks like what Aunt Minnie had, so that must be what it is." He waited for his words to sink in. "Let's go through a complete differential before we decide what to do next. To be honest, in all my many years, I've not seen one single case of pneumocystis."

Dr. Burney wrote six headings for columns on the blackboard: infection, malignant, occupational diseases, pulmonary reactions to drugs, deposits from medical conditions, and cause unknown. He solicited possibilities for each from Faith and Phineas and discussed each condition and its relevance to Levi Daniels' case. After each column was filled, Dr. Burney reached for volume 4 of Frazier and Pare's *Diagnosis of Diseases of the Chest* and found the list of conditions with an x-ray pattern that resembled Levi Daniels'. They had considered the likely diseases.

"Faith and Phineas, I'm betting your instincts are spot on. Let's go see our patient."

Dr. Burney introduced himself to Levi Daniels and reviewed his history. He inquired about recent medications, especially antibiotics and steroids.

"Tetracycline... at my family doctor."

"How about nitrofurantoin, otherwise known as MacroBid for a urinary infection. It can cause a pulmonary reaction."

"Never heard of it."

"Have you inhaled anything recreationally, like cocaine?"

"No, sir... Well, not in months."

"Do you keep birds?"

"Filthy things."

Dr. Burney agreed with their examination findings and suggested the yellow material on Levi's palate was thrush. He pulled up a chair and sat facing him. "Did Dr. Mann discuss bronchoscopy with you?"

"In excruciating detail."

"Mr. Daniels, do you have any questions for us?"

"All explained earlier." Daniels let his head fall back into his pillow.

"Dr. Mann, what time did you schedule the bronchoscopy?"

"Is 2 PM okay for you?"

"I'll meet you there." Dr. Burney stood and led Phineas and Faith into the hallway and closed the door. "You two have some research to do before the procedure. Page me if anything else comes up." He took a step before turning back. "Have you read *The Plague* by Camus?"

"Yes, sir. In high school," Phineas answered. *Why is Dr. B referencing fiction?*

"If Faith's diagnosis is correct, Mr. Daniels may be your concierge, and you are Dr. Rieux. You should read it again. As you may recall, Dr. Rieux's concierge was the first plague case he saw before the epidemic broke out."

Faith and Phineas headed to the medical library to do a deep dive looking for more information about Pneumocystis carinii pneumonia. They covered a large table with the massive volumes of the last few years of *The Index Medicus* from the reference shelves. They found only a few listings, and these referenced limited case series.

They located the journal articles in the library stacks and skimmed them. Phineas closed the last volume in his pile. "All the cases of PCP I found were in kids with leukemia on chemotherapy. You find any cases in someone like Levi?"

"Nope. Just kids with devastated immune systems." Faith looked up from her pile and wrinkled her nose. "And one said the reservoir for PCP might be rodents, like plague."

"Yuck—but interesting." Another fact had struck him. "They made the diagnosis in the kids with bronchoalveolar lavages." Phineas had performed a few lavages, generous saline washings of peripheral regions of lung that provided a way to sample the airways and air sacs. These infrequent procedures were at the request of research groups at UNC who were studying the cells recovered from this procedure.

"Faith, in the *NEJM* paper, they did biopsies, not lavages, correct?"

Faith thumbed through the Methods section of the paper. "Biopsies. Nothing about lavages," she confirmed.

"We'll do both." *Why didn't they in San Francisco?* Could he add knowledge to the new syndrome and gain professional stature?

⚜ ⚜ ⚜

Levi Daniels waited for them in the fluoroscopy room on the x-ray table, a sheet pulled under his chin. Beth had found him a warm blanket. "He was shivering."

"Has he had the topical?" Phineas asked.

"Just before you arrived."

"You should do something about...taste of that stuff," Daniels groaned. "Nastier than anything...*I've* ever tasted!"

Phineas pulled on a lead apron, then a surgical gown and mask. "Do you have any questions before we give you sedation?"

"How long will this take...and how much will I feel?"

"It usually takes around 30 minutes. Your case may take a bit longer since we plan on obtaining multiple specimens. It's not a painful procedure, but coughing can make it unpleasant. The more you can hold back the cough, the faster we will be done. We'll try to help suppress the cough with more topical anesthetic and with narcotics."

"Don't skimp on the drugs."

Dr. Burney slipped into the room and picked up a mask. He nodded at Daniels. Faith held up a lead apron for him.

Phineas positioned Daniels under the fluoroscope. "Beth, please give him fifty milligrams of Demerol IV. Be ready in three minutes with twenty-five more." He placed a thin nasal catheter into the back of Daniels' nasal passage for extra oxygen and tented a sterile towel over his mouth.

The bronchoscope passed easily into the patient's throat. A shaggy yellow carpet of thrush coated his airway from behind his tongue to barely above the vocal cords. Phineas trickled more lidocaine solution onto the sensitive vocal cords. Daniels coughed. Phineas gently advanced the scope's tip between the vocal cords, trying to avoid laryngospasm. Daniels coughed hard again. "Another twenty-five-milligram dose of Demerol IV, please, and another five cc of lidocaine through the scope." Coughing continued despite dose after dose of narcotic and the maximum safe amount of topical lidocaine.

The pungent odor of lidocaine filled the air around Phineas, burning his eyes. The bronchoscope's eyepiece and his face were inches from Daniels' open mouth. Phineas pulled the towel back over it. Faith and Dr. Burney took turns looking into the bronchoscope's teaching head connected off to the side by a three-foot fiberoptic bundle.

Phineas worked through the usual sampling protocols with brushings, washings and then fluoroscopically directed biopsies of the peripheral right upper and lower lobes. *Now for the lavage.* He instilled 60 cc of saline twice into the right middle lobe, then aspirated gently with the second syringe before he applied the more vigorous intermittent wall suction for the remainder to be collected into an attached trap. Levi Daniels coughed without pause until the bronchoscope was removed, then coughed some more.

He squawked, "Hope you got what you need...that cough is miserable!"

⚜ ⚜ ⚜

The next day Phineas' eyes were red and still burned. Goggles weren't standard, but he wished he'd thought to wear them. You only wore them if you were expecting a bloody procedure, one with potential for hemorrhage. An alarming thought gnawed at him. *Was I exposed?* Had he been caught up in the thrill of pursuing a brand-new disease and been careless?

Faith had earlier checked with the team and visited Daniels. He still had fevers and needed more oxygen. In consultation with the infectious disease specialists, the team had started the recommended antibiotic for PCP.

Phineas' pager beeped and a deep voice commanded, "Dr. Mann, come to cytopathology." Phineas and Faith stared at each other.

She spoke first. "Think that's about Daniels' specimens?"

Phineas had an uneasy feeling. "Hope they didn't mess them up in Processing."

They hurried to the basement cytopathology lab where they found Dr. Olsen staring into one head of the bulky four-headed teaching microscope. He looked young, probably early forties at the most, a push broom mustache trimmed precisely along his lip line. His pale blue shirt was pressed and his tie silk, stylish for the world of pathologists.

"Dr. Olsen, did you page me? I'm Phineas Mann, and this is Faith Oxendine."

"Where the hell did you get this specimen?"

"Which one?" *And why this tone?*

"The one in the jar marked BAL. It looks nothing like the usual washings."

"It's a bronchoalveolar lavage, a high-volume wash of a segment with the scope wedged. It's a deep alveolar sampling." Phineas was surprised that he had to explain it.

"We haven't received this type of sample from bronchoscopies. Why did you do it in this case?" Olsen's tone was less aggressive and more puzzled.

"Did you see the recent article with the pneumocystis series in the *New England Journal*?"

Olsen shook his head. "Not yet."

"They were homosexual men who frequented bathhouses for sex in San Francisco—like our patient, and they presented with the same symptoms he did."

Dr. Olsen looked startled. "And the authors did lavages?" His tone was muted.

"No, only biopsies. We searched the literature and found that lavages can give the diagnosis in kids with leukemia." Phineas was surprised he had to defend his actions.

Dr. Olsen stared at Phineas with his eyebrows raised. He blinked twice and placed a shaking hand on the microscope dial.

"What'd we get?" Phineas asked. *And why do you look terrified?*

"Sit. I'll...I'll show you." More a plea than a command.

Phineas and Faith each focused the lenses on their heads of the microscope. The field visible had a foamy blue-green background covered with what looked like numerous black-rimmed coins.

"You're looking at a silver stain. The round black organisms are pneumocysts. I've never seen *so many*." Olsen moved the slide to different fields, and all contained the same findings.

Phineas stood up to leave. "Dr. Olsen, thank you. I should warn you that there will probably be requests for teaching conferences about this case."

After the stairwell door closed on their way to Daniel's room, Faith turned to Phineas and asked, "What the heck happened to Dr. Olsen back there?"

Phineas shrugged. "You noticed it to? He looked like he just heard terrible news...Maybe he recognized the patient's name."

They climbed the stairs to explain the bronchoscopy results to Daniels, and that he was now on the appropriate antibiotic.

Daniels' gaze shifted from Phineas to Faith. "How come I'm the lucky one to get something so unusual?"

Faith told him about the recent series in the New England Journal of Medicine.

Daniels was silent for a bit after he took in the information. He rubbed his palms on his sheets. "If I got this from sex...you're gonna see more of it." He coughed and sucked three breaths through pursed lips. "Maybe not so much in Chapel Hill at first...but in other cities."

⚜ ⚜ ⚜

Phineas grumbled and hung up the phone. "No date night Saturday." He'd answered a page he received on his way home on a sunny June evening.

Iris appeared in the kitchen. "Something come up?"

"That was Ruby, Dr. Kornberg's admin. Dr. K wants me to cover the ward with him during the house staff picnic Saturday. She wanted to make sure I had no other plans. I was afraid this was coming." Phineas enjoyed those picnics and the nights off that followed when he'd been a resident. It was his turn to give back. He had to admit Dr. Kornberg shouldn't be alone on the ward. "He's a brilliant scientist and teacher but hasn't taken care of a patient by himself in years." He sighed. "It's the right thing."

Iris offered a sympathetic smile. "I'll be all right by myself for one night. I've done it before."

❖ ❖ ❖

The house staff checked out to Dr. Kornberg and Phineas at precisely 4 PM. Dr. Kornberg wore his starched pristine white coat over his usual button-down white shirt with black necktie. Phineas began to excuse himself to find a set of scrubs. He expected patient care would keep him busy all night.

"Phineas, let's talk about tonight."

"Sure, Dr. Kornberg."

"You know this is not something I do very often."

Major understatement.

"I plan to take the calls tonight *and* perform the evaluations indicated. I wanted you here to be available to listen to my assessments and show me how to carry out my plans. *I* will be the intern. *You* will function as my teacher tonight. How does that sound to you?"

"Of course, Sir. Happy to do this however you want." Phineas was stunned. He'd expected Dr. Kornberg to arrive with a briefcase full of papers to work on while Phineas went from patient to patient. Instead, his boss had a stethoscope in his coat pocket and looked ready to use it.

"What time would you like to dine?" Dr. Kornberg asked.

Is my boss asking me to join him? "I'm flexible, Sir."

"Renee has prepared a picnic dinner for us. Please call Iris and see if she can join us in the conference room. Let's say around 6:30?"

Wow! The surprises just keep coming. "I'll call Iris now."

True to his word, Dr. Kornberg instructed the operator and the charge nurse to direct calls to his pager. Phineas kept watch from the nurses' station. Dr. Kornberg answered pages, sat patiently while speaking with patients, examined them, and explained his thoughts. When he reported his assessments and decisions to Phineas, a broad smile graced Dr. Kornberg's face.

"I forgot how much I enjoy this. They seem to appreciate me," Dr. Kornberg concluded after an encounter.

In the hall on the way to the nurses' station, Renee and Iris walked and chatted. Dr. Kornberg looked pleased. "It must be 6:30. Are you hungry?" He stood to peck Renee's cheek and to relieve her of an enormous basket.

"I found our guest of honor down the hallway." Renee spoke with the subtlest French accent, adding to a lithe elegance. Her long silver hair was plaited and ended over her lower spine.

Dr. Kornberg led the group to the conference room and began unpacking Tupperware containers, a baguette, and a bottle of Chenin Blanc. He paused to inspect the label. Renee wiped the table clean before placing dinner plates, napkins, stemmed glasses, and forks on it. Iris and Phineas watched in amazement as the bounty appeared.

Renee began scooping fillets onto plates. "I hope you like poached whitefish with a lime dill sauce, rice salad and marinated asparagus."

Dr. Kornberg poured wine for the women. "Phineas, sorry, but you only get a taste." He tipped a meager splash into Phineas' glass then filled his with Perrier.

During the main course, Phineas and Iris learned how Renee and Dr. Kornberg met while he was an undergraduate at Columbia and she an exchange student from Paris. When she asked for directions to class, he walked her all the way there. Before he deposited her at the classroom doorway, he asked to see her again.

Renee reached for the basket. "I made a raspberry tart with crème fraiche for dessert."

They were about to start on the tart and a thermos of coffee when Dr. Kornberg's pager interrupted. He excused himself and soon returned to poke his head back into the conference room. "I need to check on someone. Continue your feast." Twenty minutes later he was back. "Phineas, I need to talk with you. We may be a while. You ladies take your time."

"Renee and I will be fine," Iris answered. "Do what you need to do."

Phineas stood to leave. "Thank you so much, Renee".

A chart lay open at the nurses' station. Dr. Kornberg began, "I'm sure you remember Doris Glizinski, the lady with Streptococcus pneumoniae lobar pneumonia and positive blood cultures. She was improving but is now confused and her fever has returned. I think she has a stiff neck, and we should do a lumbar puncture."

The possibility of meningitis brought Phineas to full alert. "Please remind me what antibiotic we have her on."

Dr. Kornberg slid his finger over her medication sheet. "She's on Ancef instead of penicillin because of a possible rash to ampicillin years ago."

"I don't believe Ancef penetrates into spinal fluid, so she could have meningitis, spread from the bacteria in her blood. I'll take a look at her and do a lumbar puncture."

Dr. Kornberg peered over his glasses at Phineas. "I was hoping you'd walk me through it. Just tell me where the LP trays are, and I'll gather everything while you examine her. I'll call her family to inform them and obtain consent, so we can get this done right away."

Phineas' jaw tightened. "Sir, forgive me, but I think I need to ask when you last did a spinal tap?"

"It's been a long time," Dr. Kornberg admitted softly. "But I can do it with your guidance."

Phineas listed the supplies they needed and left to see Mrs. Glizinski. When he returned, Dr. Kornberg sat expectantly next to a neat pile, which included the LP tray, gloves, masks and betadine, the iodine cleaning solution.

"Dr. Kornberg, I agree she has a stiff neck and could have meningitis." Phineas wanted to get the procedure done and adjust antibiotics immediately.

"I reached her daughter. She gave verbal consent and is on her way in." He gestured at the assembled equipment. "Now please review the procedure from beginning to end. Assume nothing." He looked eager but composed.

Phineas described the proper positioning of the patient, the sterile prep and draping, the local anesthesia, and finally the insertion of the spinal needle.

"When the tip of the needle enters the spinal fluid space, you'll sense a subtle tactile 'pop'. Then you pause to check for a fluid return and collect it in the three tubes in the tray." Phineas was less comfortable explaining it than doing it himself.

Dr. Kornberg followed every step as instructed. Phineas hovered beside him and focused on the spinal needle as Dr. Kornberg advanced it into Mrs. Glizinski's lower back.

A triumphant whisper came from Dr. Kornberg. "I felt it! I felt the pop." Cloudy fluid dripped from the needle hub into the sample tubes. Dr. Kornberg removed the needle and spoke to the patient. "All done, Mrs. Glizinski. Please stay on your back while we study the samples."

Phineas held one of the tubes to the light. "We may have our answer."

He felt relief and absorbed some of Dr. Kornberg's restrained excitement when he led the way to the microbiology lab. There they stained a drop of fluid and inspected it. Bacteria consistent with Streptococcus pneumoniae were visible under the microscope. Dr. Kornberg called the infectious disease consultant and started another antibiotic, vancomycin. He only stopped pacing and took a seat after the first dose began infusing.

The charge nurse smiled as Dr. Kornberg and Phineas sat at the workstation. "You two have been busy. Two very pretty ladies left a package for you." She held up a Tupperware container. Inside were two generous pieces of raspberry tart.

Mrs. Glizinski remained confused overnight, but her temperature came down close to normal by morning. Dr. Kornberg visited her and her daughter at the bedside repeatedly through the night. He sent Phineas to the call room for a nap with the words, "One of us needs to be rested and sharp."

On morning rounds, after Dr. Kornberg recited the events of the night to the incoming team, including the lumbar puncture, the resident nudged Phineas and whispered, "Kornberg did the tap?"

"Perfectly."

The resident's mouth fell open.

After rounds, Dr. Kornberg put his hand on Phineas' shoulder and said, "We did well." He left the hospital looking exhausted and elated, declaring he was eager to play chamber music.

As Levi Daniels predicted, an increased number of cases of pneumocystis pneumonia were presenting to hospitals around the country, first in the gay male community, next in intravenous drug users, and then in the hemophilia population. UNC's numerous hemophiliacs became desperately ill, one after another. Health care providers, including Phineas in quiet moments, couldn't help but worry about their contact with these patients. Eventually the disease was labeled AIDS—acquired immune deficiency syndrome.

Phineas came across a paper discussing the relative virulence, or potential to cause harm, of infective agents. At the top of the list, the Ebola and Marburg viruses, both occurred only as infrequent deadly outbreaks in Africa. Close behind was the influenza virus, especially the strain that caused the Spanish Flu pandemic during World War I. Next was the pneumococcus, the most common bacterial cause of pneumonia, labeled "The Captain of the Men of Death" by the great Dr. William Osler, borrowing a phrase from John Bunyan.

The pneumocystis organism was close to the bottom of the list, meaning a patient who acquired it must possess a terribly impaired immune system, one that was unable to defend against the least virulent infections. *What sort of an agent could so devastate someone's immune system? And how easy is it to catch? How long before disease shows up after exposure?* Phineas now wore eye protection during all bronchoscopies. The memory of his burning eyes following his first pneumocystis bronchoscopy repeatedly crept into his consciousness.

❧ ❧ ❧

Iris tasted Phineas' offering of sage chicken and set her fork on her plate. "So, Phineas, I saw two patients at the hospital today who were admitted with diagnoses of pneumocystis pneumonia. The doctors are saying the patients have AIDS, a new name for their disease."

"Why did they ask you to see them?"

"Trying to get them Medicaid. They were both indigent. They weren't the first we've seen at Durham County General."

"Risk factors? Drug use or homosexuality?"

"Not that they admitted to. Just poverty. One was homeless."

"We're seeing more of it at UNC every month."

Phineas sighed and placed his silverware on his plate. He and his colleagues had been performing more bronchoscopies to diagnose pneumocystis. Progressively sicker patients were being referred from smaller hospitals eager to pass them on, like hot potatoes, before the community hospital got burned with a strange disease in a critically ill patient. The referring doctors sounded anxious when they called.

"Phineas, what do you think is causing AIDS?" Iris asked. Her glacier blue stare mirrored her question.

"No one knows for sure yet, maybe an infection transmitted in blood and secretions, judging by the groups who have so far been afflicted with it. Maybe a new virus."

She raised her eyebrows. "Maybe a *Martian* virus. Revenge for *War of the Worlds*."

"*Probably* not. Some claim it's God's punishment, a new plague."

"I heard the Reverend Jerry Falwell on the news. He said AIDS was not just God's punishment for homosexuals, but God's punishment for the society that tolerates homosexuals." She pressed her lips together and appeared appalled.

"Who made *him* the judge?"

"His followers."

❧ ❧ ❧

Days later, Phineas stood behind Iris and massaged her shoulders. She closed her novel. "I think you should use condoms for a while. I'm tired of my diaphragm."

Phineas came around to face her, hoping to talk her out of her proposed change. He loved their lovemaking the way it happened now. "I'd really rather not have to use condoms. Can we maybe take turns?" He shrugged. "Besides, I don't have any." *And why is she saying this?*

"I've been using that diaphragm for years and I'm tired of it. And I bought you a box." Her tone was firm, resolute.

The discussion ended. Phineas couldn't bring himself to ask Iris if she feared catching something from him, or worse. He forced himself to bury the idea his long hours away had given her reason to be with someone else. *Someone with a more refined occupation. Someone whose job didn't disgust or frighten her.* And he wished she still kissed him the way she once had. His sadness manifest as the familiar tingling in the back of his nasal passage.

Phineas concluded Iris thought she should be careful until the AIDS mystery was solved, and she could be confidant Phineas hadn't acquired the agent during his care of so many patients. He rationalized her thinking because he respected her intelligence. That she might be thinking this way increased his anxiety. Over dinner, she mentioned, "I heard a nurse say she was looking for a way to get away from patient care."

"To do what instead?"

"She said 'maybe work for an insurance company as a case reviewer.'"

"How could she prefer *that*?"

"She said her husband was afraid."

She told him of another conversation she'd overhead at a nurses' station. "One of the anesthesiologists, Dr. Merkin, said he didn't want to provide anesthesia for an AIDS patient. He said why should he 'risk his life for someone who's sick because of their sins?'"

"God. Who's he?"

"He's this snarky middle-aged bald guy. Never see him without a surgical cap or his silly toupee. I heard him called 'Curly' behind his back once."

Phineas stifled an involuntary snort. "Did anyone say anything to him?"

"I did."

"What?" He had a feeling of foreboding.

"I asked him what his religion was."

Phineas grimaced. "And?"

"He said 'Baptist'...So I said 'Isn't what you just said the opposite of what Christ did? Doesn't the Bible teach you that he died for our sins?'"

Phineas had expected no less of a response from her. "He answer you?"

"Said he wasn't dying for theirs."

"He should find another career."

Phineas had heard of other doctors who had expressed the belief they shouldn't have to care for AIDS patients, that medical providers shouldn't have to take risks when the patients' deviant lifestyles exposed them to harm. This attitude repulsed Phineas. *How could a doctor feel that way?* They shouldn't be in medicine. They reminded him of the priest and Levite who passed to the other side of the road rather than help the robbed and beaten traveler—the Jew the Good Samaritan then aided.

⚜ ⚜ ⚜

During quiet hours, Phineas ruminated over how to find courage in his work. He rationalized that he'd invested many years in the prime of his life, as well as a small fortune he still owed money on, to get where he was professionally. He couldn't consider abandoning his work now.

He thought about how doctors historically accepted risks to care for patients. He remembered Dr. Burney's reference to Camus' *The Plague*. While it was fiction, he recalled that it reflected care during a terrifying epidemic. He decided he should read *The Plague* again. It might be helpful. The Little Professor Bookstore had a used copy. The pages were a light yellow and corners dog-eared.

The protagonist, Dr. Rieux, faced a plague epidemic that was explosive, quickly diagnosed, and without effective treatment. The city was quarantined. *At least AIDS hadn't come on so explosively and led to quarantine.* Like the Reverend Jerry Fallwell, the story's religious leader, Father Paneloux, preached that the plague was God's punishment. The innocent son of Dr. Rieux's co-worker died tragically, reminding Phineas of AIDS in hemophiliac children. Dr. Rieux and his coworkers remained motivated to help their fellow men despite misery and sleep deprivation. And the plague passed.

Phineas should go on. Science had to find a treatment for AIDS.

He wrote to Dr. MacSweeney. The return letter arrived eight days later.

Dear Phineas,

I'm glad you wrote. We're also having a tough time with this AIDS epidemic here in Boston. The medical students and your colleagues at Tufts also suppress their fears in the care of these patients.

You have taken important steps already. You have acknowledged fear and you have prepared yourself for the battle ahead. I think you and I can agree that this thing can't be that easy to catch, or we would have seen more medical caregivers with it by now. But continue to be careful in all you do, in each moment.

And thank you for your suggestion of Camus' The Plague. I have picked up a copy and will share it with others.

Cheers,
Ian MacSweeney

❦ ❦ ❦

Jerome Thomas Babineaux
November 11, 1920 – February 22, 1983

NEW ORLEANS

Jerome Thomas Babineaux died from amyloidosis complicating multiple myeloma in Tulane Hospital February 22, 1983. He was born in Baptist

Hospital November 11, 1920, the son of Robert Louis Babineaux and Brigitte LeBlanc Babineaux. He graduated from Holy Cross High School where he starred on the baseball team. He went on to graduate from Louisiana State University, majoring in physics. He began his teaching career after returning to Holy Cross High School, where he taught physics and coached baseball. As the United States entered World War II, he enlisted in the Navy and became an engineer on submarines based in Norfolk Navy Base in Virginia. Following the war, he was honorably discharged and completed his master's degree in Education at Tulane University. He then accepted a position at De La Salle High School, where he taught physics until his illness.

While in graduate school he met his future wife, then Sarah Jane Gaudet, who was at his side as he passed away. He is also survived by their son, Matthew, of New Orleans, and by their daughter Iris Babineaux Mann and her husband, Dr. Phineas Mann, of Chapel Hill, NC.

A memorial service will be held at St. Patrick's Church, 724 Camp Street, New Orleans on Saturday, February 26, 1983 at 2 P.M. followed by a reception in the church hall.

Donations in Jerome's memory can be made to St. Patrick's Church and to De La Salle High School.

He will be missed.

Iris wiped away tears after she finished writing her father's obituary. She reread it twice and decided he would have been satisfied with it. He had liked physics reports to be lean and crisp. Point A to Point B. Verbal vectors.

Her Daddy's last few weeks were awful, according to her mother, whose calls were barely coherent, weeping sketchy details of her husband's sudden illness. He'd complained of pains in his back, then constipation and the constant need to urinate. Chaos and slovenliness replaced his usual orderliness. He became lost driving home and was found in a parking lot asleep and difficult to arouse. An ambulance took him to Tulane Hospital where he was found to have a 'dangerously high' calcium level. X-rays revealed emphysema and numerous scattered holes in his bones. Blood tests showed his kidneys had stopped functioning, and a cardiac echo indicated his heart was barely pumping. Blood and bone marrow tests confirmed multiple myeloma, and a rectal biopsy amyloidosis, a condition that explained his end-stage heart failure, and for which there was no treatment.

Iris flew to New Orleans where she found her mother not eating or sleeping, and barely able to wash and dress herself. Iris drove her back and forth to the hospital, while Matthew returned home to New Orleans despite a heavy course load in his last college semester at LSU.

After Iris relayed her father's diagnoses, Phineas bought his plane ticket to New Orleans and met with Jerome's doctor to interpret medical information for Iris, Matthew, and Sarah Jane. The doctors were unable to keep Jerome's calcium level steadily in a safe range. There were periods of relative coherence when his doctor, Iris, and Phineas did their best to explain Jerome's condition to him. Iris believed preventing his suffering should be the goal, and Matthew agreed. Sarah Jane said little, rarely leaving Jerome's bedside. His intravenous fluids were discontinued, and narcotics provided. Jerome Babineaux took his last breath a day later.

Sarah Jane continued to do poorly. Her coughing awakened Iris, who found her mother wandering the house in a bedraggled state, her usual perfect hair unkempt and hanging. She ate almost nothing. Iris had to convince her to bathe and helped her put on a black dress for Jerome's funeral. Iris applied her mother's make-up and fixed her hair for her. At the service, Jerome's colleagues expressed their condolences while Sarah Jane gazed at the floor silently.

Over the next few days, Phineas listened as Iris and Matthew recalled happier memories of their father. These stories led to silent tears flowing down Sarah Jane's cheeks. Iris called her boss and told her she wasn't sure when she could return, her mother's state was so tenuous. Phineas felt guilty when he told Iris he should get back to UNC.

❧ ❧ ❧

Amos, retrieved from Ron's care, yelped, and shimmied when he saw Phineas. It was the first cheer Phineas had known since Iris left Chapel Hill for New Orleans, but it wasn't enough to heal the gaping wound of his wife's absence.

Iris' calls over the next few weeks were not encouraging. She reported that Matthew returned to LSU, would graduate in May, and accepted a job in Boston. Iris took Sarah Jane to her medical doctor, then to a psychiatrist who started an antidepressant and brought up hospitalization for electro-convulsive therapy as an option. Iris said the medical doctor, Dr. Mincey, declared Sarah Jane severely malnourished, so a nutritionist suggested supplements that Iris had to regularly push on her mother as she might an infant. Dr. Mincey mentioned the possibility of inserting a feeding tube, which forced Iris to fully grasp her mother's desperate condition.

❧ ❧ ❧

Iris soon discovered how much her father had managed the day-to-day operations of the house. He'd paid the bills, bought the groceries, and did most of the cooking and cleaning. After Iris left for Boston years ago, her mother began only going to church and occasionally visiting friends. Otherwise, she spent nice days on the screened porch day bed, and during bad weather rested inside with daytime television.

Iris tried to reminisce with Sarah Jane one sunny afternoon on the porch.

"I remember how much I loved it when Daddy read to me. He'd hold me on his lap and read until I got sleepy. When I was too big for his lap, we'd sit next to each other and read the newspaper together. Then one day he was too busy. I missed those times."

"You were capable of reading to yourself then, and I didn't want him pestering you as you became a woman." Her mother's voice was barely audible.

"He never 'pestered' me."

"Then I succeeded. I made sure he didn't. He was a man, after all."

"Daddy wouldn't have done that."

"Daddies can barge in while you're taking a bath. Daddies can touch you where they shouldn't."

Iris studied her mother. Sarah Jane rocked on the edge of the day bed, clutching a pillow and staring at the floor. Iris summoned the courage to ask, "Did Grandpa 'pester' you?" She waited several minutes for a response.

"When your grandmother found out, she put a stop to it. She packed our bags, and she and I went to stay with *her* parents. We stayed quite a while, until your grandfather convinced her he'd changed."

"I had no idea."

"And I was a skinny thing. You were developing into a glorious woman by comparison. I needed to protect you."

Iris put her arm on her mother's shoulder. "Daddy was the best daddy a daughter could have."

"I miss him so much." Sarah Jane whimpered; her head bowed into her delicate hands.

❧ ❧ ❧

Phineas studied the bowl of collard greens just harvested. "When do you think you can come home?" Cooking for one was getting old. Sleeping alone, older.

"Mom's still not where I can leave her. She'd starve and the house would crumble around her." Iris' voice in the phone sounded like she was deep in a tunnel.

"Amos and I are becoming lost souls here without you." Amos lifted his head and wagged his tail.

"Sorry. Just can't leave yet... Hey, you figure out what you're doing after fellowship yet?"

"I'm guessing I need to find a J-O-B job. Haven't heard a peep from Dr. Kornberg in Paris." He'd tried to not think about his uncertain future.

"Did you write him?"

"Weeks ago. No answer yet. I asked his admin. She said he's immersed in a project on his sabbatical, and she hasn't heard from him either. You know how he is. Probably misplaced my letter and forgot about it."

"Hate to say it, but one of us will need a paycheck in July."

"I've been spending my days with asthmatic rodents. Maybe I can get a job as a guinea pig surgeon." He appreciated her soft chuckle.

"You used to be a pretty good people doctor—I'm told."

He missed her gentle teasing. "Okay, okay. I'll hit the journal wanted ads and send out resumes."

"Try Tulane Hospital. A job in New Orleans would solve both our problems."

"I'll call soon." Phineas extracted his chef's knife from its resting place in a wooden block. "I miss you."

"Me too. Bye. Love you."

"Love you, too."

He cleaved then began chopping an onion. Its sting moistened his eyes. His nasal passage tingled front to back, a too familiar sensation. The house and his heart felt empty.

Amos sat at attention by his bowl and let out a soft whine. "Amos, I better feed you before I sauté that salt pork, or you'll be drooling all over the floor."

❧ ❧ ❧

The letter was from Baptist Hospital in New Orleans. CEO Justin Jordan explained that a colleague at Tulane had forwarded Phineas' resume. Baptist was offering to pay his travel expenses to interview.

He dialed Sarah Jane's house and felt relief and a lump in his throat when Iris was on the other end. "Babineaux residence."

"You know anything about Baptist Hospital in New Orleans?"

"Phineas! Hi! Not much. Why?"

"They want to fly me there to interview."

"A free trip. Why not?"

"Strange thing is that I didn't send them a resume. They got it from someone at Tulane." A vague uneasy feeling crept over him.

"It must be good, if Tulane recommended them." Her tone was upbeat.

"Let's hope so."

Sarah Jane made modest progress since Phineas last saw her. She remained precariously thin but was now conversant and took care of her own hygiene. Iris had taken over shopping and cleaning and struggled to enlist her mother in household duties. Both were excited to hear about Phineas' upcoming interview at Baptist. Iris suggested she should also start looking for a job if Baptist made an offer.

Phineas urged Sarah Jane to see about her constant wet sounding cough. When her x-rays revealed abnormal densities in both lungs, sputum cultures were ordered. The initial microbiology tests suggested the possibility of tuberculosis, so the health department placed her in quarantine in the home. A health department nurse came by each morning to watch Sarah Jane take a handful of pills for TB. Some days she vomited the pills soon after the nurse left. She ate more those days, her nausea partially relieved.

It took three weeks for the cultures to grow another bacterium, which had mimicked TB under the microscope. Her doctor told her she should keep taking the same medicines for the organism they identified, Mycobacterium avium complex ('MAC').

Iris reported that Sarah Jane had shot her doctor an incredulous look. "You mean I have to take the same nasty pile of pills, and it isn't TB?"

Phineas reinforced her doctor's words. "So far we have nothing better for what you have."

"But now I have to pay for it?"

"The state only pays if it is actually TB."

"I don't believe it."

⚜ ⚜ ⚜

Phineas studied the offer Baptist had mailed. They would provide a base salary and stipends for him to be their first Respiratory Therapy Director and ICU Director. A letter outlined duties for these positions. In addition to patient care, he'd have to develop and approve policies, plan for staff and equipment needs, represent at meetings, and educate therapists, nurses, administrators, and other medical providers. It would be a steep learning curve. The financial package, which also included expenses for moving, would be more than enough for Phineas and Iris to rent a decent home, even after their obligatory student loan payments.

A non-compete document was included in the papers. If Phineas left their employment, he could not practice medicine in the New Orleans vicinity for a year. Iris joked over the phone, "If you leave Baptist, you can work on your chef resume."

"If I have to leave there, I might welcome the change."

"So, you think you're going to take the job?" She sounded hopeful.

"I don't think I should turn it down. It solves all of our needs."

Then there was the life insurance policy; the hospital paid the premium as part of his income. If he died, Iris would receive one million dollars.

⚜ ⚜ ⚜

When Phineas came home from his day at UNC, Jackson Lee waited on the front steps. Amos sat next to him, enjoying having his ears scratched. Phineas noticed how Jackson Lee had aged during the five years they'd rented from him. He doubted he would ever have a better landlord.

"Sorry to hear you'll be moving. I'll miss my buddy here." Jackson Lee put an arm around Amos, who responded by licking the old man's face.

"We hate to go, but Iris isn't ready to leave her mother yet, and I have a job in New Orleans."

"I'll need to get this place painted. That'll help with the long overdue rent increase I plan to include in the ad."

"When will the painting start? Do I need to keep Amos in the house?" Amos sat at attention at his name. "I usually leave him in the pen when the weather is this nice."

"Next week. I'll be here when they start, to make sure Amos is OK. My painters will be good to him."

Phineas smiled at the pair. "Warn them not to have any food with them when they're painting the part of the house against his pen. You know he's mostly lab and eats everything."

The painters saved the wall next to Amos' pen for their last day. Phineas looked forward to the job's completion and removal of the ladders and mess. When he drove up after work, the house looked great with its dark red siding and white trim refreshed. He wished Iris were home to see it. Amos stepped out of the shade of his doghouse and stretched, chest to ground, butt in the air. He had undergone a transformation.

"What happened to you, Amos?"

A white ring around Amos' face and symmetric, perfect white feathery handprints on each side of his chest stood out on his black fur. Phineas imagined the scene, Amos with his face in a can of paint and a painter's coated hands pulling him out. If Iris were here, she would have her camera out. She would laugh nonstop. This deserved paying long-distance charges.

Phineas' eyes moistened when how much he missed her hit him. "Amos, wait till Iris hears that today you got your halo and wings."

Two weeks before the move to New Orleans, Dr. Kornberg returned from his sabbatical in Paris. He greeted Phineas from his desk chair. "Phineas, sit down and tell me about your work, and what you plan to do for us next year."

Stunned, Phineas sank into the seat across from Dr. Kornberg. "I—I didn't know you wanted me to stay on here after fellowship. I thought I needed to find a job." He looked from Dr. Kornberg to the floor. "I accepted a position at Baptist Hospital in New Orleans."

Dr. Kornberg's mouth fell open. "Of course, we want you here! I assumed you knew that."

"No one said anything." *And you lost my letter.*

"I'm sorry. I was immersed in research and had delegated administrative duties. I should have written to you directly...Can you get out of the New Orleans job?"

Phineas shook his head. "The contract is signed."

Dr. Kornberg swallowed. "I feel terrible about this."

"Please don't. Iris has been there for months caring for her mother after her father died. I'll get to be with her again soon." Phineas forced a smile. "And you've done so much for me. Thank you."

"I wanted to do more."

Phineas couldn't help but wonder "what if?" as he left Kornberg and returned to the office space he'd share with the other fellows for a few more days. He leaned against its seventh story window and surveyed the UNC medical campus, dazzling under the June sun. When he finally faced the task of clearing out his desk, six years of memories rushed by. He'd miss the place.

PART THREE
NEW ORLEANS

It is in vain that you rise up early and go late to rest, eating the bread of anxious toil; for he gives to his beloved sleep.
PSALM 127:2

From her childhood New Orleans home, Iris launched 'Operation Move to New Orleans' after Phineas signed the contract. Her former boss at Durham County General must have sent a glowing letter of recommendation to her counterpart at Tulane University Hospital when she submitted her resume, because the following Monday afternoon the social work department head's secretary called. Yes indeed, they wanted to interview her for an open position on the inpatient medical service. She was elated when an acceptable job offer followed her interview. *Job, check.*

She found a suitable rental located between Tulane University and Baptist Hospitals, necessary for Phineas to reach the hospital easily on call. She had hoped to be near Audubon Park, so they would have a park close by for Amos to frolic. She walked the neighborhoods, read bulletin boards, and studied the classifieds. Her walks and chats with residents located a small two-bedroom shotgun-style home on Clara Street off

Nashville Street. It was further from Audubon than she had hoped, but not too far for weekend expeditions. *Home, check.*

Since Baptist's offer included paying for the move, Phineas was able to hire a moving company. Matthew came to stay with Sarah Jane while Iris flew home. She and Phineas drove their two cars in a mini caravan to New Orleans. Amos took turns in the passenger seats. *Husband and dog, check and check.*

⚜ ⚜ ⚜

After early rounds during his first week at Baptist Hospital, Phineas returned to his office down the hall from the ICU. It was tiny with a metal desk, two chairs, a telephone, and no windows. He decided to try the phone and Iris' office number.

On the second ring, "Hello, Iris Mann."

"Very official. Phin here. How's Tulane?"

"Getting busy. I'd better get more efficient soon. How's Baptist?

"Still finding everything. I'm in my office near the ICU. The outpatient clinic that I staff part-time is in the office building across the street. I checked and so far, I have a lean schedule there. Should give me the opportunity to spend more time in the hospital getting my footing."

"Are they advertising your clinic?"

"Not yet. Baptist tells me their plan is to build the clinic's patient volume with referrals from the emergency department and hospital discharges. The goal is to keep uninsured pulmonary patients out of the hospital by caring for them in clinic."

"Sounds laudable." Iris, the social worker, sounded pleased.

"Actually, I bet they mostly want to keep as many as possible who can't pay away from the hospital. Good care is a secondary goal." At least he'd provide that, something most of these patients hadn't had.

"How's the hospital?"

"Slow too. I start each day in the ICU. I've only had a handful of inpatient consults, and the patients were indigent. Their doctors seemed happy to turn those folks over to me. Glad I'm salaried." *And I don't have to show a profit, yet.*

"Me too. Does your cross-cover guy get more of the consults?"

"The respiratory therapists say Dr. Cain has shown little interest for increasing his inpatient footprint, especially in the ICU. He'd rather spend his time in his clinic." Phineas checked his pager to make sure it was on. "I've only talked with him a couple of times, so far."

"So, who's done the pulmonary there?" Her Tulane Hospital had an entire Pulmonary Division.

"They tell me staff physicians at Baptist are used to calling surgeons for pulmonary procedures, anesthesiologists for help with ventilators, and doing it themselves for most of the critical care." *All things that I can do.*

"We should enjoy it while you're not busy—but salaried."

His stomach growled. "Got time for lunch?"

"Can't today. I'll put you on my calendar. What day looks good for you?"

After two pleasantly slow months, Phineas arrived for morning rounds to find requests for consultation on two new patients in the ICU. One was an elderly man with severe emphysema, an ongoing smoker, who had presented to the Emergency Department in respiratory failure. This was the man's fifth time on a ventilator in a year. The respiratory therapist, Barb, knew him well. She counseled Phineas to begin with the other patient, suggesting he may be able to have her off the ventilator quite soon. Barb was in her early 30s and usually wore the odor of her morning cigarette. Her voice was husky like Janice Joplin's, and she expressed confidence in her opinions.

Phineas followed her to the bedside of a young woman. The woman's age could have been 20 or 40. Her hair, bleached midpoint between platinum and polished brass, spilled over lean, defined shoulder muscles. An endotracheal tube was taped in place beside an oral airway splint, inserted to prevent her from biting through the tube. She was restless under the sheet. One eye, open a slit, tracked him. He studied the nurse's paper flow sheet. "Ashley James" was stamped on the label.

Her nurse, a familiar young woman with thick hair pulled back approached. A silver cross rested above her badge that read 'Angela Portier'. "Hey, Dr. Mann. How's Iris?"

"She's fine." Angela asked about his wife once before after chatting her up at Phineas' welcome luncheon. Iris mentioned that Angela pressured her to get together. He hadn't heard of that happening. "Tell me about Ms. James, please...Angela."

"Ms. James came in last night OD'd. Tox screens indicated benzodiazepines, narcotics, *and* alcohol. She was barely breathing and high risk for aspirating, even after Narcan, so they intubated her. We don't know which meds she took specifically, but they must have been short acting. We've had to give her doses of IV morphine the last few hours to keep her manageable."

Phineas lifted Ashley James' hand. Her nails were short, cracked and had dirt under them. Needle tracks violated and scarred the skin of her forearms. "Ms. James, I'm Dr. Mann. I'm going to examine you and review your x-rays. We'll need to stop giving you sedatives, so we can make sure it is safe for you to breathe without this tube in your throat. Try to stay relaxed while we do this. You'll be able to talk when we get the tube out. It should be soon."

Her examination and x-ray contained no surprises. Phineas turned to Angela and Barb and spoke softly, "Notify me when she is more alert, and we'll see if we can extubate her."

He moved over two beds and began studying the chart of the COPD patient. He noted the ventilator settings and examined the patient. He stepped into the small radiology reading room next to the ICU to review the man's x-rays.

As he stepped back into the ICU, Phineas startled at the loud crash of a metal bedside table hitting the tile floor. Standing next to it was

Ashley James with her endotracheal tube in her hand. Her defiant eyes met his as she jerked out her IV. Without a word, she bolted away from him toward the far entrance, her legs uncoiling like steel springs. Her backless hospital gown rotated around her neck and transformed into a cape, which billowed behind and above her lean and naked figure as she shot through the double door. Phineas, Angela, and Barb gave chase. "Call security!" they all shrieked at once. Phineas sprinted after her, as he might have while stealing second base in high school.

In the main hallway, Ashley James briefly paused, glanced at the closed elevator doors, and raced for the stairs. Staff and visitors froze and stared as Phineas gained on her. Phineas tried to grip her shoulder as she heaved open the stairway door. She turned toward him and slowed enough for him to sprint past her and block the opening. Blood dripped from her arm at the IV site. They locked eyes. "Ashley, let's get you back to your bed." He was catching his breath. "So we can properly discharge you from the hospital."

Phineas felt a tap on his shoulder. A burly security guard puffed behind him in the stairwell landing. "Hey Doc! Whoa! Have you just caught Supergirl?" He brushed by Phineas. "Let's find something to cover you up, Honey. Looks like you lost your costume somewheres. I'm guessing you're the reason I was STAT paged and had to run up all these stairs."

Angela appeared with a blanket and a wheelchair and coaxed Ashley James into it.

Phineas caught his breath. "She seems to be breathing fine now. May not need much more from me." Crisis averted; his pounding pulse slowed. "That's not something you see every day."

Barb wheezed and chuckled as they re-entered the ICU. "Took a super Mann to catch a Supergirl."

Angela was grinning and staring at him in apparent admiration. "Nice run, Dr. Mann! Wait till word gets out!"

Word got out. The next day, the ICU head nurse, Hilary, presented Phineas with a t-shirt with Superman's 'S' on the front and 'MANN' on the back. When hospital staff and administrators passed in the hall, they grinned and greeted him with, "Hey, Superman! Still faster than a speeding patient?" It seemed from that day forward there was a major uptick in inpatient and clinic referrals to him. He had been found.

⚜ ⚜ ⚜

Before Phineas' recruitment, Baptists' administration convinced Dr. Richard Cain to rotate being on pulmonary call with him. The respiratory therapists shared candid opinions about Dr. Cain with Phineas. He learned that Dr. Cain had been at Baptist for more than twenty years before Phineas arrived. The story was that he had trained in pulmonary medicine a meager six months past his residency at a Veterans Administration Hospital. He was therefore not board eligible, and the therapists felt he was not current in pulmonary and critical care procedures. At Baptist, he was infrequently asked to consult, and then only for help with patients on ventilators when the attending physician and respiratory therapists had given up getting these patients off life support. He preferred his solo office practice where he had purchased his office space early on, and the real estate was now valuable.

Dr. Cain freely admitted to Phineas that he preferred to stay out of the hospital and on a tennis court as much as he could. He appeared military fit and groomed. His progress notes were short, illegible, and offered little insight into his thinking process, the opposite of Phineas' notes. They reflected his impressions based on his patchy experience and not on current literature. He had agreed to share being on call with Phineas, expecting new freedom from his pager every other night and weekend.

When Phineas first arrived at Baptist, Dr. Cain advised, "Phineas, when I started, I was told that the way to build a private practice was the three A's. The order of the A's tells you the order of importance. First is affable. Second is available. Third is able." He'd let his words sink in. "I learned early on, if you do ICU medicine you want to ignore affable and try not to look very available. Let the other doctors take care of these patients as much as possible, so they don't bother you with them. Write short notes. Don't teach. They'll call you even more! You need to survive over the long haul. Office work you can control. ICU work is Hell!"

Phineas listened politely without comment and fought the urge to frown. *Well, at least Dr. Cain is someone to share the burden of being on call with. And I'll be 'able'.*

Before Phineas became too busy, before his days and nights turned to shit, there were times he could relax. He'd leave the hospital before 6 PM and arrive home when Iris did. He was usually only paged once or twice at night while on call every other night, and only had to go back to the hospital after hours once or twice a week. He often sampled savory lunch offerings at nearby cafes. On occasion, Iris joined him. On these afternoons his spirits soared. He read journals and shared articles with the respiratory therapists. He even went on a few house calls if there seemed a good reason. House calls gave fresh insights into patients' lives, but more than once he felt helpless without the option of ordering tests. House calls also set the troubling precedent he would do it again, that he was expected to do it again.

The weather was clear and mild early on this fall Saturday afternoon when he received an operator page. He hoped to join Iris soon and take Amos for a long stroll. The operator had a Donald Ross on the phone, asking to speak with the doctor on call for Dr. Cain.

Phineas took a seat at the nurses' station and rolled the chair into a far corner, out of the chatter and commotion. "Hello. This is Dr. Mann. How can I help you?"

"Dr. Mann, thank you for speaking with me. I'm Donald Ross. Dr. Cain discharged my mother, Elizabeth Ross, from Baptist yesterday. She has emphysema." He cleared his throat. "Dr. Cain told her he had done all he could. He didn't see her getting any better."

"Has something changed since she came home?"

"We can't get her to wake up today." His voice trailed off.

"Is she on sleeping pills or something for her nerves or for pain?"

"No sir."

"Does she appear in distress? Is she struggling to breathe? Any fever?"

"She always looks like she's breathing hard. She doesn't feel hot."

"Is she eating or drinking anything?" Phineas shifted in his seat, beginning to feel like he wouldn't be able to solve Elizabeth Ross' issue over the phone.

"Not since last night."

"You should call the ambulance and bring her back to the emergency room, so we can assess her and do tests. She might need intravenous fluids."

Donald Ross fell silent.

"Mr. Ross?"

"Dr. Mann, she told us to never bring her back to the hospital. I'm trying to respect her wishes. Is there any way to give her more medicine at home?"

"Was she sent home on antibiotics and prednisone? Does she have a nebulizer machine?"

"Yes sir, but she's not taking pills. I tried to put them in her mouth, but I couldn't open it. She's set her jaw."

As much as Phineas wanted to wrap up his hospital rounds and go home, he was intrigued by the mystery of Elizabeth Ross. "Our options seem pretty limited. How far away do you live?"

"2205 Octavia Street, maybe a half mile from the hospital," Ross replied.

"I'll be finishing hospital rounds soon." Phineas jotted the address down. "I'll stop by after."

He heard Donald Ross let out a breath. "That's really good of you Dr. Mann. My family and I are grateful."

❧ ❧ ❧

Phineas found the Ross home in a neighborhood he had yet to explore. The yard was tidy, and the house painted white. Donald Ross waited for him on the front porch. He was middle aged and wore a button-down shirt and khakis. He rose from a rocking chair and offered his hand. "Thank you again for coming, Dr. Mann. Can I get you something to drink? Some sweet tea?"

Phineas shook his head. "I'm fine. Where is our patient?"

"I'll take you to her."

Phineas followed him through the house into a bedroom in the back. The curtains were drawn and lights out. Three women in long dark dresses appeared as mourners seated in a row across from a recumbent woman in a twin bed next to a large window. Donald Ross turned on a dim floor lamp. A sheet was pulled up over Elizabeth Ross' scrawny shoulder. She faced away from them toward the covered window, so all Phineas could see of her was her bobby-pinned grey hair.

Donald Ross broke the silence. "Dr. Mann, I'd like to introduce my wife, Janice."

The woman on the right raised a plump hand from her lap. "Thank you for coming, Dr. Mann." Her thick blond hair framed a face that retained a measure of youthful beauty.

Ross continued. "And these are Elizabeth's sisters, Shelley and Sissy." Shelley had sparse grey hair, a moon face, and clutched a rosary in knuckles deformed by rheumatoid arthritis. Sissy, gaunt with hollowed out cheeks, dabbed at puffy, pink eyelids with an embroidered handkerchief.

Phineas leaned over Elizabeth Ross and found the cord to open the drapery. Her eyelid muscles tensed as the November sunlight shone on her face. An oxygen cannula was under her nose, and the oxygen concentrator hummed in the corner. He counted sixteen breaths and ninety-two regular heartbeats per minute, both on the high side, but close to normal. Her neck muscles contracted, and her lips pursed with each breath.

"Ms. Ross, open your eyes, please." No response. He gently tried to pry open her eyelids. The muscles around her eyes tensed. "Please open your mouth and stick out your tongue." Again, no response. He applied gradual pressure to try to move her chin down. Her jaw muscles clenched. Phineas took her head in both hands and nodded her head for her, checking for a stiff neck. She did not resist.

He extracted his stethoscope from his pants pocket and listened over her back, finding symmetric, distant breath sounds, the expected finding with her emphysema. Her heart tones were regular. He lifted the edge of the sheet. Pink nails and bony ankles. He gently pinched the skin over her shin. When he released it, it flattened slowly, suggesting severe dehydration hadn't occurred yet. He wrapped her grip around his index and middle finger. "What name does she go by?"

"Lizzie, to her friends."

"Lizzie, squeeze my fingers." Her hand relaxed. Phineas lifted her arm a few inches over her face. The arm's muscle tone was like soft wax. He let it fall. Her arm hesitated then slowly descended next to her, missed her head, and drifted back into its original position.

She wasn't dying, at least physically. Her body, while damaged from cigarettes, wasn't used up yet. There was still the chance for more good years, if the more threatening problem, her mind, could be treated. They shouldn't give up on Lizzie Ross.

Phineas turned to address Lizzie's family. "I don't think her emphysema is threatening her at the moment. She appears more psychologically than physically distressed. The physical threat would be dehydration unless she starts drinking. If she doesn't soon, she should be evaluated for another admission to Baptist, this time for inpatient treatment for depression. It could really help her."

Phineas pocketed his stethoscope and started toward the bedroom door. Donald Ross closed the drapes and followed.

The three women spoke in near unison, "Thank you, Doctor."

On the front porch, Phineas turned to address Donald Ross. "I said those things in front of her, hoping she will open her eyes and accept liquids to avoid the hospital, but she could be so terribly depressed she won't be able to rally without inpatient treatment. I wouldn't give her much longer before you have her seen at the hospital. I know what she told you about not returning to the hospital, but this is not her emphysema, and depression can be treated."

Donald Ross closed his eyes and grimaced for a moment. "She was adamant—and can be a force. Let's see if she improves here first. Thank you again."

"You're welcome. I wish I were confident that she'll rally without help." Phineas opened the Corona's front two windows to let a late afternoon breeze wash over him, hoping to cool his anger. He imagined the exchange between Lizzie and Cain before her discharge. Cain could be so brusque, and he cared little about how his demeanor affected others. He just wanted to finish up and leave the hospital. Phineas felt sorry for Cain's patients.

Monday after office hours, Phineas slouched in a corner of the 5-3 nurses' station, reviewing a chart on a new hospital consult when his pager announced the number 6137. He dialed the ward's main extension.

"6-1."

"This is Dr. Mann, answering a page."

"Just a minute, please"

"Dr. Mann, this is Dr. Perroni on Psychiatry. The family of a Mrs. Elizabeth Ross has requested you be notified of her admission."

"What's happened since I saw her Saturday?"

"She came in through the ED yesterday morning. She was taking nothing orally. Seems to be a terrible case of psychotic depression with catatonia. We started IV fluids yesterday and ECT first thing this morning. She's already responding to questions this evening. Family thinks we performed a miracle. How about that!"

"That's great. She breathing okay?"

"Doesn't seem to be in any increased respiratory distress, so we just restarted her respiratory medications."

"Thanks for the update. Mind if I stop by after I finish rounding?"

"That'll be fine. Let us know if you have any suggestions."

Phineas finished seeing his consult, called the orthopedist, and wrote his note and orders. The consult patient was acutely short of breath two days after hip pinning for a fracture. She also had chest pain, coughed up scant amounts of blood, and had a clear chest x-ray. Phineas placed her on intravenous heparin for probable postoperative blood clots and arranged a nuclear lung scan. He instructed her worried nurse to let him know if her patient's oxygen level worsened or if her blood pressure fell.

He took the elevator to 6-1 and was buzzed into the locked ward. He stopped at the nursing station to locate Elizabeth Ross' room and peruse her chart. The ward was still except for a short, loud outburst from the opposite hallway. Lizzie Ross' door was closed. He knocked then slowly pushed it open and peered in.

"Ms. Ross, I'm Dr. Mann."

She had risen with tangled hair and now perched on the side of her bed in a hospital gown. She glared at him. "You're the sum'bitch who got me into this damned mess..." The corner of her mouth twitched. "Cain't you just let a person die in peace?"

⚜ ⚜ ⚜

After sixteen months at Baptist and another long, trying day, Phineas looked forward to getting home to Iris and food. The vending machine's Nabs crackers no longer held him after he'd rounded on the ventilator patients in the ICU. There seemed to be a new scary patient with pneumocystis almost every day recently. Usually, they had lost significant weight with their AIDS. Some would respond to antibiotics and others would crash after treatment began, necessitating high ventilator pressures and oxygen concentrations. Plummeting oxygen levels and shock would herald complicating pneumothoraces, the devastating blowout and collapse of a lung. If not immediately relieved by a tube inserted into the chest between the ribs, a code blue would soon follow.

Phineas slipped out of the ICU and noticed Ava Jones, one of the respiratory therapists. She rarely attended when Phineas held his weekly educational and administrative meetings with RT. While a competent therapist, she gave the impression that what she did here was a job, and her life was elsewhere. Slender with long black hair restrained in a thick braid, she always wore a long-sleeved crew-neck shirt under her scrubs, no matter what the weather was.

"Hey Doc. I need a favor. My husband is in Emergency. I made him come in when he coughed up blood. I'm worried sick." Her hands trembled like she'd taken a chill.

"Has the ED doctor talked with you yet? Have they x-rayed him?"

"He's had an x-ray. Haven't heard from the doctor. Really appreciate it if you could look at him."

The emergency room was loud and hectic in the early evening rush hour, full of injuries, fevers, and a multitude of worrisome problems. Bright overhead lights throughout magnified the misery. Phineas found Frank, the ED MD, at the x-ray light boxes.

"Hi Frank. How're things?"

"Livin' the dream."

"Keep tellin' yourself that." Phineas looked for the clipboard list of x-rays. "Have you got Ava from RT's husband here with hemoptysis?" He stared at the light box. "This his x-ray?"

Frank nodded. "Yup. Glad you're here. Looks like he has fluid on the left and collapse of the right lower lobe. He's coughed up several tablespoons of bright red since he's been here. Want to admit him?"

"Probably. I'll go ahead and see him. Are labs back?"

"On his chart."

Adam Jones had his sheet pulled under his neatly trimmed gray beard. His head was shaved. He was easily 15 years older than Ava and had intricate and strikingly colorful tattoos on both arms. Prominent grooves between his hand bones evidenced muscle wasting.

"Mr. Jones, I'm Dr. Mann. Ava asked me to see you. I'm a lung specialist."

"Pleased to meet you, Doc. Appreciate you coming by. Scared the hell out of both of us when I spat blood today. I'd seen tiny streaks for a few weeks but figured it was my smoker's cough."

Phineas learned Adam hadn't felt his usual vigor lately. His appetite was off, and he'd lost weight. His left chest was sore when he coughed. When Phineas inquired as to his occupation, he responded, "Tattoo artist. Used to be a painter, oils mostly, but couldn't make a living." He took several rapid breaths. "Tattoos are just art on a different canvas."

Adam's chest examination was as expected with the x-ray findings, dull at the left base when Phineas percussed it with his fingers. Breath sounds were reduced at both bases. Over his low back, below the rim of his pelvis, Phineas discovered three purple, raised skin lesions.

"How long have you had these spots on your back?"

"Just recently. Meant to have them checked out. Why? What are they?"

"Not sure. Looks like what I'd expect Kaposi's sarcoma to look like from pictures I've seen, but it's a condition that has begun to show up in the new syndrome called AIDS. We're mostly seeing it so far in homosexuals, intravenous drug users and hemophiliacs." He took a deep breath and gathered some courage. "I have to ask. Any of those categories fit you in past years?"

Adam sat erect and glared at Phineas. "Christ, Doc! And I was hoping we'd get along." He paused to take a deep breath before he blurted, "None of those. Smoked dope and did a few lines of coke like everyone else in the 70's, but never shot anything."

"Sorry to have to ask, but do you ever get stuck with your needle while you work?"

"Bet you don't have any tattoos. We operate a tool with a needle that goes up and down really fast to inject ink under the skin. A reputable artist like me uses only new needles and wears sterile gloves." He took three breaths, coughed, and spat a half dollar sized bright red glob into a blue kidney shaped basin. "We run the needle with one hand, and we daub away blood with gauze in the other hand. Takes a lot of concentration to keep the timing right, so the hand with the gauze is out of the way when the needle is injecting." Another pause to breathe. "If something distracts us, we can get stuck. It happens. Comes with the turf. Knew another artist who got hepatitis."

"What about your client when that happens?"

"Usually, we stop in time. Sometimes you don't feel the stick right away and they get stuck after we do. Sometimes you're only sure after you see blood under the glove. Our needles are fine and really sharp."

Phineas digested this new information and resolved to never acquire a tattoo. He suggested two procedures tonight and one tomorrow. "We can answer the question about the skin lesions with a punch biopsy. I can do this with a local tonight. I can also place a small needle between your ribs and draw a sample of fluid from around your lung."

"I have fluid around my lung?"

"Your left one."

"Damn! Well, go ahead if you need to, Doc. Ava says you're good at what you do. Where do I sign?" Adam asked, defeat and surrender layered on fear.

"Tomorrow morning, we should also perform a bronchoscopy, to look for the source of bleeding. That's an inspection of the bronchi with a flexible scope. A biopsy from your airways may be indicated."

Phineas gave Adam's nurse a list of the equipment he needed. He washed the surrounding skin and lesions with the iodine solution, Betadine, and donned sterile gloves then surveyed the equipment and rehearsed the procedures mentally twice. With the AIDS epidemic, he'd become more and more vigilant when he worked with sharp instruments.

He dropped the punch biopsy into a formalin preservative jar before applying a Band-Aid then listened and percussed Adam's left chest for the area of dullness and absent breath sounds to localize the fluid. He marked the skin over the rib selected and prepped the area with betadine. Phineas injected local anesthetic then applied suction to the 5 cc syringe. A maroon plume squirted into its barrel. He replaced it with a 60 cc syringe and filled it with the same fluid, trying to maintain an even expression. The color rattled him. Dark bloody fluid usually meant cancer.

Adam stole a glance over his shoulder at the syringe and frowned. "That what it's supposed to look like, Doc?"

"They'll run tests on this. I'll let you know what they show as soon as I hear results." He tried to keep his tone even. Hiding his emotions and the truth were not his strengths.

"Doc, I have one request. Well, it's actually a demand." He stared into Phineas eyes. "I need to be the one to explain what you find to Ava. She might not handle bad news, and I got a bad feeling about this." He paused. "I'll let her know what I think she can handle."

Phineas protested, "But she can help you with her medical—"

"End of discussion, Doc."

The next morning, Phineas arrived in the bronchoscopy suite to find Adam signing another consent form for the nurse, and the masked and gowned technician surveying her equipment cart.

"Good morning, Mr. Jones. I need to ask if you ate after midnight."

"Followed your instructions, Doc. Ava got us a pizza before she went home last night. Nothing since. When can I expect to know anything from all these tests?"

"I'll tell you what I know as soon as I learn it. There may be something by tomorrow." Phineas pulled on a mask and arranged tight goggles in place before he gowned and gloved. "You probably have figured out I don't hide what I know. I hope that's OK with you, since I'm not a good liar."

"Just don't tell Ava anything I haven't okayed. I need her to keep herself together." His eyes closed as intravenous Demerol found his brain.

Phineas passed the bronchoscope into Adam's nose and down the back of his throat. He visualized and suctioned old blood from above the vocal cords. Timing respirations, he waited for the vocal cords to part before he advanced the tip of the bronchoscope into the windpipe. More blood was spattered throughout the airways. When he reached the bronchus intermedius, the airway between the right upper lobe and lower lobe, Phineas halted. The lumen was occluded by heaped up and nodular purple tissue. The sinister appearance shook Phineas to the core.

The bronchoscopy technician whispered, "What are you seeing?"

"Let's see if we can get some biopsies. Forceps, please."

Phineas placed the open jaws of the forceps on the purple tissue. "Close." The tech closed the forceps. Bright red blood pumped from the biopsy site until the airway lumen was filled with it. Phineas suctioned. The bleeding continued. His own rapid pulse pounded in his temples.

"Let's put some epinephrine solution on that. Start with 5 cc's and repeat if it doesn't stop right away." He held the tip over the bleeding site. The epinephrine made the purple tissue lighten, and the oozing slowed. A second spray stopped it. "OK, let's wash and trap it. Please show me the biopsy." The tech shook the forceps in a jar of formalin. The biopsy was generous. Phineas breathed a sigh of relief and removed the bronchoscope, suctioning as he retreated. "We'll stop there."

Adam roused with slurred speech. "What'd you see, Doc?"

"You have some abnormal tissue on the right. We did a biopsy. You bled some from it, but I believe it has stopped." He touched Adam's forearm. "I'll go over the findings more after the sedation wears off. Have the nurse call me if you cough up more blood than before."

When Phineas arrived that evening, the lights in Adam's room were off and Ava was lying in the hospital bed next to him. She popped up into a sitting position and straightened her long-sleeved t-shirt. "Hey, Doc. Thanks for coming by."

Adam turned toward Phineas. "You probably don't have anything new for me yet, I suppose?"

"No reports yet. Probably in the morning."

Adam patted his wife's forearm. "Ava, would you be a sweetheart and refill my ice pitcher?" She slipped into the hallway and closed the door.

Adam kept his eyes trained on Phineas. "So, what'd you see?"

"You have abnormal tissue in the right bronchus. That's what's bleeding.

Honestly, it had a different appearance than lung cancer. It was the same color as your skin lesions. We'll have to see what the biopsies show, then figure out what to do next."

"Doesn't sound good."

"I'm worried." Phineas response was subdued.

"Will we have the results tomorrow?"

"I believe so. Is there anything I can order for you before I leave?"

"Order me a miracle, Doc."

The news was as bad as Phineas had expected. Kaposi's sarcoma was in both the biopsy specimens, skin and bronchial, and in the bloody fluid he'd aspirated in the emergency room. Phineas paused at the nursing station to summon composure before he walked into Adam's room. He'd waited until the pathologist had looked at both biopsies, so it was already late in the morning.

Adam wore street clothes and sat in the recliner. His bedside table contained only his ice pitcher and the small kidney shaped basin dotted with bloody sputum.

Phineas sat down in the other chair. "Had enough of the hospital?"

"I was hoping you'd spring me today. I have a couple of clients scheduled."

"We have quite a bit to go over. I guess we can arrange most of it with you as an outpatient. You're not incarcerated. Do you want to have Ava here now?"

"Not yet. Let me hear it all first and I'll pass on what I think she can handle."

Phineas reminded himself to speak slowly and to pause after each result. "Okay. Let's go over the problems one at a time. First, the bronchoscopy biopsy did show the same tissue as the skin biopsy. They are what I told you I was worried about, Kaposi sarcoma. Unfortunately, this is a malignancy. Since it is in more than one location, surgery is not an option."

"Shit...What *are* the options?" When Adam squeezed the chair's arms, his knuckles whitened.

"We don't have a chemotherapy treatment for Kaposi sarcoma. I think we should have you see our radiation oncologist. I'm not sure how sensitive it is to radiation, but it usually works to stop bleeding in lung tumors. It can certainly be administered on an outpatient basis."

"I guess I can handle that. What else?" Adam's hands relaxed.

"The fluid around your left lung contains the same malignant cells. This means more fluid will accumulate and will eventually compromise your breathing. We can't eliminate the malignancy from this area, but sometimes a procedure to try to stick the surfaces of the lung and chest wall together can keep the fluid from re-accumulating. This procedure would require you to stay with us for at least a couple more days." No response. He'd expected Adam to at least shake his head. Phineas continued. "I'd consult a surgeon to put a tube between your ribs to drain out the fluid. He'd then put in an antibiotic, doxycycline, to inflame the surfaces. The tube stays in to keep the fluid out so the surfaces can stick together. It's called a pleurodesis. When the fluid draining slows down, we can take the tube out. The doxycycline causes pain, so they usually give a topical anesthetic and some IV morphine."

"Doesn't sound like a walk in the park." Adam grimaced. "Do I have to have that now? Any harm in waiting until my breathing is worse?"

"Hard to say. When there's more malignant tissue, it's possible that the chance of success might go down. The procedure isn't always successful, but sometimes it at least slows down the fluid accumulation." Now was probably better than waiting, but Phineas couldn't bring himself to push another procedure and a delayed discharge.

Adam closed his eyes. When he looked back at Phineas, he responded evenly, "Doc, I told you I am an artist. Between Ava and me, we make a good living with our jobs. I supplement this with regular games in the back of my shop." He coughed and spat into the basin. "You ever play poker, Doc? A good player knows when he's been dealt a poor hand…I'm a good player." He winced when he took a deeper breath. "Why don't you let me out of here and just set up the radiation appointment for now? We can talk about the other thing when we absolutely have to."

Phineas waited until he was sure Adam had finished. "There's one more thing."

"More good news, Doc?" A mock smile.

"Kaposi's sarcoma used to be a rare malignancy, which grew slowly and only occurred in the elderly. It is now being reported in younger men and has become more aggressive. It seems to be a result of a deficiency in the immune system." Phineas dreaded what he needed to say next. "The new cases are in men with the HIV virus, which was discovered recently. I mentioned this when I saw you in the emergency room."

"Is that the virus that causes AIDS? You mean I have AIDS? Shit!" Adam appeared stunned and pushed his head back into the chair's headrest. "The good news just keeps coming."

"We have a blood test for the HIV virus. It takes several days to come back. If it's okay with you, Mr. Jones, we'll get the sample before you go home. Until we have the results, you should take precautions."

"Precautions?" Query and protest.

"The HIV virus is spread by blood and bodily secretions. What you told me about accidents at your work makes me uneasy about you working on people." Phineas had to ask, "Can you still do the design and have someone else do the injections?"

"That's my art, Doc. People want *me* to do their work." Adam drummed his fingers on the recliner's arm. "I'll think about what you said."

"There's one more thing. Obviously, if you have it, you don't want to give it to Ava." Embarrassed, Phineas added, "You should wear condoms. After you talk to her, she should have her doctor test her too."

"Christ! I'll figure out some way to explain the condoms. Maybe tell her I don't want her to catch anything from me." Adam sat up and leaned into the space between them. "But what's the point in having *her* tested? You got a treatment for it?"

Phineas confessed, "I'm sorry, but there's no treatment for HIV yet."

He despaired he'd dumped a terrible load on Adam and offered little hope. "Mr. Jones, I want you to let me know when you have pain. I can prescribe narcotics for you. I don't want you to suffer." Phineas waited for a response. None. "Now, how much can I explain to Ava?"

"I *told* you. I'll do the explaining to her." Adam tapped his sternum with his finger. "I'm sure I'll need her help at some point, so I need her to keep her act together. Now let's just get me out of here." A plea.

⚜ ⚜ ⚜

As Phineas hoped, Adam's blood spitting diminished with radiation therapy, but it sapped his energy and made swallowing painful. Adam was uncomfortably short of breath within weeks; enough so that he had trouble taking a shower while sitting on a stool. He allowed himself to be admitted for the chest tube and doxycycline pleurodesis. When the raw surfaces of lung and chest wall came together, despite morphine and local anesthetic, Adam yelled that it felt like a knife in his chest with every breath. Between breaths, he reported a steady dull ache.

Phineas started Adam on oxycodone pills when needed, and also provided him with a prescription for a new product advertised to provide more continuous and smooth pain control, fentanyl dermal patches. They delivered the narcotic fentanyl from skin into the bloodstream and built up to a steady state level after a few days. Phineas' hope was that size of the patch could be safely increased every few days until the need for pills became infrequent.

Over the next few weeks, Adam's energy level hit rock bottom. His concentration was sporadic, and he reported that he now rarely had the opportunity to gamble. "Doc, no one's showing up to play poker anymore. You'd think they'd *want* to play me now that I'm not at my sharpest." His diagnosis had to have leaked out. Phineas guessed that the horror and stigma of AIDS had likely struck fear in Adam's poker playing buddies, fear of shuffling and dealing from the same deck. Adam's weight plummeted and his cheeks were now sunken. His story arc was etched in the deepening furrows of his narrow face.

Phineas pressed him about Ava. "Mr. Jones, have you told Ava everything?"

"Call me Adam, Doc. Tellin' Ava still scares the hell out of me." His sagging eyelids rolled up like a window shade and revealed dread.

"What are you worried about, Adam?"

"This ain't going to be easy. You can tell Ava's a lot younger than I am. I met her as a client." He took several breaths. "She has some of my best work under those long-sleeved shirts she wears at work."

"How is that a problem?"

Adam coughed and reached for his ribs. "She had another career before you met her. She used to be a dancer in The Quarter. I supported her through respiratory therapy school after we started dating."

"You should be proud of her."

"Oh I am. But I had to get her clean first, then keep her clean."

"Clean?"

"Jeesh Doc, you *have* to know that exotic dancers make money to support habits. Hers was coke while she worked and alcohol to come down after. Tough masters to get shed of." Adam looked surprised at his doctor's naivete.

Phineas regretted he'd asked. Some things he'd rather not know.

✤ ✤ ✤

At least the ICU staff scheduled their Christmas party during a Friday night that Dr. Cain was on call. Iris had to shake Phineas awake from an involuntary nap for them to be fashionably late at the French Quarter event. When they stepped into the festive gathering, she felt a twinge of embarrassment at how comparatively dowdy her dress was next to the figure revealing fashion statements on the dozens of young women with whom her husband spent his days—and often stretches of on-call nights. The disk jockey cued "Legs" by ZZ Top, and the space under a spinning mirrored ball filled with energetic dancers called on to use their legs.

Phineas and she loaded plates with Cajun delicacies, and he gestured at two empty seats with unused silverware and full water glasses. As Iris settled and looked up from her place setting, a young woman stood next to her. A broad grin across her round, youthful face displayed glistening teeth. Thick, wavy brown hair cascaded over the front of her black velvet dress and parted enough for impressive cleavage to prove she was amply endowed. A silver cross rested on the edge of that dark notch. The young woman must have tracked Iris soon after Phineas handed her a glass of white wine and led her from the buffet table.

Angela. That's her name.

She was the one who'd wanted to get together with her after they'd just settled in New Orleans. She'd chatted Iris up at Phineas' welcome luncheon and asked Iris to call her for "a girls' night out" back then. Busy with a new job, her recovering mother, and Phineas, Iris had promptly forgotten all about Angela.

"Hi, Dr. Mann. So glad you could make it." Angela's words burst from her. "And Iris, it's good to see you again. I'm Angela. Remember we met when you first got here."

Iris offered a polite smile. "I remember, Angela. How have you been?"

"Oh, I'm fine, and I just *love* working with your husband. Our ICU is so much better since he started."

"Well, that's good to hear, since he seems to be working there a lot, actually." Would she be stuck talking gruesome medicine tonight?

Phineas had taken advantage of the conversation to dive into his food. He sat back and chewed, wearing a contented half smile.

"And we *really* appreciate it." Angela glanced sideways, apparently scanning tables for an empty chair to commandeer and support her invasion. "So, are you guys going to start a family soon? I bet Dr. Mann would be a great dad!" Her focus on him seemed to burst with adoration.

The opening words from "I Just Called to Say I Love You" by Stevie Wonder filled the room. Iris clutched her surprised-looking husband's arm and said, "Honey, dance with me. I love this song." She vacated her chair and gave his arm a firm tug.

He lifted his napkin from his lap, wiped his mouth, and stood. "Excuse us, Angela. I'm needed elsewhere."

A disappointed look supplanted Angela's cloying smile. "Iris, don't forget to call me when you get some free time...I'll write my number on your napkin."

Iris dragged Phineas toward the dance area and called over her shoulder, "Sure thing. When I get some free time."

⚜ ⚜ ⚜

It was three days before Christmas, and Phineas was trying to wrap up his rounds when the operator paged him. She connected him with an outside call. Adam.

"Hey Doc, I need a huge favor. I have a situation here. Don't know who else to call. Ava's relapsed big time and gotten into my meds and other shit. I'm worried she might overdose." Phineas heard Adam's wracking cough. "I'm too weak to help her. Can't call an ambulance. She'd lose her respiratory therapy license. Someone needs to check her."

"Adam, do you have any family or close friends who can help?" Phineas asked, hoping someone nearby could intervene soon.

"No one that can see her the way she is now."

Phineas sighed. He'd been paged four times during the previous night and had cobbled together little sleep. He was hoping to prepare a nice dinner for Iris and to be able to stay awake long enough after for romance, a pleasure he'd had little opportunity for in recent months.

"I'm just leaving the hospital. How far away do you live?"

"Not far, Doc. 4905 Magnolia Street. You can park in our driveway. Hey, I really appreciate this."

⚜ ⚜ ⚜

The house's porch held two rocking chairs that faced the street. Whoever painted the house steel blue did a meticulous job and accented their masterpiece with a burgundy trim and highlights of gold leaf. Tall wrought iron fencing surrounded what appeared to be the edges of a lush garden in the back. The front door was cracked open. Phineas pushed it a few inches. "Adam?"

A hoarse voice. "In the kitchen in the back."

The front room contained vintage French antiques and, next to a large leather chair, an oil portrait of Ava. Deep shadowing provided contrast that enhanced her facial planes. Her eyes followed Phineas across the room. He found the hallway to the back, lined with framed figure studies of a slender woman he recognized, also Ava. He had to drag himself away from the details of her body and elaborate tattoos.

He entered a kitchen in disarray. The sink was stacked with dirty dishes. Open food containers lined the counters. A glass tray offered a single line of white powder. Adam was propped on his elbows at a table covered by a food-stained cloth. His breathing was rapid and shallow, his cheeks hollow. His voice was barely a whisper.

"Can't tell you how much I appreciate this, Doc." Adam's t-shirt hung on his bony protuberances. "I had to tell her everything, Doc. She could see I'm dying." His eyes were sunken, and when he frowned, his face sagged over his skull. "Ava's out that door in the garden drinking beer. She's not how you know her."

Leaves covered chairs and benches, and weeds sprouted from every inch of soil in the courtyard. Several beer cans, a pair of denim shorts, and a black t-shirt made a trail to a flowerbed where Phineas found Ava squatting naked, facing away from him. Her panties were around her knees and a stream of urine watered the plants.

A tattoo on her sacrum was of an apple tree. The branches spread elegantly from a trunk between her buttocks. A red, yellow, and black coral snake draped the branches, staring defiantly at him. Ava stood and pivoted slowly on unsteady legs. Her eyes were barely open. She noted his presence with a soft "Hey" then pulled her panties most of the way up. Across her breasts was a celebration of birds, butterflies and flowers in detail and brilliant hues. A parade of pairs of animals marched under her navel—cheetahs, penguins, kangaroos, and numerous other land species. Mahi-mahi, flying fish, and orca cavorted around her hips. She shivered.

Each cheek displayed a fentanyl patch. She had also applied one to each nipple and shoulder, and one over her navel. He approached her, saying, "Ava, Adam called me. He's worried about you. I need to take these patches off before you absorb too much fentanyl." Before her sluggish protest, he snatched the patches from her navel, shoulders, and breasts, and then gently peeled them off her cheeks. He supported her under her armpit, walked her into the kitchen, and sat her in a chair. Adam looked on with tears down his cheeks.

Phineas found a long-sleeved flannel shirt on a hook behind the door to the garden and covered Ava with it. He rinsed the powder on the glass tray into the sink and sat at the table with them.

"Fentanyl has a short half-life, so you should be okay now, Ava. If those patches stayed on longer, you could've stopped breathing." He waited until she nodded her understanding. "Adam, do you know someone who can help here? I can see if social work can send someone out to check on you, but it might not be till Monday. And it might be hard to arrange near Christmas."

Adam admitted he had a sister he could call tonight. She'd keep his medications for him. Ava began crying. "Doc, please don't hate me." Her words were slurred.

Phineas didn't expect the tremor in his voice. "Adam needs you, Ava. Be here for him. I know this is hard on you both." Phineas waited until she finished wiping her eyes with her sleeve. "I think it would be best for you to take some time off work. I can talk to Human Resources for you and let them know Adam is sick."

When Phineas arrived at his office in the morning of Christmas Eve, the respiratory therapy supervisor, Charles, was there waiting. His somber expression seemed out of place on a holiday. "Dr. Mann, Ava won't be in for a while. Her husband died last night."

Adam's death came earlier than Phineas had expected. Had he failed them? Missed the signals? Been too busy? Phineas couldn't help but think Adam's sister hadn't been given all the narcotics. The gambler had folded his hand.

⚜ ⚜ ⚜

Dr. Richard Cain arrived in the ICU on a dreary Friday evening in January, so Phineas could check out his patients to Cain and be off for the weekend. Over recent months Cain's demeanor had become dour during these meetings. It was obvious Phineas now unloaded much more on him than he on Phineas every other Friday.

Phineas handed a Xeroxed copy of his carefully written instructions to Cain and then discussed each patient. Out of the eight patients in the ICU, including six on ventilators, three had pneumocystis pneumonia and new diagnoses of AIDS. They were on high levels of oxygen and ventilatory support. The other five were a mix of surgical patients and smokers with chronic obstructive pulmonary disease (COPD). Phineas reviewed the ten patients he was following on the other wards. It was unusual for Cain to check out more than three or four to Phineas. As Phineas checked out, Cain's frown deepened.

Finally, Cain blurted, "Before you got here, there was no such thing as an intensive care specialist. Doctors took care of their own patients. They didn't call me to deal with arrhythmias or infections. They ordered dopamine if their patients were in shock. They let the surgeons and cardiologists place and manage the catheters. If they wanted help with a vent, *then* maybe they might call me." He was shaking his head like he was furious. "I could make quick rounds on weekends. Covering for you is misery! Family members demand meetings. And the conversations they want to have on those AIDS patients! Good God! I've always tried to get in and out of the ICU before the families arrive, and now *that's* impossible."

Phineas looked up from his patient list and made eye contact with Cain. He had a bad feeling about where this was going.

Cain continued, "I *told* you to be careful how much you give them. The more you give, the more they suck out of you. I'm tired of being paged all night covering for you." He pounded the desk with his fist. "After this weekend, I'm done covering for you. I'd rather be on call for my practice all the time than cover yours half the time."

Justin Jordan's administrative assistant buzzed him in his office to announce Phineas' arrival. She offered Phineas coffee or water. He welcomed the local coffee with chicory. He needed the caffeine.

As CEO, Justin Jordan had signed Baptist's contract with Phineas. When he called today, Phineas hadn't offered a reason for the meeting. He'd barely sipped the coffee when Justin Jordan stepped out and offered his hand. In his early forties, clean-shaven and stout with dark hair, he appeared fresh from a barber. He sported a seersucker suit and a bow tie.

"Dr. Mann, I'm hearing great reports about you and your work. We at Baptist are so glad you decided to work here. Come into my office and sit. What can I do for you today?"

"Thank you, Mr. Jordan. It's about the work. There's more than I can handle. Dr. Cain will no longer cross cover, so I've been on call every day and night for the last month." He watched Justin Jordan's smile fade.

"Oh. That's a tough one. I don't believe we have any leverage with Dr. Cain to change his mind. We don't pay him a salary, like we do you as respiratory therapy and ICU director, and he wouldn't care much if we tried to take away his admitting privileges."

"Can't you hire someone else to help?"

Jordan brushed a few clipped hairs off his shoulder. "You have to know that doctors with your training are in short supply. They all seem to want to stay in academic centers. It took us more than two years to recruit you for your position."

"Mr. Jordan, I'm hardly ever home and awake. I get paged all night when I *am* at home. I can't continue working as I am now for two more years." He raised his tense eyebrows and stared at Jordan. "And what about the vacation my contract promises? It says 3 weeks a year and one week for education. Who will cover pulmonary and ICU then?" Phineas wiped his palms on his white coat.

"I understand, Dr. Mann. I didn't realize your situation. I'll ask the CFO to review your billings and collections to see what sort of an offer we can put together to recruit a partner for you. You'd have to share some of your directors' stipends. Getting someone will take time—maybe another year or two—if we're successful."

"I won't last that long as things are now. And what about my vacation time?" Phineas hadn't yet taken a week off in 1985.

"I've heard of specialists filling in for vacations with what's called locum tenens arrangements. This is a totally new concept, so there aren't many doing this. We can explore this for you."

"Do that. I need a break soon. Can you hire moonlighters to cover for me sooner?"

"I'll ask our legal folks to look into that option. We'll do what we can, but that may also take some time." Jordan's attention seemed to shift to something he saw outside his office's picture window.

Jordan had little incentive to help. Phineas plea had found deaf ears. "I *had* liked the work here. I just can't continue with this workload."

"Good thing you're young." An offhand remark.

Phineas' spine stiffened. He was sure Justin Jordan hadn't put in a hundred-hour workweek in his life. "I'd rather not have to quit." He countered.

"As I recall, your contract indicates you're to give a six-month notice. It also has a no compete clause that stipulates you can't practice within a 25-mile radius for at least a year if you leave us...And there's the tail." Jordan, re-engaged in their conversation, tilted his head forward so his chin rested on his bowtie.

"Tail?"

"On your malpractice insurance. We pay the premium, but if you choose to leave, *you're* responsible for the tail. That's the amount to cover all the patients you've seen against future lawsuits."

"How much would that be?" Phineas tried to recall the modest figure he and Iris had recently managed to save.

"Oh, several thousand probably. We'd have to ask the insurance company. And there's the clinic rent."

"Clinic rent?"

"Your contract states that your work in the clinic takes care of the clinic rent. You signed a lease for the space. If you leave, you're responsible for the rent until your replacement is found." Jordan let escape a fleeting half-smile.

"I don't remember agreeing to that. I understood it was only while I worked there." Phineas clenched and unclenched his fists.

"Read it again. Look in Appendix B."

Phineas surveyed the framed diploma and family pictures over the credenza behind Jordan. Justin Jordan and his fashionable wife, two kids descending on each side.

"Dr. Mann, thank you for coming by today. We'll let you know as soon as we make some progress for you." Jordan stood and held the door open.

Phineas brooded silently in the hallway, his hopes sunken to the bottom of the Mississippi River. *What does it profit a man...?*

⚜ ⚜ ⚜

Iris was genuinely worried about Phineas. Concern had become worry over recent months. He hadn't had a day off in weeks. He came home late, often with time only to eat something and fall asleep. This was so much worse than his internship. At least then he'd been able to turn off his beeper and be completely off every few days. And there appeared no end in sight. When he was an intern, an end was *always* in sight, and back then he had friends who were going through the same conditions. Here he was alone. Back in the university medical center, he had experts and resources to fall back on for challenging problems. Here he had to make stressful decisions on his own. She could hardly believe she was feeling nostalgia for his internship year. How bad had it gotten for Phineas? He couldn't see how awful it was. He was so tired, he had blinders on. He was just putting one foot in front of the other.

Though not fond of cooking, Iris tried to put nutritious offerings together for him. Dinner usually went in the oven wrapped in foil.

"Iris, this chicken is really moist and tender. The meat falls off the bones."

"I've started putting a bowl of water in the oven with your dinner, so the meat doesn't turn into jerky before you get home."

"Clever. I appreciate it."

"I worry about you living on junk food out of the snack machines at the hospital. I'll pack you more lunch with healthy foods."

"The chocolate bars help when I'm tired, and those fluorescent orange crackers must have extra vitamins." Phineas chuckled at his attempted joke.

Iris frowned. "And you get no exercise. You just work and sleep."

"I walk a lot at work. I'm always on my feet."

"I wish you could walk with Amos and me, like we used to." She pointed at his stomach. "It looks like you're gaining weight."

"I haven't weighed myself, but you're probably right. I've had to let my belt out a notch—or two."

"Maybe if you wrote shorter notes, were a little less thorough, you could get home earlier?"

"I'm trying to be more efficient."

"Phineas, I get *lonely* here by myself." Her raised voice made Amos lift his head and whine.

"Sorry. I don't know what else to do at this point." His pager intruded. He placed his hand on hers then stood to use the phone. She wanted to rip its cord out of the wall and flush his beeper down the toilet.

❧ ❧ ❧

Iris understood his difficulty slacking off. Being thorough was part of his DNA, for better or worse. She recognized his discomfort with imperfection in patient care, but this strength had become his weakness. His meticulous attention to his patients' problems now took an unsustainable toll on him, making him so tired, that he was, frankly, impaired.

His sleep was terrible. Nights when he didn't go back to the hospital were infrequent. Sometimes he went back more than once. She worried about him driving through the city at night in his exhausted state. And when he was home, his pager went off repeatedly. He would barely fall asleep before being jarred awake. Then back asleep, then another jolt. Torture was the only word that fit.

Iris waited for him to lose his composure, to vent his frustration and show anger. She struggled to keep hers in check. For now, silent sadness would have to do.

They had seen the movie *Animal House* during Phineas' residency. She recalled the scene when Kevin Bacon's character was paddled during his fraternity hazing. With each blow, he shouted, "Thank you, Sir. May I have another?" And this is what her husband's life seemed to have become.

She wore earplugs, but his frequent turning over and getting up prevented her from getting restful sleep. She had to drag herself out of bed in the morning to make the strong coffee they both required.

Iris was ready to leave New Orleans, if that was what it took to rescue her husband. She had once, years ago, thought of herself as being comfortable with a solitary existence. Now she missed Phineas. Their first months here had been so pleasant. Even though Phineas had been on call every other night and weekend, those days and nights were easier. At least he'd been awake on his off days. She had enjoyed guiding him through New Orleans. They'd taken Amos on long strolls in City Park and Audubon Park, and in the Aquatic Gardens.

Now, if they were to leave New Orleans, Iris didn't know what she would do about her mother. She visited her mother at least weekly. She regularly checked her mother's refrigerator and cupboards and made notes of what to bring the next time. She made sure the cleaning service kept the place up and none of her mother's valuables went missing. Her mother had regained strength, but her world had shrunken. She watched television, sat on the day bed on the porch in good weather, and went to church—like she was saving her energy for a future effort.

More than once, her mother proclaimed how she would love to have a grandchild.

"When are you and Phineas going to make me a grandmother?"

Iris shuddered at the thought of being a single mother, and that was how it would be. "This isn't a good time, Mom. Not even a consideration at this point." That was all Iris needed. One more person requiring care.

"Daughter, you're not getting any younger, and neither am I." She gazed expectantly at Iris.

⚜ ⚜ ⚜

The alarm shattered Phineas' deep sleep. He stretched out his hand and punched the snooze button. A gentle nudge tapped the middle of his back. He smelled coffee. He peered over his shoulder and saw the space where Iris had slept, then he plunged back into sweet sleep. The alarm rattled him again. He pulled himself into a sitting position on the edge of the bed. Another tap on his back. *What is that?*

He felt like he had just gone to bed. There'd been one trip back to the hospital after midnight and at least two times paged awake after he'd returned home. He stood up and shuffled onto the cool tiles in the bathroom. Another tap on his back. Amos barreled into the bathroom and skidded across the floor. He sat panting and expectantly wagging his tail. Phineas noticed Amos' chin had begun to turn white.

"Amos, you look ready for action. I need to pee, Boy." Phineas stood in front of the toilet and studied the sign over it, "This Bathroom is Reserved for Special Events". Ron had spotted it in a secondhand store when they'd been back in Chapel Hill and proudly given it to them. Phineas felt another nudge on his back. He turned his back to the mirror and discovered a black sock pinned to his t-shirt. A round bulge filled the toe. He took off his shirt, opened the safety pin and removed the sock.

Iris sat at the kitchen table, head in hands, bent over her coffee. She peered up at him under drooping eyelids. Phineas held up the sock. Amos snatched at it and missed.

"Were you playing pin the tail on the donkey last night?"

Iris half grinned. "I *had* to do something. You snored like a freight train every time you were on your back." Her tone suggested desperation. "I got tired of pushing you back onto your side, so I found Amos' ball and a sock."

Phineas shook the tennis ball out and onto the floor. Amos fielded it cleanly and dropped it at Phineas' feet, panting and waiting for Phineas to pick it up and toss it.

"Clever girl."

"Necessity is the mother."

⚜ ⚜ ⚜

The pager fractured Phineas' sleep again. He silenced it and glanced over at Iris. She held a pillow over her head with both arms. Rather than use the phone next to the bed, he put on the battery-powered headlamp he had begun keeping next to it and crept into the bathroom. It connected with the walk-in closet and contained a dressing area with a vanity table. He sat at the table and dialed the ICU and struggled to stay awake while the unit secretary located the therapist who had paged him. Another request for ventilator orders after deteriorating blood gas results. He hoped his new orders would stabilize the patient, and he could wait to look at them until first thing in the morning.

Their bed was empty. Phineas stepped into the dark hallway. The guest room door was closed. He cracked it open and heard Iris' rhythmic breathing. He shuffled back to their bed and stared at the ceiling until sleep overcame him.

* * *

Later that month, Phineas dreamt he held a guinea pig in his hand. A 400-gram albino. He grasped it firmly with its abdomen exposed and injected pentobarbital through its tough skin. He was a fellow again, researching mechanisms of asthma attacks in a guinea pig model. He withdrew the needle and waited for it to sleep, so he could perform a tracheostomy. The white rodent violently convulsed, trembling in Phineas' hand until it stopped breathing, and its pink eyes turned blue. Dr. Ranghu PhD, the Principal Investigator, hurried across the lab and shouted, "That's one of our control group. We need it. Can you bring it back?"

Phineas frowned. "I'm not giving mouth to mouth to a guinea pig."

The animal shook again. Phineas awakened to find he was clutching his vibrating pager. The boundary between asleep and awake was now often blurred. Late night drives home from the hospital with windows wide open, trying to stay between the lines, terrified him, but the worst times were when he dreamed that he and Iris were making love, and he awakened in his recliner after midnight with her asleep in the guest room.

This time, his watch displayed 1:30. He was on the sofa with Amos wedged against his bent legs. The last thing he remembered was perusing the journal *CHEST* after a late supper. He sat up and lifted his legs over Amos then nudged and softly scolded him. "You know you're not supposed to be on the sofa." Amos slinked onto the floor and circled his pillow until he lay down.

Phineas dialed the ward. "Dr. Mann. Answering a page."

"Couture here on 5 West. Your patient, Maheu, in 5112 needs a sleeping pill."

Seriously! You're waking me up, so he can sleep? "Give him 0.5 milligrams of Ativan."

"Thank you, Doctor."

"Nurse?"

"Yes, Doctor?"

"Could this have waited? I was asleep."

"He kept pushing his call button. You can go back to sleep now."

"I've had a long day and have another tomorrow. Please try to hold off on nonemergency pages."

"I take care of my patients, Doctor, and you're not being nice." Click. Dialtone.

Jeesh! Phineas shuffled to the toilet. Before he'd emptied his bladder, he fantasized dropping his pager in and flushing.

Phineas found the bed in the master bedroom empty again. Iris hadn't slept there in weeks. He tried to recall the last time they'd made love. He decided he'd brush his teeth and cuddle next to her. She slept peacefully in what was once their little-used guest room and now had become hers. Her long auburn hair radiated over her pillow. He slipped under the sheets and pressed his torso against her warm back. She emitted a groan when he began gently massaging her shoulders.

"Phineas. I'm sleeping. Tomorrow. Go to bed. We both need sleep."

He'd returned to the exile of the master bedroom.

How had he reached such a miserable point where hopelessness filled every waking hour? Searching for answers as his eyes filled, he sifted through the milestones of the Baptist job. Before he could make any sense of them, he tumbled into a disturbing dream of an approaching storm.

Iris dripped from her nose, neck, and armpits. Her thin cotton tank top clung to her torso. Amos had embarked on his walk with his usual enthusiasm, and she'd hustled to keep up. In the late day July heat, the dog's thick black coat finally compelled him to sniff more than romp along the park trail. For some reason, while she recovered, Iris recalled dogs could only sweat from their tongues.

Phineas had called and estimated his arrival home after eight. He still had ICU rounds and a consult to finish, and he would once again have to miss Amos' evening walk. That left the task to Iris, and she now watched the fur on Amos back abruptly rise into a canine Mohawk. His tail wagging slowed, and then revved up. A wee beagle burst from the bushes, planted its feet and bayed. An attached leash trailed it. They circled each other, introductions taking place nose to anus. Amos broke into a butt-tucking circular frolic, and the beagle gave chase.

"Thank you for finding my dog. She slipped away before I had a good grip." The speaker, in running shorts and shoes, was well over six feet tall with a glistening bare chest. His curly brown hair was matted and dripped sweat. He gripped the legs of his shorts, leaned forward, and panted.

Iris called out, "Amos, here boy!" She held up her hand, pretending she had a ball or treat for him. He raced to her and sat, his eyes glued to her hand. The beagle followed closely, allowing the man in shorts to snatch its leash.

"Gracie's still a puppy. I need to take her to obedience training as soon as she's old enough." He picked her up, and she licked sweat off his tanned chin. "I'm Eli."

"Iris."

"Do you mind if we walk with you? Gracie seems to have taken a liking to Amos, and she doesn't get to see other dogs very often."

"No problem. She's obviously livened him up."

"The effect of a pretty young female, no doubt."

Iris shot an incredulous look at Eli, whose chiseled face was turned away as he bent and patted Gracie. He looked in his early thirties with a runner's lean physique. "You live near here?" he asked.

"Not really."

"My gallery is close. Gracie stays with me at work, so we walk/run from there."

"What kind of a gallery?"

"It's an art gallery and studio. I show several artists at a time. When it's not busy, I can paint in the back."

"What kind of painting?" She shouldn't be engaging him, but it was a nice change to have a conversation outside of work.

"Mostly oils. Still lifes during business hours. Portraits and figure studies on commission after hours. What kind of work do you do?"

"Social work at Tulane Hospital."

"You should come by some time. We're not far, on St. Charles near Broadway. The sign says Westerman's Art Gallery. I'm Eli Westerman"

"I don't do a lot of art shopping."

He grinned playfully and shrugged. "Hey, no problem. I'll give you the guided tour anyway."

⚜ ⚜ ⚜

Iris was surprised to find herself thinking about the art gallery as lunch hour approached. How pleasant it had been to have someone to walk and talk with! And Amos seemed to come alive with Gracie. After typing forms all morning, Iris' legs could use a stretch, and there was a break in the heat after a morning downpour. It only took ten minutes to reach Broadway and St. Charles. A bell announced Iris as she cracked open the door stenciled with 'Westerman Gallery'. The front window displayed two paintings. One was a still life of a wine bottle and half full glass above a colorful Mardi Gras mask and a peacock feather. The other was a haunting portrait of an elegant young woman cut off below her exposed shoulders. An elderly man, the lone other patron, slipped out the door as she entered. She heard a soft bark.

"Look, Gracie, it's Iris." Eli rose from a stool behind the counter, as Gracie ran around it to greet her. He wore khaki pants and a white button-down shirt with the sleeves rolled up. "Gracie, don't jump!"

"Hi Gracie. Amos is at home. I'm not nearly as much fun." She held Gracie down by the collar and patted the velvety fur on her head. "Beagles have such soft coats."

"I'm so glad you could come. How are you? Let me show you around."

Eli directed Iris to the front. He proceeded to patiently point out salient features of paintings and gave brief bios of the artists as they worked their way down one sidewall and back up the other. He pointed out his works, including the two in the front display. Iris paused along the tour to study a painting of a plump nude woman, propped on her elbow, lying on an emerald Victorian sofa. An ornate, gilded frame enhanced the work.

"My studio is behind the counter through this door. I can paint then look out when the door opens." He waved for her to follow. She stood with her back to the gallery and peered in. The room was lined with packages wrapped in brown paper, and canvases, both blank and painted. Two easels faced a table in the middle. Behind the table was the emerald sofa.

"So, this is where it all happens?" She cringed at her choice of words. "How do you decide what to paint?"

Eli kept an even expression. "I do portraits on commission. They are usually someone's spouse or a VIP. I can't take a lot of artistic license with them. Figures are rare commissions. Sometimes someone has a lover whose image they want to preserve. Sometimes I hire a model if I haven't done a figure in a while. Otherwise, when I see an object that grabs my interest, I pile it on the table until I have a collection for a still life."

Iris held her position in the doorway. "So that's how it works. And are you happy with your career choice?"

Eli approached her as he spoke. "Very. Days can be pretty routine with the business details and small talk with potential customers, but when I paint," he sighed, "that's what makes it all worthwhile." He gazed into her blue eyes, "Iris, most of my subjects are ordinary. I would do your portrait for the privilege of painting you." He looked at her left hand. "Your husband would be very pleased with the result, if that's what you're wondering."

Her heart raced. "I don't have that much free time." She pressed her right hand against her stomach and tried to stop the butterflies.

"There would be no deadline. I could work on it when you have time."

Iris surveyed the canvases around her and settled her gaze on the sofa.

"And Iris, if you would do me the honor of posing for a figure study, I'd pay above the usual models' rate."

She felt the fine hairs on her neck rise.

Eli placed his hand softly on her arm. "You could recline on the sofa. Maybe have a crystal wine glass half full of Cabernet balanced on your thigh—or your tummy. Make a great focal point."

The memory of her college date with Purple Jesus barged in. A shiver marched down her spine. Her feet seemed stuck to the floor. *Why did I come here?* The bell from the front door roused her. She backed out of the studio door as a young couple entered the gallery.

"I need to get back to work, Eli. Thank you for the tour." She hastened toward the entrance.

"Please come again soon—and think about my offer."

She barely missed stepping into a deep puddle outside the gallery before she hurried along St. Charles. The clouds that had parted earlier gathered again in the direction she walked.

Still in his dress shirt, Phineas swallowed the last of an Abita Turbo Dog beer and pushed back from the dinner table. Iris resisted the urge to mention his collapsing posture. He appeared burdened by the weight of the world on his shoulders.

"Iris, dinner was great. Thank you. I really like your spaghetti sauce. I'll help with the dishes after I sit and rest for a minute." She watched Amos follow him to the worn La-Z-Boy in the living room. Phineas settled into the impression that matched his shape.

Snoring soon came from the living room through the clatter of the dishes. Iris filled the sink with soapy water then washed, rinsed, and dried to Phineas' loud breathing. She then sat across from him and contemplated him, life, art, and Eli. *Why did I go to his studio? Am I that desperate?* Amos raised his head and moaned.

She retreated to the bedroom and pulled an envelope from her jeans pocket. She reread:

Dear Iris,

I'm glad you wrote. I'm so sorry to hear of the troublesome turn that Phineas' professional life has taken, and of its effect on you both. The hospital administrators should be ashamed of themselves.

I wish I knew how to help. I do believe that there are some things more important than a job, even if it has been a calling someone has worked hard to achieve, and these include physical and mental health. Loss of a loving partner to work stress is another. I'm glad Phineas continues to have you at his side. He needs you to help him get through this.

He may just have to quit. What's the worst that could happen? I'm no legal expert, but I suspect the burdens the hospital would try to impose on Phineas, if he quit, may be hard to enforce.

Save yourselves before it is too late. And please keep me posted.

with warm regards,
Ian MacSweeney

She peeled off her t-shirt, shorts, and bra and glanced at herself in the mirror. The memory of waking up after her date with Purple Jesus resurfaced. Then came a blurry image of an ornate, gilded frame displaying her figure study on Eli's gallery wall. She slipped on a thin cotton nightshirt and returned to the living room.

She turned the switch on the lamp next to Phineas to the dimmest setting and kissed his cheek before whispering, "It's you and me, Phineas. We're in this together. Our lives have *got* to get better."

Before midnight, she roused to hear Phineas' pager jolt him from deep sleep and, once again, eject him from his recliner.

⚜ ⚜ ⚜

The news was all weather while Iris arranged leftovers for their evening meal. Each of the national networks displayed atmospheric images of swirling clouds covering the Gulf of Mexico. Arrows pointed at Louisiana with their tips on New Orleans. Wind speeds were increasing, and the hurricane was now category 3. Forecasters urged residents to organize preparations and evacuate as soon as possible. WGNO's Phil Tomber repeated, "We believe this hurricane will intensify with dangerous winds and flooding. Please secure your residence and head north as soon as possible."

There hadn't been a Hurricane Jezebel before. The biblical reference led to the only smiles and light-hearted banter on television news and weather. Newsman Matt Sotte asked, "So Phil, is Jezebel starting her dance of the seven veils?" The image from a poster advertising a stripper called Jezebel dancing in a Bourbon Street bar now appeared on the television screen. "See her drop her veils!" it proclaimed.

"Matt, I believe you and the exotic dancer have your biblical references mixed up. *Salome* did the famous dance of the seven veils, for which she was rewarded the head of Saint John the Baptist on a platter."

"Then what did Jezebel do to have her name so well known?"

"She was known for dressing in fine clothes and wearing gaudy make-up. She was the original painted lady." Phil paused and offered an authoritative look to viewers. "More importantly, she turned her husband, the king, against God. For these transgressions, she was thrown out a window by her court, to be eaten by dogs."

"Thank you, Phil, for that clarification, gruesome as it was. How is it you know so much Old Testament?"

"I paid attention in Bible Study...and I looked it up last night, Matt."

The swirling clouds in WGNO's radar images of Jezebel reflected how Phineas' life had spun out of control, and Iris felt helpless to intervene in his storm.

⚜ ⚜ ⚜

Exhausted after another arduous day, Phineas stretched out on the sofa and patted Amos on the floor next to him. Amos emitted contented groans. Iris had already packed suitcases with her and Phineas' best clothes, and now was filling bins with people and dog food.

Phineas rolled onto his side to face her in the kitchen. "What time are you leaving tomorrow?" A lump rose in his throat.

"After I feed and walk Amos, I'll pick up Mom. I don't plan to hang around New Orleans for long." She sounded tense.

"Sounds like a good plan. I put all our important papers in a folder for you. It has our birth certificates, our renters' insurance policy, and my life insurance information. Any idea where you'll wind up?"

Iris flinched at the mention of life insurance. "I'll drive north until I'm tired and find a place that'll allow Amos, then check the news. We'll settle as close as it looks safe, then come back if conditions aren't as bad as they're forecasting." She closed the lower kitchen cabinets and stood. "I'll call Matt in Boston and your parents with where we're staying, if I can't reach you." She stared at him, her hands on her hips. "You really have to cover the hospital?"

Phineas forced himself into a sitting position. Amos turned his head to look at him and panted. "Yeah. I really do." He stood. "I need to wash up and go to bed soon. I'm dead tired. How much longer are you planning to pack?"

"Not much. Go ahead. I'll come say good night."

The sheets were soft and cool. As soon as his head settled into the pillow, Phineas drifted off and imagined floating on the mirror surface of a Vermont lake. He roused when he realized Iris had swung her knee over his thighs and straddled him. She hoisted her shirt over her head and leaned forward, her hands on his chest.

The hall light framed her as a dazzling backlit vision.

⚜ ⚜ ⚜

Toast. Phineas smelled toast. And coffee. He opened his eyes to a mug under his nose and the welcome fragrance of strong coffee. Iris stood next to the bed and leaned over him. She tilted her head and smiled. "Good morning, Sleeping Beauty. Time to face the day."

He rolled onto his back and blinked twice. "Do we have time for you to come back to bed for a bit, before I have to report to work?" He reached out to her. If last night was a dream, he wanted the real thing.

"What? Last night wasn't enough for you?" She set his coffee on the bedside table and tugged at his arm. "We need to get on the road...Don't worry. There'll be more after Jezebel."

So, last night wasn't a dream.

PART FOUR

JEZEBEL

When Lamech had lived one hundred and eighty-two years, he had a son. He named him Noah, saying, "This one will bring us comfort from our labor and from the painful toil of our hands, because of the ground the Lord has cursed." GENESIS 5:29

The memo, dated Wednesday, August 28, 1985, said that Chief Nursing Officer, Lida Weaver, would set up the Command Center in the conference room next to the administrative offices on the second floor. She was to be the incident commander by default. CEO Justin Jordan was nearing the end of a two-week vacation along the Rhine River, and transportation into New Orleans, by plane or on the ground, had been closed down. Phineas was relieved Lida would be in charge. She'd begun her career as an ICU nurse and added a master's degree in hospital administration. Justin Jordan might be a competent business leader, but he did not come from a clinical background.

Phineas had never been in a hospital during a disaster. While training in North Carolina, he was off call both when a tropical storm hit, and again when an unexpected ice storm had paralyzed the area over several days. UNC's hospital had never lost its backup power. From what he saw on the news, he worried Jezebel would shut down New Orleans for a longer time and be much more destructive.

He hurried past the ICU to his office to drop his gym bag and supplies. Then he donned scrubs and left his sports shirt and jeans draped over his desk chair. His gym bag contained socks, underwear, another shirt, and a money belt with $400. Phineas locked the money belt in the desk. He left his sleeping bag and pad rolled up and placed a flashlight and his headlamp on the desk. The cooler with ice and two one-gallon jugs of water he'd lugged from home felt excessive. His hands were sweating despite the air conditioning.

He scanned the mail he'd picked up on his way into Baptist and trashed those containing the usual ads for ICU and respiratory equipment hoping to influence him in future hospital purchases. A letter with precise printing was mingled in. The return address read Faith Oxendine and North Carolina. He tore it open.

Dear Phineas,

I am in my Infectious Disease fellowship at UNC now.

I recently heard some news I wanted to share with you. The Medicine office had your new business address.

The first patient you and I diagnosed with AIDS, 'LD', passed away. He had disseminated Mycobacterium avium-intracellulare and had wasted away to almost nothing. He looked terrible and felt miserable.

The shocking news is that the cytopathologist we worked with on LD's case just died with a severe case of pneumocystis pneumonia. Everyone here was pretty upset. I wonder what he was thinking when we discussed how LD got AIDS.

I've decided to go into AIDS research. I'm sure it will soon bring trouble for my people. Maybe I can help. The ID division at UNC is working on possible treatments with the drug company, Burroughs-Wellcome.

*From what I read, New Orleans is one of the cities being swamped
with AIDS cases. I hope it has not been too hard on you.
I learned a lot from you. Thank you for teaching me.*

Faith

Dr. Olsen had AIDS? Phineas' pulse pounded in his ears as he read the
letter a second time before he set it aside. He would have to think about
it later. Jezebel was coming.

❖ ❖ ❖

A television had been set up on a rolling metal table in the Command
Center. A swirl of clouds filled the screen, and superimposed on the swirl
was the outline of the gulf coast. Arrows were predicting the possible paths
of Jezebel. The middle arrow aimed directly at New Orleans.

Lida's black hair was pulled back and restrained by a silver clip. She
turned a worried look from the television to Phineas. "She's category 4
and may make 5 before landfall around 3 AM," In casual slacks and a
blouse with pockets, she stood alone at the conference table with the large
binders of disaster protocols and contact numbers spread out before her.
A cellular phone with its battery pack, together the size of a small suitcase,
was plugged into the wall.

Phineas began sorting the stack of patient index cards from his shirt
pocket. "I've never been through a hurricane. How do you think Baptist
will do?"

"We made it through Hurricane Betsy in '65. I was still an ICU nurse
then. There was less technology to support. Fewer ventilator patients and
no dialysis in Baptist then. Those patients went to Tulane or Charity.
Patients' and staff families rode out the storm here. Almost 800 in Baptist,
not counting pets." A half smile emerged. "And there were plenty of them."

"And Baptist came through it okay?"

"We did. The problem is that we're below sea level. Our generators are safe on the first level, but most of the circuits and transfer switches are in the basement, which flooded after heavy rains way back in '26 and '27. The Army Corps improved canals and pumping stations after that." She studied Phineas' face. "But if the levee pumps lose power, or if the canals are breached..." Her voice trailed off.

"Now I'm really nervous. Why are there still vulnerable circuits in the basement?"

"Moving all that hardware would be expensive. Other budget items always seemed to be more pressing, or more popular with administration."

"Seems pressing now." So, they weren't fully prepared. Not *mise en place*.

"Hey. There have been hurricanes since '27 and Baptist got through 'em." She raised her eyebrows and appeared to be trying to look hopeful.

"Should we get important stuff out of the basement? Just in case?"

"Everything but the electrical is packaged up and can be quickly moved at the first trickle."

"Okay. What do you need me to do and where should I start?" Phineas needed to be active to ease his tension.

"Meet with the ICU charge nurse and RT supervisor. Make lists of patients, their needs, and our manpower in those areas. I'm hearing that most of the staff scheduled to be here made it in. Let's meet back here at noon. I'll ask the kitchen to send sandwiches."

Phineas took the elevator to the sixth floor and found four empty beds in the twelve bed ICU. Six patients received mechanical ventilation. Hilary Ruth, the charge nurse, greeted him, followed by Angela Portier, the eager young RN who usually trailed him on daily rounds and had tried to attach herself to Iris at the ICU Christmas party.

Hilary was single and in her late thirties, British, and tall with red hair and freckles. She had nursed in England, Kuwait and then Columbus, Ohio before finding her way south to New Orleans.

After last year's ICU holiday party, Angela rarely failed to ask Phineas about Iris, and more than once suggested Iris contact her to get together. He hadn't remembered to follow through. As usual, Angela's ferocious mane of dark curls was pulled back for work. She started talking as soon as she saw him. "We're sure glad you're the one covering pulmonary! Did you bring Iris to sit out the storm at Baptist?"

"She left town with her mother. They're heading upstate with our lab, Amos. If he saw water in the streets, he'd have to be in it."

Angela pouted. "Lots of people brought their pets to ride out the storm at Baptist."

Hilary chimed in, "There are traffic jams leaving the city. Hope your wife made it out before then."

Phineas cringed at the news. "Iris was up before dawn. I gave her the ICU number, so she can let me know she's OK."

"She'll be fine. Ready to talk about our situation?"

"Ready."

"Baton Rouge had agreed to accept some of our patients, but the ambulances are stuck in traffic." Hilary's brow furrowed. "Ambulances that got out of the city aren't coming back, so it doesn't look like anyone is moving for now."

Phineas took out his note cards. "Let's run the list."

Phineas knew the ventilator patients. Geoffrey Ladd and Chauncey Palermo had AIDS and pneumocystis pneumonia. Both were on high concentrations of oxygen and worrisome ventilator pressures, and both were only in their thirties, but unless they began improving soon, their outlooks were guarded.

Fred Chappel and Jesse Potts had chronic obstructive pulmonary disease flares and had been slow to improve. Daily assessments suggested they were close to being able to survive without the mechanical ventilators' support.

Micah Owens, age 24, had been in a terrible car wreck, which fractured his neck vertebrae and severely injured his spinal cord. This necessitated a halo brace, a miserable contraption that surrounded his torso and attached to a metal ring bolted to his skull. He had also ruptured his spleen and undergone an emergency splenectomy. On admission his height was recorded as six foot four, and he was described as 'solid'. His muscles now atrophied by the day.

The sixth patient, Mildred Daye, was a frail 76-year-old who had been on chronic steroids for rheumatoid arthritis when she developed peritonitis from a perforated colon. She had survived septic shock and surgery but was left with the lung injury labeled adult respiratory distress syndrome. Phineas had been slowly trying to wean her from high supplemental concentrations of oxygen. She was weeks from a chance at coming off the ventilator.

"The other two are cardiac?"

Angela answered before Hilary could respond. "Correct. They both had MI's a couple of days ago. Mr. Boudreau had a run of VTach yesterday and is still on a lidocaine drip. Mr. Perrin was initially in pulmonary edema but is down to nasal oxygen. His rhythms have been OK, and he hasn't had any more chest pain. He might be stable enough to leave intensive care today."

Phineas scanned the hallways outside patient rooms. "How about nurses and RT staff?"

Hilary glanced around the unit and smiled. "We've got a good group here, the A team. Everyone who was supposed to be here made it. We have stretchers in the lounge down the hall and four empty beds for us to sleep on. Let's hope we don't get many new casualties, and we keep power." She lowered her voice with the last statement. "I've heard a few dialysis patients have shown up in the ER because their facilities are closed."

As Phineas rounded on patients, he confirmed with the respiratory therapists that all the ventilators were plugged into outlets backed up by the hospital generators. He explained the backup power to those patients alert enough to understand, and to their family members who were planning to stay through the storm.

The therapists felt it was safer to be in Baptist than in their homes, and most didn't want to evacuate New Orleans. The day shift included seasoned therapists, Judy, Barb, and Pamela. Nights were officially Sherri,

Vicki, and Ava. They were expecting shift times to be fluid, because they weren't going anywhere.

Ava had returned to work six months ago. Phineas had asked her to check in with him regularly in the difficult weeks after Adam died. He couldn't bring himself to report her drug relapse. She'd rewarded his decision by immersing herself in her work. She now participated in his weekly meetings with the therapists and never missed a shift. The other therapists had kept her close.

⚜ ⚜ ⚜

Lida shook hands and made eye contact with each individual as they arrived in the conference room that was now the Command Center. Attending were Chief Medical Officer Ted Lowry, charge nurses from each floor, and physicians from a range of specialties. Phineas' stomach churned with hunger and anxiety as he took a seat in the middle of the long table next to platters of sandwiches. On his left was Darryl Zachary Moss, Chairman of Medicine, one of the hospital leaders who had recruited him. His friends and a few colleagues called him D Z or Dizmus, Merry Dizmus during holiday season. Lida took the seat to Phineas' right. Most of the nurses had clustered at one end and the physicians at the other.

The hospital chaplain on call, Father Paul, a Jesuit priest, sat across from Phineas. Father Paul cleared his throat and requested a moment of silence he followed with, "Lord, take care of your servants gathered here in your work, and those less fortunate suffering and healing on our wards. Help us find strength and the courage to honor you during trying times."

Lida began the meeting. "You know me as your Chief Nursing Officer. Since CEO Justin Jordan can't make it back, I'll be your incident commander for the hurricane." She scanned the faces around the table. All eyes were focused on her. "Hospital census has been reduced by discharges where possible, by cancelling elective procedures, and by the few transfers we could complete before traffic jams clogged the highways. We now have 124 inpatients, including twelve neonates."

Jan Park, the neonatologist, reported that two 'preemies' required ventilators, six babies were in incubators, and the rest were newborns transitioning toward being able to go home, wherever that would be.

D Z Moss wrote notes on the chalkboard. He listed numbers by ward and included special needs such as dialysis. At least a dozen patients were severely chronically ill, some in later stages of dementia. They had come from skilled care facilities for acute problems like urinary sepsis and were awaiting return to their nursing home beds. Only a handful of the demented patients, through discussions with their doctors and families, were not to have their care escalated.

Shouting came from the hall outside the conference room. Lida shook her head. "It's troubling how many employees brought family members. Some even brought pets. Senior citizens from the neighborhood have been begging entry when it became clear they couldn't be evacuated. By an early count, we've got 280 staff and about 345 'guests.'" She paused to let the numbers sink in. "Staff will be quartered in the lounges on their wards and 'guests' where they can find space in nonpatient care areas, including the cafeteria, auditorium, and hallways. With our total numbers, we estimate food supplies are adequate for three days, if we are conservative."

Phineas raised a hand. "And medications?"

Lida answered, "The supply of drugs for today was not delivered."

She let her words linger. "If we lose power, there are three back-up diesel generators on the first floor. We have fuel for three days and hope to receive more if we need it. The worst-case scenario would be if our basement flooded. The main electrical switches are there." She took a deep breath. "It's conceivable we could then lose all power, including auxiliary. I don't need to tell you what that would mean for those on life support."

Phineas imagined bagging the ventilator patients by hand and winced.

That afternoon was a blend of a steady work schedule and nervous anticipation. There were no clinics, new admissions, or procedures, so

Phineas was able to write thorough progress notes. The televisions in the ICU rooms displayed images of the Category 4 storm and its projected path. It was still over water in the Gulf of Mexico.

By early evening, the sky over Baptist was a grim gray and a steady rain had commenced. Phineas joined the respiratory therapists' change of shift meeting in the ICU conference room. He listened as they ran their lists. Then he tossed out the question that had tumbled through his consciousness since the Command Center meeting. "What are your suggestions if we lose all power?"

Barb and Judy both started to speak. Judy paused and looked down. Barb continued. "We'll have to ventilate them by hand with the ambu bags after the batteries empty on the ventilators. Tanks are ready if wall oxygen doesn't work." She frowned. "We can't 'bag' them for days by ourselves. And our tank oxygen might not last thirty-six hours."

"Every patient will have an ambu bag." Judy took a turn. "We have extra endotracheal tubes, and our laryngoscopes are fully charged. Suction could be a problem. Our portable units need electricity. I'll call engineering to see if they can make batteries work for them."

"Thanks everyone." Phineas again. "I'll encourage Lida to keep trying to find hospitals that can take our folks ASAP, in case we do lose power. Let's keep talking."

In the Command Center Lida was on the phone trying to locate Baptist's pharmacy order. She had learned there were many unfilled deliveries and transports due to the traffic problems. As she finished her call, Phineas had another troubling thought. "Is it likely we will lose phones if we lose power?"

"That's what the cell phone is for. Plus, security and the four police on site have radio."

"How long will the cell phone battery last?"

"An hour of steady use. I have a charger for my car if we lose generators."

"I know that our neurosurgeon, Bob Proctor, has a car phone. As long as we have gas, we can make calls from the parking deck. Not a great place for the Command Center though."

"At least I could run his A/C."

"Found any hospitals that'll take our ventilator patients, in case we lose power?"

"Working on it. Baton Rouge will probably accept some. Your vent patients and the neonates would be the first to go. Dialysis patients next."

⚜ ⚜ ⚜

The televisions predicted landfall would be just east of city center between 2 and 4 AM and that Jezebel would be a Category 5 by then. Predictions were for roofs and walls to fail and for a complete power outage. People were instructed to fill bathtubs and even to have an ax on their top floors in case they had to hack through the roof to escape flooding of lower floors. The Superdome was open for those who couldn't or wouldn't evacuate. At first there'd been shuttle buses, but these had stopped running by evening.

Phineas found the ICU nurses and RTs laughing at the nurses' station. "You seem unexpectedly cheerful."

Hilary smiled broadly. "OB has a patient in labor who was freaking out about Jezebel. Everyone has been coming up with names to help calm her down. Her last name is Lagasse." She paused for effect. "Guess what the winner is. Hint: think Rolling Stones."

Phineas shrugged. "Only Gimme Shelter comes to mind."

Snickers all around. "Jack Flash" She paused for effect. "Born in a class 5 hurricane!" Guffawing followed.

A group chorus erupted "Jumping Jack Flash is Lagasse, gas, gas..."

Phineas leaned close to Hilary's ear. "Er, the words are 'crossfire hurricane.'" He instantly regretted the correction. Why provoke a question you can't answer?

"What's that mean?"

He shrugged again.

"Well, I'm sure we've got that too!"

Phineas raised his right hand. "Long live Jack Flash Lagasse."

"Long live Jack Flash Lagasse!"

※ ※ ※

By 2 AM, Jezebel had been officially reclassified as Category 5 and made landfall. Winds shook the ICU windows and rain seeped around their seals. Housekeeping, orderlies, nurses, and physicians took turns holding towels and sheets against leaks, and then mopping the slick floor.

By 4 AM, stones and other debris from nearby rooftops struck the windows, sounding like bullets ricocheting in a B Western and webbing the glass with cracks. Wind penetrated the cracks with high-pitched agonized shrieks. Phineas felt a shiver run up his spine. *Divine fury or Jezebel seeking her revenge?* When portions of glass gave way, a roar like jet engines followed.

Maintenance crews lugged sheets of plywood into patient rooms and struggled to cover the windows as glass fragments began spraying into the rooms. They had barely finished drilling the final pilot holes for the metal screws at 5 AM when the buildings and streetlights in the Freret neighborhood around Baptist went dark. A tense moment of total darkness followed in the ICU, during which the only sounds were the ventilators' alarms, the signal they had switched to battery backup. The low-pitched hum of the auxiliary generators floors below became audible. An assortment of emergency lights glowed, creating eerie reflections across wet floors.

The nurses and therapists spread out into each patient room, confirming that IV pumps, ventilators, oxygen, suction, and monitors were plugged into emergency outlets and functioning. Others mopped and frantically tried to keep up with rain leaking around plywood. It quickly became obvious that the emergency generators would not provide air conditioning. All personnel and patients began glistening, then dripping with sweat. Fans were plugged into a few remaining emergency outlets and directed onto patients.

A succession of what sounded like thunderclaps rose from below the ICU. Phineas glanced at Hilary. "What was that?"

Footsteps pounded on stairs and the metal door flew open. A security guard burst into the ICU and panted, "Windows... in the lobbies... just exploded inward." He caught his breath after several. "Visitors camped there had to run to internal rooms. A crowd's in the Chapel. Father Paul's leading prayers—and so far, the stained glass is holding."

At 7 AM, the basement began flooding. A human chain of hospital staff, wading in a foot of water that had entered from the streets, rescued stores of food, drugs, and emergency equipment. Phineas took note of the large gray metal boxes that he assumed were the panels of electrical switches. They were attached to walls two feet above the water level.

By 8 AM, Jezebel's din became less ferocious. Daylight crept around the plywood sheets. Staff discovered they could now keep up with mopping the rainwater. Windows stopped shattering. The ICU nurses and respiratory therapists tried to reassure patients who were alert. They confirmed adequate sedation for the others. None of the staff scheduled to begin the day shift had slept.

Phineas began rounds and found Ava crouched beside Geoffrey Ladd's bed surveying the contents of the ICU RT bag. She clicked the laryngoscope light on and off. As she bent over her work, her scrubs shirt hiked up and her pants crept lower displaying the snake and apple tree tattoo. She peered over her shoulder when she heard Phineas enter the room. Angela had trailed him like an eager puppy.

Ava asked, "Need anything Dr. Mann?"

Angela's mouth tightened and eyes narrowed. She shook her head in disapproval as she inspected Ava's art. Her face was glistening, and her damp scrubs were stuck to her chest.

Phineas answered Ava. "Will you be rounding with us, or are you finishing your shift?"

"I'm supposed to be finishing, but I can round."

At 9 AM, only a soft rain punctuated by gusts of wind continued. The sky began to lighten, and a faint orange ball penetrated the bleak sky. Phineas paused to survey Baptist's surroundings through a window that hadn't shattered. Water was up to car door handles on the few cars left on Napoleon and Clara streets. A few local citizens waded toward the ED ramp through dingy water topped with foam. Some had torn strips from bedsheets for makeshift bandages.

By 10 AM Phineas had examined everyone on ventilators. He, Barb, and Ava agreed that Fred Chappel and Jesse Potts had responded to treatment of their COPD flares, and both had excellent chances of being able to make it without their ventilators. Barb began preparing Fred, and Ava focused on Jesse. They suctioned their airways, removed their endotracheal tubes, and placed oxygen masks over their noses and mouths. Neither appeared unstable. Two fewer requiring ventilators, for now. None of the others would be coming off ventilator support anytime soon. They could handle current conditions for a few days, and Phineas hoped the worst was over.

Kitchen personnel, soaked in sweat, had worked over gas ranges with no air conditioning to send out trays of scrambled eggs and grits in paper cups. Breakfast with hot coffee and bottles of water lifted staff spirits.

Phineas learned that one bank of elevators near the emergency room on the first level and the operating room on the second level still functioned on the generator power.

By early afternoon word came back to the ICU that the water on the streets receded enough that a handful of the local 'guests' had waded in knee-deep water out of Baptist, hoping to find clear passage to their homes. A steady trickle of injured and sick began arriving at the ER. Dialysis patients in the nearby neighborhoods arrived, having assumed their dialysis centers would be closed for a while. A station wagon plowed through the shallow water on Napoleon and deposited a woman who had been stabbed in the chest. She was rushed to the operating room. The ICU received word that she had survived but would come to them on a ventilator. While Phineas awaited her arrival, the thirty hours without sleep planted a dull ache behind his eyes.

At least, Fred and Jesse seemed comfortable on nasal oxygen and enjoyed their first meal in days. Fred's wife, Joyce sat in the bedside recliner where she had spent the night peppering the nurses with anxious questions. Fred's nurse, Lilly, appeared totally absorbed in conversation with the two of them. Lilly was in her forties and single. Fred asked, "Where're you from, Lilly?"

"Manila."

Fred propped himself up on his elbows. "I was an officer on a submarine stationed in Subic Bay during World War II. My crew and I remained there for months after the war ended."

"I came to New Orleans from Manila but was raised in the Subic Bay Children's Home." Lilly began explaining. "I was told I was born in Dagupan."

Fred turned toward Joyce. "The crew and I used to go up to Dagupan... when we were off duty."

Lilly's tired eyes lit up when she gushed, "You must be my father!"

Fred and Joyce stared at each other with open mouths. Ventilator breaths in the adjacent rooms and the hum of generators floors below were the only sounds in the ICU.

⚜ ⚜ ⚜

Lida arrived in the ICU with the news that hospitals in Baton Rouge had agreed to accept the ventilator patients when transportation could be arranged. Ambulances capable of supporting them would need to get to Baptist and then out of the city. Traffic still failed to move at an acceptable pace for transporting unstable patients. Lida's fervent hope was that power to the city would be restored before they needed more fuel for emergency generators. The National Guard trucks patrolled the city though the water, trying to coordinate with police precincts by radio. Radio news reports indicated looting in many parts of the city and shots had been fired. More than ten thousand settled into the dark, powerless Super Dome as their last option. The reports announced over and over: *Martial Law is in effect.*

Security at Baptist reported looters carrying bags out of the pharmacy across from the hospital on Roosevelt. Security and police posted armed officers at all entrances to enforce a hospital lockdown.

Some of the staff ventured through the glass tunnel to the parking deck to get supplies and to enjoy a few minutes of their automobiles' air conditioning. Dr. Bob Proctor used his car cell phone to try to contact his wife and was unsuccessful.

While the water level around Baptist appeared to be falling gradually, the National Guard reported it was still rising in Lake Pontchartrain. At least one of the pumping stations for the canals had lost power, and back-up power to it had failed.

Before dusk, the kitchen sent out trays of spaghetti, green beans, loaves of sliced bread, and iced tea. Staff unpacked and shared snacks they'd brought from home. Lida looked exhausted but put on a brave face and announced she had found sites for the 14 dialysis patients. The National Guard trucks planned to transport them at first light. The patient census was now up to 132 counting those who had made it to the ER and couldn't be safely released. In a worn voice, Lida again expressed hope that either city power would be re-established or safe transportation for ventilator patients, including preemies, could be accomplished in the morning.

Members of the day shift tried to nap on stretchers arranged in lounges. The stifling heat and high humidity made sleeping a sticky challenge. Maintenance workers removed some of the plywood from the ICU windows to allow cross ventilation. Phineas admired the fiery sunset through shattered glass. He checked with each nurse on patients' statuses before deciding to try to get some rest in his office. Bone weary after a day and a half without sleep, he used his headlamp in the darkness of his office to roll out his sleeping bag and pad.

⚜ ⚜ ⚜

Phineas dreamt of Iris straddling him again. He felt her light touch on his chest and down across his stomach. In the moment's passion, his back arched, and he moaned "Oh, Iris." A sound beside them distracted his focus for an instant. When he looked back, Iris was gone. He came to in the darkness and sensed he wasn't alone. "Is someone there?" He heard movements next to his desk. "I *said*, is someone there?"

A strand of light created a dot on the wall then shone into his eyes. "Dr. Mann, I was hoping to get orders from you." Angela's voice.

"What do you need?" *How long has she been here?*

"Mr. Boudreau can't sleep. Can he have a dose of Halcion?"

"You can give him 0.25 milligrams. Anything else?" *How much of his dreams did she watch?*

"No. Sorry I bothered you."

Her penlight's target shifted to the office door before it opened and closed. He pondered once again why it was okay to wake up an exhausted doctor, so a patient could sleep, before he fell back into oblivion.

Someone gently shook his shoulder, but he instantly plunged back into deep sleep. More shaking, and this time a beacon blazed into his eyes.

"Dr. Mann wake up! You're needed in the ICU. We've lost all power!"

The scatter from Ava's wide flashlight illuminated her as she hovered over him in scrubs soaked in sweat. Her long hair was pulled back and tucked into her shirt. Her scrub pants had been chopped off above her knees. Body odor won the battle over her floral perfume.

Total silence had replaced the steady background hum of the hospital's generators. Phineas felt around for his headlamp and switched it on. He crowned himself with it and stood. "What time is it?"

"Just after 3 A.M."

The door flew open and banged into the wall. Ava's beam spotlighted Angela's wide-open eyes and mouth. Ava rose and pushed past her in the direction of the ICU, following her flashlight into total blackness.

Angela directed her penlight beam to the front of Phineas' scrub pants. "Dr. Mann! How *could* you? With her!" She pivoted back toward the hall.

"How could I what?" With the drawstring somehow untied, Phineas' pants had slipped to his hip bones. He turned to pull them up and secure them at his waist. When he looked back, his headlamp shone into darkness.

❖ ❖ ❖

Other than a single lantern at the nursing station, the only lights in the ICU were the ventilator displays and flashlights. Barb and Judy directed flashlight beams at Phineas. Barb spoke, "We've got two hours of ventilator batteries. There's no wall pressure or suction. We had to switch to tank oxygen. Sherri's in the neonatal ICU with Vicki and two preemies on vents."

The therapist's calm summary gave Phineas meager reassurance. "So, we have six therapists and seven ventilators. After the batteries are drained, we'll have to ambu bag them until we can get them out of Baptist. How're Fred and Jesse doing?"

Hilary appeared next to them. Her red hair was plastered to her neck. "They're troopers. They're offering to pitch in and help us."

"And the stabbing victim?"

"Her vitals are holding. We lost suction to her chest tube, but she's bubbling in the PleurEvac. Breath sounds are symmetric. Doesn't appear she's collapsing her lung."

"And the cardiac patients?"

"We kept them here rather than transfer them to the floor. So far, they're OK, but the heat is tough on them, and everybody."

Phineas swung his head from left to right to survey the scene with his headlamp. "I'll start rounds as soon as I use the bathroom."

Hilary displayed a crinkled frown. "More bad news. Plumbing's not working. No running water, no working toilets."

❖ ❖ ❖

Lida arrived in the ICU over an hour later with a sobering update after she and members of the facilities maintenance crew had shown their flashlights onto the street from the smashed second floor windows. Water was gushing from sewer vents and the level on the street was visibly rising. The maintenance crew reported water had again found its way into the basement; this time high enough to short out the power transfer switches there. After the first generator failed, the load on the other two, plus more short circuits, led to their failures. As Lida and the crew returned to the Command Center, she heard what sounded like river rapids coming from the elevator. One of the maintenance crew pried open the elevator door and pointed his flashlight inside. Water poured into the shaft below.

When Lida called the National Guard, she learned that pumping stations had failed and the levee breached at 17th Street canal. Lake Pontchartrain was pouring into the city. The water was now too high for the Guard to be able to bring their trucks to begin the evacuation, but they promised to try to get some soldiers to Baptist by boat to help with security as soon as they could. Their incident commander recommended that Lida call the Coast Guard. She dialed that number and was referred to another number, then put on hold. Finally, someone promised that an officer would assess their situation in the morning if a boat could navigate the local streets.

She brought the news to the ICU and recruited two RNs to disseminate updates to the other wards. "Patients will need to be ready to move on short notice," she said. "Obviously, we have no working elevators. When it's time we'll need to evacuate patients down the stairs to the ER ramp."

❖ ❖ ❖

The transition from the dying ventilators to manual bagging was hardest on the most tenuous patients, Geoffrey, Chauncey, and Mildred. Nurses, doctors, and therapists initially took turns trying to replicate the precise machine breaths, then nursing assistants and orderlies pitched in. To save precious batteries, oxygen measurements by oximetry were only performed if a clinical change was obvious. IV pump batteries failed, and fluids were either discontinued or run through older micro-drip set-ups recovered from storage. The laboratory and radiology shut down completely.

With the sunrise came limited window illumination followed by higher temperatures. Maintenance workers returned to remove the remaining plywood sheets from the windows, allowing more daylight and meager breezes. Patients were fanned with newspapers, magazines, or anything to move air. Sponge baths with water or rubbing alcohol helped for short periods. Nurses filled latex gloves with what was left of the crushed ice and tied them together, then draped the resulting creation around their necks.

Chauncey's nurse, Theresa, gesticulated and shouted, "Need help!"

Theresa was African American and raised near Baptist. She had worked there since graduating from nursing school, and still lived close by with her teenage daughter. Her daughter now camped out in the lounge with the ICU staff.

"He's getting harder and harder to bag! Someone check his vitals and O2 sat."

Phineas arrived to find Chauncey's pale skin was now gray and soaked with sweat. His eyes expressed terror, the whites framing his brown irises, and despite maintenance sedation, his arms flailed in an effort to reach his endotracheal tube. Linwood, an ICU orderly, worked to pin his arms.

Phineas pulled the wet hospital gown down to Chauncey's waist. "Push 5 milligrams of morphine STAT! If he doesn't settle, follow with Ativan 1 milligrams every two minutes until he does." He listened with his stethoscope to both sides of his chest, then percussed each side with his finger. The right side emitted a deep hollow sound.

"Pneumothorax. Give me gloves, a betadine swab, and a 14-gauge IV catheter. Have IV tubing and an open bottle of water ready."

Phineas pulled on the gloves as Theresa tore open the swab package. He grasped the swabs' sterile handles and painted betadine in an enlarging brown circle over the right side of Chauncey's chest. He located the top of a rib in the middle.

Ava strained so hard to squeeze the ambu bag that the tattoos on her forearms rippled. Chauncey struggled less as Theresa shrieked, "BP is 60 palpable and sat is 68%!"

Phineas poked the IV catheter between Chauncey's ribs. An instant hiss followed. Phineas attached the IV tubing and instructed Theresa to place the other end in the bottle of water. Bubbles streamed into the bottle. The oximeter reading began to slowly rise.

"He's not as hard to bag," Ava panted.

"Check his vitals again. He's going to need a chest tube. Let's try a Heimlich set-up first. It would be easier to place under our current conditions if it can keep up."

Angela handed the Heimlich packet through the door. Hilary placed it on the bedside table and peeled back its outer cover. Phineas inserted the needle from the pack next to the IV catheter in Chauncey's chest and inserted the guide wire into it. He slid the needle out over the wire then threaded the wire into the Heimlich catheter, which he advanced through skin to the hilt. He then removed the wire and attached the rubber one-way valve to the catheter. It burped a steady stream of air. He secured it with a stitch of silk.

"Page Dr. Thomas. I want to discuss a larger chest tube with our surgeon."

Hilary studied him briefly. "You haven't heard. No paging system, but we'll find him for you."

"Be generous with the morphine and Ativan. Keep him as comfortable as you can. I need to look in on the others."

Geoffrey and Mildred still maintained adequate blood pressures. RT had to feed high flow rates of precious oxygen into the ambu bags to barely keep the patients' oximetry readings at acceptable levels.

Micah had a temperature of 105 degrees. Phineas recalled that patients with spinal cord injuries are unable to regulate their temperature. The stifling conditions were roasting Micah. Phineas ordered alcohol and ice water baths, Tylenol, and more morphine.

When Phineas returned to Chauncey's room, Dr. Thomas was finishing stitching a large bore chest tube to Chauncey's chest. He carefully placed Vaseline pads and gauze dressings over the insertion site then taped it securely. Bubbles poured through the tube and out of a PleurEvac water seal device. He shook his head. "Let's step outside the room."

They entered the chaotic hallway, dark save for bobbing flashlight beams. "I doubt he's going to make it." Dr. Thomas spoke in low tones. "His BP is still only 80 and he's barely oxygenating. His lung has a massive air leak. If we had power, we'd be taking him to the OR to try to staple the leak closed. Even that might not work. His lung is probably like wet tissue paper...Then there's the whole AIDS problem. We have no treatment for it, and what if one of us catches it from working on him under these conditions? That'd be another tragedy."

Hilary, Theresa, and Angela joined them in the hallway. Theresa's scrub top was soaked through and her face dripped sweat. "What do we do if he codes?"

Phineas surveyed their faces, one by one, with the beam of his headlamp, causing each pair of eyes to blink and look down, except for Angela. She squinted and stared at him. He responded, "Don't code him. Make sure he gets plenty of morphine, so he doesn't suffer." He turned to Dr. Thomas. "Do you agree Dr. Thomas?"

Dr. Thomas nodded slowly.

"You have to code him!" Angela shrieked. "Chauncey's a young man." She inhaled deeply and glared at Phineas. "You doctors want to give up when it shouldn't be your decision. God will take him when it's his time. Miracles can happen! We have to do everything to keep him alive until we can't, even if he has AIDS because of his sins."

"Angela, coding someone doesn't change the outcome," Phineas spoke softly, "if the problem that's causing the code can't be corrected."

Over the next hour, Chauncey's oxygen level and blood pressure fell. His heart rate slowed into an irregular, slow agonal rhythm. After he died, Theresa and Angela wept softly as they removed his tubes and catheters and covered him. They moved his body to the chapel, the temporary morgue, since the basement morgue was flooded. Chauncey Palermo was Baptist's first Jezebel casualty.

⚜ ⚜ ⚜

Phineas sat to write Chauncey's death note.

> *8/30/85*
> *S: app. 2 hrs prior to death, Px with PCP and ARDS had sudden shock and refractory hypoxemia.*
> *O: BP 60 SaO2 68%. No breath sounds right. Px cyanotic, diaphoretic and agitated.*
> *A: Tension pneumothorax with PCP and ARDS*
> *Placed Heimlich after emergency catheter drainage. SaO2 transiently higher. Heimlich not able to keep up with leak. Consulted TSurg who placed a large CTube, also not adequate. BP and SaO2 continued to fall. No surgical options. Situation hopeless. Attempted to keep Px comfortable with morphine and Ativan prior to asystole. Pronounced dead at 9:32 AM. Unable to notify next of kin.*

⚜ ⚜ ⚜

Lida reported that she was finally able to get the Coast Guard on the phone and relayed the following conversation and updates.

"This is Baptist Hospital's Incident Commander and Chief Nursing Officer Lida Weaver. When is someone coming to Baptist Hospital? We can't wait much longer for some of our patients."

"Do you have a helicopter landing pad?"

"No. But we have a parking deck."

"Will it take 8000 pounds?"

"I'll ask our engineers, but I'm sure it will. It holds dozens of cars."

"Get back to me with that."

"Can't you come by boat?"

"Can't transport patients in our boats. You should call the Department of Wildlife and Fisheries. They have airboats that operate in shallow water." Her cell phone battery went dead after those words.

"Does anyone know where Dr. Proctor is? I'll need to use his car phone." She would still need to confirm hospitals that would take Baptist's patients. They needed a location where boats could land and transfer patients to ambulances. And they would need ambulances, and few operated anywhere in the city, so far.

The senior engineer reported he was certain the weight of a helicopter was less than the cars sometimes parked on the top level. The staff all parked below on the second and third levels before Jezebel. He also reported adequate space for a landing.

Patients would need to walk or be carried from the upper floors down several flights of hospital stairs, across the glass tunnel, and back up the parking deck stairs to be evacuated by helicopter. Boat evacuations, if they became available, would be from the emergency room ramp. Water lapped just below its edge.

❧ ❧ ❧

Later that day, Lida updated Phineas and Hilary further after she dragged herself from ward to ward and finished her rounds in the top floor ICU. Lida found patient rooms stifling hot with a horrific stench from feces backed up in toilets.

More and more patients had fevers. D Z Moss reported that without labs and x-rays, it was hard to tell if fevers were from hyperthermia from the heat or from infections. Antibiotics would soon be in short supply.

The kitchen struggled to send out provisions and to boil enough water for drinking and rehydration solutions on their gas ranges.

Visitors' tempers grew short. Security removed one family member who'd screamed at nurses and brought him to the emergency room, where security maintained a presence. They settled him with a sedative.

The ER staff turned away city residents, who had arrived in makeshift rafts thinking Baptist would be able to feed and evacuate them.

Lida instructed Hilary to have patients ready to move once she learned of transfer plans. There needed to be three links: transport by boat or helicopter from Baptist, transport from a landing area, and hospitals to receive patients. She left the ICU planning to return to the parking deck with Dr. Proctor's car keys.

⚜ ⚜ ⚜

It was midafternoon when an ICU nurse glanced out the window and spotted a Coast Guard officer and two enlisted men arriving in a flat bottom skiff. Hilary hurried to find Lida then accompanied her during the officer's Baptist inspection. Hilary returned to the ICU with news from his visit. The officer reported seeing several other boats on the streets. The occupants of one had stowed a rifle and motored away, disappearing down a side street.

By the time Lida and the Coast Guard officer reached the top level of the parking deck, his crisp uniform was soaked in sweat. He paced off the length and width. "We should be able to land a helicopter here. We'll leave one of our radios for you, and you have my office phone number. When you have a hospital where we can land that can take patients, let us know and we'll try to get choppers here ASAP."

⚜ ⚜ ⚜

Phineas found that Mildred's oxygen needs were slowly worsening. She had developed almost continuous explosive diarrhea, which didn't slow as her tube feeding was reduced to a trickle. It became impossible to keep her clean. The skin above her buttocks broke down to a raw, beefy red, oozing surface, and despite regular doses of morphine, she grimaced constantly.

Geoffrey had barely acceptable oxygen levels. Barb and RT counted oxygen tanks and estimated they might only have another 18 hours before they ran out.

Micah, with his blistering fever, was either delirious or sedated. Phineas endured helplessness and frustration watching the young man burn—and his chances for neurologic recovery evaporate.

❧ ❧ ❧

Orderlies and volunteers emptied bedpans into buckets, which were covertly poured through the broken window of an unoccupied room into the murky water in the streets below. The afternoon heat scalded the unit. Theresa hummed and sang gospel songs. Joyce Chappel and Angela joined in when they knew the words.

D Z Moss and Lida pushed through the ICU doors. They pulled Hilary and Phineas into the ICU conference room. Lida began, "We need to prioritize our transfers. Dr. Moss and I met with Dr. Park in neonatology. We agree the preemies on vents have top priority. We're hoping this will be later today. Second priority can be ICU patients who can be moved, the other newborns and their mothers, and dialysis patients. We'd like to get them to dialysis centers before they get unstable." She rubbed her eyes then covered a yawn. "Last priority will be the no code patients and anyone you think might be too unstable to move. Those patients who can go by boat should. We'll need to send staff with some patients, so we'll need to decide who will accompany them. The visitors should only go after patients have been evacuated."

D Z Moss waited for her to finish. His fine blond hair was plastered to his pale scalp, and his scrubs soaked, evidence of the even higher temperatures of the unventilated lower floors. "This evacuation may take a couple of days," he reported. "Pharmacy has word we may have a drug order coming by boat: some antibiotics, more morphine and sedatives. If there are patients who look like they won't make it, make sure they don't suffer. It's only going to get more miserable before we leave, and patients will continue to deteriorate."

❧ ❧ ❧

Friday evening, Phineas heard the distant throbbing sounds of helicopters through the broken ICU windows. The same sounds became louder as the Coast Guard's Sea Guard rescue helicopter came into sight. He and Hilary hurried to the parking deck. They hoped to better understand the process for the adult ICU patients.

Lida had healthy newborn babies in clear plastic bassinets arranged in a line on the parking deck one level below the top. In front of them were RTs Sherri and Vicki gently squeezing tiny ambu bags to ventilate two preemies in their incubators. Mothers stood next to their babies. At the end of the line two mothers cradled their newborns in their arms. A neonatal nurse and Dr. Park supervised.

The Sea Guard helicopter touched down on the top level. Two crewmen unloaded food and lights while the rotors continue to turn, producing a welcome blast of wind. Dr. Park approached the pilot with the information for the accepting hospital. Sherri and Vicki were helped on board with their preemies. The crewmen secured three more newborns, their mothers, and Dr. Park in their seats. The neonatal nurse and other babies and mothers would be on the next trip. They waited on the stairs two by two. The Sea Guard departed and offered a refreshing downdraft.

"Looks like another full load here," Hilary observed. "We should aim to move our patients at first light."

"It'll take that long to get them ready," Phineas answered, "and to have our staff organized for the monumental task."

Hilary and Phineas confirmed that the neonatal nurse had all she needed. In her arms were the babies' records. Hilary pointed at the top chart, labeled Jacques Flash Lagasse. It was the first time Phineas had seen her smile in two days.

⚜ ⚜ ⚜

As Hilary and Phineas re-entered the ICU, Angela yelled, "Need you here!" She leaned over Mildred's ventilator tubing and began pumping the blood pressure cuff. The tint of Mildred's face was now a similar but paler blue than her wild eyes. Mildred squirmed and emitted a small puddle of foul-smelling stool. Her daughter, Betsy, stood frozen in the corner with tears streaming down her cheeks. She had stayed with her mother and had quietly helped with trying to keep her clean.

Angela turned to face Phineas. "BP is 60 palpable. I can't hear it anymore. Her last oximetry reading was 72%. Dr. Mann, what would you like us to do?"

Phineas pulled on his stethoscope and listened to her chest and abdomen. He heard crackles over both lungs and high-pitched tinkling bowel sounds. Mildred writhed in pain when he touched her abdomen. *Bowel obstruction.* Surgery was the usual next step, but impossible now. "Give her more morphine, 5 milligrams now and repeat in 15 minutes if she's still suffering. And start a saline bolus and a dopamine drip. Betsy, please come outside with me."

Phineas waited in the hallway. Hilary put her arm around Betsy and escorted her out of the room. Betsy's chest heaved, and her words cascaded in sobs. "Dr. Mann, she's all the family I've got!" She directed a pleading look at Phineas with blue eyes she'd inherited from Mildred.

"I'm sorry Betsy." He struggled to not let weariness sabotage empathy. "Her examination suggests a bowel obstruction. We don't have x-ray to confirm. I'll place a nasogastric tube to try to decompress her bowels, but this usually doesn't fix the blockage without an operation." He let these words sink in. "We don't have the option of surgery, and it's unlikely she'd survive it if we did. She's just too sick. We'll consult Dr. Thomas, our surgeon, to get his input." He lowered his voice. "It's likely the obstruction is from a segment of necrotic bowel."

Betsy glanced up at him. "Necrotic?"

"Bowel without blood flow. Gangrenous. Betsy, I'm sorry, but your mother may not last the day." He needed to offer something. "We'll try to ease her suffering." Phineas waited for Betsy's response. She only wailed more loudly. He gestured toward Mildred. "Betsy, you can sit with her. Hilary, please ask someone to find the chaplain." Betsy's legs folded as Hilary eased her into the bedside chair.

Angela stepped into the hallway and closed the door. *Why does it have to be Angela again?* Putting his frustration aside, Phineas instructed her. "I need an NG tube, gloves, K-Y jelly, and a large suction syringe. We really need wall suction, but without power, we'll have to try manual decompression. And please ask someone to find Dr. Thomas to assess her and talk to Betsy." Angela's mouth pinched into a tight line. "Angela, Mildred may not survive the next few hours, much less an attempt to move her down seven flights of stairs and to another facility. It would take more than a miracle for her to get through this."

"Then that's what we should wait for. We have to hope and pray for one." Angela stood up straight in a defiant posture.

"It's not going to happen here. Keep her free of pain and look after Betsy."

He continued to study Angela's face. *I know what she wants to ask.* "It would make no sense to code Mildred if she dies."

Angela said nothing. She fixed him with an icy stare then pivoted and stomped back into Mildred's room on her clogs' wooden soles.

Phineas gave her a few minutes to gather supplies then returned to gently advanced the clear plastic nasogastric tube from Mildred's nose into her stomach. He suctioned what looked and smelled like thin stool repeatedly with the syringe and finally asked Angela to take over this effort. Dr. Thomas arrived and confirmed Phineas' impressions of dead bowel.

Mildred died three hours later. Phineas helped move her body next to Chauncey Palermo in the chapel.

Phineas returned to the ICU and found Hilary in an empty patient room making lists on a clipboard. "Can you encourage Angela to get some rest?" he asked.

"I have been. She says she will, then she pitches in somewhere else." Hilary sounded like she was also frustrated.

"Well can you at least assign her to the cardiac or COPD patients, those who aren't on life support?" *Someone who doesn't need a miracle.*

❦ ❦ ❦

Iris hung up the phone. She'd tried unsuccessfully to get through to Baptist's ICU since she and her mother had settled in their Memphis motel room. At first the line was busy. Now after she dialed, there was nothing.

Amos was coiled on a folded blanket next to her bed. He sighed when she reached down to pet him.

Sarah Jane opened the bathroom door wearing a shower cap, a silk kimono and gold slippers. With the robe's belt pulled tight, her scrawny mother reminded Iris of a sailboat's mast with the main sail furled.

Sarah Jane sat on the opposite bed. "No luck?'

"I reached his parents. They haven't heard from him either."

"He can't call us, since he doesn't know where we are."

"And I'm pretty sure their phones are down from what's on the news." Iris took a deep breath and let it out slowly.

"I'll bet we hear from him soon."

Amos groaned after Iris ran her hand from his head down his back. "I'm really worried."

Sarah Jane removed her shower cap to reveal that every hair was still in place, undisturbed in their escape from the hurricane. "Hospitals are safe places. What could possibly go wrong?"

The TV news contained no mention of Baptist Hospital. Images of New Orleans were terrifying. Iris was convinced she and her mother would have risked their lives if they had stayed. The trip north was arduous with stop and go traffic. Fuel, food, and restrooms were sparse. They had begun watching roadside motel signs for vacancies after they reached Memphis. The first chance was a Howard Johnsons motel. Iris had rushed to the desk displaying her credit card. She'd filled out the registration paper and watched the clerk stamp her card.

When Iris asked for an extra blanket for Amos, the clerk had shaken his head. "We don't take pets."

"He's a really well-behaved older dog. Management will understand. With a hurricane..." She pleaded with hands folded.

Then Sarah Jane stepped through the lobby door with Amos on leash. She stood behind Iris and commanded, "Amos, sit." Amos dutifully sat and stared at her, at Iris, then at the clerk with glistening brown eyes.

The clerk handed Iris the key and reached under the counter for a blanket. He waved his hand.

"I didn't see him."

On the sign in the parking lot, NO lit up in neon next to VACANCY.

As the sun fell to the New Orleans horizon, it spawned orange and pink ribbons along the water-filled streets running east to west. Battery-powered lights now surrounded the perimeter of the Baptist parking deck. The remainder of the newborns and their mothers were airlifted, heading to a distant hospital. The Coast Guard pilot assured Lida that he would return and assess the safety of a landing after dark, but he could not promise he'd land.

Lida crossed through inches deep water in the glass tunnel then waded in the dark hallways before following the thin beam of her flashlight up the five pitch-black flights to the ICU. She gathered Phineas, Hilary, D Z Moss, and Dr. Thomas along the way.

"The helicopter will be back in a couple hours." Her voice was weary. "No guarantee it'll land. We need to decide who we should have ready for transfer if they land. Obviously, whoever goes will have to be transported down the five flights of stairs and back up to the top of the deck. Suggestions?"

"I'd love to get the stabbing victim to a functional ICU," Dr. Thomas spoke first, "but moving her in the dark, and then if they can't land and we have to bring her back..."

Hilary went next. "Same for Geoffrey and Micah. It'll take a team to carry and support them. And in the dark? I believe Geoffrey would die if we moved him to the deck and then had to bring him back. Maybe the best option is to move the cardiac and COPD patients first. They can walk slowly. We can put chairs on the stair landings. We'd only need to send two nurses with them. We can move those dependent on life support at first light."

Phineas and D Z Moss nodded their heads in agreement.

Lida informed them that the helicopter's capacity was eight adults plus the crew. Hilary suggested one of the nurses should be Rebecca, who was seven months pregnant. She also pointed out that Fred Chappel's elderly wife was frail, and Fred probably wouldn't go without her. This would leave two places. Hilary decided to send two of the less stable dialysis patients from a medical ward. She repeated her goal of closing the ICU tomorrow. They could then start trying to move the numerous ward patients, visitors, and staff. She declared, "We need to get ready and be on the parking deck in less than two hours."

The doctors, nurses and available staff hurried to arrange themselves along the path from the ICU, down the stairs, across the hallway, across the glass tunnel, and up the parking deck stairs to the top. Heat and humidity delivered misery the whole way. The only illumination came from the battery powered Coast Guard lights on the parking deck and from flashlights.

As Phineas placed a chair at his station at the bottom of the parking deck stairs, his thoughts unexpectedly drifted to religion. He peered into the glass tunnel that rose to the stairs, the stairs that went up to the top deck and the lights of salvation, a Jacob's ladder. He again resolved that he should try to lead a good life, or else when he died, he would be the doctor in Baptist during a hurricane and without power for all eternity.

Mr. Perrin walked slowly down the dark hospital stairs illuminated by flashlights, then panted as he settled into the chair at the bottom. He and his chart were passed from caregiver to caregiver. He murmured softly, "Hail Mary, Mother of God..." as he stood and slid his feet through the hallway water. Angela greeted him near the door to the glass tunnel.

The code cart with drugs and defibrillator had been pushed against the door to prop it open. Phineas waited at the far end of the tunnel by the parking deck, the next rest stop. He then escorted Mr. Perrin up the stairs to the top level, supporting Mr. Perrin under his upper arm as they climbed.

Jesse Potts followed. His neck muscles tightened with each breath forced through his pursed lips. Barb pushed an oxygen tank beside him. He leaned heavily on a rolling walker as he waded through at least an inch of water in the glass tunnel. Phineas observed Jesse's labored ascent up the parking deck stairs one slow step at a time, as if he were summiting Mt. Everest. At the top, the wind from the helicopter's rotor refreshed them.

When he descended the stairs again, Phineas heard D Z Moss yell to Angela. "Need help here!"

When she shined her light on Mr. Boudreau's face, he appeared ghostly pale. He held a fist over his chest. "Pain! Can't... breathe!" He retched once and crumpled into a silent, limp heap.

D Z Moss rolled him onto his back and pressed on his neck. "No pulse!" He gave one hard thump on Mr. Boudreau's chest and started chest compressions.

Angela ripped the defibrillator off the top of the code cart, set it next to him, flipped the switch to 'on', and hit the charge button. She lifted the paddles and knelt across from D Z Moss. Her flashlight lay submerged in the water, its beam fanned across the floor.

Phineas raced from the glass tunnel door. "Angela, stop! Don't shock him in water! You'll kill yourself." He pulled the backboard from the code cart. "Drag him higher up into the tunnel."

Angela froze and glared at him as her trembling hands replaced the paddles on the defibrillator. "I...I knew that."

They struggled to move Mr. Boudreau to a drier spot at end of the tunnel. Phineas gave him breaths with an ambu bag and facemask. Angela shocked him twice, each time with his body arching in a convulsion, each time without return of a pulse. They used the paddles to scan for a rhythm and found none. Angela yelled, "Adrenaline!"

Phineas shook his head. "Doubt we can save him under these conditions."

Angela ignored him. She hurried to the code cart and returned with syringes. D Z Moss glanced at Phineas, shrugged, and resumed pumping. Angela pushed the Adrenaline in his IV and charged the defibrillator again. "Get off him! I'm going to shock on 1, 2, 3!" Mr. Boudreau's body convulsed again. No pulse or detectable rhythm followed.

Phineas put his hand on Angela's shoulder. "You tried. You and he are so soaked in sweat; you'll probably shock yourself if you keep trying. Please stop."

She pushed his hand away. "Is that an order?"

"If that's what it takes. Yes."

Phineas turned his headlamp toward the door. Fred and Joyce Chappel and Lilly stood there; their eyes directed at the floor. Lilly spoke. "Dr. Mann, can we pass by now?"

Phineas and D Z Moss tried to shield the Chappels from Mr. Boudreau's body when they shuffled past. As they exited the glass tunnel, Phineas heard Lilly murmuring. "Now you have my number and address, and I have yours. As soon as this whole mess is over, I want to come see you."

After midnight Hilary and Phineas met with nurses and respiratory therapists in each of the remaining three ICU patients' rooms to lay out plans for their more arduous transports and for decisions as to which of the staff would accompany them on the helicopter transfers. These staff members were not expected to return to Baptist. The order of patients would be Micah, then Geoffrey, then the stabbing victim. Whenever cooling sponge baths were paused, Micah's temperature shot over 105 and he became delirious. Phineas feared any chance of neurologic recovery was threatened. Geoffrey continued to require high flow rates of oxygen, and his oxygen levels remained lower than standard goals. The stabbing victim still had an intermittent leak from her lung and needed significant amounts of supplemental oxygen.

Each patient was supported with bagged breaths by rotations of whoever was available and had the remaining hand strength, and each patient would require a nurse and a respiratory therapist. This would leave only one therapist at Baptist. The amount of space the ventilator patients would require on the helicopter allowed one ICU patient at a time. Hilary guessed that four dialysis patients could fit in the back rows on each trip. The next helicopter was supposed to return just before dawn.

Phineas could barely keep his head up as he began his fourth straight day at Baptist when D Z Moss found him writing summary notes in the patients' charts. He asked Phineas to accompany him to the other hospital wards. Begrudgingly, Phineas followed, although he'd hoped to steal a few minutes of sleep before dawn.

"I could use your help on the patients outside the ICU when you have time." D Z Moss sounded spent. "After you transfer your final three ICU patients, and the twelve dialysis patients leave, we'll still have at least 90 patients on the floors. Lida is working on finding receiving hospitals for them. Some of them are ambulatory enough that they may be able to go by boat to a waiting ambulance. Looks like there will be a boat landing area near Ochsner Clinic."

"And what would you like me to do?"

"It's just plain awful on the wards. Your broken windows at least allow some ventilation. It's like an oven on the wards below. Some patients have deteriorated and may not make it out of here. I've been trying to get their doctors to be liberal with narcotics, since there's nothing else that relieves their suffering. I'm getting pushback from nurses." He glanced at his filthy tennis shoes. "I was hoping you could round on these folks with me and see if you have any suggestions. And you can help me with the staff. This is really difficult for them."

The phrase "liberal with narcotics" stuck in Phineas' thoughts as he finished the note and closed Micah's chart. *How liberal is his "liberal"?*

He followed D Z Moss and his flashlight down the pitch-black stairs to 5 East, the ward below. As they entered in darkness, he was assaulted by a more oppressive wave of wet heat and penetrating stench accompanied by ragged wailing beside him and shrill shrieking ahead of him.

... shall cast them into the furnace of fire. There shall be wailing and gnashing of teeth. Matthew something or other...

D Z Moss directed him to the wailing room. A nurse slumped there in a metal chair, a wet towel tied over her nose and mouth. Tissue paper plugged her ears. She removed one side and spoke.

"He's not eating or drinking. Throws his food. Says it's poison. Pulls at everything. I had to leave his IV out. Every time I clean him, he messes hisself again. He was trouble before Jezebel. Now he's impossible. Can't wait till 7 AM when I pass him on to some other unlucky nurse. Then I'm going to get in my car and run the A/C."

D Z Moss shined his flashlight on the open chart. "Mr. Frederick has severe dementia and COPD. He barely got by with a regular schedule and all the benefits of electricity, plumbing, and civilization."

Phineas directed his headlamp beam onto the patient's squinting eyes and grimace. His shoulders were skeletal, skin tears laced his forearms, and his forehead felt fiery against the back of Phineas' fingers. The patient's lung examination revealed diminished sounds and a few soft wheezes. Phineas lifted the sheet and discovered a puddle of liquid stool.

Mr. Frederick wailed again, "Help me. Help me!"

His nurse began pulling on gloves. "Oh Lord! Can't tell when they soil themselves, since this whole place stinks of shit!"

Phineas rotated the handle to the sink faucet. Dry. He shook his head at D Z Moss. "I don't have any additional medical suggestions. Not much you can do beyond trying to get him to take his meds, food, and then enough drugs to treat his suffering, and to keep him from hurting himself or someone else."

"Good to know I wasn't missing something."

Phineas followed D Z Moss from room to room. Piles of wet towels and sheets lined the hallways. Many of the patients he was introduced to were confused, naked without sheets, and hot to the touch. Some had family members camped in their rooms. The minute they spotted the doctors, frustrated and overwhelmed kin pleaded to know when they would be evacuated.

Phineas and D Z Moss peeked in the lounge where physicians and nurses tried to sleep on narrow stretchers. D Z Moss whispered that he didn't have the heart to awaken anyone. He stepped back into the hall and told Phineas, "I'm going to run the patient list in the AM with the physicians and head nurses. We'll need to come up with an order to follow for when we can evacuate. The demented and no code patients should go last. This means some of them will be in even rougher shape. We shouldn't hold back on narcotics and sedation for these folks. If we can't fix their problems, we can at least alleviate some of their misery."

Phineas nodded his understanding. "When I empty the ICU, I'll help with the ward patients. It's getting near dawn, so I need to head back upstairs and make sure we're ready."

They moved Micah in his halo brace gingerly onto a rigid stretcher, and two bearers arranged themselves on each side. The respiratory therapist stood at his head and squeezed the ambu bag. His nurse carried his chart and led them down the stairs, across the glass tunnel, and up to the top of the parking deck. Phineas gently squeezed Micah's shoulder. "Safe travels, Man."

Dialysis patients followed. Six were able to walk, and two who were missing legs were carried. The powerful throbbing from the helicopter's blades was a welcome racket since it whipped the muggy air around them.

The three evacuation trips from the ICU took most of the day. Phineas had no idea when he would hear if his patients had survived the transfer.

He was totally drained but felt obliged to find D Z Moss for an update.

When Phineas spotted him at a nursing station, Moss vigorously waved him over. "The Department of Wildlife and Fisheries' airboats started evacuating patients stable enough to be discharged." His smile faded when he shrugged. "But I have no idea where they're being taken. And that's the *good* news. Bad news is, with staff and visitors, we still have hundreds to move out of here. We're guessing two more days between boats and helicopters. I'm meeting with the doctors and charge nurses before supper arrives. We'll be in the second-floor lounge in 15 minutes? It stinks less there."

Phineas knew most of the doctors by name from past patient transfers into and out of the ICU. There were five internists including D Z Moss. Also attending were Lida, Father Paul, the general surgeon Dr. Thomas, the neurosurgeon Dr. Proctor, Dr. Ted Lowry from the ED, and an anesthesiologist he hadn't yet met. He knew a few of the charge nurses. Hilary stood in the back. Beside her was Angela in soaked scrubs flecked with dried blood.

Ted Lowry started the meeting by thanking everyone. He let them know the ED was having few visitors and seemed well protected by security. He'd been helping on the floors and planned to continue.

Lowry didn't mention the case the nurses had been whispering about. An unresponsive elderly man had been dropped at the ED platform. He barely had a pulse and smelled horribly. When a nurse removed his boot, his lower leg, covered with maggots, came off with it. He died shortly after, and his corpse—with leg still in boot—was wrapped, sealed, and placed in the chapel. The ED then reeked of gangrene on top of death.

Lida informed them they had used much of their three days of food and were receiving a few staples and some pharmacy supplies by boat. She encouraged those who brought provisions to continue to share. She then asked D Z Moss to talk about the remaining inpatients, since most were medical patients.

D Z Moss held up a clipboard. "I've made a list of the remaining patients. Triage will be in three groups. Group 1 has those who have no terminal conditions and had been improving and are expected to survive. Group 2 are those in a gray zone. They have severe chronic conditions. Many are elderly and most have deteriorated following Jezebel. They should be evacuated first. Group 1 will be evacuated next. Group 3 includes those with terminal conditions including severe dementia. Our goal for these individuals will be comfort. We have drugs that can alleviate suffering. Their life expectancies were short before Jezebel. Some may die before they are evacuated." He paused and surveyed faces. "We'll have copies of the list written, and we'll put numbers on charts. Comments?"

Dr. Warren, the only African American internist had joined the staff last year fresh from his residency. He spoke up. "I'm not comfortable pushing drugs if there's any chance I'll cause a death. I don't want to be accused of active euthanasia after all this is over."

"We mustn't hasten anyone's passing," Father Paul added. "That's not God's will."

Angela frowned and slowly shook her head at Phineas. Her troubled stare shifted from D Z Moss to Father Paul to him, where it lingered and bored into him, causing him to struggle to focus on the conversation. He had to look away.

D Z Moss sighed, "I can discuss individual cases. Let's get some of us back upstairs."

Phineas approached D Z Moss after the meeting. "I'm going to my office to catch a few winks. You can send someone to get me in a couple of hours and I'll help out in the evening." On the way to his office, he grabbed his dinner ration, a paper cup of rice with cream of chicken soup spooned on top.

⚜ ⚜ ⚜

Phineas managed less than two hours of sleep before Hilary gently shook him awake. "Okay Sleeping Beauty," she wearily kidded, "it's your turn to check the floor patients. I'm going to take a nap in the lounge."

He located his headlamp before she and her flashlight slipped out the door. He found the water jug he'd emptied and added his concentrated urine then capped it. He took a swallow from his other water jug and brushed his teeth, rinsed, and spit into the few grains of rice left in the paper cup.

He started with Mr. Frederick whose wailing had become less constant despite the stimulation of his nurse applying a rubbing alcohol sponge bath. Phineas noticed towels piled up against the bathroom door. "Why all the towels against the door?"

"Toilet's overflowing from emptying bedpans. Trying to keep the feces from coming in here."

Phineas grimaced. "Is he getting any nutrition?"

Mr. Frederick screamed when his nurse lifted gauze wrap to display his raw forearms. "Won't eat or drink. Tried to hold him down and start an IV. He fought so hard, tore his skin and he bled all over."

Phineas inspected the skin tears. "What are you giving him for comfort?"

"Dr. Warren wrote for 1 milligram of morphine subQ every 2 hours as needed. Doesn't touch him."

"Make it 5 milligrams. I'll write the order and come back later to check on him."

Phineas found other demented and terminally ill patients on the ward on similar stingy doses of narcotics and sedatives. He adjusted these doses upward to what he judged to be more adequate. He did find a probable new case of pneumonia by carefully listening to the lungs of an elderly diabetic man with a fever. He ordered an antibiotic and asked the nurse to notify him if the pharmacy lacked it. Vague and sketchy chart notes prompted him to take the time to write what he considered adequate documentation.

He returned to the empty ICU and stood next to a shattered window to let the soft night breeze wash over his face. A full moon cast a silver glow on the water filling streets below. Phineas savored the silence. *Where is Iris?* Three gunshots rang out, followed by an outboard engine, then another. *She had to have made it out of here.* He retreated from the window then followed his headlamp beam down the stairs to 4 East.

4 East was a contrast to 5 East. Stench, darkness, and wet heat were the constants. These patients had "Group 1" written on their chart covers. Here family members fidgeted in bedside chairs. Patients were quietly sleeping or conversing coherently. Staff, while tired and sweaty, worked with more energy and expressed hope. Phineas discussed each case with a nurse, examined patients and adjusted orders.

By the predawn hour, he'd rounded on each of the wards he'd been assigned, so he returned to Mr. Frederick. The beam from Phineas' headlamp found the old man sitting bolt upright and laboring to breathe, his neck muscles straining with each breath. He stared ahead with eyes wide open and moaned, "Help me...Can't breathe...Help me!" Phineas listened to his chest and found no change from earlier.

His nurse shrugged. "What do you want to do, Doctor?"

"His emphysema is end stage, and we've done all that we can for his lungs." Phineas inhaled deeply. "Wish he had a loved one here to comfort him. He's suffering. Do you have another 10-milligram vial of morphine?"

She nodded and handed it to him.

He gave half of the morphine to Mr. Frederick then sat and began writing in the chart. After 20 minutes Mr. Frederick continued to moan, "Help me!" Phineas administered the other 5 milligrams then held Mr. Frederick's hand. Ten minutes later the old man's breathing slowed, and his eyes closed. A hint of a smile replaced his grimace. He lay back in the bed and gradually stopped breathing.

His nurse stared silently while Phineas wrote a death note and closed the chart. "I'll help you move him to the chapel."

As they and an orderly they'd recruited opened the stairway door, Phineas' headlamp beam settled for a split second on a head of thick dark hair slipping around the corner of the hallway. An apparition, or real?

The concentrated odor of death days old assaulted them as they cracked open the chapel door. They suppressed gags and hurriedly deposited Mr. Frederick's corpse.

※ ※ ※

Phineas climbed the stairs to the shattered ICU to watch the sun rise. He had checked out to Dr. Warren and another internist and hoped to steal a nap before he returned to work. As he crept down the dark hall to his office, he found D Z Moss and Ted Lowry at his office door.

Ted directed his flashlight into Phineas' eyes. "We've been informed by the Coast Guard that they and the Department of Fisheries are going to make a big effort to get people out of here today and tomorrow by boat and helicopter. They have added another staging area for evacuations at the cloverleaf of I-10." He paused and looked at the floor. "They refuse to take pets and they can't say when anyone can come back to retrieve them."

Phineas had heard barking, mewing, and whining as he wandered the wards on his rounds. He learned that many had thought Baptist the safest place for their pets to ride out Jezebel. Most were tucked away in crates in dark offices and lounges. The animals' distress seemed to be helped little by brief releases for feeding and removing waste from the crates. "What's your plan?"

Ted cleared his throat. "We don't see a choice but to offer to euthanize most of them. Maybe some of the smaller ones can be smuggled out, but we don't know what awaits them at the staging areas."

Phineas thought of Amos. "And how do you plan to euthanize them?" Euthanize didn't feel like the correct word.

"Pharmacy has some pentobarbital, but not enough to euthanize all the animals. So, we'll sedate them with it or whatever else is left, then stop their hearts with intracardiac potassium. Phil Sanders from anesthesia has agreed to help."

"Have you notified the pet owners?"

"Some. As you can imagine, there's been a range of reactions. We won't be the ones to force anyone to give up a pet. People may have to hear from the Coast Guard that it's their only way out of here."

Phineas stared wearily at his two colleagues. "If you *really* need my help, come find me after my nap. I can barely process at this point. I'm guessing we have another couple of days before the last of the doctors can leave." He shifted his gaze to the floor. "By the way, what'll you do with all the dead animals?"

"Put them in the chapel."

⚜ ⚜ ⚜

Again, it felt like he had just closed his eyes when Phineas was awakened by a series of soft knocks on his office door. In the pitch-black windowless room, he fumbled for his headlamp and switched it on. He cracked the door open to find Jaspal, the ICU pharmacist, wringing his hands. Jaspal had come to the United States from India as a teenager. He'd often enlisted Phineas' input in development of ICU protocols and improvement projects.

"I am hoping that you can help me with a most difficult task, Dr. Mann."

"Sir?"

"I will give you a chance to wake up, and I will be out here when you are ready."

Phineas closed the door and used his urine jug then splashed a frugal handful of bottled water in his eyes and stepped into the hallway.

"Jaspal, what's up?"

"Dr. Mann, sir, I have a difficult favor to ask. I brought my wife and our two Labrador retrievers to Baptist to wait out the storm in my office. They are telling me they will not take our dogs on the boats when we leave here." He inhaled deeply and sighed. "We cannot leave them here without knowing what will happen. We care for them too much. We have had them both for more than twelve years."

"What do you think I can do?"

"I have been giving the pentobarbital and potassium to Drs. Lowry and Sanders. Sometimes the animal dies quietly. A few times I observed struggle and suffering with the potassium. Will you please, kind Sir, be there to make sure our wonderful dogs do not suffer?"

"Jaspal, are you sure you want to do this?" Phineas couldn't imagine doing the same with Amos. "You could wait a bit longer and see if the situation improves, and there's a chance to evacuate them."

"It will only get worse before it gets better, Dr. Mann." Jaspal met Phineas' gaze then stared at the floor. "My wife and I have discussed this thoroughly. Our dogs have had good, long lives. We can't leave them to starve, alone and afraid. We'll say our loving good-byes now."

Phineas followed Jaspal to the pharmacy offices. As they approached, he heard excited barking. Jaspal opened the door to reveal an Indian woman kneeling and wrapping her arms around two retrievers' necks, one black and the other yellow. Jaspal hurriedly restrained the larger black dog. Its face was trimmed in white. The yellow Lab wobbled when it stood. Wasted thigh muscles framed protruding hips. The woman stood and adjusted her sapphire blue sari.

Jaspal gestured proudly. "Dr. Mann, sir, I would like you to meet my wife, Anjeni."

"Pleased to meet you, Anjeni. Wish it was under different circumstances." Phineas offered his hand, palm down, in front of the black lab's nose. "What's his name? My black lab's name is Amos. I have no idea where he and my wife are. They drove out of the city before Jezebel." Sadness and anxiety washed over him. He detected the familiar feeling of club soda in the back of his nose before he blinked back a tear.

Anjeni murmured, "His name is Jeeval, which means full of life." She sniffed and wiped her eye on her sleeve. "I wish we had also left New Orleans."

Jaspal left as Phineas began petting Jeeval. He learned from Anjeni that their yellow lab was named Hema, which means golden. They chatted about retrievers until Jaspal returned with Ted Lowry and Phillip Sanders.

Jaspal, Anjeni, and Phineas sat quietly as Sanders drew up two syringes of pentobarbital. Phineas helped Jaspal pet and hug each dog firmly as

Sanders inserted the needles under the skin on the backs of their necks and injected the barbiturate sedative. The dogs became quiet over several minutes then closed their eyes and lay flat on the floor. Dr. Sanders produced a long needle. Dried blood was visible at its hub. He attached this to a large syringe of potassium solution and began feeling Jeeval's ribs.

Phineas asked him to pause while he tickled the hairs between Jeeval's footpads and then the openings of his nostrils. No response. Amos would have pulled back his foot or shaken his head, if sleeping. Phineas then pinched the dog's loose neck skin. Still no response. Phineas nodded his head at Dr. Sanders and looked away, unable to witness.

They placed Jeeval's and Hema's bodies on a stretcher and covered them with a sheet. Jaspal took one end and Phineas the other as they navigated the stairs and halls to the chapel. Phineas pulled open the door of the chapel to find Angela and Linwood, one of the transport orderlies. A slender corpse wrapped in a sheet lay next to Mr. Frederick. On the other side of the chapel was a pile covered by sheets. A furry paw stuck out near its bottom. Angela stared at the two bundles on the stretcher, shook her head, and left without a word.

Phineas returned to his office where he splashed drops of water in his eyes and brushed his teeth. He considered the miserable task of repeated pet killings Ted Lowry and D Z Moss faced. As spent as he was, visions of plunging the cardiac needle into beloved pets kept him from sleep. Finally, he left his office to search for Lida and an update.

He found Lida with Hilary in the lounge with the broken windows. It was already steamy, and the air was still. They wore scrubs cut off at shoulders and knees. A thermos yielded him a warm cup of coffee. Lida offered crackers and a jar of peanut butter. Phineas gratefully accepted. They sat quietly for several minutes before he asked, "How's the census today?"

Lida looked over at Hilary. "We're making progress finally. I don't have up to the minute totals, but we're moving people steadily to the evacuation areas. Those who can go by boat are lined up at the entrance to the ED. Those who require helicopter transport are lined up in the hallway on the way to the parking deck. Hard to gauge the rates, but we hope we might move the last ones out by tomorrow afternoon." She massaged her temples. "We're letting family members go with patients now. Relatives' arguing has led to unpleasant situations in the lines. Security has had to defuse some conflicts. Our nurses are struggling to keep up with patient needs for hours in those dark, hot hallway lines."

"So, I should plan on another night on the wards?"

Lida began arranging loose papers. "Hopefully this will be the final night, and we'll get the last of us out tomorrow. Can't tell you how much we appreciate your work here."

Hilary spoke softly. "I do need to warn you of possible future issues, when all this is over."

"Go on." Phineas' guts twisted. *Hunger or a stomach bug?*

"Angela's very upset and not handling some of the difficult decisions you and some of the other physicians have had to make." Hilary glanced out the window then back at Phineas. "She's told other nurses she plans to file reports that you've euthanized patients. She's convinced at least one other nurse to back her claims."

Phineas clenched and unclenched his fists. "Why would she do that?"

"Angela's father died in an ICU after a long and difficult struggle when Angela was a teenager. They'd been very close. She claimed that the doctors gave up on him. She believed that if he could have stayed alive long enough, a miracle might happen." Hilary paused and studied Phineas' face. "That may be the main reason she went into ICU work when she finished nursing school last year. Apparently, her mission is to make sure everyone has a chance to have a miracle, *her* miracle. The one she was denied."

Phineas endured a mix of nausea, fear, and furor. "So, I get through all this only to face legal charges? Can't you at least evacuate her soon? Get her out of here?"

Hilary responded, "Angela insists on staying until all the patients are out. Eventually we'll need to debrief all staff, and some patients and families."

Lida finished arranging the papers into a pile. "Let's hope it doesn't come to legal charges."

Phineas slapped the table. "How can anyone judge us? No one can put themselves in our places and even imagine how it's been here."

❖ ❖ ❖

Phineas found his way to the hall outside the ED. Dim light leaked in from an exit door. The too-familiar smells of body odor mixed with urine and feces assaulted him as he entered the department. Patients, some naked, but most in wet gowns, formed a line of wheelchairs from the entrance to the loading platform. A few cried out in bursts. Most were silent. Weary family members in sweat-stained street clothes sat or stood hovering around the patients.

He found a similar lineup in the hallway next to the glass tunnel leading to the parking deck, except many of these patients were on stretchers awaiting a helicopter trip. Again, some were barely covered and being fanned by family members or wiped as clean as possible with damp towels by worn out looking nurses and assistants. Phineas found Father Paul praying over a scrawny old man whose ribs and breastbone formed a bony rosary. The priest said "Amen" and looked up.

Phineas waved. "Got a minute, Father?"

"Of course." He walked toward Phineas, and the two entered the brilliant sunlit glass tunnel. "What can I do for you?"

"Have you spoken with Angela?"

Father Paul brought his hands together and looked into Phineas' eyes. "What are you referring to?"

"I've heard she is upset we've given drugs to terminal patients to provide comfort. She's telling others we are actively euthanizing them."

"As you know, God decides when death should occur. We should not hasten it. As a physician, *you* are a healer—not the decider."

"And if it's clear a condition is taking someone's life, and that condition can't be healed, and the person is suffering terribly?"

"Give just enough to ease suffering, but not expedite death."

"Imagine you're the one, Father." Phineas wanted to scream but managed to respond in a measured, even tone. "You're the one with a hopeless condition and you're suffering mightily because I'm not giving you *enough* narcotic. Would you not cry out, 'Dr. Mann, why have you forsaken me'?"

The priest clutched the wooden cross tethered around his neck. "I'll not duel with scripture. You are not God, Dr. Mann. God may still heal."

"You're talking about miracles." Phineas gestured up and down the hall. "Seen any of those at Baptist lately?"

"I am not the one who judges." Father Paul glanced upward.

"You're not helping, Padre." Phineas followed his gaze and saw only a bare white ceiling. Divine intervention wasn't going to eliminate Angela's threat.

"We're both too tired for this conversation," Father Paul mumbled, his eyes closed, head bowed.

"You're right on that point. And I need to get back to work."

"And I to my flock." Father Paul turned back around. "You understand, Dr. Mann, if I'm questioned, I'll tell what I saw."

"I don't recall that you *saw* anything." *He wasn't there.*

Phineas seethed as he walked away from Father Paul. *With any luck, I'll be out of this hellhole in 24 hours.*

Evacuation boats and helicopters had begun delivering bottled water and beige, plastic-wrapped packages labeled MRE, short for Meals Ready to Eat. Phineas picked up a meal and some water and went back to his office. With his headlamp, he read the label: Beef Stroganoff with Noodles. He resisted the urge to completely satisfy his hunger. The last thing he wanted to deal with was diarrhea. He figured he'd steal a nap after, but too many thoughts swirled around his brain. It wouldn't shut down. He wished he knew Iris was safe. Why did *he* have to deal with Angela's personal demons?

He gave up on sleep and went back to 5 East where most of the group

3 patients had been assigned. Two rooms were empty, Mr. Frederick's, and the one across the hall. He could hear the same shrieking he'd heard earlier coming from the far end. It was not as loud or continuous. A nurse waved at him from the shrieking room.

"Doctor, can you look at Mrs. Cormier? She's not doing well."

The patient was emaciated with wisps of white hair. She lay on her side, shrunken and ancient. When he touched her, she shrieked, "Ouch" or "Save me!" Unlike so many, her skin was cold and clammy in the heat. Her gastrostomy feeding tube was unattached and loosely taped to her damp abdominal skin, and the urine in her bladder catheter was dark and cloudy. He could barely feel her rapid pulse.

"What were her last vitals?"

"BP 75/45, pulse 130. Better earlier today. You know she has severe dementia."

"From the looks of her urine, she's probably septic on top of dehydrated. She have family?" He cleared his throat. "Is she a written no code?"

"She's a no code. Hasn't known anyone for a long time. Just lies in bed and is turned every two hours. Fed, watered, and cleaned. Don't know about any family. None here."

Phineas contemplated ordering morphine but guessed more trouble might follow. He found Mrs. Cormier's chart and reviewed her last urine cultures before he ordered antibiotics. He tried and failed to start an IV. Three times he thought he'd found a vein, but each flimsy one blew apart when he attached fluids. With each effort, she'd screamed, "Ouch" and "Save me" over and over and over. Frustrated, he changed the orders to infuse fluids and dose antibiotics through her feeding tube.

He continued to round on the remaining patients on the wards and in the hallways awaiting evacuation that night. Basic care was all the nurses and he could offer. When his headlight flickered, he hurried to the emergency room where security scrounged up replacement batteries. After the sun set, boats and helicopters arrivals were infrequent, and progress in the lines leading out of Baptist slowed almost to a halt.

Hopes were again extinguished.

※ ※ ※

Before Monday's dawn, Phineas returned to Mrs. Cormier's room. A young, plump woman, whose badge read Medical Assistant, had replaced her nurse and snored in the bedside chair. Mrs. Cormier's breathing was shallow and ragged, her high-pitched squeals barely audible. Wild eyes fixed on his face. *Doe eyes.* Her abdomen had become so distended that it resembled a globe crisscrossed by scars. She whimpered when he confirmed its rigidity. Her rapid carotid pulse was barely palpable. He clamped the feeding tube and shook the medical assistant.

"Hey, wake up! When did her abdomen get like this?"

She blinked repeatedly and rubbed her eyes. "It's way bigger than when I last checked."

"Her G-tube must have come out of her stomach. Fluids have been going into her peritoneum. Probably peritonitis by now. Find me the charge nurse." *Too harsh. Probably thinks I blame her.* "Could have happened anytime earlier, in these conditions."

Phineas wrote a note in Mrs. Cormier's chart. As he closed it, he recognized Angela at the door, spotlighted in the beam from his headlamp. "You asked for the charge nurse? I'm covering for her."

Phineas swallowed painfully; his throat was so dry. "Mrs. Cormier has severe dementia and is in shock from a urinary infection and peritonitis, likely worsened by a displaced G-tube. We have no way to correct it." He took a deep breath. "She's likely to die soon. Chart says she is not to be coded, which I agree with. I plan to give her morphine to ease her suffering."

Angela did not immediately answer. Then, "How much do you want to give?"

"Five milligrams now and repeat in 15 minutes, if she's not more comfortable."

"Write the order and I'll get it. *You'll* have to give it." Words laced with venom. She confirmed his written order. Stared at it.

When Angela returned and handed the syringe to Phineas, she announced, "I've been documenting everything you've been doing. When we get out of here, I'll make sure you don't practice medicine again. Euthanasia is a crime. I'll see you go to prison!" She pivoted and marched down the hall.

Phineas winced and slowly shook his head. Feelings of anger and frustration followed by helplessness boiled to the surface. He had to steady his hand when he gave morphine until Ms. Cormier's breathing slowed and the whimpering ceased.

The medical assistant mumbled, "What if you gave too much?"

Phineas turned his headlamp beam onto her exhausted face. "What if I don't give enough?"

He sat with Ms. Cormier as she quietly died. He and the medical assistant wrapped her in her sheet to move her to the chapel. Phineas tied a towel he'd dipped in rubbing alcohol over his nose to dull the stench before they opened the door and deposited her there. The medical assistant stopped to wretch outside the chapel door.

After five days of incarceration at Baptist, it seemed the evacuation efforts were at last more efficient. The patients, visitors, and finally the staff were being transported to one of two evacuation areas and then, reportedly, out of New Orleans.

Phineas returned to his office late in the morning and choked down a peanut butter sandwich and water. He lay on his sleeping bag in the dark and wondered where Iris was. His dry, gritty eyes moistened as he fell asleep. He dreamt they were back in school. Life was simple. A walk along Boston's Charles River in April was a sweet treat. He held her hand and was about to kiss her when he awakened. He'd been asleep for hours.

Gwen, an ED nurse supervisor, found Phineas in his office brushing his teeth with what was left of his water. "Dr. Mann, I came by because no one saw you leave. It appears you're the only doctor left in Baptist. Can you take a look at the John Doe some guys in a boat just dropped on the ED ramp? Found on his porch moaning." She leaned against his door jam. "He was unresponsive with a stiff neck. I put him in the isolation room. Doesn't seem to have a fever. Glad we have a few of the old glass thermometers. Digital thermometers are all dead. BP was on the low side, 86/50, so I started IV saline. He seems to be perking up a little. Hope we can move him to a functional hospital right away, and I hope we aren't long leaving behind him. The Guard is sending more boats."

Phineas put on a mask and gloves in the ED. In the isolation room, he found a thirty something Caucasian male on a stretcher, moaning and clutching his head. He had several days growth of dark beard.

"Sir, I'm Dr. Mann. What happened to you, and what's your name?"

More moaning. Phineas felt his pulse. Surprisingly slow at 48 per minute and thready. He pumped up the blood pressure cuff and slowly opened the valve. 95/55. There were no bruises or other signs of trauma. He found only the stiff neck, a dry mouth, and sagging skin, suggesting severe dehydration. When he tried to flex the man's neck, his entire torso lifted from the stretcher. *Really is stiff.* He fully opened the stopcock on the IV solution and watched 750 milliliters quickly empty, then swapped a full bag for the empty bag.

Gwen was writing in charts at the nurses' station. "So, Doc, what do you think about Mr. Doe?"

"He has no ID?"

"Didn't find any. Went through the clothes under his stretcher."

"It's either meningitis or a subarachnoid hemorrhage. I'd bet on the latter with his low pulse. Usually their BPs are higher, so he's probably really dry. Or, he is septic with meningitis, but then I'd expect tachycardia and fever. Do we have any IV ampicillin left? Any vancomycin?"

"I'll check."

"Let's hang 2 grams of ampicillin and 1.5 grams of vancomycin. It's tempting to get some spinal fluid, but it'd be more for my curiosity. I couldn't even look at it, since all our microscopes need electricity. Let the second liter run in, then set it at 250 per hour of saline. I'll write him up then have another look at him."

On his next examination, John Doe's blood pressure was a normal 120/85. His forehead was still cool. His face, pale and damp, wasn't flushed. He opened his eyes and peered at Phineas.

Phineas raised his eyebrows and smiled behind his mask. "Sir, I'm Dr. Mann. You're in a hospital. What's your name?"

His voice was gravelly, barely audible. "Noah...Noah Waterson."

Seriously? Parents much have been really Old Testament or had a sense of humor.

Noah coughed. "Head *really* hurts!"

"I think you had a bleed into the spinal fluid around your brain. We're also treating you for meningitis. That's why I'm wearing a mask. Mr. Waterson, do you have any medical problems?"

"High blood pressure. Ran out of my Aldomet pills after the storm."

"You have any family?"

"Parents passed. Only child."

"You a veteran?" Maybe transfer to a VA Hospital was an option.

"Nope."

"We didn't find any ID in your clothes, so I'll need to add your name to our record. Besides the headache, any other symptoms? Weakness, numbness, visual changes?"

"No. Headache and neck hurts. ID's in my boots, under the sole. Put it and some cash there when I saw I was stuck in my place." Noah winced in obvious pain when he tried to turn his head. "That was before the pain struck...Put me on my knees."

"Just a few more questions, then I'll look for some morphine for your headache. Occupation? Alcohol? Tobacco? You don't sound like you're from the South."

"Line cook. Can't stand tobacco. Drink like everyone else...Came to The Big Easy a few months ago from Pennsylvania. So far only found a few temp gigs."

Phineas found a pair of cowboy boots under the stretcher. He handed them to Noah who reached into the right one and pulled out the insert, then a thin envelope labeled 'NFW'. He handed it to Phineas. It contained papers and a driver's license.

"We'll put these in a safe place for you after we record your information."

Noah retrieved several bills from the other boot. He slowly and deliberately counted out $182, losing his place twice, before handing it to Phineas. "Hope I get this back. Don't know when I'll work next." Phineas slipped it into the envelope.

Noah groaned and he stared into space. The right side of his face drooped. His right arm and leg convulsed as he lost consciousness. His left pupil dilated into a black hole.

Shit! He's bled again.

Phineas opened the isolation room door. "Gwen! Anyone?" No response. He found the code bag and rummaged through it for the laryngoscope and an endotracheal tube. He tried to insert the laryngoscope blade between Noah's teeth, but they were clamped together. Then, in an instant, Noah's jaw relaxed, and Phineas quickly inserted the tube. He attached and began squeezing the ambu bag. Noah was completely still. Phineas felt for a pulse and found none. Both pupils were now fully dilated. He stopped squeezing the bag. There was no effort to breathe. Phineas tried again without success to feel a pulse, stared at his patient for several moments, then stepped out of the isolation room.

Gwen yelled across the ED, "Can we move your John Doe? The Guard is here, and we need to leave *now*."

"He died. No question he just had a massive subarachnoid bleed. Herniated his brain. Didn't have a chance. It was quick."

"Well, get your stuff together right away. I'll ask someone to move him to the chapel." She paused and made eye contact. "Doc, they're telling me we need to debrief soon after all this mess gets cleaned up. The CNO said hospital attorneys want to hear from us."

Phineas swallowed hard. *Can this misery get any worse?*

⚜ ⚜ ⚜

Phineas hurried to his office, removed his jeans and collared shirt from the hook on the back of the door, and stretched them across the bed. As he stripped off his sweaty scrubs, he discovered that he'd shoved the envelope printed with NFW into the pants pocket when Noah coded.

Could this be a lifeline?

He added the packet to his cash in his money belt, pulled his jeans on over it, and pocketed his hospital ID.

Gwen was in the ED hallway hurrying toward the emergency room's loading dock.

"Gwen, what's the plan? Who's left?"

"There're only a few of us. Guard is securing the hospital. I'm going to the loading dock for the next boat. You should come now."

They found two more people on the loading dock: a nurse named Phyllis, and the orderly, Linwood. Both had possessions wrapped in plastic bags and hadn't bothered to change from their scrubs. Soft vibrations of an outboard motor, at first like the wings of a hummingbird, puttered in the distance before it grew into a steady throbbing as an olive flatboat with four National Guardsmen approached. The man in the bow tossed a line to Linwood. The driver throttled down and yelled, "We can take three to fill the spots of our guys staying here. Another boat should be along soon for whoever's left."

"We're it. Can't you take four?" Gwen hollered back. The three guardsmen in the front two seats stepped onto the concrete dock.

The driver shook his head. "Boat only holds four."

"I'll wait. I can go back and move the patient to the morgue." Phineas blurted. "You three go." He gestured with his chin, urging them to accept his offer.

"Naw, Doc. I can wait," Linwood responded.

"Linwood, go find your wife and kids. Someone will get me."

The departing three stepped into the flatboat and took their seats. Phineas released the bow line and waved as the guardsman backed the boat away and motored west on Clara Street.

Phineas addressed the three remaining guardsmen. "One of you can help me move a deceased patient to our temporary morgue on the second floor." Two looked to be barely out of their teens. The third had gray hairs in his neatly trimmed mustache.

The older guardsman patted Phineas' shoulder. "We'll take care of it. Wait here for the next boat. Where on the second floor is the morgue?"

"The chapel. Follow your nose—and wear a mask."

The young guardsmen followed their leader through the entrance door. Phineas directed them to Noah Waterson's corpse and pointed at the stairway.

His beard itched maddeningly, its roots steeped in crystallized sweat. *I must also smell like death.* Alone in the uncharacteristically quiet space, he found the clean hold supply closet. Most of the bins were empty. He salvaged shaving cream and a disposable razor, and then discovered a sterilized packet containing battery-operated clippers, used for surgical preps. The staff bathroom was dark and oppressively hot, despite a propped open door to listen for more boats and guardsmen. With the guiding beam from his headlamp, he mowed his thick beard into the sink. He then blanketed the stubble with lather and dragged the dry razor over tender skin, nicking his Adam's apple and lip border. The face looking back was not one he recognized. He hadn't seen his cheeks or chin in a decade. They looked soft. They felt like a baby's skin. His eyes rested on dark crescents. *Who are you?*

Phineas scooped his whiskers from the sink and stepped outside to drop them in the murky water around the loading dock. He placed his duffle at the end of a metal bench and reclined against it while watching his beard drift away. His back, already sore, tightened on the rigid surface. The edge of his Baptist ID badge pressed into his leg. He extracted it from his jeans' pocket and studied his bearded image. Blood trickled down his neck from his Adam's apple razor cut. He wiped the blood with his fingers. It smeared on his badge before he tossed it beside an overflowing trash bin. *Angela, if you want Phineas Mann's blood, you can have it.*

The urge to drift into sleep was strong.

⚜ ⚜ ⚜

"Hey! Young man!"

Phineas sat erect, his core stiff from the hard bench. In the failing light, a stout man with a salt and pepper beard idled a skiff with outboard motor beside the loading dock. The middle seat held a woman huddled with her arm around a girl. Mother and ten-year-old daughter, Phineas guessed.

The man yelled again. "You trying to leave here?"

Phineas cleared his scratchy throat. "I was waiting for a National Guard boat."

"Not much daylight left. You might be waiting till tomorrow. We're heading to a relocation area. Got room for one in the bow."

Phineas scrambled to the edge of the platform and tossed his gym bag into the boat with one hand while holding the gunnel with the other. He stepped in and settled onto the hard metal seat. "Thanks. I'm definitely ready to get out of this place."

The boat driver offered, "Got a name? I'm Malachi."

Iris, forgive me.

"Noah."

"Seems fitting.

The flat-bottomed skiff's outboard motor growled as it gained speed through the detritus and filth covering the floodwaters surrounding Baptist Hospital. Phineas lifted the front of his shirt over his nose against the stench of rotten fish, human waste, and garbage floating in the gray-green water. Oil and gasoline streaks layered the surface and shimmered iridescent where the sun approached the horizon. He pivoted in the bow seat, searched the bearded and weathered face of the boat's pilot, and asked him, "Where are you taking us?"

Malachi, in soiled overalls and sweat-stained tee-shirt, sat sideways on the stern seat and gripped the accelerator handle of the outboard. He down throttled long enough to be heard. "I hear there's an evacuation area at I-10 and Claiborne. We'll try there first."

A young mother and daughter in the middle seat hugged each other with one arm and gripped the gunwales with the other, their faces slack.

Humid air streamed against Phineas' freshly shaved face, a sensation he hadn't experienced since before he raised his beard in college, refreshing for a fleeting moment before the events of his chaotic last five days swirled back. Angela's threats haunted him. Was it possible that after all he'd done, he could face murder charges? His money belt hid two identities. One belonged to a dead man.

The massive concrete structure of the I-10 bridge materialized in the distance. Next to its railing, an ambulance's lights flashed red and white. Phineas discerned human outlines. Some stood. Others sat and clutched their knees. Dark blue and khaki uniforms lined the road.

Malachi idled the motor, and the boat glided to the muddy slope adjacent to the abutment. "This looks promising. I'll drop you folks here."

Phineas clutched his gym bag and stepped over the bow. "Thank you, Sir."

"Don't mention it. Good luck, Noah."

PART FIVE

BORN AGAIN

Jesus replied, "Very truly I tell you, no one can see the kingdom of God unless they are born again."
JOHN 3:3

Phineas scanned the empty faces of the fifty or so anonymous and silent souls seated around him on the Greyhound bus. Pervasive body odor was an improvement over the smells of the hospital. The young African American man seated next to him by the window stared at passing land-scape and intermittently grimaced when his stomach complained out loud.

After the sweltering days and nights in Baptist, the bus's constant air conditioning made Phineas shiver. Was his nightmare over, or was more coming? Could Angela cause him more misery? He fingered his money belt under his shirt. It held another man's identity. Was it crazy to keep it, at least until he was certain he wouldn't have legal threats? *Who was he going to be? Too much to think about...So tired....Need sleep...*

✣ ✣ ✣

He spotted Iris on a park bench in New Orleans' Audubon Park, a stroller beside her. He'd been running in the city's parks before or after

209

work, hoping to happen upon her, guessing he'd eventually find her in one of them if Amos were still alive.

Two and a half years felt like forever. Would she recognize Phineas with a buzz haircut, a clean-shaven face, and lighter by 25 pounds? He was now used to living as Noah, comfortable in the assumed identity and cooking career he'd grown into after his evacuation to Houston following Jezebel.

As Noah, he'd settled into the rhythm of restaurant life, the daily wiping clean of all messes (unlike in medicine), the immaculate kitchen, and the safe harbor from the multiple murder charges. Then, at long last, the prosecution's main target's name, Dr. Phineas Mann, disappeared from the newspapers, his bloody Baptist ID badge a forgotten dead end in the energetic rebuilding of New Orleans. Time had arrived to chance a return, a rebirth.

His mouth was dry and his hands shook. He swallowed painfully. *Will Iris know me? If she doesn't, should I be Phineas or stay Noah?*

He stood still on the trail. A growl. Amos limped toward him. The old dog's face was now frosted white.

"Amos! No bite!" Her voice. It's deep south warmth. How he'd missed it. Alone in the park, she must want him to assume Amos would protect her, if she commanded. He chuckled and held his hand out, palm down, toward Amos' muzzle, who sniffed, then stiffly wagged his tail and whimpered. He patted Amos and scratched behind his ears.

When he looked up, Iris clutched a child to her chest and stared, her glacier blue eyes wide open. A glistening aura framed and highlighted the two of them against the green surroundings.

His heart pounded. "Seems to like me. Sorry to interrupt."

"He's never this friendly."

"Dogs like me." Panic crept in. *She doesn't know me...If I say I'm Phineas, she might hate me...Maybe later.* He had to clear his throat. "I'm...I'm Noah."

Iris kept her gaze on his face, studying him, her head tilted. Noah looked from her to the black-haired child and back to her. He could hardly get a breath in. She stood. "We need to be going now. Amos, come!" She buckled the child into the stroller.

"I should go, too. Have to get to work." A desperate afterthought. "I cook at The Bistro at Maison de Ville in the Quarter. Come by."

"Maybe another time," She called out over her shoulder as she hurried down the path, the aura trailing her like a comet's tail.

"Bye." Noah began running in the opposite direction. *Well, that didn't go well.* He felt sure she hadn't recognized him. He'd desperately wanted to tell her he was Phineas. And the child? Had she moved on to someone else?

⚜ ⚜ ⚜

He jogged in a different part of the park two weeks later and spotted Iris with Amos and the stroller. She perched on a bench, again easy to find, inexplicably illuminated in the center of the scene. She was conversing with a young couple hovering over another stroller. Noah slowed his run to a walk. Amos loped straight to him. This time he settled on a bench twenty yards away and allowed Amos to eagerly sniff him.

"Good boy, Amos," He whispered. Amos' whine sounded like he was saying, "Missed you."

Iris leaned back from the stroller and turned toward Amos. "Amos. Don't bother him. Come here." She held up a leash.

"I must still have delicious smells on me." Noah sat up straight and smiled. "I've been working as the roast chef at The Bistro."

The man holding the stroller turned to look at him. "Were you behind the delicious duck breast I had for lunch there Tuesday?"

"Yessir. I work lunches Tuesdays to Thursdays. Dinners Fridays to Sundays. I get Mondays off." Pride had emboldened him. "I'm Noah."

"Nice to meet you, Noah. I'm Sam and this is Lacey. I'll probably be back at your place soon." Sam eased his stroller forward as it emitted an infant's squawk. "Well, we need to get home and wrap a present for a one-year old's birthday party. See you."

Noah patted a seated Amos and hoped for a less tense conversation this time. "Are they friends?"

Iris stared at him. "Friendly strangers. Like you." She arranged a blanket on the grass and lifted her child from the stroller. She handed the child a bulging cloth sack that he began ransacking.

Noah cleared his throat. "Just moved here a few months ago, so I haven't met many people outside of work. I can leave if you prefer."

"Sorry, if I sounded hostile."

"No problem. I understand. Care to share your name?" He moved to a closer bench, across the trail from Iris.

"Iris."

Now he could say her name. "How old is your son?"

"Just turned two."

Noah turned the dates over in his head. Two years old meant Iris would have become pregnant around the time of Jezebel. He tried to remain calm as he recalled the night before the storm.

"Is his dad at work, Iris?"

"His dad passed away before he was born."

Oh? "Sorry."

"That was a while ago. One has to move on."

Amos trotted back to Iris. He lowered his chest and front legs onto the ground and wagged his tail while he studied her. She pulled a tennis ball from a stroller pocket and tossed it down the trail. Amos lumbered after it then circled back and performed a stiff old dog butt tuck run around the benches before he dropped the ball at Iris' feet.

"What's your son's name?" The child looked up from his play with wide open dazzling blue eyes and laughed out loud at Amos' antics.

"Jonah."

"Great name, although you don't look anything like a whale—oops— sorry, Iris. I shouldn't have said that."

"No offense taken." Half a smile.

"What kind of work do you do?" He knew but wanted to hear her say it.

"Hospital social work at Tulane Hospital." She threw the tennis ball again. It seemed to float, suspended in the humid air. Amos bolted after it, an old dog's bolt.

"Do you enjoy it?"

"It's a job, and we need the income. And things have finally settled down after Jezebel."

He shouldn't stay too long this time and risk her feeling afraid. "Well, Iris, I've really enjoyed meeting you. I need to get back and clean up for work. Saturdays are busy...but I'd like to invite you again to The Bistro sometime. If you can get a break." He expected rejection. "My suggestion would be to come toward the end of a lunch around 2 on a Tuesday, Wednesday or Thursday. The staff starts to relax then, and I can take a break."

Her expression softened. "I might take you up on that."

"Hope to see you soon."

Noah jogged back on the trail, slowly at first, then almost sprinting. This time it had gone *so* much better. She'd actually smiled. And Jonah *had* to be his son. He so much wanted to pick him up and hold him.

⚜ ⚜ ⚜

A young woman greeted Iris at the door of The Bistro and apologized. "Sorry, but it's 2, and our kitchen just closed."

"Noah asked me to come at 2."

"A friend of Noah?" The woman's face lit up. "I'm Dot. We thought all Noah did was work, read about food, and run. Great to meet you!" Slender and in her early twenties, dark roots led to blond hair corralled in back by a mother of pearl clip. "I'll tell him you're here. Why don't you sit by the window? Want some coffee?"

"Coffee would be great. Thank you. I'm Iris. I just met Noah—Is he as nice as he seems?"

"Wow! You cut right to the chase. We all like him here. He's not one to go out partying with us after work, but boy is he great to work with. Does his job and pitches in to help others. It's almost like he's escaped Hell and is in a happy dream." She started toward the kitchen door then stopped and spoke to the gray-haired black man behind the bar. "She's a friend of Noah. Any decent coffee left?"

The man waved at Iris. "I'm Leon." He brought her a silver tray loaded with matching porcelain cup, cream pitcher, and sugar bowl. As he poured, steam rose from the spout of the silver pot.

"I'm Iris. Thank you so much." She added cream and sipped the coffee as Leon returned to tidying his bar. Iris watched a man through the window outside on the sidewalk lift his camera and point it at a horse-drawn carriage.

"Hi, Iris." Noah stood behind her with a tray balanced over his shoulder. He set it on a stand near the table. "Iris, I'm so glad you could come. Hope you haven't eaten." He pointed from one dish to the next. "It starts with a few crawfish and small alligator bites, then an apple and pecan salad, followed by turkey and sausage gumbo. If you still have room after, there's sweet potato pie." He removed his food-splashed apron and served her samples of everything then placed a second bowl of gumbo for himself.

Iris shook her head. "This may be all the food I need for the rest of the day. It's usually a peanut butter sandwich and carrots for my lunch."

"I can go back in the kitchen and make that for you."

She skewered an alligator bite. "Don't even think about it."

Fallen leaves had been collected in the weeks before Thanksgiving, and the sounds of the city were magnified without the leafy sound barrier as dusk turned to dark. Noah had called ahead to say he was on his way over with food and news.

From outside the front door, he heard Amos announce his arrival. Iris flung open the door, and her shimmering glow erased the darkness. She relieved him of one of his grocery bags and kissed his cheek. Jonah greeted him with, "I'm hungry. What'd you bring?"

Iris shook her head. "Jonah! Say 'hello' first and be nice."

"Hello first and be nice, Noah. What'd you bring?"

Noah laughed. "Snips and snails and puppy dog tails for you, young man."

"Puppy dog tails?" With a worried look, Jonah put his arm around Amos' neck.

"It's an old saying. I did bring some snails though. We call them 'escargot'. Maybe next time maybe I'll bring frog legs!"

"Ewww!"

Iris looked amused. "Well, you certainly are broadening a two-year-old's palate." She raised her eyebrows. "You mentioned news?"

"I was going to feed you first, but now I'd better tell you. Let's sit down." He arranged two of the kitchen chairs across from a third and lifted Jonah onto one. He motioned for Iris to sit. His usual rock-steady hands trembled.

"I have been offered a promotion, from Commis Chef to Chef de Partie. This means I'll get to learn all the stations of the kitchen. It's below the Sous Chef, which is below the Head Chef, Susan. Maybe in a year or so, when she opens her new restaurant, she'll consider me for Sous Chef there or in The Bistro." He smiled with pride. "Sometimes she even includes me in business discussions with Antoine, the Sous Chef. She has to be grooming me."

Iris leaned forward and covered his hands with hers, infusing energy into him. "Noah, that's great news. We're proud of you." Her shimmering aura surrounded her and pulled him inside.

Noah lowered himself onto one knee in front of her. *Now for the hard part.* "That's not all I wanted to say." He paused to gather his courage. "Iris, I hope you know how much I love you" He looked into those blue eyes. "Will you marry me?"

Jonah twisted in his chair. "You'd be my Daddy?"

"Yes, Jonah. I'd be your Daddy." *How I've wanted to say that!*

Iris' face went blank. She stared at him for what felt like a very long time before tears rolled down her cheeks.

Have I ruined everything?

"Mommy, why are you crying?" Jonah looked and sounded frightened.

Why did I get greedy and make a mess of this? Have I hurt her and Jonah? I should have told her I'm Phineas from the beginning. I should get up and go now.

He fought to hold back tears. The room swirled around him like an ocean whirlpool sucking him down.

Iris rescued him. "I love you too...Noah." She winked. "Yes, I'll marry you. I couldn't imagine marrying anyone else."

❖ ❖ ❖

"Excuse me."

Phineas felt a nudge on his shoulder. *Iris, I'm so happy...*

"Excuse me." Louder. A deep voice. An urgent tone.

Vigorous taps on Phineas' forearm. He shook his head and blinked. The young man in the Greyhound bus window seat leaned over him, distress in his features. "Stomach's upset. Musta' ate somethin' spoilt. Need to use the bathroom. Quick!" Phineas shot upright in time for the young man to bolt toward the back of the bus. A grimy backpack remained behind on his vacant seat. Outside the bus window, the sign promised Houston in 190 miles.

Phineas tumbled from imagined bliss into reality, into his personal disaster chaos. At least no one was directing Phineas from one tragedy to another. No one on the bus was threatening him. The quandary of Noah's papers, the record of that man's worldly existence, remained.

The young passenger was soon back in the aisle, an expectant look on his weary face. "Hey, you want the window seat? I may hafta go again."

Phineas reached down to feel the gym bag tucked under his seat. "Naw, I'll let you by."

Don't have to decide who I'll be yet, maybe not for hours, days...maybe weeks...Decide later.

He settled into his cushioned seat and closed his gritty eyes...*Rest now... Back to dreaming...to Iris...*

❧ ❧ ❧

Noah had been jogging almost daily before or after his kitchen shift. He first noticed Amos sniffing a tree, barely lifting an arthritic leg to lay down his scent. His face was frosted white. Noah scanned the benches nearby and recognized her profile. The early morning sun bestowed an extraordinary yet familiar golden aura over her. She was more stunning in shorts and t-shirt than he remembered from more than two years ago. She leaned into a stroller. He summoned his courage and approached cautiously. Amos growled and made as much of a charge as he was able.

Noah held out his hand and whispered, "Easy, Amos. Good boy." Amos halted and ambled to Noah then sniffed his feet. The old dog's tail started to wag, and he whimpered. Noah scratched behind Amos' ears. When Noah looked up, Iris stood and clutched a child to her chest.

She stared at him with the blue eyes from his dreams. "Who? Do I know you?"

"Iris, it's me, Phineas," He whispered, his head bowed. "Sorry for everything you've had to go through."

For what seemed like an eternity, she only stared. Noah remembered he now looked nothing like when he'd left her. He felt like escaping. "Maybe I was wrong to stay away. With the murder charges...it seemed best for all. Please forgive me. There's so much I've wanted to tell you."

"You sound like Phineas..." She took a step back. "Tell me something only Phineas would know. How did we meet?"

"The bag lady attacked you with her cigarette."

"You *are* Phineas." Her brow furrowed, then a full frown. She glared at him. "Well then, meet the son you abandoned. This is Jonah." She turned so Phineas could see the boy's face before he buried it in her cleavage. His hair was black. He had her blue eyes.

"I have a son? How?"

"How? *I* have to explain it to *you*? The night before Jezebel. The *one* time without a condom!"

Jonah exclaimed, "Condom."

Her frown eased into the beginnings of a smile. "He's been quite the talker lately. Hope he doesn't use that one in daycare." She lowered Jonah to the ground and reached in the stroller for a cloth sack. Jonah snatched it from her and began ransacking it.

Her smile faded. "Phineas, how *could* you? How could you stay away?" She looked and sounded furious.

Noah glanced furtively from side to side before whispering, "Iris, my name is Noah Waterson now."

"You're kidding. Did you make that one up?"

"Let's just say I was provided with the necessary documents."

"So, under what rock have you been hiding?"

"It's a really long story." *She looks too mad to unload his story on her now.* "Can you come back here tomorrow an hour earlier, and I'll tell it all to you? And I want to hear about you and Jonah. I think I should stay Noah. We should be careful." He took two steps back.

"I also have more to tell. For instance, I was recently officially declared a widow." Her stare became a glare. "Okay, I guess I'll see you here tomorrow...Noah."

A widow! Well, it had to happen. He began jogging, leaving them, wondering if, now that he was dead, they'd return.

⚜ ⚜ ⚜

Sunday morning took its time in arriving. Even after a full out Saturday in the Bistro's kitchen, sleeping was a challenge, interrupted by his exploring ways to reunite with Iris and become a father to Jonah.

First to arrive at their meeting place, he jogged up and down the trails nearby. *Has she changed her mind?* Then Iris was there, behind aviator sunglasses, pushing the stroller, Amos on leash.

"You don't know what it's like organizing with a toddler." She began hastily arranging toys and cardboard books on a blanket. "At least I'm not *two years* late."

That hurt. It wasn't easy for me either.

Noah positioned himself in front of her. "I'm just so happy to see you. I barely slept." She finally stood and tentatively hugged him. The familiar lavender fragrance. The feeling of her body against his. She pushed away from him before he was ready, before he could try to kiss her. He retreated a step and bent over to run his palm from Amos' head down his spine.

Jonah yelled, "Get me out!"

Iris lifted him from the stroller and onto the blanket.

Noah waved. "Hi Jonah."

"Hi." Jonah surveyed the blanket contents while hugging a stuffed whale.

Noah held Amos' collar and began scratching behind the dog's ear. "Want me to go first?"

Iris settled on the park bench. "Go ahead. You're probably more organized."

Noah sat on the bench across from her and recounted the horrible days in Baptist and the threats Angela had made. "When the newspaper reported that I was being charged with murder, I decided to remain Noah." He hoped she understood. "I couldn't inflict my misery on you and your mother—and I was terrified I'd spend the rest of my life in jail...I hoped they'd decide I'd died my last day at Baptist."

"What about all those things they said you did?"

"Those patients were going to die no matter what we could do. It was not euthanasia. I relieved their suffering."

She stared at him, stone-faced, waiting.

"Angela thinks God wants us to keep people alive until we no longer can, no matter how much they suffer. I did nothing wrong."

"And if you'd come back as Phineas?"

"Could have been a long and messy trial. Possibly prison for life."

He told her about the Astrodome, his start cooking, first in Houston and now back in New Orleans, and his simple new life. He patted his flat abdomen and bragged that he was finally physically fit. "And no pagers waking me up all night long. I have no desire to return to medicine. I'd rather prepare food."

"So, how'd you become Noah?"

"As the last of us were leaving Baptist, a John Doe passed away in the ED. He'd told me he had no family." Noah wiped sweat from his forehead. "He didn't need his IDs anymore."

"God, that's creepy."

"Seemed like a gift I should accept."

Iris handed Jonah one of his books. Noah folded his hands and waited until she sat upright. "I'm sure you have lots to tell."

Iris told Noah about the time with Sarah Jane at their Memphis motel and a visit from the New Orleans police. As they were moving back into the family home, Iris realized she was pregnant. The news about Phineas and Jezebel's destruction of New Orleans took its toll on Sarah Jane. She ate poorly and lost weight. Her cough worsened and, during a racking bout, Sarah Jane broke a rib. X-rays at the hospital showed the fracture, but also scars and pneumonia in both lungs.

"They found bad organisms in her mucous. They thought it might be TB and quarantined her at first. It wasn't TB. Something harder to treat."

Iris described how Sarah Jane had received weeks of intravenous antibiotics followed by pills, which took away her meager appetite. "Her weight fell below eighty pounds. One morning, I found her...passed away in her bed...cold to the touch." Iris dabbed at her eyes. "I was almost nine months pregnant then."

"Wish I had been there."

"I struggled. Matt helped with the funeral and took me to the hospital when I went into labor."

"I owe him. Where is he?"

"Boston."

"I need to ask. Do you and Jonah have enough money?"

Iris explained how Jezebel had temporarily shut down Tulane Hospital for several months, but administrators eventually called her back to work. They'd had Jerome's pension until Sarah Jane died. Then she and Matt had found a few stock certificates in Jerome's name, a modest cache for them to split while they discussed whether to sell the family home. Iris planned to live there for now.

"If Phineas was declared dead, did you file for the life insurance benefit?"

"My lawyer says we can do that now, but he isn't sure they'll pay...since no body was found."

"Iris, as much as I want to move back in right away, I should keep a low profile until we figure out how to get back together without calling attention to me. Phineas needs to remain dead. I hope we can all move far away from here together before long."

Iris abruptly lifted Jonah and settled him in the stroller, then scooped his toys and blanket into the cloth sack. "I don't believe I asked you to move back." She stood erect, white knuckles clenching the stroller's handle. "Much has happened. You were gone a *long* time. Phineas died. And now... *there's someone else.*" She turned and began hurrying back down the path she'd come from.

Noah felt like he'd been punched in the gut. He bent over to breathe.

⚜ ⚜ ⚜

A blow to his shoulder. The frigid air blew on his neck from the overhead vents on the Greyhound bus. He shivered.

The young man again. "Gotta get by. Hope this is the last time. Can't be much left."

Phineas stood in the aisle. "Where are we?"

"More'n halfway to Houston." The fellow traveler jogged to the back of the bus and disappeared into the bus's bathroom.

Who am I going to be? Phineas had been given the opportunity to start a new life. *Should I seize it?* Phineas extracted an index card and pen from his gym bag. He began making lists.

> If Phineas:
>> 1. reunite with Iris ASAP
>> 2. continue medical career?
>> 3. possibly lose medical license
>> 4. potentially stand trial
>> 5. possibly go to jail
>
> If Noah:
>> 1. Begin new life with the cash I'm carrying
>> 2. Evade legal charges
>> 3. New career cooking? Simplify life
>> 4. Find place to live
>> 5. Maybe Iris gets $1,000,000 insurance
>> 6. Maybe never get to be with Iris ever again

Never seeing Iris again clinched it. He would stay Phineas, and as soon as he got the Astrodome, he'd begin looking for her. The decision made, his tension dissolved.

When the young man took his seat again, Phineas closed his eyes. *Need to rest now...to rest...for what's ahead....*

When Phineas learned from his mother where Iris was, he left a message with the motel clerk. After the lengthy breakfast line at the Astrodome, he pulled on donated jeans and t-shirt and packed his dirty clothes in his gym bag. A line of barbers stood near the third base dugout and donated haircuts. Opting for a buzz cut, Phineas felt such relief to shed his thick, matted mop of greasy hair. At the stadium exit, he asked directions to the Greyhound station then marched through a steamy Houston until he was able to hail a cab. The bus ride took all day, then another cab ride. His excitement grew with each mile.

He arrived after midnight and begged the night clerk at the motel to call Iris' room for him. She appeared at the front desk in a t-shirt and shorts, Amos at her side. The now familiar golden aura surrounded both. She took a step back when Phineas approached.

"Phineas, is that you? What happened to your hair and beard?" The clerk put his hand on the phone. Amos sniffed Phineas' pant leg, then his hand, wagging his tail and whining with increasing intensity.

"It was so hot and sweaty, and such a greasy mess I just had to get rid of it. I'm looking forward to a long, hot shower."

"I know that voice and those eyes." She wrapped her arms around his neck. "Where did you get that shirt?"

"I should burn all *my* stuff, it's so nasty after the hospital."

She wrinkled her nose. "Maybe a shower and laundromat first."

The clerk apologized that the motel was full and all the cots in use as he stacked an extra blanket and towel on the counter. Phineas said he would be happy to sleep on the floor, that the floor was where he'd stolen his few precious naps in Baptist.

The first days Phineas, Iris, and Sarah Jane pored through newspapers and watched television news reports of Jezebel's devastation of New Orleans and surrounding areas. Phineas dutifully called police and reported that the John Doe in the emergency room was Noah Waterson, and that Phineas had left New Orleans with Mr. Waterson's identification papers during his sudden evacuation.

Then came television reports of the scenes at Baptist. Vivid descriptions of the chapel stacked high with decaying corpses, human and animal, blared hourly and horrified the public. The ghastly states of the deceased's corpses appalled their family members. Autopsies were being performed.

An ICU nurse claimed physicians administered lethal doses of medications to helpless patients. The District Attorney was investigating.

The maps of New Orleans they saw on the news suggested that Sarah Jane's home might have been spared from the flood, but that their own apartment was not.

❖ ❖ ❖

Phineas, Iris, and Sarah Jane again gathered around the television for the evening news. Sarah Jane picked listlessly at a takeout helping of cold barbecue and greasy fried okra. Amos gulped a can of Alpo and belched.

Iris pinched her nose. "Phew! Amos! You're going back on dry dog food."

A loud knocking startled them. Amos growled. Iris clutched Amos' collar as Phineas squinted through the door's peak hole. He opened the door and two Louisiana state troopers stepped inside.

"Are you Phineas Mann?"

"I am."

"You're under arrest for second degree murder. You have the right to remain silent..."

Phineas didn't hear the rest. The handcuffs, the long ride in the moonless dark, being fingerprinted and placed in a cell at 5 AM by ghoulish grinning guards. He learned that Baptist's administrators knew about his arrest when a hospital attorney, Jude Savant, showed up at the city jail before 8 AM to bail him out.

Sporting a light blue seersucker suit and yellow bow tie, Savant appeared fit, his black hair cut short and parted perfectly. The faint scent of smoldering cinders trailed him as he escorted Phineas to his firm's plush suite where he offered coffee and pastries, proclaiming, "we got electricity back last week." He closed the door to his personal office behind Phineas with a disturbingly loud thud. "We hoped we could beat the press photographers and save you a perp-walk. Baptist Hospital is committed to seeing you are well represented. If you're agreeable, we'll start building your defense."

Phineas swallowed hot coffee and tasted chicory. He felt the beginnings of heartburn. "All right. What's next?" He slouched in a leather chair, feeling small next to a monstrous cherry desk.

"I'll need to hear your version of the circumstances around the deaths of each of the patients you're charged with murdering."

"I documented everything in their charts. Who am I charged with..." He shuddered. "Murdering?"

"That's one of our problems. Their charts are useless."

"How can that be? They were in their racks after I wrote the death notes."

"The charts were found in standing water with no legible notes left."

"How could that happen? Did someone take them out of the racks?" Bewilderment and panic overcame Phineas.

"We have no way of knowing."

Did Savant just suppress a grin? Phineas learned he was charged with second-degree murder of four patients, ICU patients Chauncey Palermo and Mildred Daye, and the elderly, demented ward patients, Mr. Frederick and Mrs. Cormier. Savant informed him that two nurses and a family member had reported him.

"The charge is second-degree murder and not first-degree murder," Savant explained, "because the prosecution believes the public will be more likely to accept it." He waited for his words to penetrate. "Euthanasia is considered murder in Louisiana."

"I don't believe this." Phineas felt sour acid rise into his throat and placed his hand over his mouth. "I'm feeling sick." Jude Savant passed him a shiny brass wastebasket.

"I hate to make you feel worse, but you need to know that a second-degree murder conviction carries the possibility of life in prison at hard labor without the chance of parole." He leaned back, a legal pad and pen at the ready. "When you're ready, I need to hear what happened. Start at the beginning."

Phineas recounted every patient detail he could remember from the Baptist nightmare that had engulfed him. He tried to look defiant, as though that would help him. "There was no way to save them. They were all on death's door, and their suffering was awful. I had to ease it." Defiance dissolved into fear.

⚜ ⚜ ⚜

Phineas found Iris sitting in Sarah Jane's kitchen with her head in her hands. "D Z Moss called."

"And?"

She lifted her distraught face from her hands. Her mysterious encompassing aura had faded and shifted into red tones. Tears streamed down ashen cheeks. "He's been watching your trial, since his is next, and doesn't like how yours is going. He's hiring his own lawyer instead of using Jude Savant's firm. He thinks their goal is to protect the hospital, even if it means sacrificing you...Says they don't want people to start saying the hospital should have been better prepared. You on trial shifts the blame away from Baptist's administration." She sniffed and studied Phineas' eyes. "He also says *the DA* wants you to be a scapegoat to shift attention away from New Orleans and Louisiana's inadequate preparations and disaster response...Says the DA's coming up for re-election and wants to make a name for himself." Her tears splattered on the kitchen table, one after another.

Phineas took the seat across from her. "Wish he'd said something sooner. Closing statements are tomorrow."

She began sobbing. "I couldn't stand it if you went to jail. It would probably be that horrible Angola State Prison."

If Phineas weren't numbed by the shock of his predicament, he would have sobbed along with her.

⚜ ⚜ ⚜

The District Attorney delivered his final words at a measured pace as he looked into each juror's eyes. Phineas could only see the back of the DA's black suit as he moonwalked across the front of the jury box.

"And finally, ladies and gentlemen of the jury, I want you to consider that this man, who was supposed to heal, felt he could play God as he administered lethal doses of medications to helpless sick people. Who gave him the right to kill, to murder? I urge you to find him guilty as charged on all four counts of second-degree murder."

Angela's head bobbed up and down as she smirked at Phineas from the front row behind the prosecution's table. Her necklace caught the overhead light and reflected it at Phineas.

He struggled to keep his composure when he turned to see Iris' reaction to the DA's words. She was grimacing, head bowed. He turned to Jude Savant and whispered, "Hope you can better that."

Jude Savant passed him a note as he stood to address the Jury. Phineas unfolded it and read:

> *Try not to worry. If this doesn't go well, we'll file an immediate appeal.*
>
> *Jude S.*

Jude Savant stood before the jury and reviewed how each patient had reached a state from which they could not recover and then emphasized their suffering. He claimed that their deaths were inevitable, their fates out of the hands of their caregivers. He pointed out that the doctors had no way of knowing when rescue might arrive. Finally, he asked that Phineas not be judged as if his actions had taken place under normal hospital conditions. Relieving pain for the hopeless was all he could provide.

All Phineas heard was 'Blah, blah, blah' while he trembled under his dark grey suit.

⚜ ⚜ ⚜

Phineas and Iris waited in a small room off the courtroom for the jury to return. Jude Savant's office arranged for lunch to be delivered from K Paul's. Phineas opened cartons of jambalaya and unwrapped a baguette. The aroma of onions and sausage filled the air. He tore the bread and offered Iris half. By the time they were called back, they'd consumed only a few bites. Phineas stood and hugged a shaking Iris. His hands felt numb, his chest hollow. The smell of the offered lunch nauseated him. Was it his last meal as a free man?

"I love you so much, Iris."

"I love you, Phineas." Her face left a wet spot on his shoulder.

The jury filed back into their seats. The judge asked the foreman if they had reached a verdict. The foreman, a stout, gray-haired African American man stood. "Yes, Your Honor." The judge then read the names of each of the alleged victims.

"For the charge of murder of Chauncey Palermo?"

"Not guilty."

Phineas began to feel hope.

"...Mildred Daye"

"Not guilty."

"...George Frederick?"

"Guilty."

Hope was replaced with panic. The courtroom swirled. Phineas clutched the arms of his chair. Iris shrieked.

"...Louise Cormier?" the judge asked.

"Guilty, Your Honor." The foreman sat down.

Iris wailed once more, and Phineas turned to see her leap from her seat. "You can't. It's not fair!"

The courtroom exploded with spectators' chatter. The judge banged his gavel and announced, "Sentencing will be tomorrow." A grinning police officer approached a horrified Phineas with handcuffs.

Jude Savant put his hand on Phineas shoulder. "They need to hold you in the city jail overnight." Phineas stood reluctantly and held out his hands.

When the officer opened the cuffs, Phineas shoved him hard and bolted for the entrance. He pushed his way through the crowd, scanning his surroundings. Every pair of eyes focused on him, and every oval mouth uttered, "You!"

He snaked his way out the front door as shrill whistles split the air. He sprinted around the corner and zigzagged through city blocks, looking back every few seconds. He just kept running and looking back, running and looking back.

⚜ ⚜ ⚜

"Jesus!" Phineas shrieked.

He struggled to emerge from the dark place sleep had dealt. The evacuees seated around him were staring.

He blinked and rubbed his eyes. "Sorry. Where are we now?"

The young man next to him sat back and clutched his backpack. "Just outside Houston. Man, you gotta be havin' some crazy ass dreams. You been mutterin' and jerkin' the whole trip. Sayin' shit 'bout 'youth in Asia.'"

Phineas reached for his gym bag under his seat. "I haven't slept much in at least five days."

"We all tired, man."

Phineas couldn't recall ever having dreams so long and vivid, and one followed by another. Dreams to answer questions. Dreams to make critical decisions. He'd stay Phineas, and he'd act before the accusers came after him.

The bus exited the highway and proceeded along city streets, finally stopping in front of the Astrodome. He and his fellow travelers filed out and stretched weary muscles then found the back of a line at the entrance. Inside, he was directed to one of thousands of canvas cots arranged in long rows, each with a blanket. Cot #12 in row #12. *Should be easy to remember.* He wished the crowd wasn't too big to use the team's showers, so he could wash away dried sweat and the stench of lingering death. Phineas realized how hungry he was and found a line for food. Beef stew and canned corn had never smelled so good, like food did cooked over a campfire after a long hike.

Near the third base dugout, men and women were cutting evacuees' hair. The scene looked strangely familiar. And how his greasy scalp itched! When a chair emptied, its rotund barber asked, "What'll you have, Son?"

"Buzz cut. I'm sick of this mess."

"Excellent choice."

The air conditioning in the Astrodome invigorated his scalp and naked face. He spotted a woman with a clipboard. "Ma'am, where can I find a phone, please?" She pointed to a tunnel leading to the concessions area. Phineas found a line of tables, each with two phones and a volunteer monitoring them. He took his place in line. He figured the only sure thing would be to call his parents. His mother picked up after the first ring.

"Mom, I'm okay. I'm in Houston."

"Phineas! Oh my God! It's so good to hear your voice. Your father and I have been worried sick! The news reports have been terrifying."

"Mom, have you heard from Iris?"

"She's in Memphis in a Howard Johnsons. I've got her room and a phone number." He heard the phone clatter as she put it down then picked it up again. "Here it is. You have a pencil?"

"Wait a sec, Mom." The phone volunteer, a bald man with a handlebar mustache, held up a pen and pad. Phineas nodded and smiled his thanks. He took down the information. "Mom, it was worse than you heard on TV. I'll call as soon as I get to Memphis and tell you about it. Love you, Mom. Give my love to Dad."

"We love you too, Phineas."

He held up his index finger to the volunteer. "Found my wife. Just one more, please." Phineas' tried to steady his hand as he dialed Memphis. He heard, "Howard Johnson's. How can I help you?"

"This is Iris Mann's husband. I was told she's in room 223. Can you connect me please?"

A long pause. "No answer. Must be out."

"Please leave her a message. Tell her that her husband is in Houston, and I'll try to get a bus to Memphis tomorrow."

The volunteer accepted the pen back. "You have some place to go?"

"Yessir. Thank you."

"You're lucky."

❦ ❦ ❦

He arrived at the Howard Johnson's after midnight and an interminable bus ride. During the entire trip he either fidgeted or dozed. He had forgotten how different he looked until Iris took a step back and studied him. He wore a donated faded bowling shirt proclaiming "Holy Rollers" on the back and "Zeke" over the left breast pocket. Amos pushed his nose into Phineas' hand and whimpered.

"You don't look like the Phineas I left in New Orleans."

"I'm definitely Phineas...but not the same one you left."

Her embrace and kiss almost made up for his recent travails. The Kiss of Life, this time with him on the receiving end. She pinched her nose. "You sure don't smell like the Phineas I left."

Iris approached the night clerk. "Do you have another room, please?"

"Sorry. All full. The hurricane, you know." He shrugged. "I'll let you know if anything opens up."

They'd have to share the room with Sarah Jane. At least it had two beds. Sarah Jane opened the door and greeted him with a smile, a hug, and "Phineas! It's such a relief Jezebel didn't devour you. I declare—you've been shorn! And your shirt! Who is Zeke? Come in here. I want to hear *everything*."

❦ ❦ ❦

A firm hand gripped Iris' shoulder, then shook it. She rolled toward her mother and squinted up at her. Sarah Jane's lipstick formed a scarlet heart, and every hair was in place. Phineas snored softly next to Iris, his back to both women.

"I'm going for my breakfast." Sarah Jane mouthed a stage whisper. "Back in a couple of hours with breakfast for the two of you."

"What time is it?"

"Almost eight. You two enjoy your time without me. I'll be back after ten." Amos sat by the door, his leash in his mouth. "I'm taking Amos."

"Thanks, Mom."

Sarah Jane flashed a wry smile as she opened the door. "How else will I ever get to be a grandmother?"

Iris waited for the door to close. She reached across Phineas chest and lifted his shirtfront then ran her hand lightly across his stomach and down to his boxer shorts. Phineas rolled onto his back, blinked twice, and stared at her.

"Tell me this isn't a dream," he said quietly.

"This is *not* a dream."

"Where's your mother?"

"Breakfast. Back in two hours with ours."

"In that case, I bought three condoms before I got on the bus."

"We may have to get more after breakfast," Iris giggled as she snuggled closer.

⚜ ⚜ ⚜

The knock. 10:00 AM. "You two must have an appetite by now. I've got sausage biscuits and juice if you'll let me in."

Phineas and Iris rolled out of each side of the bed and pulled on jeans and tee shirts. Phineas slipped into the bathroom as Iris relieved her mother of two Hardees bags. Sarah Jane greeted Phineas' re-entry with, "Now that you two are reacquainted, I want to hear what happened to you, Phineas—after you eat, of course."

Phineas recited, minus the gore, the events of his hellacious week with as little emotion as he could. "I'll be surprised if there isn't more misery still."

Iris shook her head. "Wasn't that enough?"

"Remember that nurse, Angela, the one who wanted to join us at the

Christmas party and kept asking me to have you call her to get together?"

"Vaguely."

"Well, she said she's going to report D Z and me."

Sarah Jane's jaw fell. "What on earth for?"

"She believes that giving medications to ease suffering is euthanasia. I need to find a good lawyer right away." *One who has my interests first.*

"Why don't you wait to see if you need one?" Sarah Jane asked.

"We need to be ready when she causes trouble. I'm sure about this. It came to me in a dream."

Sarah Jane raised her plucked eyebrows.

Iris said, "Maybe if you slept more, Phineas, you'd get more answers."

Amos sat up, stared at the biscuit wrappers, and licked his chops. "Not for you, Amos." Iris crumpled the greasy papers and shoved them in the bag. "Phineas, you should call your dad. He'll know something about lawyers."

Phineas sat at the chipped laminate desk, with its phone and a Gideon's Bible, and located his father at work. He repeated his painful account of his time at Baptist during and after Jezebel.

"Dad, I need to find a good lawyer and don't want to use the hospital's lawyers. I've got to be prepared if there is fallout. It could get bad."

"Criminy, Phineas! Lemme ask my lawyer friend here in White River Junction to have him find out who you should talk to. Should be someone in New Orleans. I agree. No reason to wait on this."

"Thanks, Dad."

"And lemme know if you need money. I can always refinance the house."

Phineas winced. "I'll pay you back."

"We'll worry about that later."

"Give my love to Mom."

"And ours to Iris. Bye."

❖ ❖ ❖

After days of calling around, they located Simon O. Serine, Esq., a specialist in criminal law with a track record in high profile cases. Over the next two weeks, Phineas spent hours on the phone with him before the long drive to New Orleans. Simon had demanded and obtained copies of patients' records. He learned through contacts in City Hall that the DA was indeed considering charging D Z and Phineas with murder.

❧ ❧ ❧

As October arrived, Phineas, Iris, Sarah Jane, and Amos rode through the devastation between Memphis and Sarah Jane's house. High water mud lines circled houses and businesses. Soaked and ruined cars filled driveways. Amos sniffed loudly out the Corona's window until they rolled it up against the stink of mold and waste.

While Phineas met Simon in his recently reopened office, Iris and Sarah Jane inspected their homes. Sarah Jane's was internally intact and waiting for the power to be turned back on. The power company workers in the neighborhood assured them this was scheduled for that afternoon.

Water had risen to the ceiling before receding in Iris' and Phineas' apartment. Iris held her breath while she pried open a window. The odor of mold and rot triggered a wave of nausea, and she barely made it outside before she vomited on the sidewalk. There, she scraped muck off the goblet she had turned and fired in Chapel Hill.

After locating groceries, cleaning, and a hasty supper, an exhausted Phineas, Iris, and Sarah Jane gave into sleep, collapsing on unlaundered bed linens.

❧ ❧ ❧

It felt like a familiar bad dream when the police took Phineas away at 5 AM. Roused from sleep, he hurried to put on pants over his boxers. While Phineas was being read his rights and cuffed, a frantic Iris dialed Simon.

In her satin robe, Sarah Jane shuffled into the commotion. "You two better treat him well. He's a doctor, you know."

The officers stuffed him into the cruiser's back seat and slammed the door.

Phineas flinched at the sound of the precinct cell door clanging shut behind him. Simon's urgent bail arrangement only marginally mitigated the unpleasant hours of Phineas' incarceration, but he was grateful to learn he would at least be spared transfer to the infamous Orleans Parish Prison. Sarah Jane agreed to leverage her house against the $100,000 bail. Simon had prepared the paperwork to process, having anticipated the arrest.

They met early the next day at Simon's office. The morning sun highlighted prominent crow's feet and his sandy hair, suggesting Simon had spent many hours fishing on Lake Pontchartrain and the bayou. His oyster-colored poplin suit and Kelly-green silk tie were wrinkle free. He sported deck shoes, but shined wingtips were on standby behind him. A fly-fishing rod, absent its reel, leaned into a bookcase. Phineas pulled up a chair to the polished oak desk. Simon dropped the *Times-Picayune* in front of him.

BAPTIST DOCTORS ARRESTED FOR MULTIPLE MURDERS!

"We have work to do."

Phineas kept his focus on the newspaper. The subtitle read, 'ICU Nurse Reports Events to DA'. He frowned. "Why did she have to do this?"

Simon shook his head. "One can't know someone else's motivation, Phineas. Some Christians believe all life, no matter how miserable, is sacred; that death should only occur when God takes it despite all efforts, and anything less could be considered negligence, or even passive euthanasia."

"Simon, I'm Catholic. If life is sacrosanct, why did martyrs give up theirs?" Phineas raised his voice. "Don't New Testament Beatitudes command mercy? When is it euthanasia and not an act of charity, kindness, or mercy?"

Simon leaned into his chair and pressed his fingertips together. "Euthanasia is from Greek, meaning 'a good death'. I think we can agree none of the deaths at Baptist were 'good'. Passive euthanasia has been invoked and charges filed when care was not escalated, as in not placing someone on life support or performing CPR. In the cases of your patients, we'll need to remind the jury that technology was not available, and convince them, that even if it were, it would not have resulted in prolongation of a certain death."

"Aren't we supposed to be judged by a jury of our peers?" Phineas struggled to respond in a more even tone. "Will the jury be *my* peers? Will they be university trained specialists in critical care medicine?"

"No. Careful. Don't get all high and mighty." Simon opened a leather-bound volume to a bookmark.

"On our side is the recent Louisiana Natural Death Act. It states that healthcare professionals are not required to apply medically *inappropriate* treatments, even when patients and families have not made a declaration of their wishes. Active euthanasia, on the other hand, means the intent was to shorten life and is considered willful homicide. It is synonymous with a mercy killing." He closed the book. "Were the patients dying? Yes. Were their deaths hastened? Did you know them well? Did they have a say in their care? These are all questions that will be put to you."

Phineas clenched and unclenched his fists. "Yes. They were dying. Their deaths were inevitable and imminent. Without anything to ease suffering they might have lingered in Hell on Earth a bit longer." Anger merged with frustration, as he remembered. "Family members weren't there. I didn't know Mr. Frederick. He didn't know himself; he was so demented. So was Mrs. Cormier. The others, I knew. Did they have a say? None of us had a say in the conditions we worked under."

"Hey, I'm on your side, man. There's more. Baptist will try to protect itself and its administrators. They don't need you or D Z to work for them anymore, so your only value to them is to deflect blame for their half-assed preparations, especially for not having moved the electric switches out of the flood prone basement. That's what they *have to* be thinking. Throw you under the trolley—if they ever get that damn thing working again."

"Shit."

"Oh, it gets worse. You and D Z Moss in the news takes attention away from City Hall. Before your arrest, the mayor was taking serious heat for being poorly prepared for the disaster and for his glacial response. He'll be pressuring the DA to keep the focus on you doctors."

"You're just *full* of good news."

"I'm *still* not finished. I'm sure you have read that the governor is also being criticized. And the federal government's response. It goes *all* the way up."

⚜ ⚜ ⚜

Sarah Jane was the one who suggested that Iris was pregnant, even though Iris blamed her nausea and missed period on all their stresses and the city's smells.

"You're living in that body and married to a doctor, and *I* have to be the one to tell you you're pregnant? Gracious!" Sarah Jane yelled one morning from the hallway outside the closed bathroom door after she and Phineas heard Iris retch.

Startled, Phineas joined Iris in the bathroom and shut the door. "I thought we were always careful." And he'd been preoccupied with his own misery.

Iris wiped her mouth with a wet towel. "There was that one time...the night before Jezebel. You were half asleep."

The news of Iris being with child both elated Phineas and filled him with dread. What if he's in Angola Prison when she gives birth?

⚜ ⚜ ⚜

MAYOR LAMBASTS FEDERAL GOVERNMENT
REAGAN CRITICIZES STATES RESPONSE
REAGAN CLAIMS LEVEE BREAKS A SURPRISE
MAYOR SLOW TO ORDER EVACUATION
GOVERNOR WAITED TO ORDER STATE OF EMERGENCY

Phineas and Simon went through the deceased patients' chart copies word for word. Simon complimented Phineas on how he had compulsively documented every examination and decision despite the conditions and his fatigue. Phineas appreciated Simon's careful detailed work, but worried day and night about the rising sum of his legal costs. He felt certain these would escalate to amounts he couldn't handle. Then he worried about going to prison.

Simon scheduled almost daily testimony rehearsals, with Iris sitting in a corner, an extra pair of ears, an extra mind. Simon wielded his fly rod and poked its tip into Phineas' chest when his speech lacked the desired emotion. "Too mechanical, too unfeeling, Phineas."

Phineas deflected the rod tip with the back of his hand. "I'm not an actor. Shyness doesn't mean I don't care."

"Phineas, it's a short stroll from unfeeling to cold-blooded, and you know what word usually follows cold-blooded."

"Yeah."

"Let's do it over, with feeling. Pause now and then when you speak. Imagine something that makes you really sad."

Phineas closed his eyes and pictured himself in an orange jumpsuit with Iris sitting in a booth on the other side of a screen, six months pregnant. Her water broke all over the prison floor. She screamed and expelled a tiny male fetus, like Baby O'Hara from his medical school obstetrics nightmare. He watched through the screen as it took its last labored breath.

Simon tapped Phineas' knee with the fly rod. "Now, Dr. Mann, is it true you told Chauncey Palermo's nurses not to perform CPR if his heart stopped?"

Phineas softened his voice. "Yes, sir. That is true." He sensed a tear forming in the corner of his eye.

"Why wouldn't you try to save him?"

"If his heart stopped, it would be because of the massive air leak from his lung. We had no way to stop the leak. No amount of CPR could bring him back." He felt the tear roll over his cheek and tasted its salt in the corner of his mouth.

"Better."

✤ ✤ ✤

As the soggy January day's light began fading, the car door shut in the driveway before the screen door slammed. Phineas stood at the sink and hurried to make a bouquet of rosemary, thyme, and chives, while Iris peeled off her dripping raincoat and plopped down at the kitchen table, her legs splayed. She sighed. "I'm whipped. There's just so much to do. I'll be glad when all the other social workers are back on the job."

Phineas presented the herbs. Iris lifted her eyebrows. "What's this?"

"From the garden."

"Gee, thanks. Um, you have dirt caked under your fingernails?"

"And we also have greens and radishes."

"What happened to my surgically scrubbed husband?" She looked him up and down. "You have blood on your jeans. And what are all those shiny things?"

"Fish scales."

"So, Finman, are you going to share with me why you're covered with fish scales?"

"I was at the fishmongers' to get dinner. Simon recommended a place called Castnet."

"Uh huh. And were you attacked by a school of dead fish?" A tired, but playful smile.

"They let me fillet my own fish while they watched and gave pointers."

"Quite a mess from one fish."

"I kept going. They had a load to do, so Pierre, the manager, let me help."

"Kind of him." Her eyelids were drooping.

"He gave me ten bucks and didn't charge me for our fish."

"Well, that's something."

"You're bringing home a paycheck, and Sarah Jane has your dad's pension." Phineas looked at the floor. "I'm not contributing. I'm just a drain."

Iris squeezed his hand. "I don't think the house has ever been cleaner. Mom and I appreciate that, and you taking care of meals. Mom is finally gaining weight." She released his hand and sniffed her fingers. "You smell like fish."

"It's hard just sitting, waiting. I've never done that."

Iris hoisted herself to her feet. "Time for a shower."

"Me or you?"

"We both could use one. Then I want to close my eyes before dinner. Did I mention I'm whipped?"

⚜ ⚜ ⚜

Nights only worsened for both. Iris would lie on her side and fidget until she found a comfortable position, then Phineas drifted off, only to be jolted awake by bizarre dreams imagining Angola Prison or the hot, dark wards of Baptist during Jezebel. The beam of his headlamp illuminated dark hallways with corpses floating toward him. Angela and her silver cross disappeared and reappeared around corners and through doorways. One night, Phineas awakened Iris with his hands on her head, examining her neck for stiffness, though he was sound asleep.

Sirens on the city streets made him sit up and reach for a nonexistent pager.

⚜ ⚜ ⚜

Phineas jogged toward Audubon Park in a light afternoon drizzle. He was generating enough heat to tolerate the cold air that penetrated his hooded sweatshirt. A bumper sticker, shaped like a fish, brought him to an abrupt halt.

RELEASE PHINMANN

What!? Smaller print read 'Phineas Mann MD Legal Defense Fund 504-798-2100'. What's going on? Who did this?" He started running again. Another one. This one was a square with bars.

FREE D Z
D Z Moss MD Legal Defense Fund 504-798-2101

Another bumper, another fish.

Before Phineas prepared the red snapper fillets for dinner, he dialed Simon. "Simon, what do you know about bumper stickers with my name and a number for a legal defense fund?"

"Heard about them from my secretary. She called the number and confirmed that any contributions would indeed go to your defense. I'm all for it."

"Seems out of the blue."

"Accept any help offered. See you tomorrow."

Over dinner, Phineas brought up the bumper stickers. Iris shrugged. "Haven't seen one yet. I'll check out the hospital parking lot tomorrow."

Sarah Jane appeared amused. She opened the evening edition of the *Times-Picayune* to Page 3 and held it up.

LEGAL DEFENSE FUND CREATED
FOR BAPTIST HOSPITAL DOCTORS

Phineas gestured for her to pass the paper to him and eagerly read. The article told readers that many, including physicians, felt the Baptist Hospital doctors were victims getting a raw deal, and that some judged Phineas' and D Z's efforts as heroic during the Jezebel tragedy.

For the first time in recent memory, Sarah Jane expressed pride, as she said it had only taken a few phone calls to make it happen. Phineas imagined the scene as she recounted the conversation with Simon.

Simon's secretary would have cracked open his office door. "You have a Sarah Jane Babineaux calling. Should I put her through?"

Simon would have searched his memory before recalling that she had put her house up against Phineas' bail. "Absolutely." He would take off his reading glasses before picking up the phone. "Simon Serine here. How are you, Mrs. Babineaux?"

"Call me Sarah Jane. I'm fine, but I need you to use that brain of yours in another direction."

"You have my full attention...Sarah Jane."

"That's better. Let me first tell you that Iris and Phineas appreciate everything you're doing for them."

"They deserve my best."

"Right. And I know you're putting in a lot of hours on his case."

"It's a complicated one."

"Well, Simon, we're about out of money, and we don't want you to have to cut back on working for him. His Daddy's talking about putting a second mortgage on his house."

"I see. Sarah Jane, my office will continue to do everything we can for Phineas. We know he'll be good for whatever he owes...eventually."

"If you keep him out of jail."

"That would be best for both of us." Simon would don his spectacles before flipping through his Rolodex. "Let me suggest an idea."

"I'm listening."

"A legal defense fund that folks on our side can contribute to. I can't be the one to create it. It would look like I'm self-serving."

"Well, how would *I* do that?"

"I'm going to give you the name of a PR firm that might help you set it up, promote it, and run it for a very modest percentage. Got a pencil?"

A quarter page ad at the bottom of page 3 displayed the phone numbers and address of the defense funds. A photo displayed the bumper stickers that would be mailed out in exchange for every donation. A list of New Orleans shops that were taking donations and passing out the stickers was printed below.

❧ ❧ ❧

Weeks later in his office, Simon handed Phineas a letter. "This came yesterday."

> *Dear Mr. Serine,*
>
> > *Thank you for taking my call recently.*
> > *I understand that it could weaken his case if the prosecution should find out that he spoke with a psychiatrist while a medical student, even if I were to insist he was sane, well-adjusted and non-violent. He actually demonstrated strong empathy for his patients.*
> > *If I can help with Phineas' case in any way, please reach out to me. He was an excellent student at Tufts and is a fine human being.*
> > *I have let the Dean of the Medical School know about Phineas' legal fund. He told me that he'd let our faculty know how to support Phineas. He is in our thoughts and prayers.*
> > *Yes, prayers.*
>
> *Ian MacSweeney MD*

"Phineas, it's possible that the DA might try to use your conversations with Dr. MacSweeney against you, so we'll keep those to ourselves."

"Nothing the DA'd do would surprise me."

"But on a positive note, your legal defense fund has been growing steadily." Simon offered a hopeful smile.

"Finally, some good news."

"I hear through the grapevine that a lot of doctors have your back and are cutting checks. And I'm seeing your fish bumper sticker all over town."

"Not exactly the way I want to be famous." Phineas had never desired the burden of fame.

❖ ❖ ❖

Phineas picked up the kitchen phone on the third ring. "Hello?"

"Phineas, it's Simon. We have a date."

"For?"

"Your jury trial. Wednesday, the 12th of February."

Phineas' legs wobbled. He fell into a kitchen chair. "What...what do we do next?"

"Come to my office first thing tomorrow. We should rehearse your testimony again."

Phineas grimaced. *More rehearsals.* "Okay. See you then."

"And I've arranged for expert and character witnesses."

"Who?"

"After he reviewed your well documented records, the chief of Pulmonary at Tulane agreed."

"It's good news that we have someone of his stature in New Orleans."

"And your former chief Dr. Kornberg said he'll have his secretary block those dates, so he can help you as both an expert and character witness."

"Wow! Thanks." *Glad I worked hard for him.*

"Thank me when this is all behind you."

Dr. Kornberg. Phineas felt honored that Dr. Kornberg would do this for him. "Simon?" Painful emotions overran his transient elation.

"What's on your mind, Phineas?"

"Shame. Him seeing me in this mess. Embarrassment and shame."

❖ ❖ ❖

60 MINUTES TO EXPOSE BAPTIST HOSPITAL DURING JEZEBEL

At breakfast, Phineas startled as he unfolded the *Times-Picayune* and read the headline announcing that the *60 Minutes* television planned an episode addressing the Jezebel disaster at Baptist Hospital, and that it was to air the Sunday before the beginning of his murder trial.

Simon called first thing that morning. "Phineas, *60 Minutes* could work for you, if we do it right. A trial in the court of public opinion will give you an additional chance to tell your story the way *we* want it told. We'll make the power of the media work for us."

※ ※ ※

Knowing Simon competed for the show's producers' ears, Phineas threw himself into rehearsing responses to likely questions from the legendary host, Morley Safer. Simon reported that he had let Safer know that Iris labored as a social worker to repair the disruption Jezebel had wrought on New Orleans, and that she was with child. And that Phineas had willingly returned to New Orleans, that he had chosen to *not* become a fugitive.

Simon also recounted his meetings with the coroner, where he had raised as many uncertainties as he could, planting seeds of doubt. He had asked the coroner how he could make *any* definite conclusions when the bodies had undergone so much decay over the many days in the extreme heat? What did drug levels mean in dehydrated, rotting tissue?

After they concluded one afternoon's work, Simon arranged the case folders in a neat pile. "Phineas, the District Attorney is an elected office. Michael Noble would not want the public to turn against him. *60 Minutes* is a huge risk for his re-election." He leaned forward over his desk. "There is also a rumor he is considering running for Attorney General of the State of Louisiana. He'll try to have the show blacked out locally. We're fighting that."

※ ※ ※

After another grueling morning of practice interviews and more pokes with the fishing rod, Simon, Phineas, and Iris found a table near the window in The Bistro, the workplace from Phineas' dreams. The sun provided welcome heat over his back. Iris declared a craving for red beans and Andouille sausage and gnawed impatiently on a baguette while she waited for her meal. Phineas and Simon had barely started on steaming bowls of turtle soup when Phineas sensed a presence behind him. A shadow eclipsed his own on the table. Iris clutched her cloth napkin to her mouth and glared at the window. The Bistro door burst open, and she positioned her hands protectively over her abdomen. "What do *you* want?" she growled, rabid hostility in her voice.

Phineas startled. *Where is this coming from?* He turned toward the door.

Angela stood at the entrance, her dark mane framing her round, youthful face. A black cape concealed her full figure.

Simon placed his hand firmly on Iris' forearm. "Ms. Portier, you're looking well. What can we do for you?"

Angela remained silent, her lips pressed together. She scanned from Simon to Iris to Phineas.

Simon continued, "We hope, after you have reflected on the events you shared with Dr. Mann, that you have reconsidered your earlier statements."

A hint of a smile formed in the corners of Angela's mouth. "You should enjoy this fine food while you can, Dr. Mann. It won't be nearly as good where you're going—and you won't have your snooty wife!"

Iris pushed away from the table and snarled, "Bitch!" but Angela was already retreating through the entrance door.

Phineas stared at Iris, then his soup.

Simon cleared his throat. "Phineas, when we get back to the office, I want you to again tell me *everything* you know about Angela Portier. Your best chance to come out of this is for us to bring her down."

"I will, but you really should talk to Hilary, her head nurse. She hired her and knows her story. She told me once that Angela was young when she lost her father, and that ever since then she has blamed the doctors for giving up on him...that they wouldn't keep him alive long enough for the miracle cure she'd prayed for."

⚜ ⚜ ⚜

Phineas bowed his head as they left Simon's office. "I don't think I did so well."

Iris squeezed his hand. "Safer really grilled you, but you had some good moments, like why you came back..."

He was grateful for the warmth in her grip. "When he asked me what I did to prepare Baptist for Jezebel, I had no good answer."

"That wasn't your job." She let his hand go and jabbed his chest with a finger. "It was the hospital administrators'. And how could you have worked any harder?" Her voice softened. "At least I got to tell him how much you were working, that you hardly slept and were paged over and over for months without any breaks."

Simon joined them in the hallway in a pressed seersucker suit, purposed to resemble a classic Southern lawyer. "I'm going to grab Morley Safer while they pack up." He ran his fingers front to back through his sandy hair. "Phineas, you had some really good responses that could help our case. Depends on which ones they use."

Phineas shook his head. "Wish I had a better feeling about this. Prison scares the shit out of me."

Simon put his hand on Phineas' shoulder. "I bet Morley will lend me his ear a bit longer if I tempt him with the 800-dollar bottle of Pappy Van Winkle bourbon I keep in my desk for such occasions." He grinned mischievously. "It'll give me a chance to prepare him for his interviews with Justin Jordan, the coroner, the DA, and *especially* with Angela Portier. We got interviewed first, and that's our opportunity."

"I hope there's magic in that bottle." Phineas tried to return the smile. "And your offer doesn't backfire."

❧ ❧ ❧

Phineas glanced at his watch. 5:59. "Almost time for *60 Minutes*." He lowered himself onto the sofa next to Iris and across from their 19-inch Zenith.

Sarah Jane dragged a kitchen chair to a spot as close to the screen as she could be without blocking their view. "Wish we had a color TV."

The ticking stopwatch filled the TV screen.

Angela's youthful face appeared. "I observed Dr. Moss and Dr. Mann giving narcotics and sedatives that preceded patients' deaths."

Then Morley Safer, in a dress shirt with its collar open, leaned toward the screen. "ICU Nurse, Angela Portier, has claimed that two doctors murdered helpless Baptist Hospital patients during five horrendous days after Hurricane Jezebel." His firm baritone voice and unwavering focus compelled the viewer to cease all else and pay attention.

Phineas groaned and closed his eyes. The other *60 Minutes* hosts introduced their segments on the space shuttle Challenger disaster and Bishop Desmond Tutu. Sarah Jane lowered the volume for the McDonald's and Advil commercials. Then, "he's back."

Safer introduced "Jezebel Ravages Baptist Hospital" with images of breeched levees and flooded streets, the chaos at the Superdome, the looting, people clinging to rooftops, and helicopters and boats evacuating weary and terrified citizens to the I-10 cloverleaf. He reviewed details of the preparations and response by the city of New Orleans, the state of Louisiana, and the federal government. The mayor and governor appeared in clips of press conferences in the aftermath, images that would forever link their faces to the tragedy.

The camera focused on the neighborhood around Baptist. Phineas relived the scenes of water lapping at Baptist's Emergency Room entrance, smashed windows, hallways with ankle deep water, piles of soaked linens and trash, and toilets overflowing. The door to the chapel was closed, bright yellow police tape crossing it. Safer described it as the "makeshift morgue," found stacked high with decomposing human and animal corpses.

Baptist Hospital CEO Justin Jordan was the first interview presented. Safer opened it with, "I understand you were on vacation in Europe when the hurricane hit Baptist."

Justin Jordan squirmed. "I came back—as soon as I learned how badly we were affected—by Hurricane Jeze-Jezebel."

"But not when you heard of Jezebel's approach?" Jezebel rolled off Safer's tongue like syrup drizzled over a stack of pancakes.

Justin Jordan evaded the probe and pivoted. "I and the Baptist administrative team helped with the city's recovery efforts in every way we could. For example, we were among the first to fund a mobile clinic."

"But what about preventive measures?" Safer asked. "Why was your hospital so devastated, more than others? Weren't you prepared for a disaster?"

"Our disaster protocols were laid out in manuals."

"When was the last time you performed a rehearsal?"

Justin Jordan inserted two fingers under his collar and tugged. "We schedule them every two years. The date was coming up."

"Hmm...And what was your strategy for power loss?"

"The generators."

"They failed early in Jezebel. Why did you still have circuits in the basement, where they were vulnerable to flooding?" Safer appeared astonished.

"Moving them is a high budget item. Other expenses had taken precedent." His voice trailed off.

Next was Lida, who recounted the horrible predicaments that had led to difficult decisions. She described the misery they'd functioned under day after day. "You can't imagine the heat, how tired we were, the smell, darkness...and the *wailing. Oh my God! The constant wailing...*". She pulled a handkerchief from her breast pocket and dabbed at tears rolling down her cheeks.

Then Father Paul painted vivid verbal pictures of the nightmare they endured following Jezebel. He praised the dedication and courage of the Baptist staff and attempted to conclude his interview with, "I counseled the physicians and nurses that God did not want them to do *anything* to hasten anyone's demise. I counseled them to have faith in the Lord."

"Did you personally witness doctors giving narcotics before patients died?"

"No, Sir."

"Did you watch these patients die?"

"I administered last rites after death."

Phineas began to recognize Simon's careful planting of subtle suggestions, seeds germinating in Safer's fertile mind.

District Attorney Michael Noble looked uncomfortable under the bright lights and twice used the sleeve of his black suit to wipe his shiny forehead. He explained that the reports from Baptist Staff demanded his office investigate, and the findings were sufficient to pursue the charges.

Safer leaned forward. "But second-degree murder? That seems extreme for doctors caring for patients during a disaster. Is the public aware that a guilty sentence can mean life in prison at hard labor for two dedicated doctors?"

"That's the only acceptable charge. If it's found that they committed euthanasia—which is illegal in Louisiana and the rest of these United States—and by the way, hard labor can include working in the prison infirmary."

"You would take Dr. Mann away from his wife and baby?"

Noble shifted in his chair. "If he's found guilty by a jury of his peers."

Safer scanned his note pad. "I understand you're considering running for Attorney General of Louisiana."

The camera came in for a close up. Noble turned to look into its lens. "We're exploring the possibility." He swallowed, stared, then remembered to smile.

"And your position as District Attorney is an elected one."

"Of course."

"So, winning a guilty verdict could give you favorable press."

"Just doing my job." Said like Noble referred to a routine chore.

"And losing your case might do the opposite. Lots at stake for you here."

Noble cleared his throat and fidgeted. "Just doing my job."

"Thank you, Mr. Noble."

Sarah Jane threw her satin slipper at the screen. "That's what he calls his *job*? The miserable worm!"

Dr. Kohler, the county coroner, did not appear to be a man who enjoyed public appearances, but someone in a career that allowed him solitude. His brown suit was rumpled, and he alternated studying the floor and Safer through black-rimmed glasses.

"As coroner, you were tasked with the autopsies."

"The bodies were transported to our morgue where I performed postmortem examinations."

"Please describe the condition of the bodies."

"Their tissues had deteriorated terribly during the several days of heat. It was a difficult task."

"Did the condition affect your ability to draw conclusions?"

"Possibly, at times."

"And you measured drug levels?"

"As well as we could."

"Could conditions have affected your measurements?"

A shrug. "Possibly...Perhaps. That's hard to answer. There's no way to know."

"Thank you, Dr. Kohler."

Phineas hadn't previously seen Head ICU Nurse Hilary made up and dressed to the nines. He commented to Iris that medicine might lose a nurse if a talent scout were watching. Safer asked Hilary about her years of ICU experience.

"I've been a nurse for fifteen years, almost all of them in ICU care."

"Do you think Dr. Mann could have prepared the ICU better for Jezebel?"

"He did everything humanly possible for us, including reviewing actions to take in the event of power loss. No one could have worked harder than he did."

Hilary's clipped British accent lent extra credibility to her assertions the staff and physicians performed optimally and appropriately for the circumstances. Her appearance and voice were steady and convincing. "I was directly involved in the care of two of the patients who died in the intensive care unit. They were dying and couldn't be saved. The doctors could only try to ease their suffering."

"You don't believe the doctors performed euthanasia?"

"Not even close."

"Thank you, Hilary," Phineas whispered. "Here's Ava." *Hope she has it together during this.*

Iris placed her hand on his knee. "She looks—um, colorful."

Ava's glossy black hair tumbled over her blouse, unbuttoned at the top. Her eye shadow had been liberally applied, and vivid tattoos escaped from her open collar.

Safer flipped a page on his notepad. "Ava Jones, you worked with Dr. Mann as a respiratory therapist. How would you describe his patient care?"

"Thorough and smart. He worked really hard."

"I understand he took care of your husband."

Her head jerked back. "I...I asked him to."

"How did your husband die?"

Ava lifted a sleeve to her face, smudging mascara. "He had a malignancy throughout his lungs. He'd reached a terminal stage when I finally got him to see Dr. Mann."

Safer offered a box of tissues. "What did Dr. Mann do for him?"

She pulled out a handful and pressed them into her eyes. "He made the diagnosis then arranged radiation and drainage of fluid from around his lung."

"And later on?"

"He tried to help him stay comfortable at the end."

"Did Dr. Mann provide him with narcotics?"

"Adam needed them. He was suffering constantly."

"You continued to work?"

"I did have to take some time off, but then Dr. Mann and my co-workers helped me get back on track. My work was important to my husband, Adam. He was proud of me."

Safer introduced D Z Moss and announced that his trial for second-degree murder was to follow Phineas' trial. D Z Moss described his role as chief of staff. He painted a graphic picture of the patient wards and how little they could do to diagnose and treat. He explained how the heat and lack of power and supplies led to the deterioration of patients. He defended his system of categorizing patients by category based on their chance of survival. "The worst possible outcome would have been patients with favorable prognoses dying due to delays, while terminal patients took priority. These were difficult and agonizing decisions."

The stopwatch ticked and showed 19 minutes. CBS News headlines on the Philippines election and rioting in Haiti flashed before a three-commercial break during which Phineas concentrated on slowing his breathing, calming the pounding pulse in his head. More loud ticking from the TV. His own face now filled the screen, and the pounding roared back.

Safer introduced him as the ICU Director and the defendant in the upcoming trial, accused of four second-degree murders. Phineas felt grateful for his rehearsals with Simon, even the fly rod pokes. He'd been able to maintain a caring and professional demeanor throughout Safer's probing, and on screen he looked more self-assured than he now felt sitting in Sarah Jane's living room.

Iris murmured, "You look good."

Safer furrowed his brow and said, "I'm told that you hadn't had a day off in the six months before Jezebel."

"Yes, Sir. That's correct."

"How could that happen?"

"I lost my cross coverage."

Safer still looked puzzled. "Cross coverage?"

"Another doctor in my specialty to cover my patients while I'm not on call."

"And how long did you plan to continue like that?"

"Justin Jordan, the CEO, said they were trying to find help for me."

"Was there any progress on that front?"

"As he explained it, there's a shortage of specialists in pulmonary and intensive care medicine."

Safer leaned forward. "Could those months of fatigue have affected your judgment and actions after Jezebel?"

Phineas kept an upright posture; displaying the confident body language he'd rehearsed. "I don't believe so. I'd had a good night's sleep before I went in to cover during Jezebel. I was no more tired than the other doctors."

Phineas' answers to Safer's questions painted vivid images of the night of Jezebel's destruction followed by the challenges of caring for patients in the heat, darkness, and misery of the hurricane's wake. Phineas recounted his escape in Malachi's boat on the last day. "I'm glad he came along when he did. The sun was setting."

"You came back to New Orleans when you could have become a fugitive. You even carried another man's identification. Why?"

"I was the only doctor left at Baptist when he died in the emergency room. There was no one to give his papers to."

"Did you consider staying away?"

Phineas looked straight into the camera, like Simon had coached. "I couldn't leave my wife, and I had done nothing wrong."

Safer posed a final question. "Your duty was to care for these patients. Tell us your reasons for giving them narcotics and sedatives when they were so unstable?"

"Mr. Safer, when these patients' records are reviewed, they will document that their deaths were imminent and inevitable when they received these medications. The conditions under which we tried to care for them prevented any interventions that might have helped at an earlier time. And we had no indication of evacuations coming." He blinked and took a deep breath. "They were at a stage where even a fully functional intensive care unit might have only briefly prolonged their deaths. All we could offer at that point was relief from suffering...and they were suffering mightily. To have done less would have been unkind and inhumane."

The tension in Phineas' spine melted. He slouched into their living room sofa's pillows and let out a long slow exhale. Iris patted his knee. "You looked good. Sounded good."

Sarah Jane's head swiveled toward them. "Shhh! She's on!"

Angela's long, thick hair cascaded over a black suit jacket. A silver cross sparkled on a chain over her white silk blouse. The months after the hurricane had not been kind to her. She'd gained considerable weight, and puffiness under her eyes made her look like she hadn't slept.

Safer gave viewers a moment before he asked, "You were the one who called the District Attorney and are their key witness. Why did you claim that doctors murdered patients at Baptist?"

"Because I observed Drs. Moss and Mann giving narcotics and sedatives that preceded patients' deaths. They put in the orders to give those drugs, but I wouldn't do it. I told them they would have to give the drugs themselves."

"And you saw them administer these medications?"

"Yes."

"Which drugs?"

"Mostly morphine. Some Ativan, a sedative." An edge in her voice, as if the drugs were pure evil.

"I understand you are not allowed to give us specifics about individual cases. Were these patients critically ill?"

"Yes."

"Were they suffering?"

"Yes."

"Were they likely to recover?"

"They might have had a chance, if we could get them to a functioning hospital." She raised her voice, like she was pleading.

"Was there an indication that their evacuations were arranged at the time these drugs were given?"

"We were waiting to hear."

"But you had no indication their evacuations were scheduled?"

She shifted in her seat. "No."

"And as it turned out, it would have been days in some cases before they could have been evacuated, if they could have survived that long."

She uncrossed her legs, leaned forward, and sipped from a glass of water on the table next to her. "As it turned out."

"So, you believe the pain medicines should have been withheld or minimized to avoid any risk of shortening their lives, even if the patients had to endure horrible pain?" Safer's last words sounded incredulous.

"Thou shalt not kill! God decides when someone dies. We don't. We should keep his children alive until we no longer can." She was almost shouting.

Safer glanced at his note pad. "Well. Was there anything else that troubled you?"

"He was in his office with Ava Jones when we lost all power."

"*You* also went to his office. What makes you think she was there for any reason other than to alert him?"

"Because of how he looked...and the way *she* is."

Safer stared at Angela, creases scoring his forehead. "You had been a nurse for one year when you were assigned to work during Hurricane Jezebel. Is that correct?"

"Actually, fourteen months, all in intensive care—and I *volunteered* to work the hurricane."

"Why did you decide to become a nurse?"

"I spent a lot of time in hospitals with my father when I was a teenager." She sniffed and blinked. "Before he passed away."

"I'm sorry. That must have been hard on you."

"What was hardest was dealing with all the doctors who kept telling me he was dying—and wasn't going to get better. They gave up on him." Her voice had risen to an angry crescendo, and she glared at him as if she also blamed him.

"And you thought he could get better?"

"If the doctors had kept him alive long enough. *Miracles can happen!* Why shouldn't *we* have gotten one? Why not *us*?" She leaned closer to Safer, the whites of her eyes fully revealed.

"I'm sorry for your loss, Ms. Portier." He spoke gently. "Thank you for speaking with us."

He turned to speak to the camera. "Dr. Phineas Mann will be tried for multiple murders this Wednesday for his actions in Baptist Hospital during the horror following Hurricane Jezebel."

Angela's piercing voice pulled the camera back to her. "My Daddy deserved a miracle! All patients should be given a chance for a miracle!"

Safer glanced at her and nodded once. "We can talk more in a few minutes, Ms. Portier. Thank you again." He stood and stepped toward the camera. "We should ask whether it is fair to try someone in a municipal criminal court when the setting was that of a war zone?"

Behind him, Angela had raised her sleeve to her eyes. "Anyone can have a miracle. Doctors shouldn't ever give up!" She began sobbing, her shoulders heaving. She stepped toward Safer and was intercepted by a stagehand.

Safer raised his voice. "We should also ask whether the charges against Dr. Mann are to distract from inadequate preparation and response by the hospital, and by the city, state and federal governments that contributed to the conditions medical caregivers had to work under and patients had to endure. Is District Attorney Michael Nobles being pressured to pursue these charges? Are these physicians being made scapegoats?"

The Zenith's screen shifted to soiled and wrinkled sheets, a stretcher parked in water several inches deep, and a dark and deserted hospital hallway. The camera feed left the ward to gray water with floating debris abutting the emergency entrance. Then the screen flashed views of the entire hospital from above, its battered structure becoming increasingly distant, as the floodwaters of the entire city and surrounding areas a sparkling sunset.

Sarah Jane turned the volume down on the ticking stopwatch. "That pitiful young crackpot is the one causing all this mess?"

Phineas answered the telephone after the second ring. Simon's voice was uncharacteristically animated. "You looked good, sounded good, Phineas! And Angela's meltdown has to take the wind out of the prosecution's sails. Oh man! I was worried the DA might be able to get the show blacked out in New Orleans at the last minute. This will really help get the city behind us."

"Let's hope so." Phineas allowed himself a flicker of quiet celebration.

"We start first thing tomorrow with jury selection. I'll see you at the courthouse."

Celebration over. "When does Dr. Kornberg arrive?"

"I've been on the phone with him. He gets in tonight. We're putting him up in Le Pavillon."

"Thanks for calling, Simon. See you tomorrow." Phineas unraveled a knot in the cord before he hung the phone on the wall.

Iris pressed her stomach against his back. It bestowed a soft kick.

"The three of us will get through this, Phineas."

The aroma of sausage, eggs and potatoes with onions brought Iris out of her dream. She had been back in the animal shelter with Amos staring at her from a cage with "take me home" eyes. She must have said his name before she awakened. He pushed the door open with his nose and scrambled to her bedside. She sat up on the edge of the bed and buried her face in his neck fur before she shuffled to the bathroom.

"At least we're still a pack this morning, Amos." She shook out and brushed her tangled hair, and tied the belt of her robe before she entered the kitchen and pleaded to anyone who'd listen, "I need coffee."

Sarah Jane was already dressed, her hair and make-up perfect. She swallowed a forkful of eggs and sipped coffee. "Better eat a good breakfast. There's no tellin' when we'll get lunch."

Phineas' parents, Norris and Maria Mann ate their breakfast silently. Their arrival yesterday for the trial had led to late bedtimes. Norris' lanky frame slouched in his only suit: a charcoal one he'd let slip had previously been for weddings and funerals. His bald scalp reflected the overhead light. Maria, tiny beside him, sat close in a new navy dress. Gray hairs had flecked her black curls since Iris last saw her.

Iris greeted them. "I was hoping to show you around New Orleans under better circumstances. First a hurricane, now *this*..." Phineas set a cup of coffee in front of her.

Maria dabbed at her lipstick, leaving a burgundy smudge on the cloth napkin. "We'll do that after Phineas is okay. He will be. He has to be."

Norris placed his hand on hers.

Phineas arranged plates of his cooking at Iris' and his places and took his seat. Amos paced back and forth, the clicking of his nails on the linoleum the only sounds.

The screech of tires on the street in front of the house made Phineas put his fork down. A car door slammed. Vigorous pounding on the front door ejected him from his chair. Amos raced ahead of him.

Iris, Sarah Jane, Norris, and Maria stared at each other. Iris recognized Simon's voice in the hallway. He shouted, "You're free! Charges have been dropped! You're free!"

Amos barked and pranced as if he too should celebrate.

Phineas stepped into the kitchen first. He waited for Simon to enter then asked, "How? What...what happened?"

"*60 Minutes* happened. Angela's raving happened! Their star witness lost all credibility on local and national television! You're free! D Z is free! It's over."

Phineas grabbed Simon's hand and pumped it. "I can't thank you enough." Iris bounded from her chair and hugged Phineas then Simon. Maria buried her face in her napkin and began sobbing.

Simon bowed toward those seated at the kitchen table. "Hello. I'm Simon Serine, Phineas' attorney."

Norris stood and reached for Simon's hand. "I'm Norris, Phineas' Dad. Great to meet you. My lawyer friend in Vermont recommended you."

"I shall have to send them thanks." He tilted his head back, sniffed and surveyed the plates and stove. "Smells great in here. Anything left for your hungry servant?"

Phineas hustled to make a plate while Iris set a place for him.

Sarah Jane waited until Simon had swallowed his first bite, then asked, "So, what did you do?"

"'Scuse me?"

"How was *your* hand in this?"

"Oh, I see what you're asking." His mischievous grin. "Morley Safer was gracious enough to have a drink of 800-dollar bourbon with me after Phineas' interview."

"And?"

"And it gave me a chance to give him some background I'd learned on Angela, for him to consider a line of questioning for *her* interview—to steer him toward lighting her fuse."

"Glad he didn't see through you."

Simon winked at Sarah Jane. "Oh, he may have. God bless him!"

Phineas still appeared stunned. "So I...I don't have to go to court?" He needed to hear that his struggle was over.

"Nope. Everyone has been dismissed."

Phineas sat bolt upright. "Dr. Kornberg! I need to find him. Thank him. Take him to dinner before he goes back to Chapel Hill."

Simon extracted a worn leather notebook from his suit jacket pocket. He flipped through the first few pages and handed it to Phineas. "Here's the number of Le Pavillon."

Phineas stood at the kitchen phone and dialed.

"Hello. I'm trying to reach Dr. Kornberg."

He twisted the cord around his finger and listened. "Thank you."

Simon raised his eyebrows while he sipped coffee.

"The front desk said Dr. Kornberg left a while ago with his violin

case. He asked directions to the courthouse and said he wanted to walk."
Phineas frowned and shook his head. "I've got a bad feeling about this.
When I worked with him, someone always had to direct him places. He
could get lost...or mugged!"

Simon speared a sausage link. "Come on. We'll go look for him." He
bit off half, dropped his fork, and headed toward the front door.

Iris stood. "I'm coming. Let me throw on some clothes."

Sarah Jane reached for Maria's arm. "Let's all go. Y'all ready to see some
of New Orleans?"

⚜ ⚜ ⚜

The rescue party in Simon's white Cadillac convertible detected no
sign of Dr. Kornberg while creeping from Le Pavillon over the length of
Perdido Street, and finally parking in the courthouse lot. As they walked
around the corner next to the building's entrance, heavenly timbres from a
violin's strings floated toward them. A small crowd surrounded the source
on the courthouse steps.

Phineas recognized the shiny head crowned with wings of white hair,
the frameless glasses perched halfway down the ridge of his nose, and the
gray tweed jacket. A well-dressed elderly man on the lowest step turned
to Phineas and said, "It's Haydn's *Sunrise*."

Phineas waved at Dr. Kornberg. He finished the movement to cheers
and clapping then called out, "Is that you Phineas? You've shaved. I might
not have recognized you without Iris."

The crowd parted as Phineas' group approached. Dr. Kornberg carefully
tucked his precious instrument under his arm, but left his violin case, filled
with random bills and coins, open at his feet. "I didn't expect to be *paid*
for playing. I had no idea there were so many here who would appreciate
classical music."

His smile faded and his bushy eyebrows pinched together. "You know
I don't sit still well. I left early, since I wasn't certain where I was going

when I started walking, figuring I could practice my violin while waiting my turn in the courtroom." Dr. Kornberg gestured with his violin bow. "I met your co-workers here." Hilary and Ava stepped from the crowd.

Brandishing the bow like an orchestra conductor's baton, he declared, "I missed an opportunity to keep you at UNC once. I didn't want to let you down *again*." A few in the crowd strayed. Most stood still, listening.

Simon offered his hand. "Dr. Kornberg, I'm Simon Serine. It's an honor to finally meet you, Sir, after our phone conversations. We bring great news. All charges against Phineas Mann have been *dropped*."

Dr. Kornberg's mouth fell open as he secured his bow against his violin and accepted Simon and Phineas' spirited handshakes.

Iris hugged the violinist and planted a kiss on his cheek. When she stepped back, Dr. Kornberg lifted his violin to his neck and ripped off strains of the bluegrass classic *Liberty* before deftly shifting to Zydeco fiddling. The crowd clapped and stamped.

When he paused his fiddling, he hollered, "I bet you thought all we play at our music retreats is classical!"

Phineas caught a glimpse of Angela standing alone on the sidewalk glaring at him. Her lips drew back enough to expose her teeth. She appeared to mouth, "we're not finished," then spun away and vanished into the shadows around the corner of the City Hall building. Despite the sunny morning, seeing her gave him a chill.

Dr. Kornberg lowered his violin. "Since you are now free, Phineas, why don't you come back to Chapel Hill?"

Phineas struggled to clear the image of Angela from his thoughts. "Dr. Kornberg, are you offering me a job?"

"I'm offering you a job."

ACKNOWLEDGEMENTS

I would like to give extra thanks to my parents, Albert Camus, Sheri Fink, and my wife, Karen Lauterbach.

My mother, Irene Powers, taught me to read more than any teacher. My father, Norman Powers, was a better storyteller in his declining years than I could ever be. Weaving an engaging tale was as natural for him as breathing. I wish he had written some of them down.

Albert Camus created Dr. Rieux in *The Plague,* who provided Phineas and me with the guts to care for AIDS patients during the early years when no one knew what caused this frightening disorder or how much risk it was to health care providers. In current pandemic times, I wish to honor all health care providers for their sacrifices.

Sheri Fink, in her important book, *Five Days in Memorial,* opened my eyes to the real-world horrific conditions that occurred during a disaster in a major city hospital in a first world country when the planning and response were inadequate.

My editor and coach, Dawn Reno Langley of Rewired Creatives, Inc., once again helped with book revisions and my education as an author.

Christy Collins and Maggie McLaughlin of Constellation Book Services designed the cover and interior, produced the e-book, and supported *Breath and Mercy*'s printing.

Martha Bullen of Bullen Publishing Services continues to guide me through the complex world of publishing and marketing.

Jeremy Avenarius, of Real Avenue Design, designed and has supported my website.

My first beta readers, Karen Silverberg and Craig Rackley, suffered through an early draft and were enormously helpful in righting my ship. My sister, Vicki Powers, was also a helpful beta reader.

Members of my novelist group, Carol Hoppe, Bonnie Olsen, Ro Mason, Phil Goldberg, and Sara Strassle, have encouraged and steered me throughout the writing of all my novels.

I am grateful to the distinguished individuals who offered feedback and wrote endorsements for *Breath and Mercy*. Their names and credentials are attached to their kind words in the first pages of this book.

And finally, I owe more than I can express to my wife and love, Karen, who propped me up and kept me sane and grounded during periods of my life when the workload imposed by my medical career could have buried me. She was there for our sons when I couldn't be, and is the best mother two boys, now men, could have.

ABOUT THE AUTHOR

Mark Anthony Powers did not anticipate writing his best-selling debut novel, *A Swarm in May*, when he retired from medicine, although he has always enjoyed reading fiction. He grew up in the small town of West Lebanon, NH then attended Cornell University, where he strayed into Russian and creative writing while majoring in engineering. After receiving his MD from Dartmouth, he went south to the University of North Carolina for an internship and residency in Internal Medicine, followed by a fellowship in Pulmonary Diseases and Critical Care Medicine.

After almost forty years in clinical practice and teaching, Mark retired from Duke University as an Associate Professor Emeritus of Medicine and began exploring other areas of his brain. Writing, gardening, IT, and magic courses were parts of his journey. A deep dive into beekeeping led to his presidency of the county beekeeping association and certification as a Master Beekeeper. Two cups of coffee and two hours of writing most mornings produced *A Swarm in May* and its prequel, *Breath and Mercy*. Mark is currently completing the third novel in this series. To learn more or connect with Mark, please visit www.markanthonypowers.com.